Lauren and Rafi

Charles Becker

First published 2025

A CIP catalogue record for this book is available from the British Library.

ISBN: 978-1-0369-2559-8

For Jenny

Contents

"See how she leans her cheek upon her hand.
O, that I were a glove upon that hand
That I might touch that cheek!"

(*Romeo and Juliet*, Act 2, Scene 2)

"We have not forgotten, we will not forget. Veins like roots of olive trees, we will return. That is not a threat, not a wish, a hope or a dream, but a promise."

- Remi Kanazi from his poem 'Nakba'

LAUREN'S FAMILY TREE

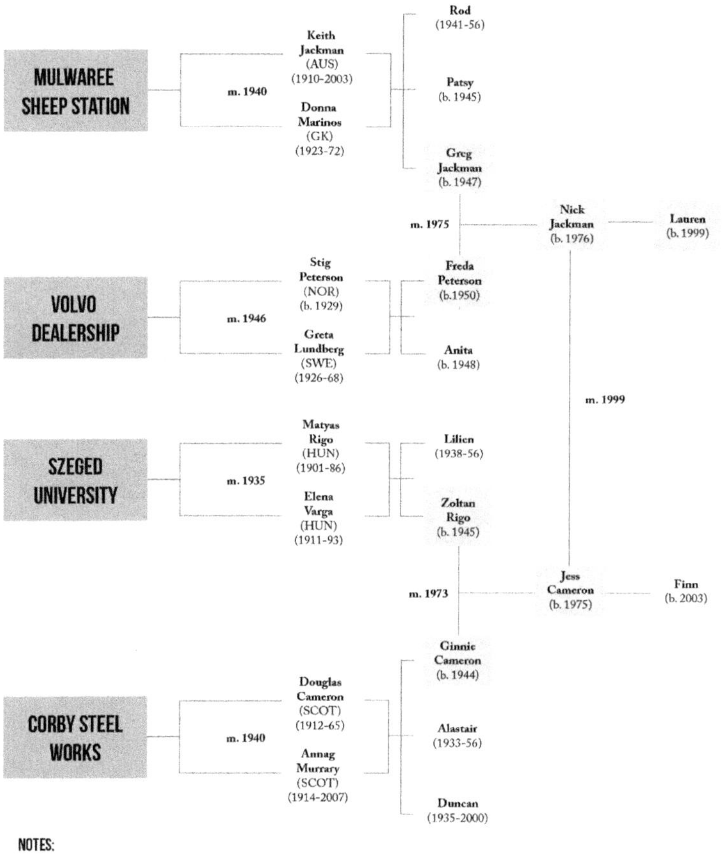

NOTES:

1. Douglas and Annag moved to Corby in 1932
2. Stig & Greta moved to Staines UK in 1948
3. Rod died in a motorcycle accident 1956
4. Lilien killed in Budapest by Russian tanks in 1956
5. Alastair died in Aden amid the Suez Crisis 1956
6. Zoltan and Uncle József moved to Slough UK in 1956 after Russian invasion
7. Ginnie's parents separated in 1956 and she went with her mother to live in Market Harborough with step-father, Dr Ramesh Shan
8. Greg moved to London in 1974
9. Ginnie kept her own surname when she married Zoltan

RAFI'S FAMILY TREE

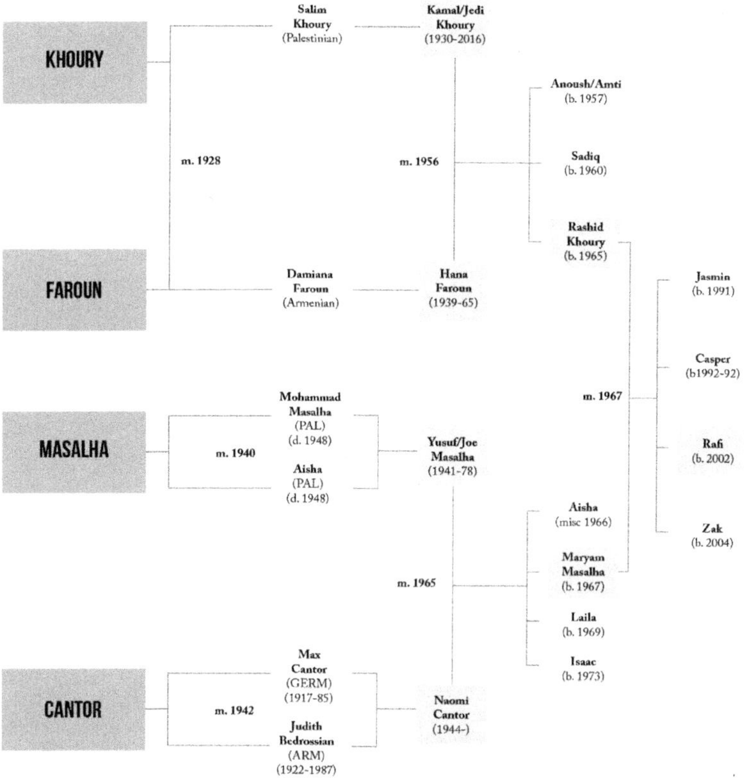

NOTES:

1. Mohammad and Aisha died during the Nakba 1948
2. Max Cantor, Jewish, moved to USA to escape the Nazis
3. Judith's parents escaped to USA during Armenian genocide 1915-16
4. Yusuf/Joe escaped to USA with his Uncle Abdul after his parents were killed
5. Kamal/Jedi was born in Jerusalem, his family becoming refugees (Jordan) after Nakba
6. Naomi remarried in 1981 to an American and had two more children
7. Naomi miscarried her first child, Aisha, in 1966
8. Casper died shortly after being born

Part One

Winter 2019

1

Lauren leant back in her chair, staring at the screen of her laptop in frustration: '*Compare and contrast the characters of Hamlet and Laertes*'.

'One makes endless speeches and the other doesn't!' was all she had to say about it. However magnificent Shakespeare's plays were, they gave her a headache. She'd much rather be out training than stuck at her desk like this. She stretched for the Penguin text and looked at the passage again, reading it aloud:

'*So excellent a king, that was to this*
Hyperion to a satyr; so loving to my mother
That he might not beteem the winds of heaven
Visit her face too roughly...'

'Beteem! What the hell does that mean?" She was fed up with having to look up the meaning of things in the notes every two seconds. 'Brilliant!' she cried, flinging the paperback back on the desk. 'Why say in three words what you can say in three hundred?'

Standing up, she moved to the window and pressed her forehead against the glass, closing her eyes to savour the icy chill of it. She was never going to get this essay done by tomorrow, not without some help. But who from, she wondered, and immediately pictured

Rafi, sitting across from her in their English Literature class, his hand raised. He actually seemed to enjoy Shakespeare.

But before she could give him any more thought, strains from Chariots of Fire burst into life; and, reaching for her phone, she saw it was Ida.

"Hi."

"You busy?"

Lauren turned back to the window and stared out into the darkness.

"Yeah, I am a bit."

"Oh, okay. Well, call me when you're through, yeah?"

"No, it's all right. It's just I'm stuck on my Hamlet essay and I was wondering whether to ring Rafi to see if he could help. What do you think?"

"What do I think?" Lauren heard Ida's amusement. "I think maybe you quite..."

"Hang on," Lauren interrupted, turning to switch off the desk lamp to see outside more clearly. "There's someone in our garden."

"No..." Ida's voice became a whisper. "What are they doing?"

"Not sure...just standing there, I think. It's dark by the bushes..."

But, even as she said it, the figure turned towards the house and she recognized the outline of her father.

"It's Dad! What on earth's he doing out there? It's freezing." She saw the white stripes of his butcher's apron becoming more apparent as he neared the house. "And he's got nothing on."

"What?" She heard Ida giggle. "He's naked?"

"No, of course not! I meant he's not wearing a coat

or anything."

"Guess he just wanted a breath of fresh air, then."

Lauren watched her father disappear; a brief shaft of light across the grass from the kitchen door and then darkness again.

"I don't know, Ida...he's been a bit odd lately."

"What sort of odd?"

"Kind of like he's there, but not there...I mean, he looks at you, but you can tell he's miles away."

"Things on his mind, maybe."

"Yeah, maybe...or maybe it's all in my imagination." Lauren shrugged her shoulders; she didn't want to talk about it. Not now, anyway. "Look, I'll call you back later. I've got to get this essay done." She paused, then added, "I think I will call Rafi, see if he can come round."

Ida laughed. "No boys till you've made it to the Olympics, remember? Anyway, why don't you ask your dad? He is an English teacher, for heaven's sake!"

"No, I need to do this on my own." Lauren hesitated, trying to understand her own reluctance. "What I mean is...I see him every day in college, right? So, when we're home, I want him as my dad, not my teacher, if you..."

"Okay, Laur, I get it," Ida broke in. "Besides, handsome as your dad is, he doesn't have Rafi's long lashes, does he?"

Lauren clicked off her phone and sat quietly for a moment, trying to fathom her own unease. Normally, Ida's playfulness lightened her mood, but she couldn't shake off the image of her father standing alone in the garden, out there in the darkness and the cold. It troubled her...he'd seemed so vulnerable, so sort of lost.

She glanced at her watch and frowned. Rafi would have to come round now or it would be too late. But she felt suddenly anxious about clearing it with her parents. Well, with her mother really. She shook her head and stood up. This was silly. Why shouldn't she ask him over? It was no different from asking Ida. A friend was a friend.

Taking her mobile, she left her room and made for the stairs. As she neared the bottom, she heard raised voices coming from the kitchen and paused, resting her hand on the bannister, the polished wood smooth under her palm.

"You've got to talk to me, Nick!" she heard her mother say, but the sudden bray of canned laughter from the living room drowned out her father's reply. Stepping down into the hall, she caught a glimpse of her brother, Finn, sprawled on the floor with his homework spread out in front of the TV. Silently pulling the door closed, she stood for a moment, warming the backs of her legs against the radiator, listening to the rising tension in her parents' voices. What was going on with them?

Coughing a warning, she moved across to the kitchen door and walked in. Her father was standing with his back to the sink. Looking up, he saw her and smiled.

"Sorry to interrupt," she started, "but I need to ask you something."

"That's all right, what is it?" Her mother dropped the pen she was holding onto the fan of papers in front of her and eased her chair sideways away from the table.

"Is it okay if Rafi comes round for a bit?" Lauren saw her mother looking at the mobile in her hand and slipped it into her hip pocket. "Don't worry, it's not on. I haven't rung him yet."

"Is this to do with homework?"

"Yeah, I'm stuck on my English essay. It's due in tomorrow and Rafi really seems to get Shakespeare. Says he's like some Persian poet he had to study at school...Hafiz or Hafez, I think....something like that, anyway."

"I don't know, Lauren. I thought we'd agreed no friends round on a week night."

"But you don't mind when I do homework with Ida, do you? I mean this is for college, so what's the difference?"

She saw her mother's eyes tighten at the challenge, anger glinting in the blue.

"The difference is you've known Ida since you were four. It's not the same. We don't really know Rafi or his family, do we?"

"What's that got to do with it?" Lauren objected. But she'd seen the warning sign and she didn't want a fight. "Look, I need his help, Mum," she went on, changing tack. "If I don't get this finished for tomorrow, I'll be in trouble. Won't I, Dad?" She looked across to him for support, but he was twisted away from her, pulling off his yellow, washing-up gloves and hanging them over the sink's swan-neck tap.

"Well, yes, you might be," he said turning back. "Old Tonks can be a bit of a stickler, I know, but with good reason. A-Levels are much more demanding than GCSEs; and, if you don't put the work in at the beginning, it's not easy to catch up later on."

"So, you're okay if Rafi comes round, then?"

She saw him glance at her mother. "What do you think, Jess?"

"Yes, all right. But no later than nine."

She didn't sound all right with it and Lauren smiled at her uncertainly. "Thanks, Mum," she said and spun away, reaching for her phone as she went.

2

Rafi found his mother settled cosily upstairs in the spare bedroom she used as a study. Sitting in her velvet armchair pulled close to the radiator, she was surrounded by papers and books, some on the coffee table beside her and the rest in pools around her feet on the crimson and cobalt rug she had brought with them from Jordan – 'a little piece of home', she called it.

"Always working, Mama," he said, smiling at her as she looked up, but she just seemed to stare through him.

"How like your father you are!" she said at last. "For a moment, I thought you were him standing there. Come." She waved him towards her and took his hand, studying him. "Same straight back...same tight, black curls." His scalp tingled as she raised her arm and ran her hand over it. "And the same deep eyes...like warm chocolate." She seemed to drift off into a reverie; but, when she spoke again, the wistfulness in her voice was gone. "Sometimes a lamb, sometimes a wolf, heh? Only, you're taller already and you don't have a beard. And you are definitely you!"

She laughed and let go of him; but he had caught a sense of sorrow in her and it unsettled him.

"Is everything all right, Mama?" he asked.

"Yes, yes," she said, clearing her throat. "Just updating my notes for tomorrow."

She took off her glasses, catching a hinge in a wave of thick chestnut hair. Freeing it, she pointed a tortoiseshell arm towards him. "Do you realize that this Nation-State Bill the Israeli government is preparing will take away the democratic rights of all Palestinians in Israel?" She tapped the papers on her lap with the same amber arm. "It changes everything." She bent forward and picked up a folder. "Maybe, you remember Aida Touma-Suleiman?" She pulled an A4 poly pocket from the folder and eased out the printed sheets it held. "She was elected to the Knesset in 2015, only the fourth Arab-Israeli woman..."

"Most certainly, I do!" Rafi interrupted, wanting to be on his way, but without offending her. "But can you tell me about this later? Lauren wants help with her Shakespeare essay and I said I would go." He took hold of his mother's free hand and held it to his cheek, absorbing the warmth of it. "I won't be there long." He went to let go, but she held on to him.

"Touma-Suleiman has warned that this bill *institutionalises an apartheid regime.* Her words, Rafi." Her eyes searched his, as if imploring him to understand the gravity of what she was saying. It was a look he knew well. "Effectively, it means an end to the peace process. Your grandfather...Jedi will never go back to Jerusalem. There will be no return of refugee Palestinians to their homeland. No reprieve for those caught in the cage of Gaza. No two state solution. The occupation will be permanent, and the US is supporting this."

His mother was a visiting lecturer at Exeter University, contracted for her expertise in Middle

Eastern affairs; and he was used to her rehearsing on him what she would be saying to her students later on. But she was usually calm and assured, and the weary dismay in her voice took him by surprise. He leant forward, kissing the top of her head.

"Have faith, Mama. We will find solutions. I believe that."

"Ah, the hope of youth," she said, releasing him finally. She looked at her watch. "But, Rafi, it's quite late. Has Lauren asked her parents if it is all right for you to go there at this time?"

"Yes, they know I'm coming." Her question irritated him. "And we'll be seventeen this year. We're not children anymore."

"Even so, I have not met Lauren and I do not know her parents. When you have children of your own, you will understand."

"But her father is a teacher at the college. He knows me and he knows I'm in the same class as Lauren for English. If he doesn't mind my going to their house, why do you?"

"Because we belong to different cultures. When you have finished your studies, Jordan will still be your home. And, while we are here, I am responsible for your well-being."

He felt exasperated. "How is helping Lauren with her homework going to affect my...my well-being, Mama?"

She studied him and something softened in her expression. "I trust you, Rafi. It's other people I worry about." She smiled and nodded. "Go on. Lauren will be waiting. And you, a Shakespeare scholar! Whatever next?"

He liked it, when she teased him; when he felt the affection of her playfulness. And he was glad to be released from his own anger. They didn't often argue and he always regretted it when they did; but, as he reached the door, she asked, "How long will you be?" and he felt his irritation rising again.

He checked his watch. "Not long. I will be back by nine."

As Rafi cycled away from the house down the lane, he pulled up the hood of his jacket, tightening the zip against the bitter wind off the moors. The night was black and the bends and hedgerows seemed to melt together in a blur. Concentrating intently on the wash of the town's yellow light ahead of him, he slalomed the rain-filled potholes as best he could.

His mother's words disturbed him. Why talk about different cultures and going back to Jordan? Everything was going as planned. They needed to stay here another eighteen months, until he'd taken his A-Levels. Then, he'd be old enough to go to university on his own to study, and his mother could return to her permanent post in Amman, if she wanted to. Meanwhile, they would have the whole of the coming summer back at home in Jordan, and he smiled into his scarf at the thought of it. But, when she had compared him to his father and run her hand over his head, he had felt a weary kind of sadness in her that worried him. Normally, she was so encouraging and self-assured. Maybe, it was because of Touma-Suleiman's warning and the thought that there would be no return to Jerusalem after all for Jedi and all the other Palestinians, who had been born and brought up there.

It touched an old anger in him at the injustice of what had happened and he pumped the pedals round faster and faster. At the junction, at the bottom of the hill, he turned right onto the minor road into town; and, as he entered the sodium vault of street lighting, he relaxed, sitting back and resting one hand on his rising and falling knee. The small town seemed as deserted as the parked cars lining either side. Freewheeling down East Street, he crossed the central t-junction into West Street, where Lauren had told him she lived, and started pedalling again as the gradient rose against him.

Immediately ahead, at the end of a short run of shops, a bunch of youths emerged from the pub on his right and started to cross the road. Recognizing them, Rafi slowed and dipped his head. But, even as he did so, a voice rang out with its familiar false cheeriness and he saw four pairs of legs stop and turn.

"Well, well, well...if it isn't our old friend, Raf... aye...el!"

Rafi braked and put his foot down to steady himself.

"Hello, Terry," he said, watching the thick lips widening in a grin under the shadow cast by the hood of the squat figure's duffel coat; and he flicked up the pedal with his toe, getting ready to move off.

"Not in a hurry, are you?" Terry said, lightly gripping the handlebars, as the others half-circled the bike. "I mean it's not very friendly rushing off when we've only just met again, after what...?" He turned to the tallest of the group standing next to him, eyes staring out above the scarf wrapped tight around his face. "What would you say, John? Getting on for a few years now since we left the seat of learning of which we are all so proud?"

John nodded.

"Longer than that for John, of course," came the deep drawl and chuckle from the figure in an army greatcoat and trilby. "Such an unfortunate incident!"

"Want another one, Larry?" John snarled, his hand snaking inside and out of his parka, a double-edged blade suddenly glinting in the lamp light.

Rafi was well aware of the antagonism between Terry's henchmen, John Knight and Lawrence Hawker; and he didn't understand what it was that bound the three of them together...well, four of them, although young Matt Smiley didn't really seem to belong. Even now, he was hovering on the edge, a step behind the others.

"Lawrence!" The brim of the trilby lifted, revealing long planes of cheeks and jaw under high-ridged cheekbones. "Never Larry, as you well know." Rafi saw the thin smile widen. "Or, do I need to remind you?"

"Now, now, lads," Terry crooned, his eyes still fixed on Rafi's. "A bit of decorum, if you please...a bit of politeness in front of our distinguished guest."

"Guest?" John's hand with the knife disappeared into his parka again. "Who invited 'im? I didn't!"

"I need to be going," Rafi said, shifting his weight to roll backwards and go round them; "or I will be late."

"Late?" Terry tightened his grip, holding the bike fast. "Late for what? Or, even, for who...or should that be whom?"

Terry Curnow and his gang had picked on him from the start of his first year at Ashbrook College and Rafi knew only too well the familiar rhythm of this gradual escalation of taunting. His father's advice about dealing with aggressors came back to him: "If words fail, target the leader."

Deepening his breathing and loosening his muscles, Rafi fixed his attention on the fleshy bridge of Terry's nose. "Please let go," he said.

Terry smirked and slid his hand further along the bar till Rafi could feel the soft, warm touch of it next to his.

"The thing is, Raf...aye...el, we're all wondering why you're over here, at all." He looked round. "Aren't we, lads?" And, nodding at the growls of assent, he turned back and went on. "Yes, yes, indeed we are. Let me put it this way. Do you watch 'Nothing to Declare'? It's a real life TV series about Australian border security."

Rafi shook his head impatiently. "No, I don't! And that is enough now!"

But Terry merely chuckled, phlegm rattling in his throat, and continued: "They don't want unapproved plants, animals and foodstuffs coming into their country, you see, because of the threat these pose to their own flora and fauna...you know, through parasites and disease preying on their own home-grown species. And you can't blame them, can you?" As Terry bent closer, Rafi recoiled from the sour smell of his breath. "After all, they don't want the likes of myxomatosis killing off all the roos, do they? Just as we didn't want grey squirrels taking over from red ones, if you see what I mean. They want to preserve their own native stock and keep them safe, keep them as they are."

Rafi could hear the excitement in Terry's voice building, and he clenched his teeth against it. "Yes, indeed! Keep them pristine and undefiled! That way, the red squirrels can go on living happily where they are and so can the grey squirrels, wherever they come from." Terry paused, before smiling again. And Rafi felt the rising menace behind it. "Do you get my drift, Raf...aye...el? Do you begin to underst..."

The diesel knock and clatter of an approaching SUV blotted out Terry's voice, as hands were raised against the glare of its headlights. It slowed to a rattle and died, and the driver's window slid open.

"Everything all right?" came a man's voice. Rafi recognized the warm burr of Ida's father, Henry Downes, who had his small-holding a bit further up Druid's Lane from Windhover, the house his mother had rented.

"Yes, thank you," Terry called back pleasantly. "Just chatting."

"Middle of the road's not the best place for that." The car door opened and a middle-aged man emerged from the shadows into the light. He was wearing wellingtons and a lumber jacket with its collar turned up and he took a couple of steps towards them. "That you, Rafi?"

"We were just admiring his bike." Terry let go of the handlebars and nodded to the others. "Time we were on our way, lads." Then, grinning at Rafi once more, he said, "Good to see you, Rafael. We'll be in touch again...soon." And, as he walked away, he looked back over his shoulder and added, "Yes, yes, very soon; you can count on that."

"They're a useless bunch," the man said, standing beside Rafi, watching them go. "Don't understand why young Matt's got 'imself mixed up with them; he's a decent enough kid."

Rafi was glad for the solidity of the man's support. "Thank you for stopping, Mr Downes."

"That's all right." He looked Rafi up and down.

"You okay?"

"Yes, I'm fine."

"Good." He gave Rafi a clap on the shoulder and went back to his car.

3

Resting his bike against the wall just inside the front door at Laura's suggestion, Rafi followed her through an inner second door into a more spacious hall than he had expected and he was surprised how the house seemed to grow wider the further he walked into it.

"Thanks for coming," Lauren said, starting up the stairs, her hand round a carved pineapple topping the newel post. He stopped; and she paused, looking back at him. Raised voices and a gun shot came from a room to his right; while, further along, he heard a kettle come to the boil and click off. "Come on up. Much less noise in my room."

"Couldn't we use somewhere down here?" he said, uncomfortable with her suggestion.

He saw her frown dissolve into a smile of understanding. "Hey, no, that's okay."

She came down and touched his arm. "Listen, we often work together in our bedrooms, but we can use the music room. It's really just the front sitting room, but it's got a piano."

She led him into a high-ceilinged room, with a startling, emerald green carpet and book-filled shelves lining the alcoves either side of the chimney breast. On the other side, past the armchairs by the fireplace, where the room grew wider, he saw the upright piano. Its lid was up, with music sheets on the stand and a jumbled pile of others on top of it. The abandoned coffee mug next to them and the cushioned stool pushed back at an angle gave him the sense of someone recently there; and he wondered who the player was.

While Lauren went to fetch her things, he settled into one of the wooden chairs set round a table in the corner. With his back to the wall, he looked at the unlit log burner, its cylindrical, cast iron body and flue dark and cold in the recess under the mantelpiece. Despite the central heating, the room felt draughty, cool currents of air circling his legs. He eyed the small stack of logs, longing to get the stove going. English winters and staying indoors were things he would never get used to.

Closing his eyes, he dreamed of the coming summer, of his grandfather's small farm, willing himself back into the warmth and fragrance of the terrace there, where they all gathered to eat and chat. Conjuring it up, he wandered past its pink and red anemones, purple poppies and tomato plants, out from under the trellis of hanging vines and down the steps into the short shadows of the peach and olive trees. His chest tightened with longing for the rough stubble of his father's embrace and for the laughing protestations and teasing of his sister and brother. Lowering his hand to stroke the head of their dog, the tips of his fingers jarred against the table leg and broke his reverie. As he opened his eyes, the terrace and its plants were dissolving into the room's reflection in a mirror opposite, when the door opened and a woman walked in.

"Oh!" She stopped in surprise, taking him in, before

stepping forward again. "Sorry," she smiled, coming across; "I didn't realize anyone was in here. You must be Rafi."

"Yes, I am," he said, standing up and stepping clear of the table. "Good evening, Mrs Jackman." He held out his hand and felt the warmth of hers, as she took it in her own.

"It's Cameron, actually," she said, "on my mother's side; but, please, call me Jess."

Rafi was struck by how different she was from Lauren. Lauren was tall and spare with rich brown hair, like her father, and she had his air of calm. But here was her petite mother, blonde hair swept back in a ponytail, eyebrows dancing up and down over sparkling blue eyes, an infectious energy animating her smiles and gestures.

"So, how are you finding life over here?" She pulled out a chair and sat down, motioning him to follow suit. "And what about your family?" she went on, before he could answer. "You must be missing them."

"Yes, I do sometimes. But I like being here...apart from the cold."

She laughed. "Yes, English winters, I know. But I can light the fire...well, wood-burner, if you like."

"No, that's all right," he said, wishing Lauren would hurry up and come back. He had told his mother he would be back by nine, but he hadn't bargained on Terry and his gang or on Lauren's mum, come to that.

"Well, if you're sure?" She tilted her head questioningly, her eyebrows dancing again, and looked at him intently. "These old houses with their high ceilings can be a bit draughty."

He nodded. "Yes, I am sure. Thank you."

"And your mother, Rafi; she must have her hands

full, lecturing at the university, as well as looking after you. And Windhover is such a beautiful house, but it's big and I know how much there is to do to..."

Before she could finish, Lauren appeared through the doorway, holding a laptop like a tray, with books, pad and pencil case balancing on top of it. "Mum, we're going to work in here, if that's okay."

"Yes, of course," her mother said, standing up and making way for her. Lauren was a head taller; and, as she bent to lower the laptop onto the table, her long hair spilling forward and screening her face, Rafi was struck again by the contrast between them.

Her mother caught him looking at Lauren and smiled. "Right, I'll leave you to it," she said. "It's nice to meet you, Rafi. You and your mum must come and have a meal with us." And, before he could think how best to reply, she was gone, closing the door behind her.

"Well, she likes you!" Lauren said, shaking her head. "I'll have to watch out." He saw her blush, as she quickly busied herself, clearing the top of the laptop and opening it. "Anyway, come on. Let's get going. Here, have a look at what I've written so far."

Rafi drew his chair in close to her; and, lightly pressing on the corner of the laptop with his thumb, he angled the screen more towards him and read carefully through the opening paragraphs. "Okay. So how can I help you?"

She turned to look at him, her face close to his. "I get confused with 'compare and contrast'," she said; and a cinnamon spiciness trailed on the warmth of her breath, as she spoke. "They're always starting essay questions like that. Why can't they just use plain English?"

Rafi tried to concentrate. "It means what are the similarities and what are the differences." He looked back at the screen. "And, as far as I can see, you're answering that." He glanced back at her. "It seems fine, so far."

"Okay." She sounded unsure. "But I'm stuck. I don't get this guy, Laertes. I mean I see the differences, but what's the same? Hamlet's nothing like him."

There was that scent again. Maybe, she'd just eaten cinnamon cake...or a biscuit. He felt overwhelmed by the closeness of her. He wanted to put out his hand and draw her hair back from her face over her shoulder. He wanted to see her more clearly.

"Rafi?" she nudged him with her arm against his and he felt burned by the contact.

"Sorry," he said, standing up. "I need to let my mother know I'll be later than I said." He moved away towards the armchairs, half-sitting on the arm of one, while he rang home.

He saw her watching him out of the corner of her eye and he looked away in confusion, as his mother answered.

"What's up?" Lauren asked, as he came back and sat down again, edging his chair slightly apart from her. "You look flustered."

He hesitated, unsure how to answer, wanting to be truthful, but not daring to.

"Come on," she said, lowering her voice. "We trust each other, don't we?"

"It's just..." he faltered, burning with feelings he couldn't find words for and continuing in desperate betrayal of them: "Terry and his friends stopped me just before I got here." He hadn't meant to tell her.

"Saw me as they came out of the pub."

"The Exeter?"

"Yes."

"What happened?" She pivoted round on one chair leg, facing him directly. "Terry's such a pillock!"

She was sitting up straight, her face taut and alert. He saw the steel in her eyes and was glad of her anger on his behalf. He thought of the red and grey squirrels.

"They pretend to be friendly, but they don't like me," he said, "and they don't want me here. But nothing happened. Mr Downes came along and that was that."

"Terry's just ignorant!" she hissed. "And so are the rest of them."

Half-rising, she pulled her chair round back to the laptop. "We all like you, Rafi. We all want you here." She tapped the machine, adding as the screen flared into action again, "Friends stick together; that's what they're for."

It was almost half-past ten by the time Rafi started his journey home with a hot glow in his chest, despite the cold. Lauren liked him. They were friends. She had said so. The streets were deserted and he raised his scarf over his lips and nose against the ice in the air. He knew his mother would be waiting up for him and he thought about what she had said earlier. She would want to talk more about the Nation State Bill and its implications. International Relations were her passion and he had known since he was seven that he wanted to follow in her footsteps and to redress the wrongs being done to Palestinians. But, try as he might to focus and separate the different issues in his mind, his thoughts constantly went back to Lauren and to the touch and scent of her.

As he stood off the seat, pedalling hard up the hill in the lane home, he stretched his chin free of the scarf and shouted at himself, "No ties! Remember? Degree first!"

4

The ice in the air sliced at Lauren's cheeks and the bone of her nose, stabbing at her eyes and forehead, as she strode home, linking her arm through Ida's to hurry her along. Turning in at the gate, she unhooked herself and felt in her pocket for the key. As she pushed the door open, golden light poured out into the darkness; and, engulfed by the sudden wave of warmth from the central heating, she hurried through into the hall, leaving Ida to close both the front and inner doors.

"Shut the door! It's freezing!" a voice rang out.

"We have!" they chorused back, laughing now and hauling off their bags and coats, dropping them on a chest under the window, woolly hats on top, and stuffing their gloves into the coats' pockets.

"Mum home yet?" Lauren asked, looking round the door into the living room.

"No, just me," came her brother's spluttering reply, his apple cheeks moving up and down in time with his chomping, his eyes still riveted to the screen of his mobile, his thumbs flying.

"You're spitting crumbs," she half-laughed, half-complained, seeing his mouth full of the triple-decker sandwich he always made himself after school: peanut butter with banana on top and apple underneath.

"No, I'm not!" He slid the phone onto the coffee table and peered at the carpet round his feet. "Where?"

"There!" she pointed. "On the sofa, right beside you! And you're still doing it!"

"Hi, Finn," Ida smiled, stepping past her. "Don't worry, she's only jealous!"

"I know," he gurgled, sluicing his mouth clean with Coke and widening his big eyes over the glistening red can, a huge grin on his face as he lifted it away and burped loudly.

"Gross!" Lauren protested, watching him pick up the rest of his sandwich using both hands to hold it together. How could he look so angelic with his halo of rusty curls and be so revolting, at the same time? "Come on," she said, tapping Ida's arm, "let's leave the ginger gremlin conquering the universe and get some tea of our own."

"It's Minecraft, if you must know, Laury-longlegs!" His half-choking cry pursued her down the passage.

"'Laury-longlegs'," Ida laughed. "Haven't heard that before."

"Yes, well, you know..." Lauren flicked the light switch, springing colour into the kitchen and blackening its windows. "I think he was about three when he came up with that one."

It had been the morning she'd looked round while crossing the road on her way to school and found him following her in his Harry Potter dressing-gown with its pointy hood. How he'd wailed and protested, when she'd hauled him home and had to unlock his chubby little arms clinging so fiercely to her leg, before setting off again. And how excited and beaming he had been, when she got back in the afternoon, rushing towards her, arms flailing and crying out, "Laury! Laury! Come play with me!" while grabbing her hand before she'd even had time to lift her satchel off, and tugging her after him. She couldn't imagine a time now when he hadn't been there.

"I don't like Finn being a latchkey kid," Lauren said, eying a thread hanging down from the back of Ida's skirt and watching it rising and falling against the dark mesh of her tights, as they climbed the stairs. There had been no mum to look after her! Not since she was a baby, even though Henry was great with her and always had been. Lauren had felt safe at their house from the start; and, if anything ever happened to her own parents, that's where she wanted to go to live and she'd take Finn with her. Not that she didn't love her all her grandparents, she did. She smiled, thinking what life would be like living with them: noise and mess with her mum's parents, Ginnie and Zoltan; order and efficiency with her dad's, Pop and Mormor.

"He's not on his own for long though, is he?" Ida said, turning sideways to bump the bedroom door open with her hip, while holding her mug and plate safely away from her body. "And what are you grinning at, anyway?"

"Oh, just who we'd live with if anything happened to Mum and Dad."

Dumping her bowl on the desk, Lauren quickly cleared a space for Ida's things on the low, oak chest-of-drawers she used as a dressing table, where a small panda bear sat crooked against the mirror. "Hang on," she added as Ida went to sit down in the armchair next to it. "You've a thread." She took a pair of nail-scissors from a terracotta pot sprouting nail files and orange sticks. "Turn round."

"Bit morbid," Ida said, turning and twisting to peer down over her shoulder. "But who would you choose?"

"That's the point, really." Lauren threw the thread in the bin by her desk. "I love all my grandparents, but I wouldn't want to leave here...you know, the running club, college, all my friends, particularly you and..." She trailed off.

"And?" Ida cocked her head and tapped her chin with her forefinger. "Let me see."

Knowing perfectly well what was coming next, Lauren sat down on her swivel chair, picked up her bowl of yoghurt and banana from the desk, and spun back towards her. Despite the pursed lips and feigned frown of concentration, Ida looked so fresh, even in winter, even in artificial light, with her tumble of straw-coloured hair past her shoulders, radar green eyes and band of pale freckles, like a skein of flying geese, across her cheeks and the bridge of her nose.

"It couldn't be the delectable Rafi by any chance, could it?"

Ida's face broke into the same beckoning, mischievous grin Lauren had latched onto in the playground, all those years ago. But Lauren felt weary, almost too weary to answer her, and dipped her head. Where was Mum? She was always out these days. It wasn't fair on Finn. Was that the matter with Dad? Or were those rumours true...fancying Jan Rawlings?"

"Laur, you ok? I was only teasing."

And what if they split up? That was more likely than them dying. Who would she and Finn live with then? Oh, God, she didn't want to have to choose between them. Finn would want to stay with Mum, but she was always out. And Dad worked full-time, but at least he was home evenings and weekends.

"Hey, what's up?" Ida was leaning forward, touching her arm.

"What?"

"You've gone a bit misty. Have you come on?"

Lauren looked up, annoyed. "Misty?"

"Yes, like you do sometimes...you know, not quite there." Ida sat back. "Mine's started, too; but I know it's worse for you."

It was true. And it was just something she had to put up with, this cycle of heaviness and headaches. She couldn't train when she was like this...couldn't run 40 metres let alone 400 without getting stomach cramps... had to use tampons instead of pads, if she tried, because of the Lycra. Oka, the club coach, had suggested she should go on the pill. "Make your hormone levels more stable and minimize your symptoms," she'd said. Maybe, she was right; but she didn't want to use drugs. It wasn't a road she wanted to go down. No, she'd put up with it...her performance would be her own.

But lucky Ida! Her periods always seemed so light by comparison, hardly bothering her at all. Anyway, 'misty' wasn't the right word. Lauren felt dreamy, like she wanted to be left alone and go into herself and be with her own feelings...whatever they were...she didn't know. That was the point. Go into the woods of herself, into the darkness and the stillness. She'd like that now. She'd like Ida to go home.

"You're disappearing again. I think I'd better be going. I'll give Dad a ring." Ida put her mug down on the empty plate and stood up. "But, look, we can talk about your dad and everything tomorrow, when you come over."

What was tomorrow? Friday? Already? "Yes...yes." Lauren put her bowl back on the desk untouched and went across to Ida. "Sorry," she said, giving her a hug.

"And Rafi, of course!" Ida smiled. "You still haven't told me how the homework went."

After Ida's father had come and she'd waved them off, Lauren wandered back upstairs and closed her door. She drew the curtains, sat on the edge of the bed and slipped off her shoes. She stretched for the earphones on the bedside table and then changed her mind, putting her mobile down beside them instead. Leaving her uniform draped over the armchair, she checked her pants before rolling up the pad and sliding it into a bin liner. Maybe, they could invite Rafi round to Ida's on Saturday; he only lived five minutes down the road from her and he seemed quite solitary, even in college. He wasn't unapproachable exactly, just sort of self-contained; and, although other people were curious about him, it was with the same caution as if they were watching tigers at the zoo. But they were wrong, she decided, as she tightened the belt of her bathrobe and made her way down the corridor. She'd felt it sitting beside him over her essay; there was a quiet strength about him, but also something kind of gentle and trustworthy. She couldn't quite put her finger on it. And the picture of Terry Curnow and his gang threatening him in the street in the dark had stayed with her. Narrow-minded, little racists they might be; but they were dangerous. John Knight had been expelled because of his violence and there was something quite sinister about Lawrence Hawker underneath his jokey disdain, as if everything and everyone were beneath him...almost as if he was untouchable. No, Rafi would be safer with her and Ida than going about on his own.

After having a shower, Lauren pulled on jogging bottoms and a sweatshirt, switched off the lights and lay down, her long hair still wet and clinging, a towel spread over the pillow. Now she could sink into the darkness and the silence. She closed her eyes. But her thoughts wouldn't settle. She wanted to think about her parents, but not about the rumour that her dad had a thing for Jan Rawlings. That was just gossip, kids trying to impress each other, making things up, embellishing things. Jan and her dad were colleagues...work friends. Of course, they collaborated over joint Art and English projects, like the college play. Even so, something was going on with him. Maybe, she could talk to Mormor about it; she always kept confidences. Besides, she was his mother, she might know something, anyway. Oh God, she mustn't forget to let the club know she wouldn't be there for training this weekend! She picked up her phone and saved a reminder. But what had Dad been doing out in the garden at night in the freezing cold? Just standing there in his apron looking at nothing; it didn't make any sense.

And what about Ida? Compared to her, Laura knew she was lucky. She had four grandparents, not to mention umpteen uncles, aunts and cousins, but Ida had none. She'd never known her mother's parents and Henry's had both died while she was still at primary school; first her grandfather from lung cancer and, not long afterwards, her granny from breast cancer. That's when Henry had given her two hamsters to look after:

Bubble and Squeak. Lauren smiled in spite of herself. Ida chose the names, of course; they reminded her of her granny and her cooking. But now, apart from her dad, Ida only had her bachelor Uncle Joe as family, although she was close to him. Ever since she was little, he'd made a fuss of her, taking her out in his fishing boat and always coming up from Newlyn for visits on her birthday and at Christmas. Even so, having no mum...or, rather, having a mum who'd gone off and left you...it wasn't the same.

What if Mum and Dad did split up? A low pulsing pain began throbbing above her right temple. "Oh, no!" she groaned, opening her eyes and leaning up to stretch for the blister pack of migraine pills the doctor had prescribed. Hormonal migraines, he called them. She didn't care what they were called, they wiped her out and she desperately wanted to stop this one building now. She lay back, closing her eyes again, and concentrated on her breathing, trying to relax and steady herself like she did before races. Somewhere below, she heard a door close followed by a rumble of voices. Her dad was home. He'd get supper going; she had an hour.

5

The mountain lion was trailing her, gliding through the snow and the trees, getting closer...low-slung, dangerous, eyes glittering as she glanced back. Rafi's hand shook her shoulder urging her to run, but she was afraid to. "Suppertime," he said, shaking her again. Her door was open, light spilling in and she screwed her eyes against it. She felt the warmth of the cougar's breath on her neck. "Food's ready." Finn's face came into focus bending over her. "Okay...okay," she said, lifting her head, and he let go of her shoulder.

By the time she had come to and brushed the tangles out of her hair, she found Finn and her dad already eating, the air in the kitchen hazy with the smell and smoke of grilled meat.

"Hi, sleepy, you okay?" her father smiled, looking up, still chewing.

"Yeah, sorry, Dad, I had a headache...must have drifted off."

"All right now?"

She paused to check. "Yes," she said, glad to find the throbbing had subsided. "Yes, I'm fine, I think." She crossed her fingers at him.

He understood and nodded. "Good. Your plate's in

the oven. It's the one on top."

Lauren retrieved it and sat down opposite Finn; but before she could pick up her knife and fork, she heard the front door opening and closing.

"Good old Mum," Finn grinned; "perfect timing!"

Not really, Lauren thought, watching her dad going to the oven to fetch the other plate, before setting it down carefully at the end of the table and straightening the cutlery on either side. Why doesn't Mum ever get home in time to do the cooking like she used to, she wondered.

With an eddy of cool air, the door swished open and her mother came sweeping in, a determined smile on her face, which Lauren recognized as one her mother adopted when she was going to confront one of them about something they had or hadn't done. Lauren watched and waited.

"Ah, let me guess." Jess closed her eyes and tilted her nose in the air. "Pork chops and baked potatoes!" Pausing for a moment with her hand on Finn's shoulder and kissing the top of his head, she sat down. "Sorry I'm late. I got stuck behind a horse-trailer for miles."

"So, how did it go?" Nick asked. Lauren heard the false note and saw the enquiring smile belied by the tension in her father's eyes.

"Really well! The bank's agreed the loan and I think I've found a good builder to work with. Looks like The Canoe's going to happen."

"Cool name," Finn said. "Better than Red Emma any day."

"Red Emma was an amazing woman and don't you forget it!"

"Woah! Child abuse!" Finn giggled, swaying away

from Jess' light tap to his shoulder. "You're all witnesses."

"And what's more," Jess went on, talking over him, "she's brought good luck to that place. It's doing fantastically well and there's a lot of competition in Exeter. That's why the bank's so happy with me. Also..." She hesitated, flicking a quick look at Nick, who was busy cutting his meat from the bone; and Lauren knew that what she said next was different from what she'd been going to say the moment before. "That is, I bumped into Rafi's mum at the petrol station first thing...Maryam... Maryam, I can't remember her surname."

"Masalha," Nick said, spelling it out, "which is confusing, as the family name is Khoury...you know, Rafi Khoury. But apparently she uses her maiden name professionally."

"Yes, that's it. Rather embarrassing, actually." She gave a little laugh "I was stuck behind her at the pumps first thing and running late...you know, for the staff meeting at Red Emma's...and I tooted my horn, because she wasn't moving off. Of course, I didn't know it was her...I didn't know who it was. Anyway, she got out of the car and came over; and to cut a long story short, I've invited her and Rafi round for Sunday lunch."

Lauren wondered what Rafi's mother would be like and wished he was coming on his own; even so, she was glad they were coming and the heaviness inside her began to lighten. She was probably going to see him at Ida's the day before anyway, but having him to herself would be different.

"I'm thinking..." Finn's voice was an octave higher than usual and his face turned scarlet. Lauren spat the mouthful of water she was just taking back into her glass and burst out laughing, while Finn made a great show of clearing his throat.

"Sorry! Sorry!" Lauren spluttered, raising one hand towards him, while grabbing her sheet of kitchen roll with the other and wiping her chin.

"Be kind," Nick said to her and turned to Finn. "Go on, Finn, what were you saying?"

"I think I'm going to be a vegan." His voice was croaky, deeper; and he flushed again. "I don't want to exploit animals anymore. We shouldn't, should we, Dad? I mean..."

"A Vegan?" Lauren giggled. "I always thought you were a Martian."

"Lauren!" Jess warned, as Nick looked up at her. It was a look of parental supplication, of an old intimacy; a tacit acknowledgement of uncertainty and the need for support. Lauren saw it and a wave of sadness swept through her.

"That's quite a big step, Finn," Nick said. "It's not just cutting out meat and fish, it means no dairy either. You know, no milk or cheese or eggs...no ice-cream."

"Yeah, but there are other things instead, aren't there? Trev's family have cheese and milk and everything, only they're made from plants and..." He looked up in the air, screwing his eyes tight and shaking his fist. "Um...not yoghurt...oh, you know..."

"Soya?" Lauren offered.

"Yes, yes, that's it, soya!" His face cleared in relief and a sort of triumph. "Can we, Mum? Dad?" He looked from one to the other. "We don't have to kill animals; we can let them be free, like we are, can't we?"

"Well, count me out," Lauren said. "I need protein."

Finn spun round to face her, his green eyes flaring in anger. "So, you're happy for animals to die, are you, just so you can go on running?"

"Hold on," Nick said, stretching out his hand and resting it on Finn's arm. "It's okay, we can sort this out." He glanced at Jess. "Can't we?"

"We can," Jess agreed; "but two things, Finn. This is your choice and that's fine, but everyone else is equally free to make theirs. And the other point is a practical one about cooking two lots of meals every time. It's going to take some planning."

Finn nodded and fell silent, while Lauren double-checked that they would still be having a roast on Sunday for Rafi and his mother. And it wasn't until Nick was handing round bowls of apple crumble that Finn spoke again.

"When are we going to see Pop & Mormor?" He looked at Nick and then at Jess. "And Ginnie and Zoltan?"

"Probably Easter," Jess said,

"But that's ages away!" Finn protested. "Why can't we see them before then? Otherwise, how am I going to get this stupid homework done?"

"Hold on, Finn," Nick said. "Don't get upset. Tell us about it. What do you need to see them for? I mean, what's the homework about? Maybe, you could just ring them, speak to them over the phone; or Skype them, if you like."

Finn was close to tears. "I've got maths to do and a history essay and somebody's poetry...can't understand a stupid word of it...and now this project, as well." His voice trailed off, his head drooping forward. He wasn't often upset; and, when he was, Lauren always felt a strong protective urge to comfort him, which she could do when he was little, putting her arms round him and holding him tight, but which seemed more awkward now. And she was relieved when Jess moved her seat next to him and put her arm around his shoulders.

"It's okay, sweetheart; we'll help you."

"That's right," Nick said. "You tell us what's needed by when and we'll help you tackle them, one by one. Okay?"

Finn shrugged, not looking up; and Jess gave him another squeeze.

"So, tell us, what's this project about?"

Finn mumbled something into his chest.

"Come on, Finn," Nick said; "talk to us properly."

"We've got to do a family tree back to our great-grandparents to see where we come from." Finn straightened up and grabbed some kitchen roll to blow his nose.

"Actually, that sounds quite interesting." Jess let her arm rest on the back of his chair. "Zoltan's from Hungary, Ginnie's Scottish, Mormor's family's from Sweden, and Pop was born..."

"In Australia, I know," said Finn, "on a sheep station!"

Nick laughed. "We're all immigrants. But, anyway, we can tell you everything; you don't really need to speak to them."

"Yes, I've got to," Finn said, desperation edging back into his voice. "Mr Frazer says so. I have to interview them about their parents and families and where they grew up and show it on a map and find out what they all did, where they went to school, what jobs they had, whether they fought in a war, and...oh, I don't know... he's given us a whole list of stuff."

Lauren shifted in her seat. "Sorry, but I've got work

of my own to do," she said, getting up; and, picking some grapes from the fruit bowl on her way out, she went back up to her room.

Finn should be having fun, not getting depressed over homework, she was thinking, as she switched on the lamps on the chest-of-drawers and by her bed. The overhead was too harsh and she turned it off, her eyes relaxing in the softer light, with its rising shadows. Kids were in school all day; they ought to be free to do what they wanted after that...especially in the summer. They ought to be outside playing, having adventures, getting exercise, being creative on their own account, not cramming for more tests, more exams. What the hell was the use of education, if it reduced you to tears and killed off your pleasure in being alive! Finn's full of curiosity and fun. Stop squashing him into your mean little box and let him be...let him find his own shape!

She sat down at the desk and pulled her straight-backed chair in close, so that her own back was firm against it. Despite the central heating, her fingers felt cold. A draught from somewhere. She tucked her hands under her thighs and stared at the closed laptop in front of her. There was homework and there was homework. She didn't mind the prospect of hers. In fact, she was looking forward to starting it. She felt in the mood. It was more of an art project really. It would count towards her grade for Art, at the end; but there was never any sense of compulsion or judgment with Jan Rawlings, much more a sense of exploration and collaboration.

The guidelines were clear and simple:

Choose a person of interest to you and represent them in paint, charcoal or clay, with an accompanying 500-1000 word account of their significance to you. Your representation may be figurative or abstract and should illustrate aspects of the character and values of the individual concerned.

Two women had leapt instantly to mind, when she'd first read the instructions: Emma Goldman and Christine Ohuruogu, one dead and the other very much alive. They both stirred strong feelings of attachment in her: Red Emma, with her courageous campaign for female equality; and Christine, for her sporting dedication and achievement. She hadn't known anything about Emma Goldman, until her mother had named the restaurant after her.

Lifting the lid, Lauren turned on her laptop and pressed the button-switch on the black, bendy-neck desk lamp. Losing herself in the screen's revolving circle of white dots, she pictured the framed poster that hung inside the restaurant's front door near the coat stand. Its sepia monochrome resembled Wild West 'WANTED' posters she'd seen; but, instead of some bearded desperado, it portrayed a young woman seated at a table, her hands clasped across a book in front of her. She was wearing a high-necked dress with an elaborate bow beneath its collar, as if some magnificent butterfly had just landed on her chest with outspread wings. But what had really caught her attention the first time she'd seen it was the accompanying newspaper extract, its content so at variance with this respectable-looking woman:

27 September 1895 – The Dutch police are anxious to find Emma Goldman, "very dangerous anarchist woman; comes from New York, is in London, and wants to go to Germany."

"You bet she was dangerous!" her mother had told her. "She wanted equal rights for women, sexual freedom and contraception, trade unions and freedom of expression. She was a great hero...or should I say heroine...of Zoltan's and Ginnie's all through my childhood."

The dots petered out, replaced by the beaming face of Christine Ohuruogu, hair caught up in a bunch, her Beijing 2008 Olympic 400m gold medal on its red ribbon around her neck and her hands in the side pockets of her red, white and blue UK tracksuit top.

It was a face and a smile Lauren saw everyday and she never tired of gazing at it, imagining the moment, as well as looking for some trace of the secret of her success. She'd been eight years old then and knew at once that was what she wanted to be: an athlete, a 400 metre runner and an Olympic gold medal winner for her country. And when Richards-Ross beat Christine into second place at the London Olympics four years later, Lauren had cried and had felt even more despairing than she had at not winning her own school event that same summer.

Emma or Christine? Her head said Emma, but her heart said Christine. She pushed back her chair and went across to her bed, sitting down on the end of it and looking at the poster on the wall opposite above the armchair. This was triumph. This was the reward of dedication and determination: C. OHURUOGU across her running top, Moscow 2013 underneath, her arms in the air, holding up a Union Jack flag spread out behind her, and a big smile on her face. She had just won back her World Championships crown in a thrilling photo-finish, catching Amantle Montsho on the line with a late surge. Lauren nodded, acknowledging how much she had learnt from her! How to be patient and hold back until, coming off the last bend into the home straight, she would let herself go, finding that extra gear that drew the leaders back to her as she powered past them in the final few yards. She owed all her ambition and success to Christine Ohuruogu.

Going back to her desk, she could already feel the flow of Christine mid-stride forming under her fingertips, a clay maquette to express Christine's significance to her and the values she embodied. She admired Red Emma, but there were times when she was Christine Ohuruogu.

She brought up a Word Document and copied out the assignment title. She knew where she was going now. The accompanying text would be straightforward, but it was the maquette that excited her; and she'd start on it over the weekend round at Ida's. She leant back frowning. But what about Rafi? She couldn't very well work on it if he was there. Ida wouldn't mind. The work bench was in her room and they just chatted and did their own thing.

"No boys till you've made it to the Olympics, remember?" She could hear Ida's teasing voice. Yeah, first things first; but she wanted to see him again out of school. It was different, more...more *personal*. That didn't seem quite the right word, but she couldn't think of another. And Sunday lunch wouldn't count with his mother and her parents there, unless she could get him on his own. Besides, what about Terry Curnow? Much better if Rafi was with her and Ida. More *intimate*, maybe. No, that wasn't quite it either. She shook her head; she didn't want boyfriends distracting her from training. It hadn't been a problem before; but there was something different about Rafi...something visceral, something in her skin.

"No!" she growled and typed '**Christine Ohuruogu**' in bold, as her heading.

6

Terry was sitting comfortably at the corner table by the fire, fondling the pint of bitter in front of him. Friday night and the weekend in prospect, he had his back to the wall and could watch all the comings and goings in the dimly lit bar; although, as yet, it was early and the pub quiet.

"Cheers!" He raised his glass and smiled.

"Yes, cheers, Terry!" Matt, sitting opposite, leant forward and clinked his glass against it. And, as he did so, Terry saw his young protégé's face redden under the springy, auburn curls and savoured the moment. John and Lawrence could be unpredictable; but Matt was an open book and devoted to him, he knew that.

"I have exciting news, Matty," he chortled. "Yes, indeed. However, we must be patient and wait for the others. But, in the meantime, you can regale me with all the latest tittle-tattle from college." He reached for the packet of crisps beside his glass, tore it open and took several, before sliding the remainder into the middle of the table. "Help yourself."

"Well," Matt started, taking one, "I'm not sure there's anything very..." A sudden burst of coughing stopped him saying anymore, as he grabbed his coke and gulped it down. "Sorry," he spluttered, wiping his mouth with the back of his hand, before coughing again and taking another swig.

"Hope it's not the gossip choking you," Terry laughed, knowing perfectly well that Matt was often flustered in his presence. "Although it must be rather..." he hesitated, licking his lips, "spicy, if it is."

"Crisp went down the wrong way...sorry."

Terry nodded and sat back, linking his fingers across the rise and fall of his stomach. "Pray continue."

For a moment, Matt stared blankly at him. Then, like sea mist, the vacancy cleared and intelligence reappeared in his eyes. "Okay. So, Ida's in trouble again...had a disciplinary with Mr Meadows."

"Hope she took a chaperone with her!" Terry raised an eyebrow. "Not entirely trustworthy our gallant Deputy Head, when it comes to the girls, I believe...a bit light-fingered, if you catch my drift." He stretched for his glass and a handful more crisps, before settling back again. "My! My! That naughty Ida! What *has* she been up to this time?"

"She brought her pet python, Coil, into college." Terry heard the sparkle of excitement in Matt's voice and saw it in his eyes. "They were going to draw him in Art, 'cause Ms Rawlings doesn't mind. But Coil woke up in the science lesson before that and slid onto Geraldine Fawcett's shoulders before Ida could stop him." Terry couldn't help smiling back at the boyish grin. "And I was there! I mean Geraldine just started screaming, making poor old Porky drop his test-tube. And you know what he's like! Seeing Coil, he utterly panicked and pressed the fire alarm. And then everything went mad, I mean..."

"Hold on," Terry interrupted, holding up his palm and looking past Matt to the door. "Here comes John." He gave a wave. "He'll want to hear this...has a bit of a soft spot for Ida, does our John."

As John shoved back the hood of his parka and made for the bar, Terry saw the door open again, a familiar trilby bending in under the lintel.

"Good evening, pilgrims," Lawrence said, striding over to them; and, taking off his coat, he tossed it onto the table next to them.

A worm of unease wriggled into Terry's stomach, as Lawrence sat down facing into the bar, leaving John the chair opposite; which meant John would be left looking at both Lawrence and the night-dark window beyond him, neither of which he would like. John would be angry and Lawrence amused. What was it with these two? When he was planning something, there was no-one he would rather have along aside him than the pair of them. At college, nobody had dared challenge him, because of them. He smirked in spite of himself. Yes, indeed, they were his praetorian guard...his Dobermans. But the moment they were off duty, they went for each other. Lawrence liked to tease John; he was floating a fly now and John always rose to the bait.

"Come, Come, Terence!" he chided himself. "Mixed metaphors, indeed! Dobermans eating trout, I don't think so. Or should that be Dobermen?" He burped and laughed. Well, he would deal with them, as he always did. He'd find a new ball for them to chase. He already had one ready in his pocket anyway; that's why he'd called the meeting.

"You seem cheerful," Lawrence smiled. "You must have some new wickedness in mind...I do hope so!"

Terry watched John walking towards them with his pint of Guinness and was aware of the tension in Matt's face; but, when he reached them, John simply turned the empty chair sideways and sat down, stretching out his long legs into the body of the pub.

"Several reasons to be cheerful, as it happens," Terry said, glancing at Lawrence. "First of all, Matty is in the middle of a story about a new college drama involving the irrepressible Ida and her pet python."

"And that's not all of it," Matt chipped in; "there's...."

"All in good time," Terry continued. "Where was I?"

John groaned. "Fuck's sake! What about Ida?"

"Ah, have patience, John; and, once Matty has told his tale, I have some exciting news of my own to share with you...indeed, I have!" Terry leant forward, picked up his glass and raised it in the air. "Here's to the four musketeers, protectors of Queen, country and our own futures!" And he clinked glasses with the others, their arms all outstretched to a single meeting point.

"Right, Matty? On you go."

As Matt began again the story of Coil and Geraldine Fawcett, Rafi's face, gleaming in the lamplight of the night before, swam in front of Terry's half-closed eyes. He curled the fingers of his right hand into a loose fist and slowly released them again, remembering the ice-cold handlebar and the sudden heat of Rafi's wrist, as he'd slid his hand next to it. What was he going to do about 'Raf-aye-el'? He couldn't ignore him; his very presence in their midst was a challenge...a provocation. No, ignore him and how many more would there be? Something needed to be done to send him on his way... but what? It would have to be subtle, no obvious stirring up of racial hatred. Don't want the boys in blue to come knocking. Something hard to trace, then...something to make him want to go back where he came from of his own volition...something to frighten him, maybe, like...

"Are you with us, Commander?" Lawrence's sardonic drawl displaced him for a moment, like being disturbed from a dream.

Looking round the blurred figures in front of him, Terry struggled to reconnect. "So...er, tell me...what did happen to...to dear Ida?" he asked, Rafi and the lamp-lit street fading into the crackle of the fire, replaced by Matt's puzzled face gaining definition. "In the end, I mean."

"Christ, Tel! Get a grip!" John grabbed his smeared glass and headed for the bar.

"And a pint of scrumpy for me, if you please," Lawrence called after him. "I have the wherewithal."

"It's like I've just been saying," Matt frowned. "Geraldine's father complained to Mr Dalby..."

"Ah, our blessèd headmaster," Terry beamed, crossing himself, now fully restored to the present and filled with pleasurable anticipation at the prospect of the evening ahead; "the good Saint Marcus of the unlit pipe!" He waved at Matt to carry on.

"Right...so, Ida had to go to see Meadows and something happened. I don't know what exactly...only that afterwards there was some kind of big confab in the Art room with Jan Rawlings and Ida and Lauren and Lauren's dad, Mr Jackman."

"Forgive me for interrupting," Lawrence broke in, "but for the sake of brevity, the point is, as Matt has already told us, that, quite apart from Ida's likely exclusion for a short period, banished home with her snake, there is a rumour that Nick Jackman is enamoured of Ms Rawlings of the paint-spattered dungarees, and..."

"Four pounds twenty!" John banged down the mug of cloudy cider, pushing it towards Lawrence and placing his free hand open on the table, palm up.

Withdrawing a handful of change from his pocket, Lawrence carefully extracted four pound coins and a fifty pence piece. "Here you are," he smiled, standing them in a funnelled stack beside John's hand. "Please keep the change for your trouble."

John hovered for a moment, glaring down at him. "I will!" he said finally, taking up the coins and sitting down legs outstretched once more.

"Now, where was I?" Lawrence looked at Terry. "Ah, yes, the paintbrush and the quill. What a delightful prospect! But, more interesting still, as Matt was just telling us, it seems romance may also be in the air between our hero's daughter and the infidel from Jordan."

"That's not quite what I..." Matt began; but John drowned him out, swivelling round, his face a mask of irritation: "What the fuck are you talking about?"

"Lauren and Rafi!" Terry snapped, but his eyes were on Matt. "Who told you?"

Of course, that's where Rafi must have been going on his bike last night; and the realization infuriated him.

"Who told you?" he demanded again, even though Matt was already trying to answer him.

"People in the canteen were talking about it at lunchtime. Something to do with..."

"What people?"

"Um, well...Jason and Kerry really, but..."

"How do they know?"

"I'm not sure, Terry. But, you know...maybe they..."

"No, I don't know!" Matt's dithering, scarlet face exasperated him. "It's what I'm trying to find out, isn't it?"

Terry drummed his fingers on the table in increasing irritation as Matt opened his mouth as if to continue, only to close it again and then lick his lips.

"You seem a bit worked up, Commander," Lawrence's languid drawl sounded amused. "Everything all right?"

The storm in Terry abated as suddenly as it had erupted. He took a slow drink from his glass and sat back, folding his hands over his stomach once again, before turning to Lawrence.

"Indeed, it is. And thank you for asking." He had lost control and he shouldn't have attacked Matty like that. It wasn't good for morale; no, not at all. "The idea of our friend Rafi becoming involved with one of our own girls," he looked round at Matt and John, "is... distressing, is it not?" He needed to bring them all back under the blanket of his calm, of his self-assurance.

"Yeah, well, it ain't going to happen," John snarled. "White girls are for white boys! So, we'll deal with him, won't we, Tel?"

"Deal with him?" Lawrence's long face split into a mischievous grin. "Now there's a thought!"

"We'll need more drinks all round, Matty, if you would be so kind." Terry held out his credit card to him and then lifted it away for a moment. "This is to celebrate a happy turn in our misfortunes, which I shall reveal as soon as refreshments arrive." He handed Matt the card and watched him walk away.

"He's a good lad and useful to us." He looked from John to Lawrence on either side of him, nodding and smiling at them both. "Yes, indeed. He has the halo of innocence about him...unlike our good selves."

A bubble of delight fizzed up inside him and burst out in a roar of laughter that ignited the same in the other two, until they were all rocking with it, taking it in turns to exchange glances and explode again; so that, by the time Matt returned carrying a tray, half the heads in the pub were turned in their direction, some laughing too and others frowning their disapproval.

John turned his chair to the table and, after they had all helped themselves, Matt slid the tray under his chair.

"Right," Terry said, pausing to take in the three sets of eyes trained on him. "What I feel we have been lacking is a sense of direction, a sense of purpose. We've been a bit aimless, am I right?"

"So?" John grunted.

A slow smile stole across Lawrence's face. "So, our noble commander, the keeper of our dreams, has come up with a plan, I fancy."

"Indeed, I have. Yes, yes, a dream of a plan, exactly!" Terry leaned forward, lowering his voice, so that the others had to follow suit. "Now, tell me, John, you're not happy at Bradley's, are you?"

"'Course not!" John shot forward, his face tight and angry. "They're taking the piss, right? I'm on an apprenticeship there, aren't I? They're meant to be teaching me construction, not just using me as cheap labour. Almost two years and I'm still doing the same fucking things I was doing the day I started!"

Terry beamed and nodded. "I know...I know, you've told me before. But you've also told me why you're not making any progress. There's no room further up the ladder..."

"Up the ladder!" Lawrence broke in. "Very witty, Commander!"

"...is there?" Terry continued, ignoring him. "And why is that?"

"Bloody Polaks, that's why! Know how to do everything already and willing to work for the same shit wages as me. So, Bradley takes them on rather than spend time training me, doesn't he?"

"Quite," Terry said soothingly. "Absolutely!" He shifted his gaze. "So, Matty, what do we deduce from this?"

He waited, watching Matt's face reddening and enjoying his confusion...enjoying both his power over him and his desire to comfort him.

"Well," Matt started, "Deduce? I mean...that is, John isn't getting the support he should, is he?"

"No, he's not; that's right. But the crucial point is: why isn't he?"

"Because of the...you know, because of the others doing the work instead."

"And who are the 'others'?" Terry persisted.

Matt's cheeks went from pink to crimson. "The... erm, the...you know...the workers from Poland."

"Yes, indeed, Matty! Immigrant workers from Poland taking jobs from us, taking jobs from you and me and John, jobs meant for those who were born here, who belong..."

"Happily not mine, though," Lawrence cut in. "You have to be a British citizen or member of the Commonwealth to serve in Her Majesty's Armed Forces."

"You're not a proper soldier," John jeered; "you're just a territorial, like fucking Dad's Army."

"Commando, actually," Lawrence paused and smiled, "like your dear old dad. But, of course, ignorance is your forte, isn't it? Besides, I've decided to join up full-time and have some proper overseas adventures." He laughed and turned to Terry. "'Fraid I'll be changing units, Commander...you know, off to do battle with all those grey squirrels."

Terry saw John stiffen, and he put his hand on his arm.

"Now, now, come on, let's not fight among ourselves. We have much too much to lose by falling out, and I have such interesting news to tell you."

"Outside...later," John growled, leaning forward. "You and me goin' to settle this once and for all. You get me, Larry?"

Lawrence took a slow drink from his glass, licked his lips and set it down softly. "If you like," he said; "but, for now, I'm rather more interested in hearing our leader's interesting news."

"So am I!" Matt broke in, the panic in his voice changing to a kind of plea. "Go on, Terry, tell us. What is it?"

This was not at all how Terry had envisaged the evening going and Lawrence's army plan was disturbing; it left him feeling oddly vulnerable, as if a part of him was suddenly unprotected. Even so, at least they had stopped their squabbling and were now looking at him, waiting.

"As we were saying a moment ago," he started, struggling to sound calmer than he was feeling, "we are all agreed, are we not, that immigration is the reason for our woes? Yes, yes, our island is a small one. It cannot accommodate an endless flow of foreigners." He shook his head, looking briefly at each of them. "No, not at all. A boat, if you like, has a limit to how many passengers it can carry before it sinks. And we are already sinking, yes, indeed. So some passengers must be returned to shore and no more allowed to get on. Do you follow me?"

"Yeah, Tel, I do. Stick all the wobble-heads and Pakis in fucking boats and send 'em home, right?"

"Just so, John," Terry nodded.

"And we'll need ships for our West Indian and Oriental friends," Lawrence joined in, "a veritable convoy!"

"There you are!" Terry held out his arms palms up in satisfaction. They were all coming back under his sway. He took a crisp and, looking expectantly at Matt, popped it in his mouth.

"And...and there won't be any more from the EU getting on our boat, will there...because of Brexit, I mean."

"Exactly, Matty! Nail on the head. Brexit was the start...was the moment when the tide finally turned... when the flood waters, if you like, began to recede. Yes, indeed! And it's more than just about having too many people in the boat; it's about making sure those left on board speak the same language, have the same heritage...the same traditions, the same customs. And that's..."

"The same food!" John snorted. "Bloody wankers!"

Sometimes, Terry wanted to punch John's aggressive, bony face right on his protruding nose. He took a deep breath, briefly closing his eyes, and let it out slowly.

"And that's why," he went on, "I have arranged a meeting with NAN this Sunday, here at the Exeter."

"Christ's sake, Tel! What's your Gran got to do with it? Thought she was dead, anyway."

"She is, John...she is," Terry repeated, his voice dropping, more amused than exasperated and trying to conceal both. "NAN stands for the National Accord Network, an organization that stands for what we stand for."

"Not a movement then?" Lawrence smirked; "All that standing, I mean."

Matt laughed and John frowned, fingering his knuckles. Terry decided to ignore him.

"NAN's membership has exploded, ever since Steve Langton, its leader, made mincemeat of Ian Hislop and Paul Merton on TV. He certainly had news for them," Terry paused to appreciate his own joke. "He was smarter than they were and the audience loved it. Maybe, you saw it?"

Lawrence shook his head, "Not exactly cutting edge, are they?"

"'Fraid not," Matt muttered.

"Never mind TV, why's he coming 'ere?"

John's tone was always most belligerent when he was most confused, and Terry felt a pang of remorse. John couldn't help being slow on the uptake; what he needed was support, not irritation.

"Good question, John. Only he's not coming, his right-hand man is...Tony Gardner, and a couple of others."

John's knee was pumping. "What for?"

"Yes, indeed! What for?" Terry looked from one to the other, a bubble of jubilation rising in his chest. This was his coup...this was his surprise. "They are coming to discuss our setting up a regional centre for NAN down here. It means training. It means being on their payroll. It means becoming actively involved in where this country's going." He banged his fist on the table out of sheer exuberance and pride. He had worked so hard for this. "It means we will..."

Shadows fell across the table, as two figures moved past Matt to the table in the corner behind Lawrence. Terry paused to take them in, as they struggled out of their dripping jackets and hung them over the backs of two of the four chairs.

"Excuse me," the man said, lifting Lawrence's greatcoat off the table, "is this yours?"

As he turned towards them, Terry took in the friendly, middle-aged face and drew in his legs, pushing back in his seat, sitting up straighter. The man was West Indian. He watched Lawrence twist round awkwardly to take the coat and then lean sideways to dump it on the floor beside him; and, as he did so, Terry saw the woman clearly for the first time, the fingers of both her hands combing her ruffled hair back into place... chubby, white fingers!

"Nice to be in the warm," she smiled, catching his eye; "lovely fire."

"Yes, indeed," Terry nodded and looked away quickly, taken aback at being addressed by her.

"Go on, spit it out, Tel! It means we will what?"

Terry was so affronted by the couple next to them that he found himself staring at John in mounting fury, unable to get his thoughts together to reply.

"What?" John's injured voice sounded distant, far removed from the throbbing pain between Terry's eyes.

"They're flaunting it," he muttered, glaring round at the others. "Here, in our very own pub!" Anger stormed through the confusion of his thoughts, clarifying them, purifying them like fire. "The grey squirrel is preying on the red squirrel under our very noses and we're not going to put up with it lads, are we?" He didn't wait for an answer; he wasn't interested in one. "We're not going to put up with the contamination of our line. Not here! Not now! Not in the pub where Sir Walter Raleigh drank. Not in the county where Sir Francis Drake drove the Spanish Armada onto the rocks and into the depths. We are the inheritors of that golden age and of the greatest empire the world has ever known that grew from it. And I'll tell you..." he drilled his will into the three sets of eyes focussed on him, "we're not going to let our birthright be stolen from us by any intruders who think they can barge in here and help themselves to everything our forefathers fought and strove for. No, sir! Certainly not! No way!"

He stopped to gulp at his beer. The storm was abating and he was taken aback to find that the couple had moved to the other end of the bar. Their table was empty and he hadn't even seen or heard them go. He kept his eyes on the deserted table. The others were watching him, he knew, waiting to see whether he had finished.

"Storm's over," he smiled, looking back at them, and then let the smile go. "We will act. We will begin. There will be no relationship between Rafi and Lauren and that's what's up my other sleeve, because we're going to ensure he and his mother go back where they came from much sooner than they intended...oh, yes, much sooner!"

"Sorry, but I've got to go," Matt said, standing up and pulling on his reefer jacket. "Promised I'd be back by ten."

Terry studied him, holding him in suspension by remaining silent. He looked like a young sailor in his navy-blue serge, with the collar turned up and his hands sheathed in the slanted side-pockets. Even the rosy bloom in his cheeks looked as if it had been freshly stung there by the wind and the spray up on deck.

"Yes, of course, Matty," Terry said at last, releasing him with a wave of his hand. "Mustn't miss the tide."

"E's goin' 'ome, not sailin'!" John laughed. "Ain't you, Matt?"

Matt grinned, withdrawing a hand and holding the palm up towards them. "See you," he said and turned away for the door.

Terry missed him when he was gone, he liked having him there. Matty was always agreeable, always willing. He didn't have to worry about him like he did with the other two. He'd known John longer; they'd teamed up in junior school, after John had punched the boy who was bullying him in the face. And, in a sense, he'd been his protector ever since. "You've got the brain and I've got the brawn, eh Tel?" Terry shook his head. Just when you thought John was oblivious to the nature of their friendship, he'd come out with something like that. No, John was volatile and too quick to whip out that knife of his, but he was...what was he? He was...staunch! Yes, that was the word; he was 'staunch'. He could depend on him absolutely.

"I need a pee," Lawrence said.

"And I need another pint." John stood up. "What about you, Tel?"

Terry looked at his glass; it was still a third full. "No thanks. This'll do me."

He watched John march to the bar and stand waiting, as the barman said something to him and disappeared out the back.

"Fathers, I suppose," he muttered. That's what the three of them had in common. He thought about Lawrence. They'd befriended him in secondary school, after his parents were killed in a car crash on the moor. Lawrence had missed his dad the most, even though the accident had been his dad's fault, overtaking where there was a dip in the road. Lawrence had gone mute, wouldn't talk to anyone, and so fierce no-one had dared challenge him, not even the teachers. But he and John had got through to him...well, John mainly...at the start, anyway. John was as angry and unpredictable as Lawrence was. He hated his father, a Royal Marine, who beat him with his belt every time he came home on leave for...what was it?...oh, yes, for 'insubordination' and 'to teach him proper self-discipline'. John's so-called insubordination had been about trying to protect his mother from his father's violence. So, it was a good thing really that his dad had been blown up in Afghanistan before John got hold of his commando knife or he'd probably have killed him. Terry nodded to himself. Yes, indeed, John would have done so and he knew the feeling. And that was it, wasn't it? Lawrence had seen a rage in both of them to match his own.

"I'll tell you what, Gary" Terry whispered, picturing his own father. His mouth was dry and he reached for his glass. "If you ever show your face round here again, I'll set the hounds on you...yes, yes, the hounds of hell!"

"Giving yourself a pep-talk, Commander?"

Terry was too taken by surprise and his mouth too full of beer to reply at once, as Lawrence resumed his seat.

"Just reflecting on what we were talking about and what we're going to achieve through NAN." Terry forced a smile over a sudden lurch into grief, as the sensation of riding pillion on his dad's motorbike threatened to overwhelm him. He'd been so young and excited and terrified, feeling the roar and power of it through every bone of his body; and he'd clung on to his dad, pressing the side of his face against the back of his leather jacket.

"Bad timing," John said, arriving back. "Eddie had to change the barrel." He flicked his finger against the side of his glass, condensation glistening against the black. "Still, nothing better than a virgin pint," he grinned and took a slow mouthful, creamy foam clinging to his upper lip as he sat back. "Bloody delicious!"

"Your Guinness moustache suits you," Lawrence nodded. "Gives you the air of a fighter pilot...you know, chocks away!"

"Actually," Terry dived in, seeing John's eyes narrowing, "I'll tell you more about NAN after Sunday's meeting, when I'll have more concrete information about what we're going to be doing and when. But, in the meantime, as regards my other plan, I know exactly what we are going to be doing about our friend, Raf...aye...el. Oh, yes! We're going to be paying him a little night-time visit." He couldn't keep the gurgle of excitement out of his voice, as he beamed at them both. "Are you with me, lads?"

"Blood brothers all the way!" John fired back, without a moment's hesitation. "Time we taught that uppity little Arab a lesson!"

A flood of affection and gratitude welled up in Terry at the fierce loyalty he saw in the hawkish eyes fixed on him. He reached out and gripped John's shoulder. "You're always there for me," he said, squeezing and letting go; "you always have been!"

He turned to Lawrence, who returned his gaze in silence.

"Well?" Terry demanded, irritated by his withholding, but more by his impending desertion. "What about you? Are you with us in this?"

A slow sunrise of a smile began to break across Lawrence's high-cheekboned, nonchalant face, brightening the blue in his eyes. "A crusade against the infidel, I like it! On our white charger, we will storm his fortress and drive him into the sea!" He raised his empty glass and brought his fist crashing down on the table, making the other glasses jump. "For Terry, England and St George!"

"TIME, GENTLEMEN, PLEASE!" Eddie boomed from the bar.

7

When Rafi woke, he heard the wind moaning through the trees and lay with his eyes closed savouring the warmth of his duvet cocoon. Saturday and time to himself; time to dream of being back home and soft-footing it out to his grandfather on the terrace, careful not to disturb his sister and younger brother. Spring, as always, the scent of blossom from the fruit trees wafting in on the breeze across his pillow. He helped himself to a piece of his grandfather's bread smeared with olive oil and Za'atar, his mouth full of the sweet nuttiness of the toasted sesame seeds. "The secret is in the sumac," his grandfather says. Dear Jedi, how he has missed him; but they will see him for his birthday.

Rafi half-opened his eyes to the dull grey light coming through the curtains. Winter in Devon was dreary; always raining, always dark, always cold. What was he going to do today? He wished he were home in the hills of As-Salt with Jedi and Baba, and Amti Anoush, and Jasmin and Zak; back meeting his friends, Yousef, Amal and the others, at Aktham's for coffee and halva...or borma even better, the honey and pistachios so delicious. As it was, Mama would be busy with conference calls and her preparations for her trip to London, and he'd be on his own most of the day. Maybe, he could call Ida. She'd said he was welcome to go round to her father's house anytime. But it didn't seem right. At home, it would mean something more.

Getting up, he crossed the room and threw back the curtains. Besides, it was Lauren he would rather see. He stared out at the grey fields behind the swaying, skeletal branches. He rubbed his breath's mist from the glass with his sleeve and turned away, shaking his head. It wasn't possible. And, anyway, he wasn't going to do that was he? Girlfriends and all of that would have to come later. Right now he had to get on with his studies; that was why they were here.

No, he would email his enquiry to Utrecht University to see for sure if their English Language BA would qualify him to go on to do the International Relations MA his mother had recommended. She said that afterwards, with one of the internships the course offered, it could be 'a stepping stone' to joining the UN's Young Professionals and pursuing the Palestinian cause...Jedi's cause. His family may have been forced to flee their home in Jerusalem by Israeli paramilitaries, but he would fight for the rights of the dispossessed.

He whipped the belt through the loops of his black jeans and tightened the buckle. It was still happening, people having to flee their own countries, lose their homes and livelihoods, and become refugees, stateless, belonging nowhere; families torn apart and treated like criminals. Well, his family had a home, thanks to Jedi; they had the farm at As-Salt. But that was only because Jordan, humane Jordan, had granted citizenship to many of the refugees like Jedi after their violent expulsion in 1948, during the Nakba.

The Nakba! He still couldn't get his head round it. 750,000 Palestinians forced out of their homes and country or be killed, as many were. And this perpetrated by Jews who had just lost 6,000,000 of their own in Hitler's gas chambers. It didn't make any sense. How could they? It was a question he carried into the kitchen, where his mother was sitting drinking coffee and scrolling through the news on her laptop.

"Come, have some breakfast," she said, indicating his chair and pouring coffee into his cup from the cafetiere.

He sat down and spooned some muesli into a bowl, adding yogurt and honey, before looking up to find her watching him, a familiar warmth in her attentive eyes.

"Yes, why would they? It's a good question." She paused. "No, it's a difficult question. Why do the abused so often become abusers?"

He expected her to answer her own question. Instead, she took a spoonful of dark jam from the earthenware pot and spread it evenly over her toast, before looking up at him again and taking a bite. He should have known. With all of them, she encouraged them to think for themselves. That was her mantra: "Not my thoughts, but your thoughts!" Her students must long for a straight answer, he was sure, but that wasn't her way.

"Oh, I don't know, Mama. Can't you tell me? I've only just woken up."

"Ah, the pocket-money smile, Mr Charmer!" She laughed and a gold filling glinted in the artificial light. "But you're not a little boy anymore. So, let me make the question more concrete." She took a sip of coffee and sat back again. "A father abuses his son. The son grows up and abuses his son. I give your question back to you. How could he?"

Rafi frowned. "I don't know. If I were the son, why would I want to...," he paused, searching for the word, "...to inflict the same pain, the same shame, on my son? No, I definitely wouldn't! I would do everything in..." The muffled jangle of his mobile vibrated in his pocket. "Sorry," he said, easing it out.

"Hi, Rafi, it's Ida. Are you..."

"Just a moment, Ida." He stood up, smiled at his mother's raised eyebrow and walked out into the hall. "Sorry, we're just having breakfast."

"Oh, look, I didn't mean to disturb you. I can call back later if..."

"No, it's fine." He started up the stairs to his room. "Please, go on."

"Okay, if you're sure."

"Yes...yes, I'm sure."

"Great. So, Lauren and I wondered if you'd like to come round, if you're not doing anything...you know, nothing special, just hang out. Lauren's working on her model and I'm experimenting with some plants for Dad, but we can chat and catch up and you can stay for lunch if you like."

Rafi closed the door and moved to the window. "Will your father be there?" His voice was calm, the reflex question hiding the sudden conflict inside him.

Ida's giggle gurgled in his ear. "Yes, he's here, Rafi; but he doesn't bite, you know!"

"No, it isn't that." He was going to explain that in As-Salt he would not be allowed to visit a girl at home on her own; but he felt embarrassed at the implications of that, caught between a taboo that didn't seem to apply in the UK and his own guilty excitement at the prospect of seeing Lauren again. "I like your father," he said instead, remembering Henry Downes coming to his aid outside the pub. "He is a good man, I think."

"Not bad!" Ida laughed. "So, you'll come?"

A wave of rain slashed at the panes of glass.

"I'm afraid I can't," he said, furious with himself even before he had finished. "I have to finish an application to Utrecht University and to help my mother prepare for her trip to London."

"Oh, right...er, that's a shame. But look, never mind, another time, hey?" He heard the disappointment in her voice, even as she tried to disguise it; and he felt stupid, cowardly.

"I'm sorry. It is kind of you to ask me. But, yes, another time; that would be good."

"Ok, bye, Rafi."

He stared at the screen...'Call ended'. "What's the matter with you?" He hurled the words at himself, spinning round and then back again. "You're a fool! No, you're not; you're a coward! Too scared to...to what?"

Another squall of rain beat against the window and he marched out of his room, flinging the door wide open and clenching his teeth along the landing. At the stairs, he stopped, staring down into the shadows of the hall. He closed his eyes and banged the side of his fist against the bannister. He wanted to see Lauren. Why on earth had he said no?

Eventually, he made his way down to the kitchen again, wondering if he could call Ida back and change his mind. But it felt too awkward; and instead, sitting down, he concentrated on his bowl of cereal and avoided looking at his mother. He wished she would go to her study and leave him in peace; but, when he saw the flash of amber from her ring as she reached for the cafetière, he knew she was waiting for him to say something.

A flake of nut stuck between his teeth and he tried to curl it out with the tip of his tongue. He always told her everything. She never judged him. And, often when he had a problem, just telling her about it helped him decide how best to resolve it. Even so, he didn't feel ready to talk about what had just happened. He finished his muesli in silence, knowing he needed to say something. He left the spoon in the bowl and picked up his cup. If he looked at her, she would know.

"I've been..." He cleared his throat and began again. "I think it's stress, stress and conditioning." He set his cup back in its saucer and looked up.

"What is?" she asked.

"The reason why the son abuses his son." He knew what he was going to say and met her gaze. "The reason why Israel persecutes us. It is because, when we are under stress and we don't know what to do, our conditioning takes over. What I mean is Jedi told me Baba says the same things to us as he said to him and Amti Anoush, when they were children and arguing like Zak and me and Jasmin...you know, things like, 'Chickens squabble. Are you a chicken?'

"That's not so terrible," she laughed. "Not really abuse, is it?"

"Well, no; but, if the father used to say something like, 'Fetch me my stick!', the son might say the same thing to his son...if he's angry and not thinking clearly, I mean."

His mother pursed her lips. "I see. But why then

is that not always the case? Why do some abused sons treat their sons only with love and kindness? Also, violence does not necessarily breed violence; think of Mahatma Ghandi's peaceful opposition to the military might of the British Raj."

Rafi knew his mother was waiting for an answer; but he was wondering if he could ring Ida back and suggest going round after lunch after all

"I don't know, Mama. Maybe, some do and some don't, and there is no reason why."

"And maybe you have had enough of this subject for now and your thoughts are elsewhere." She smiled at him and the knowingness of it infuriated him. "Do you want to talk about it?"

He shook his head. "No, there's nothing to say."

"Well, if you change your mind, I'll be upstairs." Halfway to the door, she turned and added: "As we will be having lunch at Lauren's house tomorrow, I'm going to ring Baba this afternoon, instead. Will you be here?"

"Yes, I will be," Rafi said, smiling with relief. If he was going to see Lauren tomorrow anyway, he didn't need to call Ida after all.

Clearing away the breakfast things and washing them up, he started humming.. He was looking forward to speaking to his father and the others. By the time both he and his mother had spoken to everyone in turn, often an hour or two would have passed. Of course, being a Saturday, Sadiq would still be at his office in Amman; so he'd miss all the latest stories about the wonders and misadventures of his uncle's air-conditioning units.

Whenever he thought of Sadiq, he couldn't help smiling. Although his uncle and his father were brothers, they were different in so many ways. While his father was calm and thoughtful, as well as fit and active through his building work, Sadiq always talking at ninety miles an hour, his hands flying through the air, while demolishing any warbat or baklava Amti Anoush had made and washing them down with glass after glass of Petra Amber, his favourite beer, his shirt straining against the swell of his stomach.

Thinking about his family carried him up to his room and his French A-Level essay on Moliere's 'Candide'. Everything was fine; he would spend time with Jedi and everyone on the phone that afternoon and with Lauren the next day. Perhaps, Professor Pangloss was right and 'all is for the best in this best of all possible worlds', even if Moliere was having fun at the Professor's expense, as the notes said. With his mother there at Lauren's tomorrow, he wouldn't be so much in the spotlight as he would have been at Ida's today. He would be there with Lauren without that being the reason for it. There would be no pressure on him...no expectation.

8

Lauren started to jog home from Ida's the next morning. The sun was low over the hedgerows, bathing the hoar-frosted fields in a pale daffodil glow. Cramps and headaches gone, she was enjoying the crisp air and she felt powerful, her breathing steady and the muscles in her calves and thighs warming and relaxing, as she ran. She heard the rolling peal of church bells echoing off the hills. Almost 10.30 am. She accelerated, exhilarated by the energy she felt and the excitement bubbling inside her. She was Zatopek racing past Chattaway to take 5000 metre gold in the 1952 Olympics, Grandpa Zoltan's hero. She could hear his whooping voice, see his exultant eyes: "Emil Zatopek, the greatest runner of all time, even if he was Czech! Ha! We can't all be Hungarian, can we?" And she laughed, as she breasted the tape and slowed. All her grandparents were coming down together to help Finn with his project apparently, although she felt there was more to it than that. In any case, she loved to see them; and, not only that, Rafi was coming round for lunch with his mother.

Running helped her think. She felt clearer, more herself; and problems became more distinct, leaving her less enmeshed in them. If there was tension between her parents, Mormor and Ginnie would sort it out. And Rafi's not coming round yesterday wasn't a rejection; it was short notice and he had commitments. He'd be there today and she wondered what his mum would be like. Judging by Rafi, she'd be a solid sort of person.

Lauren liked solid people; people you could trust and count on, like Ida and her dad, and Jan Rawlings and Rafi. They were straightforward, not sarcastic or two-faced, and they didn't try to please you. They were just themselves and you knew where you were with them, which made it easy to be yourself, in return; no hidden agendas, no double guessing. Except...

Lauren marked time at the Y-junction by the bridge on the outskirts of the town, waiting for a horsebox to go by, before crossing to the pavement on the far side and running down North Street alongside the little river, which ran shallow and gurgling through the centre of the old stannary town.

...except she'd not been quite straight with Ida, had she? She'd been irritated at Ida's disappointment that Rafi was busy and couldn't come over. She'd felt possessive of him and didn't want to share him; and, feeling cross with herself about that, she started running faster again, lengthening her stride and pumping harder with her arms. She and Ida told each other everything, always had. And yet, she wasn't telling her how she felt about Rafi. Well, she would tell her. She didn't want secrets between them. When, then?

She cut up past the car park and down the service lane. Tomorrow, after Ida and Henry had been to see Dalby about Coil, they could have a heart-to-heart then.

Coming through the garden, she pushed open

the back door into the kitchen and was immediately swathed in fragrant warmth and the blur of busy hands. The smell of freshly baked bread soothed her unease, as her breathing began to slow.

"Hello, darling," her mother smiled, glancing up from the roasting tin in front of her. "Just in time; there's lots to do." As she spoke, she went on making slits in the leg of lamb and pushing slivers of garlic and short sprigs of rosemary into them.

"Too right!" Finn joined in, dropping two halves of a potato into a large saucepan of water. "You can help me with these, for a start." He took another King Edward from the sack beside him and started peeling it into a plastic bucket. "Here, you can..."

"No, cloakroom needs a clean first!" Jess broke in. "Top priority. And then the bathroom."

Lauren shrugged off her backpack, letting it dangle loosely in front of her. "Ida and Henry have got to go and see Dalby first thing tomorrow about Coil. That stupid Geraldine Fawcett making all that fuss! Ida'll probably be excluded because of her."

"What happened?"

"I told you what happened, Mum! Coil went for a sleep on Geraldine's shoulders and she freaked."

"Yes, well I think I would too," Jess laughed, "if I found a python round my neck."

Lauren saw Finn smirking at her and stuck her tongue out.

"That's what you said last time." Didn't her mother take in anything she told her anymore she wondered and gave up. "Anyway, where's Dad?"

"Making up beds for your grandparents, hopefully." Jess carried the roasting tin across to the oven, still talking as she did so. "Anyway, with luck, Ida will just get a telling off. I don't see the point of exclusions; you just get behind in your lessons. But, come on, let's get on with it. Maryam and Rafi will be here before you know it." There was a belch of hot air into the room, as she opened the oven door and slid the tray in. "Are those potatoes ready yet, Finn?"

"I'm going as fast as I can." Finn pointed to the sack with his peeler."But you gave me hundreds!"

Jess put out a hand, as she passed him, and ruffled his hair. "Just wait till you see the carrots!" she said.

"I'm not one of your KPs, you know," Finn muttered, before adding with sudden enthusiasm: "How much do you pay them?"

"I'll just go and find Dad," Lauren said, moving for the door. "Let him know what's happened."

"Cloakroom!" Jess called after her. "Don't forget. And then the bathroom."

Upstairs, Lauren saw Nick through the open door to the guest room. He was standing motionless by the window, looking out over the street towards the church opposite. She was about to go to him, when she saw his shoulders shaking; and, realizing he was crying, she wheeled away into her own room, scalded by the nakedness of the moment.

She'd never seen him cry before. She stood near her bed, staring down at the wobbling flecks in the carpet, and swiped at her own unbidden tears. What was happening? He'd always been so... What had he always been? He'd always been so *there*! He'd just always been there...always been there whenever she needed him. He was her calm, reliable, loving Dad. What was happening to him? Was he breaking up with Mum?

What would happen to the house? What would happen to her and Finn?

"Stop it!" she hissed, shaking herself and looking up. It might be anything. Maybe Mormor was unwell or Pop. The room felt cold and lonely and she didn't want to stay there on her own. She'd go and find him, ask him what the matter was. She left her own door open; she didn't want closed doors. The guest room was empty, as was the other one in the attic, and so was her parents' bedroom; but the bathroom door was shut and she moved across to it. She could hear water running and she raised her bent finger to knock; then thought better of it. It wasn't the right moment; she'd find him later on after everyone had gone and he was on his own. Oh, God, Rafi and his mother! She raced down to the cloakroom and took the bleach and cleaning things out of the cupboard under the sink.

The cleaning didn't take long and she was just slotting the loo brush back in its holder, when the sudden clamour of the doorbell jolted her upright.

"It's them," her mother said, hurrying past, closely followed by Finn.

A draught of cold air swirled around Lauren's legs.

She listened to the greetings, the closing of the outer and inner doors and the rustle of coats being removed. The current of cold air died away. She pushed the door to, hearing the voices growing louder and then fading into the living-room. It was too soon. She wasn't ready. No, she had to go. This was rude. She flicked her hair behind her shoulders and took a deep breath, closing her eyes, which was when she heard the soft creak of footsteps on the stairs. Pulling the door back a crack, she saw her father going by on tiptoe. Two seconds later, he crept back the other way, holding his jacket. Surely, he wasn't going to... She pulled the door open wider, watching him steal into the kitchen, and followed him. Without stopping, he let himself out of the back door and disappeared into the garden. He was escaping! He was going away. He wasn't going to be there for lunch.

She chased after him; but, by the time she reached the service lane, he was nowhere to be seen. What on earth was he up to? What on earth was she going to tell her mum and the others? How could he do that? The sadness she'd been feeling for him earlier turned to anger. He was letting her down in front of Rafi. He was letting them all down. She stomped back into the kitchen and tore at the mat with the soles of her feet. Right, well she'd deal with him later; but right now she had to go and join the others and find some way of warning her mum.

As she walked in, she found the room glowing with the warmth and crackle of the open log fire.

"Ah, there you are!" her mother said as Rafi, sitting beside her, stood up. But, before she could respond, an elegant woman with rich chestnut hair rose from her armchair to greet her and stood silhouetted against the long sash window with the garden behind.

"You must be Lauren," she smiled, holding out her hand. "I am so happy to meet you."

Lauren skirted Finn on his beanbag. "Yes, me too, Mrs Masalha," she said, taking her hand. Not only was her grip firm and warm, but so too was the steady gaze from her large intelligent eyes. "Please, call me Maryam." She smiled again, and Lauren was aware of her subtle scent, like jasmine.

"Right, let's have a drink," Jess said, springing up,

"And you come and sit here Lauren, while Finn and I go and get things sorted. Is sparkling wine all right for you, Maryam? Or a gin and tonic or a sherry, if you'd rather. Or a soft drink, of course."

"A glass of sparkling wine will be lovely, thank you. It always feels festive."

"And you, Rafi? What would you like? We have beer as well...or lager, at least."

"Yes, a beer would be good. Thank you."

Lauren caught his eye. "Hi, Rafi," she said, circling her mother coming the other way. "You okay?"

"Same for me, thanks," Finn chipped in.

"In your dreams," Jess laughed, pausing and draping an arm over his shoulder.

"Yes, I'm fine." Rafi said; but he seemed embarrassed, still standing like he wasn't sure what to do with himself.

"Good. So look, do sit down," Lauren gestured to the sofa, "and I'll just go and help Mum."

"Excellent!" Finn said, giving her a thumbs-up.

"And you can entertain Mrs Masalha and Rafi, in the meantime," Jess grinned, giving Finn's shoulder a squeeze.

Lauren followed her out to the kitchen, anxious to tell her what she knew, but waiting till they were out of earshot.

"Dad's gone awol," she said, closing the door. "He's not here. I don't think he's going to be here."

Her mother's back was to her, bending to open the oven door. As she pulled out the roasting pan, a belch of fragrant steam whooshed up to the ceiling; and she started turning the potatoes and basting the lamb, slowly, methodically, as if she hadn't heard.

"Mum! What's happening? Why isn't he here?"

Her mother slid the pan back in, closed the door and pushed the oven cloth into place on its rail. When she turned, there was a steely glitter in her eyes. Lauren knew it well. So did Finn; he called it her 'ice eyes'. Their mother was usually bright and cheerful; but, when she was angry, it was a cold anger. Something hard and withheld that felt far more threatening than rage. She didn't go red; she went pale. She was pale now.

"Tell me," she said; and Lauren did. "I see." She crossed to the fridge, stooped to lift out the bottle of sparkling wine, put it on the side next to a plate of smoked salmon blinis and stooped again for a bottle of lager. "Get one of those small beer mugs for Rafi, will you?"

Lauren did as she was asked, handed it to her mother and waited as she put it on the tray beside the champagne flutes and Finn's tumbler. "We won't be needing this one," she said, removing a flute. She held it up in front of her and, for a moment, Lauren thought she was going to smash it; but, after a pause, she reached up, lifting her heels, and slid it onto the top shelf behind the wall unit's glass-fronted doors.

She turned back, straightening her jumper. "Put the blinis on the other tray with the crisps and nuts and I'll take the drinks and glasses. Oh, and get a can of coke for Finn," she added, moving to open the door.

"But what about Dad, Mum? What are we going to tell them? And what's going on, anyway?"

Her mother gave a rueful smile, some warmth coming back into her eyes. "I don't know, sweetheart. A mid-life crisis of some sort, maybe. People get to middle-age and start questioning where they're going... where they've been. Maybe, it's something like that."

"I saw him crying this morning...upstairs, staring out of the window." Tears filled Lauren's eyes, as she said it, and she brushed them away, embarrassed. "And I heard you both arguing in here the other night. Are you splitting up? Is that what this is all about?"

"No, darling, of course it isn't!" Her mother reached out to take her hand, but Lauren crooked her arm, jerking it away from her.

"It's so rude!" she flared. "What are Rafi and his mum going to think? How could he do that to..." she was going to say 'me' and checked herself, "to us?" She felt shamed before Rafi, anger boiling inside her, blood pounding in her head. Not knowing what to do with herself, she stood glaring at her mother, unable to think or move.

"Lauren, it's going to be all right," her mother's voice was calm, her gaze steady. "I'll talk to your Dad and find out what's going on and we'll sort it out, trust me. As for now, we'll just say, as a key-holder, he's been called into the college unexpectedly and gives his apologies." Her mother paused. "Ok? Do you feel ready to go back?"

More than anything, Lauren wanted to go up to her room and be alone; but she nodded, flicked her hair behind her shoulders and picked up the tray of nibbles.

9

"So, you've never been to the Rec?" Lauren checked, as she and Rafi walked away from the house towards the town centre. The clouds had cleared and pale, watery sunshine was brightening the early-afternoon streets. Finn was round at his friend, Tom's; and they had left their mothers in the music room, where Maryam was listening to Jess playing the piano. She felt lighter and excited to be on her own with Rafi.

"No, I haven't. I have heard it mentioned in college, but I don't know what it is."

"Oh right, of course, why would you? Sorry. Rec's short for recreation ground. It's a park...you know, grass and trees mainly, but with quite a big skateboarding area down the far end. Very popular!" She laughed. "Somewhere to hang out with your friends on your own...there's nowhere else in town."

"Isn't it cold in the winter? Or, is there a cafe there?"

"No, not in the park itself, but there's a shelter; you'll see."

A learner driver went by and turned off left at the t-junction, leaving the street deserted, apart from a couple with a small dog coming their way.

"Let's cross," she said, tapping his shoulder as she

stepped into the road. She felt his recoil at her touch and flushed. She hadn't meant anything by it. It was instinctive, a kind of 'hey' to draw attention to what she was about to do. She often did it, no matter who she was with.

They walked on in silence.

"This way," she said, turning off down a side street, which felt instantly darker and colder, the low sun blocked now by the rooftops. She pulled her hood up over her woolly hat and glanced at Rafi, stuffing her hands back deep in her coat pockets.

In profile, although his eyes were shaded by the peak of his baseball cap, he seemed thoughtful, preoccupied, looking straight ahead, his strides matching hers, but saying nothing. Maybe, he didn't want this...to be out with her. Maybe, he'd rather be on his own. But he'd seemed ok about going to the Rec. She'd thought he might like it. She didn't understand the change in the atmosphere between them.

Lunch had gone well. She'd been surprised how smoothly her mother's explanation had been accepted; and conversation had flowed easily after that. Rafi and Maryam had seemed relaxed answering questions about their family and the farm in Jordan. In return, Jess had told them all about her giving up teaching to open her restaurants. And, when asked, Lauren had been happy to talk about her running, as had Finn about his veganism. She liked Maryam; she was serious, but she was genuinely interested in what they said. She hadn't just been being polite. Rafi, though, had been quite quiet, not really saying anything unless he was spoken to. Even so, nearly every time she had glanced at him, she had found him looking at her. So, why was he being so silent now? It had to be about the touch, didn't it?

"You all right?" she asked.

"Yes...yes, I'm fine." He didn't look at her.

She stopped. "What's up, Rafi?"

He looked round. "Nothing," he said, taking half a step back towards her.

"Come on, something is. You've gone all silent."

"No, really, I was just..."

"Is it because I touched your shoulder? I didn't mean to offend you." She hadn't known she was going to say it, but she was glad she had. She felt stronger, less self-questioning. "Just wanted to let you know I was going to cross the road."

"Yes, I'm sorry." His voice was muffled by the black-and-white scarf covering half his face and he pulled it down. "This is different for me." He glanced away up the street. She knew he was embarrassed, but she wanted him to go on and so she waited, saying nothing. "We don't do this at home," he said finally, facing her again.

She stamped her feet. "Look, it's freezing out here, why don't we forget about the Rec today and go to Zeno's."

"Zeno's?"

"Yeah, it's just up there on the corner." She pointed. "I really fancy a hot chocolate and it'll be warm in there. Come on, and I'll show you the Rec another day."

He seemed hesitant. "Race you!" she grinned and took off.

She was inside and holding the door open by the time he caught up with her.

"Hey, you're fast!" he panted, unwinding his scarf as she led him to a corner table at the back.

"Log burner's doing a good job," she said, unzipping her jacket and pushing back the hood. She hung it over the back of one of the chairs. "So, what can I get you?"

"No, no. It's my turn, you gave me lunch." He smiled and she thought how beautiful he looked, the flash of his eyes and the sheen on his skin. "Hot chocolate you said, yes?"

She nodded and watched him go, loose and graceful like a cat. She noticed a woman staring at him, as he passed halfway to the counter, and saw her whisper something to her companion, an ugly sneer on her face. The man looked round at Lauren and she stared him down. How many Terry Curnows were there in the town, she wondered. It made her think of Christine Ohuruogu. What prejudice had she had to fight her way through? What was the problem with people? Well, she'd decided long ago that racism was just a form of fear...fear of what was different. Even so, it was so stupid. "For God's sake," she muttered, "what's skin colour got to do with anything, anymore than eye colour or hair colour? It's nonsense!"

She looked around at the other tables: two elderly women, heads bent, deep in conversation; a young guy on his own, who she recognized from the hardware store, preoccupied with his mobile; a young family with two little girls playing cards, their parents watching and prompting. They weren't paying Rafi or her any attention; but she was still seething by the time Rafi came back with their drinks.

Steam was coming off the frothy, chocolate-dusted top, as she took the mug from him "Thanks," she said, clasping it in both hands. She waited while he settled. "I have the same," he smiled, a vanishing smile replaced by something veiled and apprehensive in his dark eyes.

"So, tell me. You said something is different for you. What did you mean?"

"Yes, I need to try to explain this, but it's not easy." He paused, looking away into the café.

"Just spit it out, Rafi! I won't mind."

He cleared his throat, took a sip of his chocolate, wiping away the moustache it left with the back of his hand, and looked back at her.

"You and I are friends, yes?" She nodded. "We can meet and go out together, like now, and it's normal." She nodded again. "But at home, where I come from, it's not like this. At home, a boy does not go out with a girl alone unless there is an understanding between their families that this is all right, and even then there will be a chaperone."

"You mean going-to-be-engaged-or-married 'all right'?"

"Yes. Otherwise it will be very bad for the girl's reputation."

"What about the boy's?"

"Yes, his too; only it won't be so serious for him, unless the men in the girl's family go after him."

Lauren felt conflicted. She wanted to honour his culture, but was incensed against the double standards. Besides, this was about them, that's what they were really talking about.

"Ok, I get it. That's why you went quiet after I tapped your shoulder, right? Back at home that would be absolutely forbidden...touching in public, I mean."

"Completely! Things are changing slowly; but Jordan is still mainly a Muslim country and the rules are still strict."

"Are you a Muslim?" She hadn't thought about this before.

"No, my family is Christian, although I have both Muslim and Jewish ancestors."

Lauren sipped her drink slowly, watching him over the rim of her mug and wondering how she would feel if she was at college in the town he came from.

"It must be really difficult living in a different country with different customs," she said, putting the mug down. "Like not being sure what you can or can't do."

"Yes...sometimes!" he laughed, and she flushed. "But I can always ask my mother."

A wave of cold air swept over her. Glancing up, she saw the door was open, three men coming through and standing inside looking around without closing it. "Shut it, for God's sake!" she wanted to yell, until one of the elderly women at the window table said something to them and the last one in raised his hand in apology and closed it. In heavy overcoats but without hats, they seemed out of place. Lauren didn't recognize them, and she felt annoyed when they passed a couple of empty tables and sat down noisily at the one next to them at the back, laughing and arguing and all talking at once.

She thought about Rafi's mother and his family. She could see they were close and she wondered about his sister and brother, knowing she'd miss Finn if she was living in another country. But, before she could ask, Rafi said, "I was just thinking that customs may be different, but underneath people are the same, aren't they?"

"Well, should be, yes." She frowned; she wanted to think that, but she wasn't sure they actually were. She thought of Brexit Remainers and Leavers and the woman in the cafe with the sneer. She thought about what they'd been talking about earlier over lunch. "But are they? I mean, what your mother was saying about the..." she couldn't remember the name, "you know, that time when your grandfather's family were forced out of their home in Jerusalem and escaped to Jordan."

"The Nakba."

"Yes, the Nakba. Those paramilitaries that killed your mother's grandparents...I can't remember their name either."

"You mean the Haganah?"

"Yes, that wiped out their entire village. How can they be the same as the people they killed...you know, like you said, underneath?"

He nodded, his eyes holding hers thoughtfully. "Yes, that's hard. Why do we hate and kill each other?" He fell silent again, but it was a comfortable silence. Lauren knew he was going to say more and waited. "What I meant was that we are the same, because we all have family and friends, we all have hopes and fears, we all know happiness and sadness. The killers and the victims are the same in this, I think."

Even though she could see what he was getting at, something was in revolt inside her. "Maybe...yes and no. All right, the killers may have family and friends, but the victims are not full of hatred and violence like they are. They're different, not the same, are they?"

"Yes, even in this, they are the same," he insisted, leaning closer towards her. "There are Palestinians who hate and kill, too. They had the Haganah, we have Hamas. They wanted their own country, their own state, and were called terrorists; now it's our turn. They wanted it for the safety of their people, for the Jewish nation, because of Hitler's Holocaust...that's how the State of Israel was born; and now we want a State of Palestine for exactly the same reasons."

His intensity excited and alarmed her. She picked up her empty mug with both hands and held it in front of her. She felt out of her depth; she didn't really know anything about Israel and the Palestinians, except she was on the side of Jewish people and against terrorists. But Rafi was Palestinian and...and, well, she really liked him. And he wasn't being anti-Jewish, was he? He was saying they were the same as each other. How could they be? It was totally confusing. And, besides, she didn't want to be thinking and talking about politics right now; that wasn't why she'd suggested going for a walk. But she needed to say something; he was still leaning forward with his arms on the table, waiting for a response.

"I hadn't thought of it like that before," she said; "I need time to think about it." He nodded unmoving, as if he expected her to think about it there and then go on. "But, actually, there are two things I want to ask you."

"Yes?"

"Right, going back to what it's like for you over here, do you miss your sister and brother? I know I'd miss Finn a lot, if I was doing what you're doing."

"Jasmin and Zak?" He seemed surprised at her change of direction and sat back. "Yes, I miss them. But we speak on the phone every week and we will go home for the summer holidays."

"Will you?" She hadn't expected that...that he wouldn't go on being around; and a sudden emptiness drained the hope from her.

As if sensing it, he added: "Yes, but we'll be back again in time for college." He yawned, stretched an arm in the air and stuck out his legs, tangling his feet in hers.

"Sorry!" His feet jerked away.

"That's ok," she smiled. "I don't think it really counts as touching."

For a moment, he looked nonplussed, then relaxed. "What was the other thing you..."

But before he could finish, a voice from the table next to them cut across him: "Excuse me, do you live round here?"

Lauren looked round to find the nearest of the three young men half-turned in his chair towards them. He was flat-faced, bland looking, with a St George flag tattooed up the side of his neck, which looked strangely at odds with his neatly parted hair.

"We're looking for the Exeter Inn," he went on. "Meeting some friends of ours there. But we must have taken a wrong turn."

Lauren didn't trust him. He was smiling and being pleasant, only there was a glint in his sharp eyes that wasn't either.

"Ok, it's not far from here," she said. "Go back to the road at the top, turn left and it's about a hundred yards up on the right, just past the t-junction."

"Thanks." His gaze slid past her to Rafi. "Don't suppose you're local, eh? Just visiting like us?"

"I go to college here."

Lauren saw the other two look over. With their coats off, she saw they were all wearing dark suits and ties. Not Jehovah's Witnesses or Mormons, surely? Not the rowdy way they came in.

"Do you? Do you?" The flag creased and straightened

as the man nodded. "Now, that's very interesting. So, you live here?"

"Yes." Rafi's voice was even, non-committal; but she sensed a new tension in him, something coiled and alert.

"But you're not a Devon man, I take it?" the man persisted, looking round and gesturing inclusively to the other two. "What I mean is, we're from Essex, born and bred. And we were just wondering where you come from...you know, originally."

"Sorry, we have to go," Lauren interrupted, standing up and screening Rafi, while pulling on her jacket.

"That's a pity," the man continued from behind her. "That is a pity. But thank you for the directions." And, as they moved away, he added: "Take care. This situation, shall we call it, isn't going to last." He laughed and she heard the other two joining in: "Yeah, change is coming"..."In fact, it's already started!"

"Let's go home," Lauren said, as soon as they were outside, and set off without waiting for an answer, afraid the men would come after them. She took long, fast strides and only slowed once they had passed the Exeter Inn and were close to home.

"How do you cope with that, Rafi?" she asked, as they eased up and turned in at the gate, fear turning to anger now they were safe. "They were just looking for trouble!"

"I follow my father's advice."

"What's that?"

"Don't argue, stay calm and leave when you can."

"And, if they attack you?"

"Then, you fight." And, as she led him round to the back of the house, he stopped.

"But before we go in, what was the second thing you wanted to ask me?"

Light from the kitchen was spreading across the path onto the grass and she paused in the shadows.

"We were talking about different cultures...different customs, right?"

"Yes."

"Well, is that the real reason you didn't want to come round to Ida's yesterday?"

Before he could answer, she heard muffled voices coming up the lane behind them and jerked her palm up at him to be silent, until a woman laughed going by, and she started breathing again.

"Sorry," she said, putting her hand down; "I thought it was...you know..."

He was standing very still, looking at her, not saying anything; and, even in the darkness, she felt the intensity of his hesitation.

"I did want to come," he said finally. "It was silly. You were right. I am in England, not Jordan." His paused again. "In fact, I changed my mind, but then it felt too late."

"You should have called! Even Henry was disappointed when Ida told him you weren't coming. We all were."

It was more than she had meant to say and she turned away for the back door, glad of the warmth of the kitchen as she led the way in and relieved to find her mother and Maryam sitting side by side at the table, family albums open in front of them.

After Rafi and his mother had gone, Lauren went upstairs and lay on her bed with the curtains open, looking out at racing, wispy clouds veiling and unveiling a shimmering moon, imagining the black silhouette of a witch on a broomstick flying against it. Sometimes, when she'd given her all in a race she'd won, she felt both elated and drained. She was feeling that like now, remembering the flash of Rafi's eyes in the darkness. "I did want to come." It was an admission, wasn't it? But who had he wanted to see, her or Ida? Or was it nothing like that and just his being friendly? But that wasn't what she'd felt, was it? Something had passed between them; that's why she'd talked about being disappointed. She'd wanted him to know that she had wanted to see him, too. Why was it so difficult to say what she was feeling straight out?

The front door closed below, followed by a brief silence, before Finn's excited exclamations pierced it, flaring and fading against the familiar low monotone of her father's replies. She lay still, listening to a sudden hail of canned laughter chopped off, as quiet blanketed the house again. So Dad was home...what was going to happen now, she wondered. Hearing a creak on the stairs, she lent up on her elbows. Another creak and then her mother's echoing demand rang out in the darkness. "Is that you, Nick? I want a word with you."

10

As the English class ended and she slid her returned essay into her backpack, Lauren avoided catching Rafi's eye. She had Art with Jan Rawlings after the break, but she wanted to try to see her on her own beforehand. Losing herself in the crush for the door, she stared at the mullet's tail on the back of the otherwise shaven head of Eddie Laing, who was blocking out the light ahead of her, together with his mate, Ray.

"Stuff Hamlet!" Eddie said, pushing his way through. "Wish Ghost would give us a break and kill the lot of them!"

"Too right!" Ray laughed. "Stuff old Tonks behind the arras, as well!"

Once out into the corridor, Lauren joined the clattering flood down the stairwell into the entrance lobby, but veered away from the stream of students heading for the canteen and pushed through a swing door into a labyrinth of echoing green corridors. Passing the emptying classrooms, the hubbub faded to a murmur and then to silence behind her. At the far end, she pushed through a door marked 'FIRE EXIT', the sudden rawness of the air outside catching in her throat, as she hurried across the courtyard to the art room in the old school.

Since her grandparents had arrived, particularly her grandmothers, Ginnie and Mormor, Lauren was feeling less alone and more confident about talking privately to Jan. After the bleak grey of the day, the bright light and blaze of colour that met her as she opened the door was like stepping into sunshine. The art room glowed with vibrant paintings and textiles circling its canary yellow walls.

"Hi, Lauren," Jan smiled, setting her mug down beside a replica Ball Python, coiled in sleep and beautifully glazed, its pale gold markings and cream underbelly vivid against the dark brown of its skin. "You're early...you okay?"

With her spiky orange hair and mustard dungarees, Jan's comfortable presence usually released a sense of ease and relaxation in Lauren; but she was seeing her differently now. Was she having an affair with her father? Would she do that? For all her friendly informality in class, where she created an atmosphere of everyone working together to a common end, full of encouragement and free of judgment, Lauren had always had a sense of her integrity...her trustworthiness. She hesitated, watching Jan folding the sculpture in bubble-wrap. Surely, she wasn't a phoney, was she?

"What's up?" Jan said, tearing a strip of sellotape off the dispenser and glancing up at her.

"Is that Ida's?" Lauren asked, moving closer. She knew it wasn't, that it was too accomplished for Ida, but she had to say something. She couldn't just blurt out, "Are you and my dad...?"

"No, it isn't, but it is for her." Jan brushed her fingers against the bib of her dungarees and picked it up. "I was going to ask if you could give it to her for me. I know you'll see her before I do and I'd like her to have it sooner rather than later. I'm sure you already know she's been excluded for a week for bringing Coil into college."

"Yes, I do. She called me on her way home."

"How was she?"

She'd been jokey, but Lauren knew she was angry.

"Upset, really."

Jan took a sip from her mug and sat down.

"So would I be." She gestured towards a nearby chair and Lauren pulled it closer to the table, sitting down and slipping her backpack off onto the floor. "And excluding her?" Jan shook her head. "In the run up to A-Levels? It's senseless! Besides, if anyone's to blame, I am. I said she could bring Coil in and I told the Head that."

"What did he say?" Lauren was confused. If Jan had taken responsibility, why was Ida being punished? But, also, it was typically decent and straightforward of her to take the blame. It's why she wouldn't start an affair with a married man...she just wouldn't!

"He said taking responsibility for one's own actions was an important lesson for her to learn." Jan smiled. "Ironic really, seeing as that was what I was trying to do. Anyway, I suggested if a member of staff said it was okay, maybe the rule should be more flexible. Also, I explained what good work had come out of Coil being here and asked him to come and have a look."

"And did he?"

"Here...there's a note, too."Jan pushed the neatly packaged sculpture towards her, together with a small envelope with Ida's name on it in italics. "No, he didn't.

He said the point was that instead of bringing Coil straight to me, Ida had carried him around college, resulting in another student having a panic attack."

Geraldine! Lauren slipped the sculpture and note into her bag. Ok, she'd been frightened, fair enough... but why had she made such a fuss and caused so much trouble? She knew perfectly well Ida hadn't meant her any harm...or Coil, for that matter.

"Right, almost time," Jan said, checking her watch. "Can you give me a hand and put these out?" She moved to a chest by the window on the far side.

"Sure." Going across to her, Lauren waited as Jan eased several large sheets of coloured card from one of the wide, slim drawers. When she went to take them, their hands touched.

"I need to ask you something!" Lauren blurted out and then hesitated, unsure what to say next.

"Ok," Jan said, hooking her thumbs into the shoulder straps of her dungarees. Her gaze was steady and she seemed perfectly relaxed and open.

"I don't know how to put this exactly..."

"Well, don't worry," a smile of encouragement flickered in Jan's eyes, "just say it."

"There's a rumour going round..." Lauren stopped again; she sounded ridiculous to herself.

"A rumour? Look, give me those." Jan freed her hands and took back the sheets of card from her, setting them down to the side on one of the work tables. "It's all right, love. Just tell me."

"It sounds so silly!" Lauren looked away for inspiration and then back again. "But people are saying there's something going on between you and my dad and...and, well, things are really tense at home between him and Mum and I just want to know if it's true or not." Now that she had said the unsayable, the words were gushing out of her. "Because I know you're not like that, but something's going on and..." Hot tears were crazing her vision and she swiped them away.

"Hey, come on," Jan's hand was on her arm, "come and sit down."

Lauren followed her and sat with her head bowed, her hair falling forward covering the sides of her face. She felt exhausted and closed her eyes..

"The others will be here soon," Jan said eventually. Her voice was calm and gentle. She wasn't angry. "So, why don't you come back this afternoon after classes and we can talk properly then, ok?"

Lauren looked up and nodded. Jan was watching her, concern in her eyes.

"Your dad and I often work quite closely together," she said. "You know, on college plays and one or two coursework projects...but that's it."

Later that afternoon, the Art Room windows were blazing like beacons in the shadowed darkness of the courtyard. Lauren knocked and walked straight in. Jan, sitting at her table with charcoal sketches fanned out in front of her, looked up and waved her over.

But, as she sat down, now that she was here, Lauren wasn't sure what there was to talk about. Jan's earlier openness had left her convinced nothing was going on, after all. So, what was there to say, really? And yet, something wasn't right.

"Think the heating's already going off," Jan said, leaning forward and pulling on a woolly mauve cardigan from the back of her chair. "So, tell me," she went on, "what's happening at home?"

"I don't know. It's just Dad's not being himself, somehow."

"In what way?"

"It's like I said to Ida, he's there and not there. I mean physically he's there, but in his head he's completely somewhere else. And he's not happy. The other day, I saw him..." Lauren checked herself, feeling suddenly disloyal; that seeing her dad crying was private and not something she should be talking about.

As if reading her thoughts, Jan said, "I don't want you to tell me anything you're not comfortable with. But I also want you to know that anything you do tell me stays between us."

Lauren nodded. "Ok...so, he was upstairs in a room by himself and he was just standing there, looking out the window, and his shoulders were shaking...he was crying. I'd never seen him cry before." She could see him now and the same helpless fear gripped her again, as it had then. "He didn't see me..." She was trembling and her mouth was dry. "I should have gone to him... said something...anything, but I just hid away in my room." She closed her eyes, a plume of sick rising like smoke and burning the back of her throat.

"It's all right, Lauren, I'm here." Jan's chair scuffed on the linoleum, and Lauren felt the warmth of Jan's hand closing over hers. "Just breathe in slowly...that's it...in to the count of four, out to the count of eight... and again, keep going."

Gradually, the nausea subsided and she forgot about counting in and out.

"Sorry," she said. She felt embarrassed and was glad when Jan gave her hand a squeeze and let go.

"No need to be. Parents hold up our world...not easy to find out they're as vulnerable as we are."

Lauren looked away into the room, turning over what Jan had just said. It was a new thought and it wasn't. She had been worried about what would happen to her and Finn if their parents separated; but she hadn't really thought about her mother or father not coping. They'd always been so dependable, so...in control. She'd just taken their being there for granted, like the ground under her feet. She looked at her shoes, lifting the toes and pushing them down again.

When Jan asked quietly, "Have you told your mum about it?", Lauren jerked up, almost as if she'd forgotten Jan was there.

Despite her bold colours and straight-ahead manner, Lauren only ever saw kindness in Jan's face. Of course in the eyes, because that was where feelings showed themselves; but, it was more than that, something to do with the attention she gave you, as if she was really listening to what you were saying...as if she was really interested in you. She was doing it now: sitting back, waiting patiently, her shoulders relaxed and her gaze steady.

"Yes, I did. I wasn't going to, but Rafi and his mum came round for lunch on Sunday and Dad ran away... that's what it felt like. I saw him go, just after they'd arrived...watched him creeping out of the house like a thief and then running across the garden." Remembering how betrayed she had felt in front of Rafi, hurt and anger flared through her. She didn't feel sick anymore; and, when she spoke again, her voice was stronger. "We'd never met Mrs Masalha before. It was meant to be a special occasion and he just disappeared!"

She stared at Jan, wanting her sympathy, wanting her endorsement of the way she was feeling.

"Lunchtime, crept out of the house and disappeared," Jan said softly, almost to herself. And, for a moment, her eyes lost their focus, leaving Lauren feeling she was looking through her, not at her. Jan seemed lost in thought; but, with a quick nod, the focus came back and she went on, as if there had been no pause. "And what did your mother say?"

"She didn't know...not until I followed her out to the kitchen to warn her." Lauren remembered her mother's icy reaction. "She was angry...but, in a cold way. She didn't blow up or anything. She just said something about people Dad's age suddenly questioning where they've got to in their lives...something like that. And she'd speak to him."

"And do you think that could be it?" Jan asked. "That your dad may be going through some sort of mid-life crisis? It's not unusual..."

"Well, he hasn't bought a Harley, has he?" Lauren snapped. "Or run off with his secretary!" Then, seeing Jan's raised eyebrow and rueful smile, immediately regretted it. Why was she so angry? She wanted to smash something. It was like her blood was on fire.

"I know. I know. Very confusing, but..."

Lauren wasn't listening. "I've got to go!" She jumped up, grabbed her bag and raced to the door. "Sorry!" she yelled, yanking it open and running out. She didn't stop running. She ran through the deserted corridors, across the lobby and out of the college grounds into the road. She tore through the dusk, flying along on and off the pavements, pumping her knees, her arms, oblivious to traffic, to people, a raging energy powering her on, the biting air as sharp as her fury.

Once home, she fled straight upstairs to her room and closed the door, wishing she could lock it. Throwing off her bag and coat, she stood panting at the window, hands on hips, staring out into the darkness of the garden, imagining him, looking for him. He wasn't there. No turning figure. No striped apron. Just the merging shadows. But he had stood there, alone and in the cold. And it went with his crying and his running away. She smashed the side of her fist against the window frame and it didn't help, so she did it again and again.

Not knowing what to do with the anger still boiling inside her, she kicked off her shoes and lay on her bed, staring at the ceiling. 'He hadn't run off with his secretary,' she'd said and Jan had raised an eyebrow and given that little smile. What did it mean? That she was...wasn't the secretary? And what was that other odd moment? Something was nagging at her. The rumble of people below suddenly cracked and Pop's voice rang out, "No, it's all right. I'll get it." She listened to the creaks on the stairs and his long stride passing by outside, soon returning and disappearing again.

She should talk to Ginnie, not Mormor or Mum... they were too close to Dad. Ginnie would be more objective. Besides, she'd always been able to tell her troubles to Ginnie ever since she was little. She was more open somehow, didn't fuss or get worried...a kind of everything's-going-to-be-fine confidence about her that made Lauren feel stronger and less anxious about whatever it was. Bit like Jan, in a way. Well, they were both teachers...how come she'd never thought of that before...and drama was expressive like art. But hang on... Lauren drew up her legs and shoved them out straight again. That was it...that moment when Jan had suddenly got lost in thought. What were they talking about?

Lauren swung her feet round onto the floor and sat up. She'd been telling Jan about Rafi and his mum coming for lunch and her dad disappearing. What did Jan say? But it wasn't that, was it? Lauren closed her eyes, trying to recapture Jan's face. She'd just repeated what she'd told her...something about lunchtime and his running away...and then she'd gone sort of glazed, as if the words had triggered some other thought.

"Oh, no!" Lauren shot up. Surely not! Surely, Jan hadn't been lying to her! Was that it? Had Dad dashed off to be with her? She started pacing to the window and back. It didn't make any sense. If he was having a secret affair with Jan, he'd hardly want to draw attention to it by doing something so outrageous, would he? He's not that stupid. But maybe he's obsessed with her, thinking about her all the time, standing in the garden in the dark in the freezing cold, crying upstairs in secret. It makes sense. Couldn't face Sunday lunch...couldn't face having to pretend.

Lauren stopped by the bed and picked up her phone. She'd go through it with Ida, see what she made of it. But, as the contact list appeared, she hesitated, banging her knees in and out against the side of the mattress. She scrolled down. She didn't want to talk to Ida; she wanted to talk to Rafi. She stood still, her thumb poised, rehearsing, paralysed, trying to summon up the courage. She went back to Ida, then down again to Rafi. "Just do it!" she shouted at herself, glancing round at Christine Ohuruogu for support.

"Lauren?" A loud knock on the door. "Can I come in?"

Ginnie! She clicked off the phone and moved for the door. "Yes...yes, come in."

11

With the house full and with the whole family gathered in the music room every evening after supper for Finn's nightly interrogation of the 'Grandies', as he called them, the week was rushing by. Thursday already and she'd only spoken to Ida once, as she'd gone to stay with her uncle in Newlyn for a few days. "Going fishing with Joe to blow Geraldine and Dalby out of my hair. Just hope the weather's good enough," she'd said. "Back on Friday." That was tomorrow and she could tell her everything then.

From her vantage point on the piano stool at the far end, Lauren glanced along the crescent of faces circling the log burner. Supper was over. Mugs and glasses littered the coffee table in front of them. Beyond Ginnie, who was next to her, Zoltan was in full flow, while Finn on his beanbag was scribbling furiously in a notebook perched awkwardly on his knees. "Buda...B.U.D.A... Pest, Hungary's magnificent capital city on the River Danube, where I was born and grew up until I was eleven...until my parents sent me over here with Uncle Jozsef to keep me safe after Lilien was killed, mown down by Russian..."

Lauren knew the story of the Hungarian Uprising

and the death of Zoltan's eighteen-year-old sister, killed in the centre of Budapest in November 1956 by Russian tanks sent to reimpose Soviet domination. And his fleeing to the UK with his uncle made her think of Rafi's grandfather and his family forced into exile in Jordan. Why was there so much hostility to people who had lost their homes, their families, their way of life and who were desperate for shelter, for safety?

"Those brave Russian soldiers," the anger in Zoltan's voice hooked her back to him, "took the bodies of the young, unarmed protesters and tied them to the back of their tanks and dragged them behind them through the streets, as a warning!"

"Your sister, too?" Finn whispered into the silence.

Zoltan's eyes glistened and Lauren saw his flowing moustache quiver. "I didn't see it, but we were told." He banged his fist on the table and a teaspoon flew off onto the carpet. "And that was the day I became an anarchist! No more governments! No more power over others!" His voice softened. "You must understand, Finn, we only need each other as equals to get along. You see..."

"If you don't mind me interrupting," Pop Greg broke in, "I think it might be a good idea to let Finn read his notes back to us. You know, make sure he's managed to get everything down all right and give his poor hand a rest." Even after forty-five years in England, Lauren could still hear traces of Australian rhythms in his speech, not least the light, questioning lift at the end of his sentences that she found herself doing when talking to him.

Zoltan waved his arm in the air. "Quite right, I talk too much! At least that's what Ginnie tells me." His teeth flashed as he turned to her. "Don't you?"

"Perish the thought!" Ginnie grinned and added, as if in a stage whisper to Jess on the far side of him, "Such a quiet and unassuming man!"

Jess laughed, as did Mormor Freda sitting on the sofa beside her. And seeing their faces turned towards her, Lauren was struck afresh by how similar they looked, both blue-eyed and fair-haired, although Mormor's hair was paler now, white-gold with age. If you didn't know, you'd think Mormor was Jess' mother, not Ginnie with her unruly ginger mass. A wave of affection for her two grandmothers surged through her, making the tension between her parents seem more manageable and less catastrophic.

But the relief didn't last long; for, looking from her mother to her father next to Finn, she saw her dad staring at the floor, his face drawn and tired, his cheeks hollowed out and dark shadows bagging under his eyes. Remembering what Jan had told her, she didn't know whether she wanted to hug him or hit him. All the surprise of that meeting was still alive and undigested in her. She glared at him, going through it all again, not caring if he looked up and saw her; because it was like looking at a stranger, not her dad...like looking at someone separate, someone no longer a part of her.

When, unexpectedly, Jan had asked to see her again the day after their last meeting, she'd gone in her lunch hour, feeling apprehensive and steeling herself before walking in. But Jan had taken her by surprise. "I want to clear the air with you," Jan had begun. "I needed thinking time after we spoke yesterday. When you said about your dad disappearing last Sunday lunchtime, you caught me off guard. The point was...is...your dad had rung me then. He was up on the moors and said he wanted to see me urgently. But I had friends round and we were in the middle of eating, so I told him whatever it was would have to wait till Monday back here at the college."

"So, what happened on Monday?" she'd asked and Jan had given her a sad kind of smile.

"Nick...your dad...told me he thought he was in love with me. It didn't sound real and I told him he wasn't, or he'd know for sure. But he looked so...so lost that I suggested a quick drink at the Horse on the way home after work. I wasn't offended. I knew he was going through something and I just wanted us to go on being friends."

That's when Lauren had first known for sure that the rumours were true, or at least half true. Her dad was obsessing over Jan, but it was all in his head. There was no affair going on. Did her mum know, she wondered. She looked back to the sofa. Both Mormor and her mum were listening to Finn, with their hands linked between them. Her mum was still smiling, but Lauren recognized the defiance in it and saw how her back was straight and held away from the cushions behind her... on alert, like when she was driving. She was holding it together, putting on an act. And, although Lauren admired her for it at one level, at another she hated the falseness of it and wanted her mother to show her real feelings...show the sadness and the anger she was feeling in herself.

Maybe it was her mother's fault, anyway. She was so busy with the restaurants, she was hardly ever home. And, even when she was, she always had her head buried in brochures and notebooks. Dad was doing all the cooking and clearing up. Maybe he felt neglected.

She did at times, although she felt it more for Finn than herself.

"...killed your brother and your mother," Finn was saying, as she glanced at him. She hadn't been listening.

"Yes, Rod was only 15 when he rolled the tractor, as I told you, and I was 9." Pop Greg stretched his long legs out in front of him and drew them in again. "But, when my mom died, I was already grown up."

Finn flipped back a page of his pad, scanning what he'd written. "I haven't got that," he said, looking up. "What happened?"

"Poor soul," Greg said, "she went out to the barn in the dark, trod on a tiger snake...they come in after the mice. Venom paralyses you, dead before we found her." He shook his head. "Sheep farming! Tough way to earn a living, I can tell you."

A log slumped and hissed in the burner, flames rearing up, hot on the side of Lauren's neck and face; and, in the sudden sparking brightness, Lauren saw the streaks glistening on Mormor's cheeks. Who was she crying for, she wondered; her husband or her son? Or was she simply caught up in sad memories of her own? Lauren couldn't disentangle any of it...all these stories from their pasts...all these currents under the surface. They were only making her feel more confused.

"Sorry, everyone," she said, standing up, "I've still got stuff to do for college in the morning." She went quickly down the line, kissing and being kissed, apart from Finn, who swayed away from her, two fingers raised in a cross, intoning, "Back to your crypt, Drusilla!"

She made her way upstairs and sat on the end of her bed with the lights off. A high moon, out of sight, was flooding her desk and a slice of the carpet in a ghostly, white light. "Good night to be a vampire," she muttered. She wouldn't mind being Drusilla, wouldn't mind having her powers. She fell back on the duvet, giving way to the fantasy. Would she sink her fangs into Jan and save her dad? Remove her from the picture... out of sight, out of mind. Bite into her pale neck just below the line of her jaw and cropped orange hair? She bared her teeth and closed on the flesh, rolling her head away at the last moment, disturbed by her own desire.

Changing into the comfort of her pyjama bottoms and long sleeve t-shirt, she thought about the coming weekend instead. Ida would be back, so she'd have her usual Friday night sleepover at her house. She was looking forward to it. She'd missed having her to talk to, which reminded her she mustn't forget to take Jan's sculpture with her. Also, as Rafi's mother was going to London and not back till the day after, maybe they should ask him round. Not much fun being on your own at the weekend. She unhooked her bathrobe from the back of the door and pulled it on. After tying the belt, she stood, hands in pockets, staring out at the moonlit branches and thinking of Rafi and the cat-like beauty of him that made her want to reach out and touch him. She'd much rather sink her teeth into him. The thought caught her by surprise and she laughed out loud. Maybe he'd stay the night...there was a spare room and Henry wouldn't mind. And they could have the next day together; much nicer for him to be with them rather than out and about by himself with the likes of Terry Curnow on the prowl.

Terry Curnow! She took a hand out of her pocket and curled her fingers. If she had Dru's killer nails, he'd be in for a surprise.

12

Terry was looking forward to the night out in town with the boys and, not least, to the bit of fun he had planned for dear Rafael at the end of it. He savoured the thought. It would be his reward for a difficult week, yes indeed. Not only had his mother come into his room uninvited to 'tidy up' just as he was enjoying a wank, but later on, after he had gone out, she had returned and thrown away the folder he'd left beside his desk. "It was by the bin. I thought it was rubbish." He could hear her infuriating voice now. As a result, despite the wind and rain, he had had to plough through the assorted trash in the wheelie bin down by the gate to retrieve it, containing, as it did, not only all the notes he had made during his meeting with Tony Gardner and his two colleagues about getting NAN established in Devon and Cornwall, but also all the costings involved.

"We might be interested in involving you," Tony Gardner had said, "but, if we decide we are, you'd be responsible for raising the necessary funds to pay for leasing an office and all its related expenses. Every centre has to pay for itself. So, if you want to become the DO... or District Organizer...down here, you're going to need to provide us with a detailed viability report, showing relevant costings and sources of revenue...you know, as proof of your commitment and abilities. You up to the job, Terry? We don't want to go wasting time on people who ain't."

"I certainly am!" he had assured him. "Yes, indeed."

So far, however, he hadn't made much progress. Office space in Truro had proved to be far more expensive than he'd imagined, with thousands of pounds required upfront just to obtain the lease, quite apart from the hefty monthly charges on top of that. He had no savings of his own and would have to borrow money to get started. It was hopeless; the only person he knew who could possibly help was his Uncle Nathan, his dad's elder brother. But he was a solicitor and shrewd; and Terry was well aware his uncle didn't think much of him; not since the fiasco over the fake football shirts and tees.

Terry shook his head; he'd been making a killing then. Perfect pitch, Plymouth University, 18,000 students looking for a bargain. Maybe he could start that up again...post something on Facebook. He still had the contacts.

"Giddy up, poltroon!" shouted Andy, as a white Transit van pulled out into the fast lane in front of them and then failed to make any progress in overtaking a low loader, which was itself barely managing to overtake a petrol tanker, all three of them side by side and making hard work of the gradient rising against them.

"Friday night, the weekend ahead of us," Terry said, glancing across, "we've all the time in the world."

Andy flashed him a grin, slung like a hammock between his sideburns and chinstrap beard, and eased back from the Transit's bumper. Terry wished he was more dependable. Andy was teetotal and made a perfect driver; but, more than that, he had certain lock-picking skills, which would be very helpful later on. Problem was you never knew how long he'd be around or if, in fact, he would ever show up again. He was part of an extended family of Travellers; sometimes they stayed for months and sometimes just for days.

"Will you be here for a while this time?"

"Depends which way the grass bends."

Why don't you cut it then? Terry kept the thought to himself and went back to ruminating on tackling his uncle for a loan. If he got the viability report for NAN right, perhaps it would be good enough to convince him. It just had two weak points at the moment: costings for an office and potential membership fees. Well, maybe he should simply go and ask for his help with those as well. His practice was in Truro and he'd have all kinds of contacts and insider knowledge.

A slow smile played at the corners of his mouth. His uncle would pull his report apart and hand it back to him in tatters. But he knew his uncle's Achilles heel. "I understand, Uncle," he muttered to himself, "and thank you for giving my proposal such careful attention. Mum'll be very disappointed, of course. She thought this was really going to 'set me on the right track', as she put it. But I'll explain what you've said." Ever since his dad had run off with that young Jamaican woman from the post office, Uncle Nathan had taken it on himself to look out for his and his mum's well-being. His uncle was very protective of his mum and she thought the sun shone out of his backside.

He chuckled, picturing himself getting up to leave and Uncle Nathan growling, "Wait a minute!" and seizing hold of the folder again. "Give me that and I'll think on it."

"Share the joke," Andy said, regally holding the old Volvo in the fast lane and ignoring the flashing lights of the car behind.

"Let him through," Terry growled. He didn't want their night out ended prematurely by some officious cop in an unmarked car, like it had been once before. "We've got bigger fish to fry."

Andy eased back on the accelerator, as Terry watched the needle sink below 60 towards 50 mph.

The car behind swung into the middle lane and Andy swerved in front of him.

"Stop it!" Terry shouted. "Are you deaf? I already told you, didn't I?"

"Careful, Jeeves," crooned a voice from the back. "Don't want the Rolls damaged." The figure in an army great coat and trilby was slouched in the corner behind Terry.

"Certainly, Sir Lawrence." Andy was grinning. "See who it is, Terry? Look." He stayed in the middle lane, as a vintage Jaguar pulled out and roared by, blowing its horn.

"That's Meadows' Jag, isn't it?" said a smaller, younger figure, who was crushed in the middle of the back seat between Lawrence's sprawl and John's unyielding legs and elbows. Matt's voice was soft, his face barely visible between his woolly hat and the upturned collar of his reefer jacket.

"Ah, our vertically-challenged Deputy Head!" Terry had rather admired Leo Meadows for his strutting self-importance and stentorian pronouncements. "Probably fleeing Ida's python and her wrath!"

"Better not muck 'er about, fuckin' ponce!" John yelled. "I'd 'ave 'ad 'im by now, if 'e lived out our way. Where does the fucker live?"

"Lives in Plymouth," Terry said, lowering the sun visor on his side and looking at John in the rust-spotted mirror.

"Well, let's follow him 'ome then, re-introduce ourselves, like." John seldom smiled. Smiles didn't sit easily across his gaunt features. But when he did, as now, the thin lips pared apart in a canine snarl, revealing stained and crooked teeth.

"Not tonight," Terry said. "Tonight, we're going to have some fun in Union Street and then..."

"Will that just be the duelling, or will there be some romancing, too?" Lawrence drawled from under his hat.

"To conclude, if I may Lawrence...there most certainly will be romancing if the price is right, and then we're going to pay young Rafael a visit in his nest... in the small hours. Yes, indeed."

Matt cleared his throat. "Won't there be other people in his house? They'll call the police, won't they?"

"Ah, the boys in blue, Matty. No, no need to worry about that, not at all. Put your..."

"The sainted nuns of Sainsbury," Andy observed, as the white sails over the supermarket came into sight. He flicked the indicator left and took the exit for the 'City Centre'.

"I had a nun once...well, a novitiate, in fact," Lawrence commented. "Very capacious dresses they wear. She was...what was she? Tender, shall we say?"

John jerked round to face him. "You're full of shit!" he snarled. But, before the words were out, Lawrence's fist was in front of his nose, the fingers riveted together in a brass knuckleduster.

"Have a care, John Knight," Lawrence smiled, "or it could be lights out, good night."

"Fuckin' throat out, more like!" John's arm flashed out of his parka and metal rang on metal, as he swept the fist away from him with the flat of his father's seven inch Commando blade. "Fancy some of this, do yer?"

Terry caught its lethal blackness in the mirror, lit up in the glare of the headlights behind. In the silence of the standoff, Matt shrank further down.

"As I was saying," Terry continued, glancing over his shoulder as if nothing had happened, "put your trust in Uncle Terry. It just so happens that our friend, Rafael's, mother is away in London, which means he's going to be all alone tonight and longing for a little company, I shouldn't be surprised. Right?"

"Right." Matt nodded.

"And we wouldn't want to disappoint him, would we, boys?" Terry's face hardened. "No Henry Downes this time!" He paused and then added. "Be in his pyjamas, won't he?"

Behind them, the wailing of a siren grew louder. Andy watched the flashing blue light coming up fast, other cars slewing to the side out of its way. John slid his knife away and Lawrence's hand vanished back into his pocket.

"Good forethought, Jeeves," Lawrence said; "switching plates."

The wail became a scream as the high-visibility squad car blasted past them, disappearing out of sight through the river of red tail lights ahead.

"'Ow d'yer know where his ma is, anyway?" Andy

asked.

"It's my job to know. That's what I'm here for, isn't it?" Terry's fat lips spread in a satisfied smirk, as he tapped the side of his nose with his forefinger. In fact, his mum's friend, Linda May, worked as part-time cleaner for Mrs Masalha and he'd overheard them talking about it; but he wasn't going to tell Andy that... far too banal. No, mystery was power. Instead, he said, "We've been doin' a bit of detective work, haven't we, John?"

"Lock'll be a piece of piss for you," John said, eyeballing Andy in the mirror.

For a while, a thoughtful silence filled the car, as they made slow progress through the linked lights approaching the city centre. On their inside, traffic was queuing for the turn off to Sutton Harbour and the Barbican.

"Well, well," Lawrence said; "I think I spy our former camp commandant up ahead." And the others strained to see what he was looking at.

The lights changed and the cars on the inside started to move.

"I see it," Andy said, indicating and jinking into a gap, as the train of cars in front curved away left and Leo Meadow's Jaguar became clearly visible further up the queue.

"What yer doin'?" John shouted, pulling himself close to Andy's ear. "Union Street, we said. Not the fuckin' seaside!"

"It's okay, John." Terry kept his voice low and calm. "We'll just see where he lives. Bit of research for another time." He turned, with a knowing smirk. "Know what I mean?"

"Yeah." John moved back, catching Matt in the chest with his elbow. "That's all right, then."

"Sorry," Matt said.

John drew out his knife and cut short, stabbing lines in the air. "I'm gonna carve my initials on that cunt's balls!"

The venom of his words hung in the air, until Lawrence's laugh punctured it.

"I like trouble," he said.

13

A wafting aroma of cloves and cinnamon and other spices his mother used, cumin and coriander, told Rafi his supper was ready. He crossed to the oven and took out the pot of warmed-up maqluba she had left for him. Spooning the rice, chicken and aubergine onto his plate, he carried it back to the table. He pulled a small bowl of yogurt and cucumber closer to him, glancing up at the clock as he did so. 6.38 pm. There was no rush; his father's call wasn't due for another twenty minutes. He looked across at the note his mother had left on the dresser, with its numbered points in her clear hand. And, even though his father would already know from her text message about the London conference and her night away, Rafi felt tense about the call. It was the first time he would be speaking to his father alone in charge of the house, and not as a child under the protection of his mother. He pushed his plate away, the food half eaten, and drank from his water glass until it was empty.

His mother always took the call from Jordan first; and only after she had finished speaking to his father would she beckon him over. But tonight he would talk to his father more as a grown-up than a child; for the first time, he would have autonomy as an adult. He pulled his plate back towards him and started to scoop tzatziki onto it, when the phone rang. He hurried into the hall, coughing as he lifted the cordless handset, his throat dry.

"Salam!" He coughed again, hurrying back to the kitchen for his mother's messages.

"Hi." It was Lauren's voice. "Is that you, Rafi?"

"Lauren! Yes, hello, it is me. I was expecting my father."

"Oh, okay. Shall I ring back later?"

He looked at the clock. "No, it's alright; we have a little time. He will not ring till seven."

"I'll be quick, then. It's just I'm at Ida's and, knowing you're on your own tonight, we wondered if you'd like to come round."

Should he? He wanted to. Only, what if his mother rang on the landline? Would she mind his not being there? But he wouldn't be gone long; Ida's house was just up the lane.

"Rafi? You still there?"

"Yes. And thank you. I will talk with my father and then I will come. I may be a little while." He laughed. "First there will be my father and then my grandfather; and, if my sister or brother is there, I may have grown a beard by the time you see me."

"Cool. See you in a bit."

"Oh, one more..." There was a click, then nothing. "Lauren?"

He replaced the handset and stood in the shadows of the hall staring at it. Would Henry Downes be there? If not, it would not be right for him to go. He moved his hand towards the phone, but remembered the conversation in Zeno's. He wasn't in Jordan; over here, things were different. He turned away and went back to his meal. He wanted to see Lauren; and was she just being kind or did she want to see him, too?

Forty minutes later, he was cycling up the lane, skirting the puddles, the nervous anticipation he had felt after Lauren's call replaced by a deeper sense of longing. It was a familiar feeling of homesickness he often experienced after speaking to his father; as if speaking in Arabic reconnected him immediately to some core sense of himself where he belonged. He only had to hear his grandfather's voice to close his eyes and be transported to the warmth and scents of the small farm and the silver leaves of its olive trees. Aunt Anoush had been there, too, his father's elder sister, who had mothered her baby brother after their mother died giving birth to him.

He squeezed his tongue against the roof of his mouth, remembering the honey cake with almonds, which he had helped her bake as a child, watching her sturdy, potter's arms stirring the mix and placing the tin in the oven with the same practised ease as she loaded pots into her kiln. Wouldn't it be better to go home altogether, as his mother was suggesting? Back to Jasmin and Zak. The bump and lurch of a concealed pothole nearly unseated him and he cracked his shin, his foot failing to find the pedal again. But, as he regained his balance, the sharp, stabbing pain died away and he became aware of a dull orange glow in the darkness ahead, coming and going through dips in the hedgerow and the black branches of trees. He would soon be there.

"So, my little brother, have you yet captured the heart of some unfortunate, short-sighted girl?" Rafi grinned, recalling his sister's teasing. He missed her and his younger brother, also. Zak was always getting into fights over taunts at school about his blue eyes and what his mother had been up to; and, frequently Rafi had had to come to his aid against much older boys, who were bullying him. A fierce loyalty tugged at him to be at his brother's side; and he was still thinking of Zak as he turned in at the open gate to the Downes' smallholding and passed the trestle table, where most days Henry left out trays of vegetables and plants with an honesty box beside them. The beam from his front light lit up the SUV's towbar and tailgate. Henry was home, after all; but the relief he felt was tinged with disappointment.

He leant his bike against the garage wall, went up the short flight of steps to the front door and rang the bell.

"I'll get it!" he heard Ida call out; and, a moment later, the door opened and she stood illuminated, her hair tied loosely back, making her face seem broader than usual. "Hi, Rafi." She gave him a smile and stood back. "Come on in. We're in the den."

Rafi followed her, taking in the bungalow's interior for the first time. It wasn't what he had expected. Instead of a hallway with a staircase and rooms leading off it, a short lobby gave way to a large, open-plan space, with a sofa and easy chairs on one side and an eating area with a solid wood table on the other. In the middle, in a stranded chimney breast, he saw the glow of a log burner and felt the warmth radiating from it. Other than that, as he followed Ida, he was aware only of sanded floorboards and tall pot plants near windows, richly green against the white walls.

"Watch the step," Ida said, glancing over her shoulder, as she led him through an arched opening and down a level. "You've just missed Coil having his supper," she added, as they passed what looked like a couple of bedrooms and a bathroom. "But he can be quite shy with strangers, so I'll leave him in his tank for now. He always sleeps after he's eaten, anyway."

Rafi was secretly relieved, remembering his cousin, Haroun's, death from a viper bite, while he was walking in the hills near their home. He didn't trust snakes at all.

At the end of the passage, they went down another step and through a second archway, with a heavy, rust-coloured curtain caught back in a swag. Following Ida into the den, the first thing that caught his eye was Lauren stooped over a wall-to-wall work bench at the far end, her back to him. But, even as he looked at her, she half-turned.

"Hi, Rafi," she said, brushing her hair off her forehead with the back of her hand. "Nearly done." And she went back to whatever she was doing, her arms and shoulders moving, but her hands screened from him.

The room was warm and he slipped his jacket off, looking round for somewhere to put it.

"Here." Ida took it from him and hung it on a peg over a canvas apron. "Let me give you the tour."

The room was split in two: a carpeted bedroom-cum-sitting room one end; and a work area with quarry tiles the other.

"Here's Coil." She led him to a tank against the wall opposite. "Sleeping, like I said."

"There's a change!" laughed Lauren.

At first, he couldn't see the snake, only foliage and branches with shredded bark underneath.

"There," Ida said, pointing. "At the back."

Then he saw it; curled up, brown and gold, camouflaged in the hollow of a branch in one corner. He nodded, not knowing what to say about it and wondering how to engage with Lauren.

Ida tapped his arm. "Want to see some magic?" She steered him back past Lauren to another tank at the opposite end of the bench. "Look."

All he could see was a row of plants suspended in water.

"Tomatoes one end, potatoes the other!" She grinned at him. "Amazing, isn't it? Same family...the wonder of hydroponics!"

As he moved to get a better look, he saw Lauren step backwards, rubbing her hands together. Catching his eye, she looked again at the clay figure in front of her. "What do you think?"

Rafi was so absorbed in trying to make sense of what he was looking at that he whirled round in surprise when he heard Henry Downes' voice behind him: "Room for another?"

"Hi, Dad." Ida beckoned him over. "I was just showing Rafi the wonder plant."

Rafi's eyes flicked between her father and the divan bed with cushions in the far corner. "It's her bedroom. I shouldn't be here," he thought, as Henry walked towards him.

"Evening, Rafi." Henry raised his hand and Rafi's own was hot and sticky as he took it. "I was in the cave, didn't hear you come in." He looked round at Lauren and Ida. "Fancy a cuppa? I've just put the kettle on."

As they sat round the table in the kitchen with their mugs of tea, Henry drained his and stood up. "No rest for the blessed," he said, carrying it to the sink. "VAT man wants his pound of flesh." He looked at Rafi. "Keep all my paperwork ...well, have my office, if you like, in the basement." As he moved past them for the door, he stopped and turned. "Your mother away, is she?"

Rafi nodded. "Yes, sir; she's in London till tomorrow."

"Hey, Dad!" Ida whooped. "Proper respect!"

A smile flickered at the corners of her father's mouth. "That's all right, Rafi, Henry'll do. But I was thinking, you're welcome to the spare room, if you want. Save you being on your own tonight."

"Thank you..." Rafi hesitated, unable to bring himself to say 'Henry' and caught, also, between longing to stay and feeling he shouldn't. "But my mother has asked me to look after the house while she is away." He was aware, from the corner of his eye, of Lauren and Ida exchanging glances as he spoke.

"Right then," Henry said, turning to go. "I better get on, but you're always welcome."

His departure left them momentarily suspended, as they listened to the double click of a door opening and then closing.

Rafi's arm was resting on the table and Lauren nudged it with the back of her hand. "I know, why don't you ring your mum now and ask her if it's ok to stay?"

"Yeah, good idea," Ida said. "Then we can all watch 'Men and Chicken'."

"Oh, no!" Lauren groaned. "Not more copulating

horses and swimming out to sea for vodka." She tilted her head towards Rafi, continuing in a theatrical whisper, "She's a bit weird; she's got this thing for obscure Polish and Romanian films with subtitles."

"Danish actually, this one." Ida flicked a biscuit crumb at her. "And the other one was Icelandic and you loved it!"

Rafi was struggling to get his thoughts together. He was only half-following what they were talking about, because he desperately wanted to stay, desperately wanted to reach out and touch the tumble of hair bunching on Lauren's shoulder leaning so close to him; but reason was telling him he mustn't do either.

"Go on, why don't you?" Ida said, and he looked up to find her eager eyes on him

"No, that's all right, thank you." He felt caught out and answered more stiffly than he meant to. "I would like to see the film; but I need to go home afterwards."

As if sensing his discomfort, Lauren looked round at him. "That's okay," she said, nudging his arm. "There'll be other times." He couldn't hold her gaze and felt burned by it. He picked up his empty mug and pretended to drain it.

"Right." Ida stood up. "Back to the den, then."

14

"You drive," Terry said, tossing the key at John. It fell short into a puddle. "Andy's not comin' with us, after all."

"Why the fuck not?" John grabbed the key from Matt, who had fished it out by the fob and was drying it on his coat cuff. He turned it in the driver's door and the locks popped all round.

"His cousins call and off he goes," Terry said, his voice thickened by the beers and shots he'd been drinking. "Always does. Travellers, aren't they? It's what they do."

"Don't matter." John climbed in and slid his seat back till it banged against Matt's knees. "Don't need him, do we? I'll just kick the fuckin' Arab's door in." He started the engine and looked round. "Where's that other cunt?"

"Not sure," Terry said, crossing his arms and hugging himself. "'How long till the heater comes on?"

"I think he's walking that girl, Tania, back to her place. Shouldn't be too lo..."

"Fuckin' wanker!" John exploded, cutting Matt off short. "Who's 'e think 'e is, fuckin' Sir Prancealot?"

"Prancealot! Like it." Terry cleared his throat,

half-opened his window and spat into the illuminated darkness, fine rain slanting across the glare of the street lights. He closed it again. "Maybe he does see himself as some sort of...what's the word?...you know, round table...Arthur...all that."

"Like knights, you mean?" Matt offered.

"Yeah, that's it." Terry twisted round briefly to look at him, as if he'd forgotten he was there. "Chivalrous knight; that's what he is; but he's a soldier through and through."

"Is 'e? Right, five more minutes and then he can find a fuckin' 'orse and ride 'ome!"

John switched the fan full on to clear the steamed-up windscreen, while Terry used the sleeve of his duffel coat to clear the fog off his side window. Small hillocks of clear glass began to appear behind the steering wheel.

Terry chuckled, remembering what had Just happened at the club. "It's Lawrence," he said, attempting an imitation of Lawrence's laconic drawl, "or would you prefer a visit to the dentist."

"It were that bloke's fault," Matt said. "He deliberately called him 'Larry'...twice."

"Yeah, well he won't be calling anybody anything now for quite some time, will he?" Terry tapped John's arm. "State of his mouth! Did you see it?"

John grunted and looked at the clock on the dashboard. "7.20! No, it fuckin' ain't!" He hit the dial with the heel of his hand and looked at his watch. "2.29," he muttered. "I'll give 'im one more minute, that's all."

"We're not leaving him..." Terry started, when the door behind him opened with a blast of cold air and Lawrence slid in.

"Good of you to wait, driver," he said, settling back and pulling down the brim of his trilby.

It was a little after 3.00 am by the time they passed the entrance to Henry Downes' smallholding. Not long afterwards, they spotted the gateway to Rafi's house ahead of them, on the right. "'Stop here!" Terry said, and John pulled in tight against the hedge on the left in one of the narrow lane's passing spaces. As the lights and engine died, no-one spoke, their eyes adjusting to the darkness. Gradually, the gateway became apparent again, twenty yards further up.

"Very bloody convenient!" Terry said, struggling to get his trailing leg over the gearstick and under the steering wheel. He glared up at John standing in the road.

"Well, lads," Lawrence said, sliding across the back seat and stepping out, "I rather fancy some eggs and bacon; how about you?"

Terry, hopping on one leg and finally extricating himself, tapped his lips with his forefinger. "Sssh! Don't want dear Rafael hearing us coming, do we?" And he led the way across the road and into the driveway.

"Now," he whispered, beckoning them into the deeper shadows of a large rhododendron bush. "No more talking. Gloves on and panther quiet. Lawrence, you and Matt check the back for ways in. John and I'll take the front and sides. Whoever finds anything comes and gets the rest of us, okay?"

As Lawrence went to move away with a nod to Matt, Terry put a hand on his arm. "One more thing," he whispered, "once we're in, follow me and not a sound, not until we're all standing round his little bed, eh?"

He took his hand away. "Let's go."

The house loomed large and dark as they crept over the grass by the drive. At the corner of the building, Terry paused, watching Matt and Lawrence stealing past the bins and merging with the blackness beyond. Turning, he pointed John towards the far side, with two short jabs of his finger. He saw John check the front door and push at a window further past it, before vanishing round the far corner.

The front windows on his side were firmly locked; PVC frames, tight-fitting and secure. Turning along the side of the house, he found a side door and a small window just beyond it also locked. Looking up, he made out two more windows. They were the same size, but the upper half of the one further back seemed blacker, its darkness denser. He was still squinting up at it when he heard a scuffle of leaves and glanced round to find Lawrence's trilby and greatcoat emerging from the shadows. As he neared, Matt stepped out beside him; and they came up shaking their heads.

Terry tapped Lawrence on the shoulder and pointed up at the second window. "I think it's open," he whispered. "Maybe Matt's small enough."

"I'm as thin as fuckin' Matt," came a low voice and they all spun round, Lawrence's gloveless right hand clearing his pocket in an instant.

Seeing John, like some graveyard ghoul, head cowled in a hood, only his nose scything out, Lawrence's hand disappeared again. "True, although your hobnail boots aren't."

"Enough!" Terry hissed. He looked at John. "Any luck?"

John shook his head, his eyes never leaving

Lawrence's.

Simultaneously, the growl and flickering lights of a vehicle coming up the lane propelled them close aginst the wall, their backs to it, their faces angled towards the drive. As they waited, the engine note changed, the driver dropping a gear against the hill, swiftly followed by arcing beams of light raking the gateway, gravel and grass before dying away, the darkness swallowing them up again.

"Terry," Matt said, so softly that Terry had to move round Lawrence to hear him. "I think I saw a ladder by the shed over there."

"Show me."

Terry followed him past the end of the house to a patio area with a shed at the side. On the ground, leaning almost invisibly against it, was a wooden extension ladder.

"Might do," Terry grinned, putting his arm round Matt's shoulder and giving him a squeeze. "Well spotted."

Once they got the ladder back, John took it and, holding it vertically with Matt's assistance, he slid the extension quietly to its fullest reach and gently angled it into the wall close to the window.

"Piece of piss," he said, looking at Matt. "You can step straight off it." He put his boot on the bottom rung and waited till Matt had started up. "'Ere, give me those!" He pulled the nearest of Matt's shoes off, then stepped up a rung and tugged the other away. "Don't want you fuckin' clatterin' about in there."

"Not just a pretty face, then," Lawrence muttered and swayed to the side as the second shoe flew over his shoulder.

"For fuck's sake!" Terry hissed, glaring at them both. "Absolute schtum, both of you!"

Heads raised, they saw Matt give a thumbs up and ease a leg through the top half of the window. The ladder wobbled as he did so, and Terry shot out a hand to help support it. Matt's shadow seemed to hover half in, half out; then the ladder moved again and the shadow was gone.

Terry turned away, flicking his arm for them to follow, and rounded the corner of the house, making for the front door. They grouped in front of it, waiting, straining to hear. Behind them, high up in the pitch black of the moor, the distant whinny of first one pony and then another sliced the night; and, in the echoing silence that followed, they heard a muffled click and saw the door opening slowly inwards.

Once inside, Terry stood still, listening again. But, apart from John's adenoidal breathing and the muted ticking of a clock, he couldn't hear anything. At first, he couldn't see much, either. Gradually, however, as his eyes adjusted to the grey light from a window above, the denser shapes of things began to emerge from the spaces around them: a coat stand and table nearby on his left, a wide staircase in the middle, two doorways on the far side separated by something tall and narrow.

Turning to the others, he put a finger to his lips, then bent to unlace the tops of his Doc Martens, before pulling the tongues up and easing them off, setting each boot down carefully, silently. Lawrence followed his lead and then moved to the stand, taking off his trilby and greatcoat and hanging them there. Rejoining the others, he gestured at John's feet. John looked at Terry, who nodded. Sitting on the floor, John tugged his boots off angrily, still gripping one as he stood up again, facing Lawrence.

Lawrence grinned and turned away, following Terry towards the stairs. Matt, waiting to go last, saw John slide his knife from inside his parka, before he moved after them.

15

Rafi came to, opened his eyes, saw the darkness and closed them again. He tried to slide back into his dream, but couldn't catch its fading tail, as thoughts of the evening before sailed into its place, of Lauren's hand on his shoulder leaning in to kiss his cheek as he was leaving and that faint cinnamon scent of her again. Maybe he could ring her, suggest something? But he would see her in college on Monday. He shouldn't be too...What was that? Someone's breathing? Everything inside him went rigid. Someone was there, by the bed. Pretend to be asleep...crash out sideways...no warning... grab your phone...race downstairs...lock yourself in the loo...call the police. Right...now!

Bringing his knee up and pushing off from the edge of the mattress with his lower hand, Rafi exploded out of the side of the bed, his eyes wide open, as he catapulted straight into Terry's chest, bowling him over and tripping over on top of him. Before he was halfway up again, a hand grabbed the neck of his t-shirt, yanking him backwards, while two more seized his arms.

"Not so fast, Ali Baba!" Lawrence chuckled, hauling him clear of the bed. "Get a chair, Matt."

Someone switched a light on; and, as John stepped

towards him, Rafi caught sight of Terry struggling up behind. The next thing he knew was electric pain and all the air punched out of him, as John caught him in the solar plexus. He tried to buckle over to catch his breath, but the arms held him upright.

"Fuckin' behave yourself! Or, I'll really 'urt yer." John stuck the tip of the blade under Rafi's chin, forcing him to look up.

"Well, well, well. Look at you," Terry said, tapping John on the shoulder, so that he moved to the side, taking his knife away. "We've come to give you a surprise, Rafael. But have a seat. Thank you, Matt."

Before Rafi could react, the chair was shoved into the back of his knees and he collapsed onto it, bending forward, feeling he was going to vomit, trying to grab some air against the spasms still knotting his stomach. Immediately, a hand grabbed a fistful of tight curls on the top of his head, jerking it backwards and upwards until Terry's leering face leaning in closer was all he could see.

"There's no-one here to save you this time, is there, my little Rafi?" The voice was low and rhythmical. "No Henry Downes to come riding to the rescue. Oh, my word, no."

Rafi tried to twist his head sideways away from the putrid stench of Terry's breath; but his scalp burned, as if his hair was being torn out at the roots, forcing him to look back again.

"Thing is, Rafael, me and the boys..."

"Leave me alone." Rafi's throat was scorched and his words came out in a rasp. "I have nothing to do with you."

He saw Terry look away over his shoulder, tutting

and shaking his head, before turning back. "Manners, manners, Rafael. Didn't your mother ever tell you it's rude to interrupt?" The open-palm slap cracked across the side of his face, stinging like a whip. "Now, where was I? John? Lawrence?"

But, before either of them could answer, a sonorous chime from the depths of the house wrenched their heads around, and, as they stared at the doorway, it rang out three more times.

"Phew!" Matt gasped. "Thought it was the doorbell."

Terry checked his watch. "Four o'clock. We better get on, boys. Want to be fast asleep in our beds by sun-up, don't we? Innocent lambs, eh?"

"Why don't we scour 'im with some bleach?" John grabbed Rafi's chin, holding it like a vice, forcing him to look at him. "See if the fuckin' brown comes off."

"It might work, John," Lawrence intervened and Rafi watched the knife turning away from him. "But to achieve the...um...pigment lightening you seem to favour, you would have to apply it all over and the problem there is..." He paused, with a sigh and the wisp of a smile. "You'd probably cause permanent tissue damage and, maybe, who knows, even kill him. It's the sodium hypochlorite, you see; burns like buggery."

"Up your fuckin' arse!" John snarled, raising his knife.

"Quite," Lawrence laughed. "That is what the word means all right. Well done."

And, before the flood of blood to John's enraged face could reach his muscles, Lawrence stepped inside his knife arm, parrying the blade to one side, and smashed John's jaw with a right cross he never saw coming. As he fell, he caught the back of his head on the corner of the wooden bed frame.

"Lights out!" Lawrence said, while Rafi watched John slump, eyes closed, his chin skewed sideways against his shoulder.

"For Christ's sake! What did you do that for?" Terry had his hand flat against Rafi's chest, as if to support himself. He stared at Lawrence, then down at John and back again. "What the fuck are we going to do now?"

Lawrence eased his fingers free of the knuckleduster, gently massaging them, as the brass bar disappeared into his pocket. "Well, I don't know about you, Skip, but I'm going to review the egg-and-bacon situation. I'm hungry."

Rafi watched him go, feeling the warmth of Terry's hand on his chest against the drumming of his own heart. "John's tough." Was Terry talking to him or Matt, or was he just thinking aloud? "He'll have a headache when he comes round, but he'll be all right." Maybe he should make a run for it now. "Except, when he comes round, he's going to go after Lawrence, for sure...kill him, if he can." Terry's eyes lasered into Rafi's. "How the hell am I going to deal with that, eh?"

Over Terry's shoulder, Rafi saw Matt sliding silently out of view.

"But..." Terry's face softened unexpectedly into its habitual look of oily relish, like a greedy man eying his supper, "that leaves us, doesn't it, my little Raf...aye... el? And I have bones to pick with you. Goodness me, yes! Juicy thigh bones..." a roar of laughter exploded from him, spattering Rafi with flying spit, "yours and Miss Jackman's." Terry leaned in closer. "Never the twain shall meet, Rafi! Not while I'm here. Oh, no...

absolutely not!"

Ducking his head from the rancid breath, Rafi pushed forward to stand up. "Not yet!" Tarry barked, gripping his shoulders with both hands and forcing him back down. "I haven't finished." He was smiling again. "You see, I've taken a bit of a shine to you...yes, indeed, a bit of a shine. And I'm going to offer you my protection. That's why we're here...that's what we've come about. We want to ensure..."

"He needs an ambulance," Rafi interrupted, pointing at John, "and you're the only one left to call it."

"Matty?" Terry glanced round, first over one shoulder, then the other; and, knocking his arms away, Rafi jumped up, wincing as he straightened.

"Sit down!" Terry lunged at him; but he side-stepped and Terry's momentum carried him forward, stumbling into the chair and knocking it over.

Rafi raced for the door. "Lawrence!" Terry screamed, coming after him. "Stop him!"

Rafi raced down the stairs, leaping the last five, and, as he fled across the hall for the front door, the incongruous smell of fresh coffee brewing banged up against the metal taste of fear in his mouth.

"Hey!" It was Lawrence's voice. "Leaving so soon?" Rafi wrenched the door open and sprinted down the drive, the gravel and ice of the night slicing at his feet and throat. He could hear the crunching feet behind him. He didn't dare look round...didn't have time, didn't want to see the knuckleduster flashing his way.

He spun into the lane. The tarmac was smooth and the jagged pain in his bare soles eased. Was that a car? It seemed buried in the hedge. Must be theirs. He swerved past it, wondering if he could make it to Ida's before they used it to overtake him. What was that? A stunted tree, maybe? But wasn't it moving? As he peered ahead, his foot landed on something soft that slid and his leg went away from him, tearing at his groin. Hopping clear on his good foot, he tried to run on again, but his left leg was weakened and he had to keep his weight on the right one, as much as he could.

Gradually, the strength came back and he picked up speed again, avoiding the leafy slush at the sides of the lane. He saw the black shape of someone moving ahead of him and he was gaining on whoever it was. Behind him he heard an engine fire and die, then fire again and catch. They were coming. The gradient was against him and his legs felt like they were dragging through glue. His thighs were burning and acrid vomit erupted into his throat and mouth and subsided again. He realized it was Matt, jogging slowly, hands jammed into the pockets of his coat, and he ran past him without a word. A glow from behind, coming and going, began to grow brighter. The gradient was levelling off. It couldn't be far now. The drum of the car's engine was growing louder and, as it rounded the bend behind him, the beams of its headlights lit up the lane around him. He could see the turn into Ida's. He charged past the produce table and on towards the house.

As he passed the SUV and leapt up the steps to the front door, he heard the squeal of tyres and skidding gravel. Jabbing the bell and pounding on the door, the shelter of darkness was stripped from him by the dazzling lights. A hinge creaked in the blackness. "Quick, grab him!" The voice was low, urgent. Rafi glanced round, still banging on the door. A shoeless leg and the hem of a long coat moved out into the light.

"I'm coming! I'm coming!" he heard Henry Downes shouting, as the hall lights went on.

A car door slammed and then another. The front door opened, but Rafi turned away, watching the headlight beams ricocheting crazily as the car hurtled backwards into the lane and took off with screeching tyres back the way it had come.

"Rafi! What on earth? Look at the state of you! Come in. Come in." Henry's warm arm circled his shoulders, guiding him into the house.

16

Lauren woke feeling sick, her stomach tight and uncomfortable. She opened her eyes, alert to the night's disturbance and the memory of Rafi barefoot in the hall, shuddering and hugging to his chest the blanket Henry had thrown round him.

The blinds over the work bench and near the bed were down. The room was still dark, but no longer impenetrable, the spaces between the black shapes of things fogged in the wintry grey light of early morning.

Ida turned over, dragging more of the duvet with her, leaving Lauren stretched out along the edge, her front uncovered and chilled. Attacked in his own house in the middle of the night by that fat slob Terry and his mates. In the small hours, when she'd given up her bed in the spare room, she'd been afraid. The banging, the car's roaring and Rafi's face, his staring eyes and gulping breaths had frightened her. She had followed Ida to the lobby and, as soon as she had seen him, she had wanted to rush forward and put her arms round him, make him feel safe, make him warm; but she hadn't dared to.

All she felt now was anger, pure vengeful fury. She wanted them sent to prison, wanted them to be picked on and beaten up. But, most of all, right now she wanted to see Rafi, make sure he was all right. She swung her feet down onto the rug, kicked her way into her trainers and grabbed Ida's bathrobe from a peg by the curtain.

"Hey, where are you going?" Ida called, propping herself up on her elbows and squinting at her.

"Just going to check on Rafi; won't be long," Lauren whispered, holding the curtain aside and slipping past.

She paused. The house was silent and the doors to the bathroom and Henry's room were partially open. Stealing past them to the guest room, she knocked softly and waited. When there was no response, she pressed the handle down carefully and nosed the door open until there was space enough for her to slip inside.

Pale daylight was seeping through a gap between the roughly-drawn curtains and spreading across the foot of the double bed. At first, she thought the bed was empty; but, as her eyes followed the covers up to the pillows, she saw a deeper darkness in the dip of one on the far side. And, as she tip-toed round the foot of the bed, Rafi's head and profile came into focus. He was on his side facing her, eyes closed and the duvet up over his chin. She took another step towards him and stopped. He seemed at once so peaceful and vulnerable, so undefended, so boyish, like Finn.

Something changed in the room, darkening it. She glanced round to find Ida gliding through the shadows towards her, her hair sleep-tangled and bushy above her nightdress. Lauren raised a finger to her lips and looked back; but the spell was broken by Ida's presence and she wished she still had Rafi to herself.

"Come on, you two," came a hushed voice from the doorway. "Best let him be."

Once they were out in the corridor again, Henry

closed the door behind them.

"Sleep's what he needs," he said, briefly resting his palm on his daughter's head. "He'll be all right."

Later, after Lauren and Ida had dressed and were sitting round the table with bowls of cereal and a pot of tea, Henry joined them. He'd had his breakfast earlier, but he wanted to be with them. He poured himself a fresh mug.

"Are you two okay?" he started, looking at them in turn. "Sort of," Lauren nodded. Her thoughts and feelings were so churned up, she didn't know what else to say and she was relieved when Ida cut across her, "What are we going to do, Dad? Have you rung the police yet?"

Henry sat back and studied them both again for a moment before answering. "We need to think this through a bit," he said. "I went over to Windhover after you'd all settled down again last night. Wanted to check Terry and his friends had left...make sure the house was secure."

"And had they?" Lauren's head jerked up from the milk she was pouring.

"Yes. No sign of them. But the front door was wide open and the gas was lit in the kitchen...on the cooker, I mean. I turned that off and had a check round. Found a window open in the bathroom. That's probably how they got in. Anyway, it's closed now and I bolted the front door." He patted the pocket of his overshirt. "I went out the back way and took the key with me. Should be safe enough for now."

"What about the police, though?" Ida persisted. "Aren't you going to call them?"

He was gazing at her without answering.

"Dad?"

"Sorry, love...I was thinking of your mum. You look so like her sometimes." He smiled. "Mind you, she was terrified of snakes." He picked up his mug and took a swallow. "The police, right?"

Ida nodded and raised her eyebrows at Lauren. "No, I haven't contacted them, yet. I think we better speak to Rafi first, don't you? Get the facts clear. It was all rather a muddle last night. Besides, it's his decision to make; he may not want the police involved."

"But he was attacked!" Lauren flared. It had never occurred to her they wouldn't tell the police. "They broke into his house, knowing he was on his own. If he hadn't managed to escape, who knows what they might have done to him! And they might come after him again. Surely, we have to tell the police, don't we?"

Henry was studying her, frowning slightly, and she was relieved when he started speaking again.

"Sometimes, it's better not to poke about in a hornet's nest, Lauren. Sometimes, it's better just to accept the sting and take precautions." He lent towards her, resting his forearms on the table. "What I mean is, it's not always best to involve the authorities. Things get taken out of your hands, out of your control." He paused. "No, let's discuss it with Rafi first and then with his mum once she's back. And, needs be, I'll go to see Terry...and his uncle too, come to that, Nathan Curnow. He was a lock back in my rugby days. 'Mayhem' they called him. Solicitor now, of course." Henry gave a wry smile. "But he'll put a leash on Terry all right, if I ask him to."

"But what about the others?" Lauren started,

incensed that maybe there would be no retribution; but she was cut off by the sudden blare of the landline, as Henry quickly crossed the room to answer it. Glancing at Ida, Lauren waited, her chest tight and jittery.

"Henry Downes...ah, morning Colin...no, that's fine...yes...all right, let me just make a note." She watched him pick up a pen and angle the shorthand pad towards him. "Right, ready...got it...after lunch, ok...'bout two...right you are, bye now."

"More potatoes?" Ida asked, as he came back.

He nodded. "And beetroot and celery. Which reminds me..."

But, before he could continue, there was a cough and they all looked round to find Rafi standing in the archway in a pair of Henry's oversized pyjamas. His eyes were sunken, their sockets charred and hollowed out. But it was the patch of scalp showing through the dark mat of his hair that caught Lauren's eye and stirred up the fury in her again.

17

Henry insisted on accompanying Rafi back to his house; and, although he protested there was no need, Rafi was secretly relieved not to be going there alone. Strong winds had swept through in the small hours and the lane was littered with pieces of dead twigs and broken-off branches strewn along it. It was calmer now, although there were still fast-moving clouds chasing each other high up, and a squally, dark bruise was spreading across the skyline to the north.

Rafi had woken feeling angry and wanting revenge; but now, as they retraced his desperate flight of the night before, this gave way to a brooding anxiety; not so much out of fear of Terry and the others coming back, as from worry about his mother's return. Even though the break-in and the violence wasn't his fault, nevertheless they had happened while she was away and he was in charge. He blamed himself, feeling that none of it would have happened if she had been there. And, while he dreaded her disappointment in him, he was struggling also to resist his longing for the comfort and security of her being home.

As if reading his mind, Henry broke the silence between them. "Don't you go worrying about your mum, now. I'll help you get things straight and I can hang on till she gets back, if you like."

Rafi glanced at the figure striding along beside him in his wellington boots and heavy jacket. "Thanks," he said, wondering if he could trust this man. His mother had told him a fear of foreigners ran deep in the British and that they disguised it with surface politeness. From his own experience, he knew it was true and that some were just out-and-out racists, like Terry and his friends. But Henry and Ida and Lauren and her family, they weren't like that. Even so, his colour marked him out. In Jordan, he was invisible on the streets; but here, he felt under constant scrutiny. Maybe he should forget about studying in Holland. Maybe his mother was right after all and it was time to go home.

In fact, once they were inside, Rafi found there was very little to 'get straight'. It seemed as if Henry had accomplished all that on his last visit. He went from room to room checking to see if anything was missing. Coming to his mother's study, he paused before opening the door. Everything she valued most, she kept here. His eyes skipped along the family photographs in their silver frames. They were all there. So was a small selection of his aunt Anoush's pots set along the top of the oak bookshelves. He glanced down at the floor to the crimson and cobalt rug from her father's home, which carried him and her origins with it. It, too, was there and unharmed. He breathed a sigh of relief. And then, remembering, he rushed to her desk and tugged open the bottom left-hand drawer. There it lay, cushioned in silk, the 19th century pottery Hookah base that she had bought only recently at auction to give to her father-in-law, Kamal, for his forthcoming 90th birthday. Coming from Jerusalem, where he was born, and painted with traditional vines and flowers, Rafi knew how much it would mean to his grandfather. For a moment, he wondered if Kamal had watched his father or uncles passing such a pipe between them, drawing the smoke of opium or cannabis through the water in its glass base before inhaling it.

"Alhamdulillah!" he breathed, closing the drawer and stretching across to its partner on the right, where his mother kept her jewellery box and a wallet of emergency cash and US dollar travellers' cheques. There was no give; it was still locked and undamaged.

Later, as they were sitting in the kitchen drinking coffee and at Henry's request, Rafi was explaining the flight of Palestinians from East Jerusalem and the West Bank. "Both of them spoils of the Six-Day War, along with Gaza and the Golan Heights," he explained, "after Israel crushed the neighbouring Arab forces in 1967."

"And were your family affected that time, as well?" Henry was listening carefully; and, realizing he was genuinely interested, Rafi was feeling more and more at ease in his company.

"No, although it meant that..." A draught of cold air swirling round his legs and the rattle of wheels on floorboards cut him off short. "Excuse me," he said and hurried out into the hall.

As his mother turned from closing the front door, pushing back her headscarf at the same time, he saw her initial smile die at the sight of him. "Whatever has happened to you?" she gasped.

"Let me take that, Mama," he said, kissing her on both cheeks and taking the small suitcase from her. He set it aside and helped her off with her coat.

"Thank you," she said, straightening her hair and starting, as she turned. "Mr Downes! Forgive me, you took me by surprise. Is everything all right?"

"Afternoon, Mrs Masalha." Henry stepped forward and held out his hand. She shook it and gestured to the sitting-room. "Shall we go through? It's quite draughty here."

Sitting down on the sofa, with a flourish of her hand, she invited Henry to take the armchair nearest to her. "Please," she smiled.

"You'll be wondering what I'm doing here, I expect," Henry began, glancing at Rafi as he settled beside his mother. "Truth is, there's been some trouble, while you've been away. Nothing to worry about now, mind. But young Rafi here's had a bit of a knock and I thought I'd keep him company till you got back."

Rafi started to tell her about the break-in and what had happened, struggling at times to keep his voice from faltering. And he saw the anger and concern wrestling in his mother's face as she took hold of his hand and held it in her lap; and, by the time he got to his escape up the lane, she was squeezing his hand so hard it was hurting. But he felt too full of shame to say anything. He should have defended himself...he should have defended the house, not run away like a little boy.

As if reading his mind, she softened her grip, bringing her other hand up to cup his between both of hers. "There is no shame in this, habibi. Your grandfathers, your uncle, they all had to flee to survive."

"But these weren't the Haganah!" Rafi objected, embarrassed by the comparison.

"Who knows what the one with the knife will do when he wakes up," she said quietly, releasing him and turning to Henry. "I'm very grateful to you, Mr Downes. Thank you." But, before he could reply, she sprang up and wheeled round, taking in the room. "Everything seems to be as it was. But that gang were here on their own." She twisted round again, double-checking.

"It's all right, Mama," Rafi said, "Henry...that is, Mr Downes came back."

"That's right," Henry nodded. "Once I knew Rafi was safe and unharmed, I came down here to make sure they'd gone. And they had, but the front door was open and I decided to have a proper look round." While he was speaking, Maryam sat down again, adjusting the cushions behind her. "I closed the bathroom window where they'd got in. They'd used a ladder to get up there. I found it after I'd locked up." Shifting his weight to one side, he stretched out a leg and took some keys from his trouser pocket. Leaning forward, he handed her two on a ring, one chrome and the other black, heavier and longer. "I took these from the front door, and this one," he passed her a flat Yale key, "as I went out the back."

"I see," she said quietly, holding the black key apart and gazing at it. Rafi felt Henry was waiting for some kind of response and he wanted her to go on. "My father had one like this," she said at last, "but bigger, heavier. My brother has it now." She looked at Rafi. "Your uncle." He nodded, and she turned back to Henry. "My father's parents were Palestinian and they were killed in 1948 by Jewish paramilitaries. Their village near Jerusalem, Deir Yessin, was attacked in the middle of the night and the inhabitants massacred."

Henry frowned and shifted his feet.

"Have you heard of the Nakba?" she asked him.

"Young Rafi's mentioned it to me, yes."

"In Arabic, it means 'catastrophe'. In 1948, more than 700,000 Palestinian Arabs fled or were expelled from their homes, as a result of the Jewish insurgency." Maryam held up the key. "Many of them took their front door keys with them believing that British forces would intercede and that they would be returning in a few weeks or even days." She paused, shaking her head. "But it didn't happen. And here we are over 60 years later and there has been no return...nor will there be."

"Ah, right, I see," Henry said, nodding; "and that's like the key your brother still has...the key to your grandparents' house."

"It is."

In the silence that followed, Rafi thought about the links his mother was making with his own experience: the attack in the night, the violence and intimidation, his flight from the house and the keys. But the scale and the context were quite different. It was just him and a few ignorant locals. No murders, no fighting to establish a new state, no mass exodus, no refugee camps, no history with other countries involved. She was overreacting.

"Come on, Mama," he said, touching her arm. "I'm all right, thanks to Mr Downes. And, you see," he gestured to the room, wanting to lighten her mood, "we have returned; we are safely home."

"This is not our home." As soon as the words were out, she seemed to regret them; and, resting her palm against his cheek, she added, "But you are right. You're safe and that is what matters." She looked round at Henry. "We are very much in your debt, Mr Downes. Thank you again for looking after my son and for all your kindness."

She held out her hand; and, with some awkwardness, he half-rose to shake it.

"That's all right, Mrs Masalha," he said, releasing his hold. "Neighbours need to look out for each other." And he sat down again.

"Maryam. Please, call me Maryam. We are friends now, I think."

"Henry," he nodded, returning her smile.

Rafi found the warm sturdiness of Henry's presence reassuring; but, as his mother went to settle back, he saw her straighten again and his earlier sense of anxiety returned.

"Have you told the police?" she asked, looking first at him and then at Henry and back again.

"No, not yet." He glanced at Henry. "I wanted to talk to you first, because Mr Downes...," he saw Henry's grimace and corrected himself, "Henry, I mean, says he will deal with Terry; he knows his uncle. And he thinks it may be better not to involve the police...that it might make things worse."

"Hmm, make things worse?" Maryam paused, staring at the carpet. "You may be right," she said eventually. "I remember in Santa Barbara, where I grew up," she looked up at Henry, "in California, that is." He nodded. "It all happened on the same day. I was coming home on the school bus...I must have been about ten...and I saw a young Mexican with his hands in the air being shot by a white policeman. His body crumpled and then there was just a line of trees as the bus moved on."

Rafi watched her fall silent. "Mama," he said, touching her hand, "are you okay?"

"Yes, yes. Poor boy, he was only in his teens. He

couldn't have been much older than you, Rafi. He was unarmed and his hands were in the air, and the policeman shot him...shot him in cold blood." She shook her head. "I couldn't make sense of it," she went on. "I wanted to tell my parents. But when I got home, they were out in front of our garage, furiously rubbing at something on the door. And then I saw it: FILTHY ARABS spray painted in giant, red letters." Rafi saw something harden in her eyes. They still burned, but seemed to be locked inwards. "The soapy water was useless; it simply ran off. 'Call the police!' my mother was saying. 'Let the city clean it up!' But my father went on scrubbing. 'The police won't do anything,' he told her, 'and drawing attention to ourselves will only make matters worse!'"

Maryam stressed the last three words and let them hang in the air for a moment, before adding, "Is that what you think, Henry...that we shouldn't draw attention to ourselves?"

"It is. There's no point beating about the bush; there are people down here who want things to stay the way they always were."

Rafi snorted, angry in the moment, remembering the violence against him and the reason for it. "No foreigners, you mean...especially dark-skinned ones!"

"That's part of it," Henry said evenly. "Trouble with prejudice is people don't even know they've got it till something unfamiliar happens and sets them off. It's fear at bottom."

Maryam slumped back; and, when she spoke again, Rafi could hear the weariness in her.

"Very well, we'll take your advice and let you talk to this 'Terry' and his uncle, if you are happy to do that for us."

"Certainly, I will." Henry stood up. "Time I was going." Buttoning his jacket, he turned to Rafi. "Try to keep what happened in perspective. Difficult, I know; but you and your mum are well thought of round here by most. So, don't let these layabouts go putting you off your stride."

At the front door, Rafi and Maryam stood side by side, watching Henry push first one foot and then the other into his wellington boots.

"Right, I'll be off then," he said, his face flushed from bending. "And, don't forget, Rafi," he added with a quick smile, "you're welcome any time. Ida and Lauren'll be pleased to see you, I know that."

18

The raid on Rafi's house had been a disaster. Terry stood looking out of his bedroom window. Further down the road, a white Transit van stopped and reversed into a space. The headlights died and a figure got out. 4.00pm and already growing dark. He half expected a police car. Well, never mind; he had his own version worked out and he'd spelt it out to John and Lawrence. As for Matty, he wasn't answering his calls or messages and he'd have to waylay him after college. Too late today; it would have to be tomorrow.

More headlights were coming up the close, driving slowly along the corridor of semi-detached council houses, with cars and vans parked either side. Like the Transit, a car stopped and backed into a gap. The lights died. An Audi estate. It seemed familiar. A burly figure got out, opened the rear door, pulled out a jacket and shrugged it on.

Terry watched him walk up the path to their house on the corner and turn in at the gate. He took a deep breath and tried to ignore the lurch in his stomach. Uncle Nathan was a trial at the best of times; right now he was the last person he wanted to have to deal with.

He took a step back into the shadows as his uncle

stopped halfway up the garden path to look about him, before moving on and disappearing under the porch. Terry crossed to the bedroom door, opening it a crack, as the shrillness of the bell burst the silence of the house.

"Can you get it, Terry?" his mother called up from below. He didn't move. He wanted to know in advance why his uncle had come.

"Terry!" A pause, then her footsteps from the kitchen. "You could 'elp me, I've enough to do."

The suck of air, warm out into the cold, and muffled voices becoming clearer.

"Goodness, Nathan, wasn't expectin' you of all people. Come in, come in."

"I know, Cathy." The deep, Cornish voice stirred ancient anxieties in Terry. "I'm sorry; it's been much too long."

"That's all right." Silence...rustling...Terry slid out near the top of the stairs. "Ah, that's a nice hug, I needed that." His mother's voice again, softer...warmer; then louder again, straight up the stairs, "Terry! Your Uncle Nathan's 'ere!"

He backed away to his room. "Give me a minute," he called.

"Come on through and I'll..." The voices faded into a blur.

Swapping his slippers for thick-soled loafers, he grabbed a rust-coloured, corduroy jacket from the wardrobe and slipped it on over his v-neck sweater. He never wore it at home; but, as he soft-footed his way down the stairs, he was reassured by the sense of protection it gave him, like a carapace.

The kitchen door was pulled to and he paused outside to hear what was being said.

"...looking so different..." his uncle was saying.

"'Ere, have one of these." Through the crack, he saw his mother's wrist moving against the table.

"...very neat and tidy. Not like when Gary was here...all those rusting trail bikes strewn over the grass... disembowelled parts for that precious bike of his. What was it?"

"Honda TLR. Quite sought after these days, I 'ear."

Terry clenched his teeth. Why was she always justifying him, even now?

"Yes, that's it." A pause, followed by the knock of a mug put down again. "No, you've made a proper job of it, all right. I saw the greenhouse up the side and a vegetable patch behind, maybe?"

"Yes, well, you know, Gary wasn't all that bothered with plants; but I get a lot of pleasure from being out in the garden after being on the tills all day. And we're lucky having a corner plot, 'bout twice the size of the others."

Terry was growing impatient. He wasn't interested in all these pleasantries; he wanted to know why his uncle had come. Nathan liked his mother, he knew that; and he'd been a big support to her after his father had run off. But he didn't make the journey up from Truro these days without a reason. Terry was about to make a move when his mother made it unnecessary.

"So, this a social visit, Nathan, or what?" she said, then added quickly, "Don't get me wrong, mind, you're always more than welcome, but...you know...it's been a while."

"No, I'm afraid it isn't." His uncle's tone was weary with regret. "To be frank, Terry could be in serious trouble and I need to have a word with him."

"You better tell me then," his mother said. "I'd rather hear it from..."

Terry bustled into the room before she could finish.

"Uncle!" he beamed, advancing with his hand outstretched. "This is a nice surprise."

His uncle stood up to take it, squeezing and keeping hold, while looking him over, taking him in.

"We need to have a word," he said finally, releasing him, and he turned to Cathy. "Okay if we use the other room?"

"'Course it is." She paused and turned. "I don't know what this is all about, Terry, but you listen to your uncle; he's 'ere to 'elp you."

Fuck off! Terry thought, despising her kowtowing to his uncle. He was sick of her long, concave face and dented nose, bent and flattened to one side that, nevertheless, always seemed to be meddling in his affairs, and her little hazel eyes always getting under his skin with their love...with their hurt.

He glanced around the neon-lit room at the white, melamine units and worktops and the checkerboard grey-and-white linoleum tiles, so different from the oak, marble and slate he'd seen in his uncle's kitchen, his wife, Della, standing there, so confident and polished, so worlds away from the life of an abandoned Co-op assistant.

"Come along," Nathan said, standing up and towering over the short table, waiting for him to lead the way.

Once in the sitting room, his uncle closed the door. Terry watched him decide against the narrow, wood-framed armchairs either side of the tiled fireplace, sitting down on the sofa instead, which sagged under the weight of him. Best to take the bull by the horns, he quipped to himself.

"Well, Uncle," he said, standing with one elbow resting on the mantelpiece, "I'm yours to command, as they say."

"You sit down and stop playing the fool." His uncle pointed to one of the armchairs. "It's a serious matter I'm here about and I don't want any of your nonsense."

Terry froze for a moment, his fingers curled into fists. 'I'll give you nonsense, all right!' But, as he pulled round one of the armchairs to face his uncle, his breezy smile returned.

"Just pleased to see you, Uncle, that's all," he said, sitting down and running his hands along the arms of the chair. "But you said you're here about something important."

He saw his uncle bristle. "Don't play games with me, lad; I'm warning you."

A shimmer of a smirk ghosted the corners of Terry's mouth. "Of course not!" he said; "I wouldn't think of it."

His uncle stared at him, not saying anything, until Terry couldn't stand the intensity of his scrutiny any longer and looked down.

"Ever thought of joining the army?" his uncle said at last. "See the world. Learn some discipline. Get yourself a proper career."

"Not quite my thing," Terry laughed. "Not really into killing people, if you know what I mean."

"Yes, I know what you mean." His uncle leaned forward, eyes glinting. "You prefer breaking into houses and roughing people up while they're sleeping, don't you? That's more your kind of thing, isn't it?"

Terry struggled to catch his breath, as if he'd been punched. "I don't know what you're talking about."

"You know very well what I'm talking about." Spittle flew out of his uncle's mouth, his voice raised in exasperation. It was warm on Terry's cheek, but he didn't dare raise a hand to wipe it away. "Don't lie to me! Henry Downes has been to see me. I know all about you and your friends' attack on a Jordanian boy, Rafi Khoury, on Friday night."

Terry couldn't look at him, couldn't think.

"You broke into his house while his mother was away and assaulted him in his bedroom, where he was asleep. That's right, isn't it?"

Enough! He wasn't ten years old anymore. Just deny it. Tell his own version.

"Isn't it?" his uncle demanded again.

"No, no, not at all!" Terry said, shaking his head. "We all know Rafael from college. We called round on our way back from a night out in Plymouth. He let us in. We had a drink. And then, you know how it is," he nodded at his uncle, "Rafi said something untoward, which John took exception to. One thing led to another and there was a bit of a...well, a bit of a fracas, if you like. And Rafael ran off and we went home. No harm done."

He felt reinflated, confident again. Yes, indeed...the same facts simply cast in a different light.

"It could be Gary speaking." Terry wasn't sure if his uncle was talking to him or thinking aloud. "You lie and lie, and slip and slide, and take no responsibility for anything you do."

"Come, come..." Terry started.

"You think we're all fools, don't you?" his uncle

exploded. "You think you're so much cleverer than everyone else that you can do whatever you like and get away with it!"

Terry opened his mouth to protest, but his uncle put up his hand. "I haven't finished and you'd better listen very carefully to what I'm going to say next. Rafi and his mother haven't been to the police yet, because Henry Downes has persuaded them to let me come and talk to you first. So, take it..."

A knock on the door interrupted him; and, as it opened, Cathy's fingers and face appeared round the edge of it. "Everything all right, is it?"

"Everything's fine!" Terry bit off the words, not turning to look at her. He didn't want her to know anything about this...he wanted her gone.

But his uncle looked round, clearing his throat and softening his voice. "Not entirely, Cathy, but it will be." Terry saw his uncle's reassuring nod, as he added: "Don't worry, I'll come and find you before I go."

The door clicked shut.

"You're not going to tell her about this, are you?" Terry asked, the moment she was gone.

"Exactly what I tell her depends on you." His uncle arched his back and grimaced and stuffed a cushion into the hollow behind him. "Now, where was I? Ah yes, whether to inform the police or not. The point is, Terry, it wouldn't take them five minutes to disprove your cock-and-bull story and to charge you with breaking and entering and aggravated assault. You'd be looking at two years, minimum."

"But nothing happened!"

His uncle waved his protest away with the back of his hand. "The judge would look at intent, as well as any actual physical or psychological harm."

"They can't prove..." Terry blustered, but was drowned out.

"I'm not here to argue with you, boy!" his uncle roared, standing up and blocking Terry in his chair with a single stride. Nathan's hands were locked on either arm and he was leaning down, his chest and shoulders shrouding Terry in shadow. "You're going to do exactly as I tell you or you'll be in the dock quicker than you can fart again! Understand me?"

Terry nodded, ashamed of the rank smell wafting between them, but never taking his eyes off him.

"You are never...NEVER...going near Rafi Khoury or his house again! Is that clear?"

Terry nodded. "What about Mum? You won't tell her, will you?"

"Stop whining and act like a man for once!" Disgust wrestled with contempt in his uncle's face as he straightened up, but stood glaring down at him still. "Your dad was older than me and all the time we were boys he teased and tormented me. But, one day, I was sixteen by then and playing for the Redruth Colts, I'd had enough. I don't know why I hadn't realized it before, but I'd grown bigger and stronger than him. And I got him down on the ground and sat on his chest, pinning his arms with my knees. My fists were free and I was going to batter him." Terry winced as his uncle balled his fists and held them in front of him. "But you know what?" Terry shook his head. "I changed my mind. All I could see beneath me was a weak and empty loudmouth. There was nothing worth hitting."

Terry hadn't realized he was holding his breath till his uncle took a step back from him and he gulped in air.

"No, I won't tell your mother what you've been up to. I won't tell her that you're a bully and a racist and a violent little thug. She doesn't deserve that, not after all the sweat and tears she's put into loving you."

Nathan wasn't going to hit him; and, although he was still afraid of him, the tightness across his chest and shoulders was easing.

"But I wish to God that, if you have no respect for yourself, you'd at least show some for her! How old are you, nineteen?"

"Twenty-one." Terry's voice was barely audible.

"Twenty-one. Right, then, let this be the moment you decide to grow up and do something useful with your life."

His uncle paused and stepped back from him; and, when he spoke again, his voice was calmer. "You're not your father and I didn't come here to crush you. All I want is to shake you into some kind of decency."

"Yes, Uncle," Terry said, adopting a tone and expression of contrition. "I know that," he added, with a sudden burst of coughing to cover the laughter erupting inside him.

"I hope so." His uncle was already relenting and he knew how to play him from here. "The thing is, Terry, change your ways and I'll try to help you. But there's got to be an end to these shenanigans of yours, once and for all."

"Yes, you're right," Terry said, looking up at him. "I need a change of direction, I can see that." A quiver of a smile twitched at his lips. "A change of direction, yes indeed."

"Right, then," Nathan said, moving for the door,

"I'll just go and say goodbye to your mother and then I'll be on my way." As he opened it, he turned, raising his forefinger and pointing it at Terry like a gun. "But you remember what I've said now; you stay away from Rafi Khoury!"

"NAN direction! Politics direction!" Terry laughed as soon as he was gone, the room suddenly brighter. "And, yes, plenty of money helps, Uncle, you can count on that."

Anxious to avoid his mother and her inevitable questions, Terry was halfway up the stairs, humming "money that's what I want...", when he stopped midstep, the Beatles' tune extinguished. "Yes, yes...of course!" he muttered. "You're the problem and you're the answer!" He grinned and stood with one foot resting a step above the other, astonished at the revelation. No, he could see it clearly now. He would stay away from Rafael. Lauren Jackman was the key. Absolutely! He shook his head and moved on up the stairs. "Cherchez la femme!" he said aloud, closing and bolting his bedroom door.

Women were the problem, like the one with the West Indian boyfriend in the Exeter the other night...like his Dad's mistress, Maisie. They were the ones who mixed the races, who contaminated the stock. His eyes rested on the newspaper cuttings pinned to his noticeboard, his gaze moving between Nigel Farage holding up a pint in his local and smiling affably into camera and Boris Johnson's triumphant Brexit 'freedom' moment, thumbs up, Union Jacks massed behind him. Well, not for much longer. Johnson and Farage had won Britain's independence back. They were putting an end to immigrants pouring in. They were on the same side as NAN and he was going to join forces with them. No more mixed marriages...no more half-caste children! Each to their own. And that went for Miss Jackman! Yes, indeed!

He would teach her a lesson and dear Raf-aye-el, as well. Ideas were tumbling over themselves and excitement drove him pacing up and down, nodding in agreement with himself. Yes, yes, she was blind to what she was doing and all her kind like her. Well, he would make her see! See, ha! Yes, that was it and she'd be a lesson to others. He would blind her to make her see. That's what she needed...something to give her insight. Get rid of her outsight and then she'd have insight. Acid would do it. "Acid'll make you ugly!" he cried out. "Acid'll twist and scar that haughty, unspoiled face of yours and Rafael won't want you then, will he?"

His yell brought a rattling at the door. "Terry what're you doin' in there? Why's this door locked?" More rattling. "Come on, open up. I want to talk to you."

"Not now, mother!" he shouted, "I'm busy. I'll be down in a bit."

"Busy doin' what?" she demanded, then added, "No, I don't want to know", her voice trailing off as a floor board creaked. He knew she was going back downstairs and he waited for the telltale drone of music from the kitchen.

"Lauren Jackman, I'm coming for you," he whispered, closing the curtains. "No more running...no more Rafi...no more silky brown skin against yours!" He closed his eyes, already back in the dark of Rafi's bedroom.

19

The sun was dying through the trees as they stood outside the college gates, the end-of-day flood of students milling past them. Lauren had seen Rafi ahead of them; but, now that she and Ida had caught up with him, she wasn't sure what to say. Or rather, she knew what she wanted to say, but she wasn't sure how to say it without sounding angry, which she was. And the tension of her self-restraint seemed to bind them all in a moment's awkwardness of nervous smiles and colliding eyes.

"Nice one, Nell!" Ida laughed, as a moon-faced girl bobbed in front of her and kissed her, leaving a scarlet imprint of lips on her cheek. Ida pointed to the open lipstick in the girl's hand, its bright red tip poking out from the shiny black casing. "Looks like a randy dog's willy!"

"Share a kiss and save the world!" the girl cried, running off.

"Huh, well, there's a thought!" Ida grinned, looking at Rafi and rubbing her cheek with a tissue.

Don't you dare! Lauren glared at her, but couldn't catch her eye.

"I have to go," Rafi started, but Ida cut across him.

"By the way, I meant to tell you Terry Curnow's uncle has been to see him. Gave him a proper hard time, Dad says."

"That was good of him," Rafi nodded. "Please thank your father for me."

"Why haven't you told the police?" Lauren burst out at him, infuriated by his passivity, his politeness. "He and his mates broke into your house! They assaulted you...punched you, tore your hair out! They chased you up the lane in a car!" She was almost shouting now, dimly aware of other students stopping to listen, but she didn't care. "They intended to do you serious harm, Rafi! What good is Ida's uncle telling him off? What he did...what they did is a criminal offence and he'll do it again, if you don't do something to stop him."

"Hey, Laur, calm down...we've been through this." She felt Ida's hand on her arm and shook it off.

"Do you want to get beaten up again? Do you want these creeps to feel they can go around battering and abusing people and get away with it?" Rafi's eyes were locked on hers, but he wasn't saying anything. "Well, do you?"

He frowned, looking puzzled. "I don't understand, Lauren. Why are you so angry with me?"

His question enraged her all the more. She didn't want to have to explain herself to him...tell him how frightened and vengeful she'd felt that night at Ida's, seeing him standing there barefoot in his pyjamas, looking so vulnerable. Or how protective of him she'd felt the next morning watching him curled up asleep in the guest room. Her feelings were private. Instead, she whirled round on the bystanders. "What are you all gawping at? Mind your own business!" Ignoring their reactions, she turned back to him. "I'm not angry with you! I'm angry that nothing's being done...that those thugs are going to get away with it. I bet Terry gave his uncle the finger the moment his back was turned. Do you really think a telling off's going to stop him?"

"Come on," Ida broke in, "this is embarrassing. Let's use the cut-through and talk on the way."

"I'm afraid I can't. I have to go," Rafi said, tightening the zip on his jacket. "I'm sorry, Lauren. I know you are upset because of me. But, please, I will be all right." He smiled at her, his eyes softening and crinkling at the corners, as he shrugged his backpack into a more comfortable position and raised his hand. "Yalla," he said, turning away, "see you tomorrow."

Lauren watched him weaving his way through the mass of kids heading home, until they swallowed him up and she lost sight of him altogether.

"Come on, I'm hungry." Ida's arm slid through hers and tugged at her.

"Well, if he won't do anything about it, I will," Lauren said, falling into step beside her.

The cut-through, known locally as the 'Terrace', was a popular route back into town from college, being more direct and quicker than by road; and, picking their way past the worst of the puddles and muddy patches on the path up through the scraggy wood at the top and down the grassy hillside on the other side, they walked on in an uncomfortable silence.

"So, what are you thinking of doing then?" Ida said finally.

Lauren glanced away from the trail of students strung out ahead of them to the shadowy shapes of a bunch of cows far down to the right. She didn't know what she was going to do, only that she wanted to confront Terry in some way to make him understand other people knew what had happened and to warn him off...threaten him with the police, maybe. She didn't want to talk about it, anyway.

"You were being a bit flirty, weren't you?" she said instead, her grievance slipping out before she could edit it.

"Who, me?" Ida laughed. "When?"

"You know when." Lauren affected a simpering rise and fall to her voice. "'Share a kiss and save the world. Well, there's a thought!'" She paused and then added with more venom than she'd intended, "Remember?"

"Whoa!" Ida stopped, forcing Lauren to turn to face her. "What are you being so arsey about?"

Ida was glaring at her, her smile gone, her lips closed and her chin up. Lauren knew the set of her expression well. Ida was easy-going; but, if confronted, she didn't back down. They'd had several scraps and fallings out over the years, and, although Lauren had always been taller and more athletic, Ida could be fiercely tenacious under attack; so that, more often than not, Lauren had been the one to back off or to apologise.

"Sorry," Lauren relented, "I'm being stupid, I don't know what's got into me. I feel so angry and I was just taking it out on you. Sorry."

"So, come on, Laur," Ida took her arm, moving off again. "What's going on? Tell me."

Lauren didn't know what was going on. She felt close to tears. "Oh, I don't know." She shook her head. "It's like everything's wrong...I don't know...up in the air...you know...Rafi being attacked, Mum and Dad on the verge of breaking up, all the Grandies gone home and..." She stopped. "And..." She stopped again.

"And what?"

Lauren unhooked her arm and turned aside, standing looking down at the cows below, half-merged now with the hedgerows in the gathering dusk. "The thing is..." she murmured, almost to herself.

"The thing is?" Ida repeated, moving closer.

Lauren sucked in air and blew it out again. "Look, you know me, I'm a runner. That's what I'm good at... that's what I want to do. I want to be the best I can be. I have to train. I have to be totally committed...no take-aways, no drugs, no alcohol, no boys...no distractions!"

She stopped to move out of the way as a line of younger boys came hurtling down the slope behind them passing a rugby ball, hips twisting, arms swivelling.

"Ok, I get it," Ida said, as they shot past. "Hormones in rebellion, right? Certain urges not willing to be taken off the menu?"

She knew. Lauren saw it in the grin she gave her.

"I haven't felt like this before."

"Come on, I'm getting cold." Ida linked arms with her again as they regained the path. "Haven't felt like what?"

"I can't stop thinking about him." Just admitting it, saying it out loud, relaxed her. She'd dropped the bomb and, instead of napalm, the air was sweeter, clearer.

"And you thought I was flirting with him." Ida gave her arm a squeeze. "Guess I was," she laughed, and then added more seriously, "but I was just having fun. I know you're keen on him and I wouldn't, you know..." She let go of Lauren at the kissing-gate, where the paths from the fields and hillside converged, and then led the way down a steep flight of granite steps to the road.

"Besides, it's you he's got his eyes on, not me."

Lauren paused by the curb, waiting to cross. "Oh, I don't think so," she said, remembering the look he'd given her in the garden after their walk to Zeno's, but discounting it.

"Trust me, Laur. I've seen the way he looks at you, pretending he's not...eyes swooping away and back again. And there's like this tension in the air whenever you two get together." She tapped Lauren's arm, "Come on!", and she darted into a gap in the traffic. "So, thing is," she went on, after they'd crossed and turned towards the town, "does it have to be running or Rafi? Can't it be running and Rafi! You know, he's a quiet sort of boy...what I mean is, there's something thoughtful and trustworthy about him, isn't there? He's not going to mess you around."

"No," Lauren agreed and then added, after a pause, "but maybe he's too serious, too caught up in his family's past and wanting to put it all right. He's only seventeen and he's already talking about working for the UN."

"Well, you've been talking about going to the Olympics since you were thirteen!" Ida interrupted. "So what?"

"No, it's not that." Lauren was struggling to get hold of what was really worrying her. "It's more about his not staying here. As soon as A-Levels are over next year, he'll be going back to Jordan and then to uni... in Holland, I think. So, things can't go anywhere, can they?"

"Ah, things!" Ida said, as they walked on in silence; and Lauren knew she was thinking about her former boyfriend, Sam. She had liked him too and been happy for Ida; and then he'd gone and cheated on her. The only time she'd seen Ida cry like that before was when they were in junior school and saw a dog run over by a lorry outside the playground. It was more wailing than crying...wild and unstoppable like the way she laughed sometimes.

Sam had tried to get back with her, but Ida said she didn't trust him anymore. "I don't want him touching me," she'd said. Lauren understood that; it was such a betrayal. He'd been Ida's first real boyfriend...her first sexual relationship; and she'd gone on the pill for him.

'Well, I'm not going to do that!' The thought of it caught her unawares and she tried to smother it. 'Terry Curnow!' she insisted to herself, as they passed the line of shops at the top end of North Street and turned right for home. 'How am I going to get him on his own?' But it didn't work. Pill or no pill, she wanted Rafi to touch her and she wanted to touch him; and she'd known that ever since that night of the Hamlet essay when their arms had brushed and a physical excitement had raced through her. She'd felt the damp between her legs even as she was sitting there. She'd never experienced anything like it before...being so aroused without doing anything.

As they turned in at the gate, she was still arguing with herself. She didn't want to be a drug-assisted runner; but she didn't want to get pregnant either. 'Oh, for goodness sake!' an inner voice chided her. 'You're jumping the gun a bit, aren't you?' And, taking out her key, she laughed in spite of herself. She didn't want to jump the gun, she wanted to jump Rafi!

"What's got into you?" Ida asked, nudging her.

"Nothing," she said. She put her key in the lock and paused, looking round at Ida. "Did it hurt...you know, the first time with Sam?"

"So, that's it!" Ida half smiled, half frowned. "No, not really...more messy than anything else."

'You're way ahead of yourself,' objected the familiar voice, as Lauren turned the key and stepped inside. 'You've someone-else to deal with first, haven't you?' It was a statement, not a question.

20

Where to confront him, that was the question. Lauren didn't feel frightened of Terry. If anybody was going to be violent, it was her. She'd given that slimeball Dean more than he'd expected when he'd come on to her on a college outing to Blackpool Sands - a strong knee in the balls had reinforced her message after he'd ignored her "No!", and he'd left her alone after that. But she wanted Terry on his own...no John Knight, no Lawrence Hawker...just him and her. He was a bully and the best way to deal with bullies was to stand up to them. Without his gang, what was he? Just a podgy creep!

When the moment came, it took her by surprise. She was on the last leg of a late afternoon run before supper, passing St Gudula's Well on the Old Totnes Road before merging with West Street close to home; and, as she rounded the last bend, she saw him up on the right by St Andrew's Church. Easing to a halt in the shadows of the terraced housing to her left, she stood, hands on hips, watching him and getting her breath back.

He seemed to be patrolling, walking slowly away and then back again. As a woman towed along by a Westie passed him, he checked his watch, looking up and down the road as if waiting for a lift. And he did the same thing again a few moments later, when two workmen in hi-viz jackets crossed the road towards him. Maybe this wasn't a good time to tackle him, Lauren thought; not if he was expecting someone. But, as she waited, it suddenly hit her that every time he came towards her and turned, he paused to stare across the road; and that what he was staring at was her house.

Without a second thought, she sprinted towards him. "Hey, Curnow!" she yelled; and she was almost up to him before he wheeled round.

As he took her in, an amiable smile quickly chased away the momentary confusion in his reddened face.

"Well, goodness me, if it isn't young Lauren," he said, taking a step back and regarding her, his hands loosely linked in front of him. "And what can I do for you? You certainly took me by surprise calling out like that."

With his neckless head and protuberant eyes sticking out of the shell of his body-warmer, he looked like a turtle. "What are you doing here?" she demanded. "Why are you watching our house?"

"Watching your house?" He peered up and down, as if unsure quite where to look. "Do you live here? Well, well, well."

"Oh, come on!" Despite her anger, she had intended to be cold and calm with him; but his fake surprise infuriated her. "You know bloody well which house it is! I saw you staring at it. I've been watching you from over there," she pointed to where she'd been standing, "pretending to be waiting for a lift or something every time someone walked by."

"Pretending?"He shook his head. "No, no, there's no pretence, Miss Jackman, I assure you. I am indeed expecting a lift, as you put it. And, if you don't mind my saying so, you seem a little over-excited, a little...what shall we say...over-imaginative?" He smiled and glanced at his watch. "Goodness, is that the time? I think my friend must have been delayed. Anyway, I really better be going, I'm afraid. Don't want to be late home for supper."

"I didn't imagine you watching our house," Lauren snarled, raising her voice, as he turned and started to walk away. "And I didn't imagine you and your mates breaking into Windhover and attacking Rafi while his mum was away, did I?"

She watched him stop mid-stride, standing motionless with his back to her, the air around them suddenly still and silent. She glanced behind her, but the street was deserted...no traffic, no walkers. And a shimmy of fear fluttered through her as he turned.

"Dear me, there you go again, conjuring up evil where there is none," he smirked, sauntering up to her. "Breaking into Rafael's house and attacking him? No, indeed. We just called on him on our way home from a night out, as friends do...you know, old college friends, no invitations needed."

Hearing Rafi's name used so slimily in his wheedling, pompous voice, all her pent-up anger erupted again. "You don't terrorise friends! You don't rip their hair out and chase them up the lane in their pyjamas in the freezing cold in the middle of the night, do you?" She saw him grimace and brush his cheek with the back of his fingers. She was spitting and she didn't care. "DO YOU?"

She was glaring at him so hard, she didn't even notice the couple approaching, until she heard a voice saying, "Are you all right, love?", as a worried face fringed with grey curls under a cherry bobble hat leaned in front of her. Lauren thought she recognized her from the Co-op.

"Yes," she nodded, taking in the man just behind her. "Yes, I'm ok...thanks."

The woman hesitated, glancing at Terry. "Well, if you're sure."

"We can see you home, if you like," the man joined in, moving level. "No trouble."

"No, I'm fine." Lauren gave him a quick smile. "Really."

"Right, then," the woman said, touching Lauren's shoulder. "You take care, now."

"Good-hearted people!" Terry announced, as they walked away. "That's how true British citizens behave... being neighbourly, looking out for one another. We can get back to that...no need to lock your doors, safe to walk the streets at..."

"You haven't answered my question," Lauren interrupted him and, before he could reply, she added, "I'm not interested in your answer, anyway. All I want to do is warn you to stay away from Rafi."

"Warn me?" His smirk guttered and caught again. "So, on your say-so, I am to stay away from dear Raf... aye...el or...or, what?"

"Or I'll go to the police, that's what!"

He shifted his weight, rolling his shoulders; and, when he looked back at her, his bulbous eyes were as cold as his voice.

"I wouldn't do that if I were you."

"Well, you're not me!"

Cars in the far lane were now queuing behind a stopped DPD delivery van, its hazard lights winking, as the driver talked to someone out of sight in a doorway further up. She wasn't alone and she wasn't going to be intimidated. "And, if you or any of your gang go anywhere near Rafi again, I'll make sure the police know all about what you were up to the other night!"

He stood staring at her, saying nothing.

"Do you understand me?"

From the corner of her eye, she saw the driver walking back to the van before climbing in again.

"It's against nature. You foul things up. You contaminate the blood." He was nodding. "Indeed, you do. And once there's a hole in the dam, you won't be able to stop the flood. The valley will be drowned and everything good in it despoiled forever...forever, you can be sure of that. Yes, indeed...absolutely!"

"What are you talking about?" All his oiliness was back in a flash, in the smugness of his expression, in the rhythm of his words, and it confused her. "That's not an answer," she objected; but he ignored her.

"No, the hole must be filled at once...and, so too, all the cracks. And the riches of the valley must be preserved at all costs...all its good fruit, all its honourable people, all its noble ways." He took a step forward, gripping hold of her arm, his face up close. "Surely, you must see that."

"Stop it!" Lauren tried to shake him off, but his fingers only dug into her more tightly. "I don't know what you're talking about!"

"You're a white woman, the daughter of white parents. One day, you'll be a mother...the mother of a white child. That's how the goodness of the valley will be maintained. There can be no Rafi for you...no, no, not at all." He smiled, relaxing his grip. "You may not see that now, but you will. Oh yes, mark my words, you will. Yes, yes...always darkness before the light."

"Fuck off!" she yelled, wrenching herself free. "You stay away from Rafi and you stay away from me!"

He shook his head. "No holes in the dam," he said softly, turning away; and, as she watched him go, he glanced back at her over his shoulder. "And no grey squirrels!"

Part Two

Spring 2019

21

Lauren carried the banana protein drink she'd just mixed up to her room. Being the Easter holidays and able to follow her own timetable, she'd eaten a bowl of chicken and pasta earlier on. She liked to eat early on training nights, as it gave her the energy she needed when the time came, while leaving her feeling nourished but not weighed down. "Just comfortable and ready for action!" she told herself, putting the stainless-steel shaker down on her desk.

She checked the clock by her bed, a wooden puppy with brown rotating eyes, hours in one and minutes in the other. Pop and Mormor had given it to her one Christmas when she was little and she had loved its friendly strangeness and knowing it was there keeping watch over her. Even now, she still liked to have it beside her in the dark, the yellow flecks, luminous at night, circling in each eye to point out the time.

5.20 pm. The Harriers' Arena was open again every Tuesday and Thursday, and Thursday it was! Training was at 7.00, which meant she had just over an hour before they'd need to leave; plenty of time to sort out her kit and finish her thank-you email to Ginnie and Zoltan for the new laptop they'd given her for her seventeenth.

She went back to her desk; and, as she read through what she'd already written, the flapping of a moving shadow outside her window made her look away into the garden, where a pigeon was landing next to another one. She watched them waddling across the grass like a pair of well-fed bishops, their necks popping in and out as if in conversation.

She sat back, losing herself in the slow-moving clouds drifting beyond the treetops. Perhaps winter was finally over. March had been so wet and cold...like being trapped inside a washing machine. Despite occasional glimpses of sunshine promising spring and lighting up the pinks and yellows of the garden's camellias and daffodils, Atlantic gales had kept sweeping in, blurring land and sky into smudged grey dampness. The moors higher up had had the worst of it, bleak and sodden week after week; but, even in the town, the unrelenting mist and drizzle had sucked the colour out of the landscape and the energy out of her.

The laptop's screen blanked into darkness, drawing her back. And, as she stared at it, she reached for the protein shaker, remembering how lethargic she had felt back then. She'd struggled to keep to her training schedule, as she'd meant to. She hadn't tackled her parents, as she'd meant to. And she hadn't followed up on her feelings for Rafi, as she'd meant to. Instead, she'd allowed herself to be carried along by the routines of college and weekends at Ida's, as if she had no will of her own to determine anything. She banged the shaker down. Thank God that was changing!

Even so, was the change just to do with the end of term and having more time for herself? Maybe. Certainly, now days were warmer and evenings lighter, she was enjoying running again and she was looking forward to restarting at the club. Running had always lifted her and cleared her head. But the question now was, what was she going to do about her parents? And what was she going to do about Rafi? She closed the laptop's lid; they'd have to wait, while she got her running schedule sorted.

After changing into her tracksuit, she grabbed the small panda bear sitting by the mirror on the chest of drawers, which her dad had given her when she was seven and ill with chickenpox, saying: "He'll look after you and bring you luck." "Well, I nearly forgot you," she whispered, sliding the little bear beside her running shoes, towel and water bottle in the black sports bag on the bed and zipping it up.

She was ready to run. She wanted to run. Ever since she'd joined the Exeter Harriers in Year 5, training and competing had become not only her life, but also her sense of who she was. Every time she rounded that final bend and felt the surge of her own power as she kicked for home, she experienced a sense of fulfilment she found nowhere else. The Devon County Track and Field Championships were less than a month away and she had a lot of work to do. Glancing up, she saw Christine Ohuruogu beaming at her and she grinned back.

Grabbing her bag, she went downstairs to the sitting-room.

"Okay, time to go," she said, coming through the door. She saw her father in his easy chair by the window, spot-lit by the lamp behind him and reading a book. "Are you still all right to take me, Dad, or shall I ask Mum?"

"You can take yourself now you're seventeen," Finn chipped in before Nick could answer, grimacing as the brush Jess was wielding caught in his curls and tugged his head back. "Do a five day intensive driving course and ask Pops for one of his Volvo bangers. I'm sure..."

"No, we'll both take you," Jess interrupted, "won't we?"

"Yes...yes, if you like." Lauren saw her father's head jerk up. "Although, if you're busy, I don't mind going."

Jess's smile was brittle. "Finn and Tom are going to work on their climate project for next term, so we can drop him off at Tom's on the way."

"Awesome!" Finn looked up from his smart phone, his thumbs still flying. "I can stay the night, save you coming back."

Jess laughed and put the hairbrush down on the coffee table. "Nice try. Very considerate. But, no, we won't be late...back by about 9.30 and we'll pick you up."

"Curses!" Finn said, flashing a grin at Lauren.

"You're not going to watch me, are you?" Lauren said. "I mean, I'm into parental support and all that, but...you know...a tad embarrassing now I'm not six anymore."

She ducked as a cushion flew overhead.

"Wish you were," Jess said, moving to retrieve it. "We thought you were going to be a jockey, not a runner," she went on, clutching the cushion to her. "You rode that rocking-horse Zoltan made for you all day long. We couldn't get you off it, could we?"

Nick nodded, a flicker of a smile relieving the strain in his face.

Lauren flushed. "Mum!"

"Anyway, no," Jess said, putting the cushion back on the sofa, "don't worry, we won't embarrass you. Your father's taking me out for a meal while you're training."

The book slid off Nick's knees and he scrambled to retrieve it.

"Bit of a shock, eh, Dad?" Finn said. "Going to have to unlock the old wallet again!"

Lauren laughed, feeling a flood of affection for him. She loved his sense of the absurd...teasing sometimes, but never mocking or hurtful...more a sort of sideways smile at life, really.

In the car, Lauren buckled herself into the backseat behind her mother; and, after they'd dropped Finn off and merged onto the dual carriageway to Exeter soon afterwards, she kept her eyes on her father. He was sitting straight-backed, his head clear of the padded rest behind and both hands on the steering wheel.

"It's nice not racing," her mother said, breaking the silence. "You see more in the slow lane."

Lauren saw the pink of her father's knuckles turn cream and fade back to pink again.

"We're in good time, aren't we?" he said.

Her mother didn't reply and his question was left hanging.

"Yes," Lauren volunteered, "there's no rush."

She found the silence uncomfortable. She could see that her dad was tense, his gaze locked on the road in front, and she wished she could see her mum's face to gauge what kind of mood she was in.

"Where are you going to eat?" she asked.

"I thought The Hare," her mother said, after a pause. "The food's good and it's quiet and comfortable...good for talking. Isn't it, Nick?"

"Er, yes, I suppose it is...yes. No awful music and the carpet helps...and the curtains...you know, help absorb the noise, other people's chatter and so on."

He sounded...what did he sound? Lauren couldn't quite put her finger on it. He wasn't being his usual humorous self, but then he hadn't been for some time. And he didn't sound down exactly... his tone wasn't flat; it was more kind of neutral or non-committal, maybe? Yes, non-committal, like he was being careful what he said. 'Careful', that was it...but why?

"Well, don't be too enthusiastic!" Her mother's profile poked out from the headrest, the curve of her nose like a parrot's beak.

"No, I am," he said quickly. "It'll be...you know... it'll be good."

There wasn't a trace of enthusiasm in his voice.

"Good?" the profile disappeared. "I was hoping it might be more than that."

"No, you were the one who said it would be 'good' to talk. That's what I meant."

Lauren saw his jaw clench and she looked away out of the side window, wishing her mother would leave him alone.

Nothing more was said; and, after they dropped her off, she took their simmering silence into the changing rooms with her. She didn't want to talk to anyone and, once she'd warmed up, she pounded out her anger on the rubberised track, glad of the evening chill and the fading light.

Oka was waiting for her as she completed another circuit and took her aside.

"So, talk to me. What's up?"

Lauren didn't know what to say. She stood, breathing hard, looking at the steady, familiar face. Oka had been her coach for the last seven years. Sometimes, she felt she knew her better than her own mother did, although she wasn't in the least maternal. She was more like an older sister who looked out for you, but didn't hesitate to challenge you if she felt you needed it.

"Well? You just going to stand there or you going to tell me something so we can get some proper training started before the night's out?"

She was taller than Lauren, a former Nigerian heptathlete powerhouse, but sleek-looking, her hair raked back into a tight, looped ponytail, her broad cheekbones gleaming.

"Sorry," Lauren said, shaking her head. "Sorry, Oka...it's Mum and Dad, that's all."

Later, driving home, oppressed by the silent tension between her parents, Lauren sat staring out into the dark, mulling over Oka's response to everything she'd told her. "They're not your responsibility, you are," she'd said. "Best thing you can do is live your normal life." Her words had seemed empty at the time...meaningless. But, as she rummaged through them again now, something seemed to shift, as if changing her point of view, like stepping back from the trees and seeing the wood. The choices were theirs, not hers. Of course, she wanted them to stay together, but that wasn't up to her. And what else could she do than go on with her own life? Go on running. Go on doing exams. Go on being there for Finn, he'd need her. Go on spending time with Ida. Go on...go on with what? Go on with Rafi!

The car turned sharply and she lurched sideways, the seatbelt catching and holding her. Rafi disappeared into cold air, lights, voices and driveway shrubs.

"We're building a tree-house!" Finn announced excitedly, scrambling in beside her and immediately opening his window to shout goodbye to Tom.

"I thought you were meant to be working on your project!" Jess objected.

"We did! And then we started making plans for the rest of the hols." Finn leaned forward, grabbing hold of the driver's seat. "It's really high up, so we'll need a longer ladder. And we're going to have a water tank, but first..."

"Live your normal life," came Oka's voice, and Lauren smiled as the car swung back into the lane and Finn raced on. This was her normal life, family life, and she wanted it to continue.

22

Once they were home, Lauren went for a shower. Slipping off her bathrobe, she spread it across the radiator and stepped into the bath, drawing the shower curtain across. As she stood with her back to the steaming spray, her head bent forward, and giving herself up to the heat flowing over her neck and shoulders, she thought of Rafi. Her angry outburst all those weeks ago about his not going to the police had spoilt the ease between them and she regretted it. He was still friendly, still came over to Ida's at times, but gone was the unspoken closeness she'd felt with him before, replaced by an awkward tension every time they met now.

She squeezed some shampoo onto the top of her head and began washing her hair, closing her eyes against the suds. She wished he was here with her now... in the shower...literally stripped bare, so that there was nothing misunderstood between them and no words needed. But words were needed, and she'd caused the rift, so they'd have to come from her...to start with, anyway. "Why are relationships so hard?" She yelled into the spray. "Why can't even Mum and Dad keep it together!"

Finn's hammering on the door finally broke through

her trance. "You fall asleep in there?" he asked as she emerged, towering over him, her hair turbaned in a towel. But it was more of a complaint than a question. "Mind the bugs don't bite," she said and crossed the landing to her room, closing the door behind her.

As she dried her hair and got into her night things, she thought about Rafi again. She liked watching him; the catlike grace and power of him as he moved...a contradiction of muscular softness. And yet sometimes he could seem so stiff...his politeness, maybe...or a kind of formality that made her wish he'd loosen up. But wasn't that just part of his seriousness, part of his wanting to do something to help Palestinians? And wasn't it his seriousness that attracted her, as well? He wasn't like the other boys she'd grown up with. And maybe that was it. Maybe it was his very otherness that appealed to her.

But there was something else too, she thought, as she put her brush down and slid the hair dryer back in the drawer....his smile, his vulnerability. Ever since watching him curled up and asleep at Ida's the morning after the attack, she'd felt protective of him, as if it was down to her to make sure he was okay; and she still felt that. Terry was constantly hanging about outside college and the very thought of him sent a chill through her. Several times she'd felt she was being followed, but had seen no-one there when she'd looked round. Terry was slimy, like a toad; and she hated that she couldn't get him out of her head...that he had a hold on her.

Well, she'd go to the police if he tried anything...yes, she would, without a moment's hesitation. "God, if I had a baseball bat!" she burst out, imagining smashing him with it...knocking him down, smashing his teeth, smashing his arms and legs. She saw his popping eyes, his slug-like body lying crushed, all the threat smashed out of him, and the violence in her burned across her chest and into her arms.

She got into bed. Her hair would be a mess in the morning. She didn't care. But she couldn't let go of her anger and kicked her legs from side to side trying to get comfortable. She tried thinking of Rafi with her in the shower and slipped her hand under her shorts, but couldn't concentrate. She was too wound up, too wide awake to sleep. Maybe a mug of decaf tea would help. She kicked off the duvet, put her damp robe back on and went downstairs. But before she'd even reached the bottom of the stairs, she heard her parents' voices coming from the kitchen, taut and antagonistic.

Her mother's first, low and inaudible, followed by a cry of exasperation from her father and then his voice, angry and louder. "Love...lust...desire! Is that what you wanted? It sounds banal, doesn't it? But it was so much more than that...so much more."

Instinctively, Lauren half-turned to go back. She didn't want to hear this. But as he went on, his tone changed, becoming more anguished, and the desperation of it held her where she was. "I don't know how to put it...something spiritual...something volcanic...something that made me feel ten feet tall...I didn't want her....well, yes I did...but I wanted to be her...I wanted to put her on like a sweater, climb into her and stretch myself up through her body and be her."

It had to be Jan he was talking about. Lauren sat down, holding on to the bannister strut beside her, too riveted by shock at the sound of her father's brokenness to tear herself away.

"Pathetic, I know," he added much more softly, "but you asked."

Silence echoed through the vaulted emptiness of the hall and stairwell, and all she could hear was the pounding of her own blood.

"Love...lust...desire." The calm of her mother's voice, as if repeating a shopping list, was more menacing than her anger. "And did you act on them? What happened between you and Jan Rawlings?"

"Nothing happened!"

"Nothing?"

Her mother's snort of disbelief twisted inside Lauren like a knife and she longed for her father's convincing denial. But when he spoke again, his voice was weary with self-contempt.

"I told her I loved her. She told me I didn't. We had a drink afterwards and that was it."

Her mother laughed. "I like her better than I thought I did!"

Lauren relaxed her grip on the strut. That was exactly what Jan had told her. Why had she ever doubted her?

A chair scraped back. "I'm tired, Jess," her father said. "I need to go to bed."

Lauren yanked herself up ready to dart back to her room, but her mother ignored him.

"What are we going to do, Nick? Do you still love me? Do you still want us to...to go on together?"

She was remorseless. She would hold him to the flame and watch him burn; and Lauren could see no way of his escaping her. Her mother was waiting for his answer and so was she. "Just say 'Yes!'" the silent scream ricocheted between her temples. "Just say 'Yes!'"

"Look, I'm knackered," he said eventually. "I'm too tired to think straight. Can we go on with this tomorrow?"

"That's not a 'yes', is it?"

Hearing the door handle turning, Lauren raced up the stairs. She paused in the shadows at the top and looked down in time to see her mother sweep by and disappear into the living room.

Back in bed, Lauren pulled the duvet tight around her, her eyes locked open as she tried to clear her head against the dizzying, whirling questions. "I wanted to put her on like a sweater, climb into her and be her." Her father's voice went round and round inside her, but something he'd said was missing...she couldn't remember what exactly. None of it made any sense. He wanted to climb into Jan, be her. What did he mean, "Put her on like a sweater"? Was he going mad? Was he having a breakdown? Was this what a breakdown was? Would he ever be okay again, or was he going to stay like this...stay...stay damaged? "No!" she shouted and buried her face in her pillow. She wanted him back the way he'd always been, happy, jokey...solid. She wanted him normal again.

She couldn't breathe; she twisted onto her back. They couldn't just split up...he needed help...someone who understood these things...a counsellor...like the one they had at the college...yes, maybe he could see her... well, maybe not...but someone! She'd talk to her mum... suggest it to her...tell her to stay home more, spend more time with him...they could work this out.

She reached for her phone on the bedside table. She'd call Ida...or maybe Ginnie would be better. She looked at the puppy...10.25...no, it was too late for Ginnie...she'd call her in the morning. Even so, the thought of speaking to her calmed her and she scrolled to Ida instead, hoping she would still be up...she was.

"Hi, Laur...hang on a minute, I'm just trying to tempt Coil into having his supper. Honestly, if I hadn't eaten anything for a couple of weeks, I'd be tearing my hand off!"

Watching Coil winding himself round a mouse or a rat before consuming it was something Lauren tried to avoid, as it both fascinated and sickened her. Even so, as she waited, she couldn't help but picture it.

"Right, sorry," Ida was breathless, "I tried feeding him earlier, but he was still half-asleep. All he ever does. Anyway, all done now...you okay?"

Suddenly, Lauren didn't want to go into it. Something in Ida's upbeat, busy tone made confiding in her feel like too much of an effort.

"No, it's all right, I shouldn't have called. I'll tell you about it tomorrow."

"You sure?"

"Yeah, just too tired now...sorry."

"That's ok. Whatever it is, we can sort it in the morning, yeah?" Lauren was about to click off, when Ida added, "Oh yes, one thing, though. Dad says we're in for a hot spell and he's suggesting having a barbecue on Easter Saturday and maybe inviting Rafi and his mum round. What do you think?"

But before Lauren could answer, Ida laughed and went on, "Never know your luck; maybe his mum won't be able to come!"

"Can we talk about it tomorrow?" Lauren said, wanting to stay with her thoughts about her dad. "My head's cabbage right now."

She pushed her phone onto the table, drew in the duvet again and closed her eyes.

23

"So, looks like our Arab friend's getting friendly with the natives," Terry said, watching John roll a thin cigarette between his calloused fingers. "Whaddya think of that?"

The Royal Oak's beer garden was a sun trap and he was enjoying the midday warmth of it.

John flicked his tongue along the edge of the paper. "I don't give a flying fuck about it! Got other things to worry about." He smoothed the roll-up closed, placed it in the side of his mouth and struck a match, cupping his hands round the flame as he bent to it.

Terry chuckled. "My, my, John! I so admire your finesse, your delicacy. A flying fuck, indeed. What would I do without you?"

John's head jerked up. "You taking the piss?" The smoke streaming from his nose and mouth tangled in the breeze and blew across Terry's face.

"Not at all! Not at all!" Terry said, fanning the smoke away with his hand. "You are the one I respect, the one I count on."

He took a drink from the pint mug on the table between them and then exploded with laughter, whipping his head sideways as cider spayed into the air.

John grinned. "What?"

"Oh, dear." Terry took a paisley hanky from his pocket and mopped at his face and shirt. "I was just remembering when..." he struggled to control the rising gurgle in voice, "when you kidnapped Ms Bird's cat and...and..." He couldn't contain the roar of laughter that burst from him, causing the other users of the pub's garden to look round. "Sorry, sorry," he said, raising his palm to them.

John was watching him with his legs stretched out, an amused smirk on his face. Welded to his bottom lip, the roll-up waggled as he spoke, "Got you outta detention, didn't it?"

"It did. It did." Terry folded the hanky again and dabbed the corners of his eyes. "Bet she'd never had a ransom note before. How did you put it? 'Let Curnow go or your moggy gets'...gets something. What was it?"

"Let Curnow go or moggy goes in the spinner." John's eyes glittered. "Sent you straight 'ome, didn't she?" He sucked in on his cigarette and Terry waited for the drooping tail of ash to drop off, but it didn't. "Cat still went for a ride, though...looked like a fuckin' astronaut in orbit!"

"Want another?" Terry said.

John drained the dregs of his lager and handed him the glass. "Yeah, go on then."

When he came back, Terry put the drinks on the table and settled himself again.

"Thing is," he said, keeping his voice lower than before, "I need your assistance in a little venture I have in mind."

"Do yer?" John's flat response was not encouraging.

"Indeed, I do. Let me explain. As you know, our little band of brothers is sadly depleted."

John pulled a stringy bit of tobacco from his tongue and spat on the ground. "Speak fuckin' English, Tel!"

"Andy's away travelling," Terry continued, ignoring him. "We never know when he'll show up again. And young Matty has decided to devote himself to football and a life in shorts!"

"Matt's a girl!" John snarled. "Always was a fuckin' useless cunt."

"Succinctly put, as ever." Terry raised his glass. "Cheers!" He took a mouthful and set it down again. "Sadly, however...well, to me, that is, although not to you, I know...Lawrence has also departed...gone to join the crusade against the 'Infidel', as he put it."

"Departed!" John jerked round to face him, his hand sliding inside his parka. "I'll 'elp him depart this fuckin' life, if I ever get the chance! Runnin' away more like...knew I'd be comin' for him, didn't he?"

The black knife slid out, sinister in the midday sun.

"Not here!" Terry hissed, glancing round. "The point is, John," he went on, relieved to see the blade disappear, "there's an infidel of our own needs taking care of, if you get my meaning."

"Not back to that bleedin' little Arab again! All right, Tel, I'll 'ave 'im for yer, don't you worry. Send 'im 'ome where 'e belongs..." He threw his fag end on the gravel and stamped on it. "In a fuckin' box!"

"Yes, well, I appreciate your support, but we'll need to be a bit clever about this...yes, indeed." Terry raised a forefinger and tapped the side of his nose. "A little bit foxy, Jonno."

"Yeah, right." John pulled the tobacco tin and Rizlas closer to him. His eyes narrowed and he sat staring at the table, his nail clicking up and down on the lid.

"It's all right," Terry said, "I've had an idea that I..."

Without looking up, John's hand shot into the air cutting him short. "I got it! First thing, I'll be in the bushes down Druid's...get 'im on 'is way to college... take 'im from behind. 'E won't know nothin' 'bout it, till it's too late." John grinned his stained teeth grin and mimed slitting a throat from behind. "That foxy enough for yer?"

"It's not a bad idea," Terry said. "It has the element of surprise, certainly. But there may be a couple of problems I can see."

John's grin disappeared. "Like what?"

"Murder may be rather excessive, for one. It would cause a lot of police attention and I imagine they would soon discover that I...and you, of course...have...how shall I put it?...Well, that we have...er...encountered young Raphael before, shall we say?"

"That all?" John snorted. "'E doesn't 'ave to die, does 'e? Just 'as to learn 'e's not welcome 'ere. Besides, I'll do it on me own. You'll be 'ome with yer mum, perfect alibi."

He sat back satisfied and laid some loose strands of tobacco in the paper.

"Yeah, good alibi, I see that," Terry nodded. "Only problem is that people...not least my uncle...know we're good mates, you and I, and they'd come checking up on you, for sure."

"Right then, you got a fuckin' better idea, 'ave you?"

Terry paused, searching for words to defuse John's anger before it boiled over. "I don't know if this is a better idea than yours," he began, as calmly and soothingly as he could, "but let me set it out for you and then you can tell me what you think. All right?"

John grunted and went on rolling, as Terry continued.

"What is it we really object to...you know...about all these other people from other places coming over here to live? What's the worst of it?"

"They're takin' what's ours! They're stealin' my fuckin' life!"

Whether at the force of his words or at the glasses jumping on the table, as he smashed the side of his fist down on it, several heads turned to glare at John.

"Who're yer lookin' at?" he snarled, starting forward.

The couple at the table nearest to them picked up their glasses and went inside, while two elderly men further away drained theirs and walked off towards the car park.

"Yes, yes, taking what's ours," Terry agreed, a hardness entering his voice that hadn't been there before. "Taking our houses, our jobs, our benefits, while we get...what? What do we get, eh, John?"

"Shafted!" The match flamed in the mean, dark eyes.

"But you know what's worse...much, much worse?" Terry dragged his chair round, facing John directly and leaning in towards him across the table. He lowered his voice. "They take our women. They pollute our stock. If we don't do something, before you know it there won't be any proper English left. There won't be any more you and me. No more pure Anglo-Saxon yeomanry that made this country great...that built the greatest, most glorious empire the world has ever seen."

Their eyes were locked and smoke from the roll-up drifted between them.

"So, we're not going to let that seductive little Arab

get away with it. This is where the tide turns. No more mixed blood, Jonno. This is where we stop it, right?"

"Yeah," John nodded, "but how? Yer 'aven't said what yer plan is."

"No, I haven't, have I?" Terry sipped at his cider and sat back. His face unclenched and a smile played with the corners of his thick lips.

"There's more than one way to skin a cat, Jonno. Yes, indeed...more than one way. And the way I have in mind will send out a warning that not only young Rafael's going to listen to, but also everybody else, particularly..." He paused, thinking how impressed Tony Gardner would be. "Particularly any English maid attracted to the sheen of sun-kissed, brown skin! Know what I mean?" He giggled. "These young women, these mothers-to-be, are *blind...*" he stressed the word, "blind to the consequences of their actions; so, it's up to us to open their eyes. Except...and here's the beauty of it..."

A great rumble of laughter rolled from his chest and exploded into the afternoon still.

"Except fuckin' what?" John said.

"Except we're going to open them by closing them."

John's hand slid inside his parka. "I told yer before, stop fuckin' messin' with me!"

"Oh, John!" Terry sighed. "John, John, John...what am I goin' to do with you? Okay, let me spell it out." He lent forward again, beckoning John towards him. "You may have noticed that our Rafael has become very friendly with the daughter of a certain teacher we know." He waited for the penny to drop, but John's scowl of incomprehension remained.

"I'm talking about Nick Jackman and his daughter, Lauren...Lauren the runner...Lauren of the long legs and long dark hair...Lauren the holder of Rafael's hand, metaphorically speaking, and who knows what else! Now do you get it?"

"'Course I fuckin' get it!" The tip of the roll-up flared as John drew in heavily. "You're goin' to open 'er fuckin' eyes, in't yer?"

"Not exactly, no." Terry adjusted the angle of his chair, leaned back with his hands behind his head and stretched out his short, thick legs. "I...that is, we...are going to close them for her, so she can see better. And you're going to help me."

"I don't know what you're fuckin' talkin' about! Close 'er eyes to see better?" John shook his head and laughed. "Too much fuckin' cider, Tel, that's your problem! Rottin' yer brain, in'it?"

"No, it's foxy. Yes, indeed, cunning as a fox. Seeing doesn't just mean looking, does it? It means understanding, too...if you *see* what I mean." He chuckled. "Oh yes, Rafael's little friend is going to view things very differently once we've...well, once we've given her our attention, shall we say? And so is he! Yes, indeed. He won't want to be responsible for a blind girl, will he? No, he'll be booking his camel out of here before you can say..." Terry paused to empty his glass and push it across the table. "Before you can say, 'same again, please'!"

24

Rafi had been surprised when his mother told him Henry Downes had invited them round for a barbecue lunch; and, as they walked up the lane, he was feeling oddly nervous. Of course, he wanted to see Lauren. She was in his thoughts all the time. Yet, being with her, he just couldn't be himself, couldn't say what he wanted to. She was still friendly, not angry with him anymore; and, during term-time, he had lunch with her and Ida in college almost every day. Except, whenever Lauren was there, he was on edge, wanting to feel closer to her again, like he had back in the winter in her garden, but not knowing how to; so that usually it was a relief to get away, even though it left him feeling cowardly and frustrated. What was he afraid of? All he had to do was ask her if she would show him the Rec, like she had said she would. Why was that so hard?

"Look at all these flowers!" his mother exclaimed. "Aren't they pretty?" And she beckoned him over, dipping her face close to the hedgerow. "Mmm, just smell these bluebells!"

He came up beside her. "Bit like honey," he said, stepping back again.

"And these yellow ones, they have no scent. Do you

know what they are? And these pink ones?"

"No, Mama, I don't." He liked the citrusy fragrance of the orange and lemon trees at home and he liked the colours of these flowers without wanting to know their names...blue ones, yellow ones, pink ones was enough.

"These are primroses and those are called pink campions, I think. But look at them, Rafi; such a delicate tapestry. Really, these Devon lanes are quite beautiful in the spring!" She gave a little laugh. "When it's not raining, anyway."

They walked on again and, as they turned in at the gate, Rafi's mouth went dry and his stomach cramped, so that he couldn't catch his breath. He lagged behind, as his mother made for the steps to the front door, wanting to run away...to disappear...to not be there. He watched her in a blur as she rang the bell and waited until Ida appeared around the side of the house, smiling broadly as she came up to them

"Hello, Mrs Masalha...hi, Rafi. We're round the back, trying to get the barbie going." She led the way along a narrow stone path, half-turning in her continuing welcome. "So glad you could come. It's such a great day!"

Rafi didn't want to arrive, didn't want to follow them round the corner to the terrace at the back...didn't want to leave the shade for the glare of the sun.

Henry saw them first and waved from the brick barbecue he was tending. He came across, shaking their hands. "Maryam, Rafi, good to see you both. Charcoal's still smoking, but it won't be long now." He pulled back a couple of chairs from the table. "Here, make yourselves comfortable and Ida'll get you something to drink while I put the food on."

As Henry moved away, Rafi caught sight of Lauren emerging through the sliding door from the kitchen; she was carrying a tray. Pretending not to see her and raising his hand to protect his eyes from the sun, he stared at the row of polytunnels curving away down the slope to the fields below and the shadowy hills of Dartmoor rising behind them.

"Hello, Mrs Masalha. Hi Rafi."

Lauren was sliding her tray onto the table and glanced up at him as he turned.

"Oh, hi!" he said, his voice rising in feigned surprise. But his mother was already speaking.

"Here, let me help you with these." She stood up, leaning across the table to unload dishes from the tray, screening Lauren from his view as she did so. "And please, Lauren, call me Maryam. Mrs Masalha makes me feel so...so stuffy." She gave a little laugh. "Is that the right word?"

Lauren said something in reply, but her voice was too low and muffled for Rafi to catch it.

"Cider or lemonade?" Ida grinned, arriving at his elbow and setting down a tray heavy with tumblers and two large, glass jugs filled to the brim, one clear and honey-coloured, the other cloudily opaque. "Both home-made, you know. Dad's special brew, the cider."

"Thanks, I'd like to try that. We have lemon trees at home and make our own lemonade, but we don't have cider."

The golden halo of Ida's hair blocked out the sun, as she bent to pour him a glass; and her smile was so friendly and disarming as she handed it to him that, for a moment, an easy peacefulness settled through him.

"This is like being home," he muttered, "back at

the farm with Jasmin and Zak...with Damiana!" He laughed in spite of himself, picturing the huge ears and bared teeth of their ancient donkey.

Ida put her hand on his shoulder. "Must be hard being away so long," she said softly. And as she turned to offer his mother a drink, he saw Lauren look quickly away. She had been watching them and he felt guilty, caught out, and he wanted to explain, to tell her that it wasn't like that. It was precisely because it wasn't Ida that he wanted that made it so easy to be with her.

While he was wondering how or what he could say to tell her this, Lauren leant forward out of the shade, reaching for her glass; and, as she did so, the dark fall of her hair came alive in the sunlight, as if shot through with red, ginger and gold threads, sudden shimmers of colour he had never seen before. So lost was he in gazing at her that, when she sat back again and looked up, her eyes caught his, trapping him. Bright flashes fizzed, blurring his vision; and, as he opened his mouth to say something to make sense of his staring, no words would come, so that he grabbed for his glass instead, embarrassed and ashamed.

Afterwards, he carried home the despair of his dumbness before her. The remainder of the barbecue... the food...the sudden shower...were all hazy and muddled in his thoughts and only Lauren's puzzled frown stayed indelibly clear to him.

"You're very quiet, Rafi," his mother said, relieving him of the tray of geranium cuttings Henry had given them as they left and carrying them through to the conservatory at the back of the house. "Is everything all right?"

"Yes, Mama, I'm fine. I'm just thinking about all the

homework I have to do for next term."

He didn't like lying to her and from the thoughtful look she gave him, he knew she wasn't fooled.

"Treat yourself gently," she said, setting the pots down carefully. "Being comfortable with new feelings takes time."

He stroked one of the geranium's tiny leaves, soft between his fingers, noticing its variegated heart shape. "I need to go and get on with my Zola essay."

But, out in the hall, he changed his mind; and, taking the key from the dish by the front door, he went round to the garage. Once inside, clicking on the strip lights, he stood with his back to the work bench and, pressing the fob-button again, watched the electric door unfolding from the ceiling, gradually blocking out the day and sealing him in.

He had enjoyed woodwork at school and also at home in the space Anoush had made for him in the outhouse where she had her kiln. He turned to the shelf over the bench and took down the box he was making for his aunt, rubbing his thumb along the smooth grain of the wood and over the interlocking, hand-cut, dovetail joints that he had fashioned so meticulously. Walnut was new to him and he had found the texture a bit coarse at first; but, as he held up the box, rotating it under the harsh, neon lights, he loved the richness of the light brown wood, knowing how waxing and polishing would bring out its beautiful, swirling burr.

At the farm he had made bowls and dishes from branches of their own olive trees, attracted by the wood's wavy patterns; and later on, while experimenting, he had discovered the satisfying heaviness and tight grain of acacia, making a chopping board for Baba, who still used it in the kitchen every day. Whatever he was making, the real pleasure lay in the feel of the wood as he planed and chiselled and sanded it, working with the grain, breathing in the resinous smell, hand and eye absorbed in concentration, and losing all track of time.

He set the box down and opened the lid, wondering where he could get the cotton velvet he was going to line it with and what colour it should be. Ruby or emerald maybe, he wasn't sure. He liked jewel colours, but Anoush might prefer the simplicity of black. And anything she put in the box would show up well against black...wouldn't be in competition with a more vivid colour.

Reaching for a jar from the shelf, he twisted the lid off and smelt the sweetness of the carnauba wax, which he liked best for bringing out a wood's colour and pattern. He pulled open one of the deep drawers at the side of the bench and drew out a soft cloth. Twisting a corner of it around two of his fingers, he began to apply the wax in small circles.

As he worked, he felt calmer; and, by the time he finished, he had decided he would ring Lauren to ask her to show him the Rec. If she said no, then he would know where he stood and deal with it; but, if she agreed, then the logjam of his worrying would be cleared and things between them could flow more easily again.

25

Easter Sunday and Bank Holiday Monday stayed fine; and Lauren was pleased for all the families and especially the children, who had been cooped up in their cars for hours driving down on clogged motorways, but who could now enjoy the fun and freedom of playing on the beaches and swimming in the sea.

Taking a cushion with her, she wandered out into the garden and sat down on the wooden bench, avoiding the side with the chalky smears of pigeons' droppings. A distant buzz-saw seemed only to emphasise the silence rather than to disturb it. She eased her phone from the front pocket of her jeans and laid it on the bench beside her, not ready yet to make the call and wanting instead to come to rest and think about what she wanted to say.

The sun had already risen above the trees. Leaning back, she closed her eyes savouring the heat of its rays on her bare arms and face; aware, too, of the warmth on her shoulders and the tops of her thighs, even through the cotton of her jeans and t-shirt.

Her father had gone off early, she didn't know where, and her mother was dropping Finn off at Tom's, while on her way to a site meeting with the builder at the new restaurant in Totnes. Being alone was a relief.

It meant she could confide in Ginnie without worrying about being overheard or interrupted. Ginnie would listen. She wouldn't judge or give advice. Lauren loved all her grandparents, but Ginnie was the one she felt closest to. She couldn't quite put her finger on why that was: Zoltan and Pop were playful and fun to be with, but somehow she always found herself being jokey and upbeat with them, never sharing any of her worries or doubts, even though she knew they both loved her. And Mormor?

Mormor always treated her seriously; but there was something anxious and over-protective in her seriousness, as if she was anticipating problems and on standby to come to her aid. Perhaps that was a Swedish characteristic; Lauren wasn't sure. Or maybe it was the result of Mormor's parents' experiences during the war. When the Nazis had invaded Norway, Mormor's father, Stig Petersen, had escaped on a fishing boat to Sweden, where he met and fell in love with Greta Lundberg.

A blackbird landed on the edge of the stone dish resting on the low patio wall and hopped into the shallow pool of water. Watching the sudden flurries of splashing, black wings, orange beak and spraying droplets of water all glinting in the sunshine, Lauren sat transfixed. She didn't want the mesmerising dance to end; she stayed motionless, barely breathing until, without warning, the bird shot off across the garden in a low trajectory and disappeared into the hedge opposite.

She felt momentarily bereft, wishing the blackbird would fly back and bathe again; but the stone dish remained deserted, like a stage with the actors gone. She picked up her phone and stared down at the blankness of its screen.

No, Ginnie would be easier to talk to. Lauren clicked it on and scrolled down.

"Hi Lauren. What a lovely surprise! And how is my favourite granddaughter this fine day?"

The sound of her grandmother's faint Scottish burr, with its warmth and the soft rolling 'r' in her name, loosened something inside Lauren and she struggled to control the quaver in her own voice.

"You've only got one and I'm okay." She tried to laugh, but choked on it. "Actually, no, I'm not."

"Ah, all right. Just bear with me a moment while I go out into the garden. Zoltan's singing and you know what that's like!"

As the sound of her grandfather's chanting faded, replaced by the distant thrum of Chiswick traffic, Lauren pictured Ginnie going through the French windows out into the little walled garden of their terraced house up a lane from the river; a garden she had loved as a child for its strange, echoey privacy, which felt so safe and mysterious all at the same time.

"Right, almost with you...just pull this chair over into the sunshine." Lauren heard dull scraping, followed by a sigh. "Ah, there we are. Now, come on, I can hear you're upset, but we won't be disturbed. So, take your time and tell me what's the matter."

"Okay." Lauren took a deep breath and held it. Where to begin? "Okay," she said again, letting it go. "It's about Mum and Dad. And, the thing is...the thing is, can I talk to you about them without your telling them? Because I think they're going to split up and I don't know what to do to stop it."

"Ah, well, why don't you tell me what's happened and it'll just be between the two of us?"

Lauren started with the freezing night she'd seen her father standing alone in the garden in his apron and gradually recounted everything she had seen and overheard between her parents since then. As she neared the end, she began to falter; partly because of the catch in her throat when she got to her father's wanting to put Jan Rawlings on like a sweater and climb into her and be her, and partly because her grandmother wasn't saying anything.

She paused, noticing another bird now splashing in the birdbath, spray flying around its brown wings and speckled chest.

"Are you still there, Ginnie?" she asked quietly, not wanting to frighten the bird away.

"Yes, I am. I'm listening to you. Is that everything?"

The calm assurance in her grandmother's voice steadied her and Lauren went on again.

"Almost. The last thing, really, was the other night when they were in the kitchen. I was on the stairs going down for a drink. Mum seemed to be having a go at Dad and then I heard her ask him if he still loved her. And he didn't say anything for ages and I wanted to scream at him to say 'Yes!' That's all he had to do; but in the end, he just said he was tired and they could talk about it in the morning, as if they were talking about the shopping or something."

Her grandmother gave a little grunt. "And what did Jess say?"

"Um, something like, 'Well, that's not a yes then, is it?'"

"No wonder you're upset," Ginnie said, "and I'm glad you've told me. It's not a worry you should be carrying on your own."

Something in the safety of her grandmother's support, like a lifeboat coming alongside in a storm, released the sadness in Lauren and she leant forward, bowing her head so that her hair hid her, and licked the salt from a tear trailing at the corner of her mouth.

"Thank you," she whispered.

For a while, Ginnie was silent; but Lauren didn't mind. She knew her grandmother was still there and she waited, drawing in deep breaths from time to time until Ginnie went on again.

"When we all came down in the winter, it wasn't just to help Finn with his project. We knew things weren't quite right. I mean, we could see Nick was...was... what would you call it? Distracted or even lost, maybe. Anyway, Freda had a long talk with him and, afterwards, she told Jess that rather than being angry with him, she should try to get him to talk about whatever was going on...you know, get him to talk about his feelings."

Lauren still found it strange hearing her parents and Mormor referred to by their first names, even though Ginnie and Zoltan had always done that. Somehow, it seemed to put them outside her, rather than inside; she both liked it because it made her feel more equal and adult, and disliked it because they didn't feel so especially hers anymore.

"And what did Mum say?"

Ginnie gave a short laugh. "Jess is like me, she doesn't like being told what to do. She told Freda she'd think about it."

"But Mormor's right, isn't she? They need to talk, don't they? And Mum needs to listen...I mean really listen. Otherwise, how else are they ever going to sort anything out?"

Lauren knew Mormor was right. She'd never thought about it that way before; but it was obvious now. And, before Ginnie could answer, she hurried on.

"It's like when Ida and I fell out, because she was going home with a girl called Tamara every day after college instead of with me, like we'd always used to do. And it was only after I'd stopped being angry with her and started listening to what she was trying to tell me that things got better."

"Go on," Ginnie said. "How did that work?"

"Well, what I remember is that once I knew what was going on, I just wanted to help...help Ida and Tamara too, because it turned out Tamara's brother was cutting himself and she couldn't tell their parents, as he'd made her promise not to. I thought Ida was blanking me, but she was just trying to help Tamara sort things out. And I realized I was the one causing the problem, not her!"

"Ach, I do it all the time to Zoltan," Ginnie gave one of her throaty chuckles. "Make assumptions, don't listen to him. I should know better by now. But just because I'm older, it doesn't make me any wiser. Anyway, there you are, you've set it out plainly enough. Like Freda says, Jess needs to listen to Nick so that he feels heard not attacked; then, maybe he'll feel safe enough to let her know what's got into him."

Ginnie stopped and Lauren was about to say something, when Ginnie sighed and added, "But that's not as easy as it sounds. Or, at least, it's easier with people you don't care about so much. It's the ones you love that are the problem."

A picture of the confusion in Rafi's face when she had berated him flashed into Lauren's mind. But Ginnie was speaking again with a new intensity that drew Lauren back to her.

"When my mum left my dad, I was 12. Suddenly, without warning, I was living in a new town with my mum and a man I'd never met before and going to a new school, where I didn't know anybody. And I can tell you I wasn't interested in listening to anything my mother had to say, I just wanted my old life back. I wanted my friends back...and my dad back. I wanted my bedroom back!"

"Why? Why would she do that to you?" Lauren broke in, startled at the thought of it happening to her and Finn.

"She fell in love...no, that's not accurate. She needed love and she got it from an Indian doctor, Ramesh Shah, who was kind and good to her. I didn't realize it at the time, but my father was a dour, uncommunicative man, although not to me." Her voice softened. "I was his 'wee lassie' and I loved him; but I think she felt...oh, I don't know...neglected, taken for granted, starved of affection...all those things."

"Were both your parents Scottish, then?" Lauren asked. She'd always felt muddled about her grandmother's life before Zoltan

"Aye, hen, as my mother used to say, they were. Douglas Cameron, steelworker, and Annag Murray, teacher; they don't come much more Scottish than that...both from Glasgow."

"But I thought you grew up here...in England, I mean."

"We did, in Corby with all the steelworkers from the Clyde. The company they worked for, Stewarts and Lloyds, moved there in the 1930s and Dad went with them." She paused. "I was happy in Corby. I had lots of school friends and I liked the grittiness of the place. People were straight with you, no false politeness; you knew where you were with them."

"So, what was it like living with this Indian doctor, instead of your dad?" Lauren stood up and started circling the bench. "Suddenly living with a stranger, I mean?" There was no way she'd put up with that. She'd leave. She'd go and stay with Ida. But what about Finn?

"It was difficult, Lauren...at first, anyway. But the point is I was hurt and angry. Nobody had told or asked me anything and my life was being turned upside down. And, if Nick's not been talking to Jess, not letting her know what's going on, she must be feeling the same." Her grandmother's voice had regained its usual composure and Lauren sat down again. "So, if you're happy for me to do so, why don't I talk to her and try to persuade her to listen to Nick with an open mind.... actually an open heart would be better?" She paused and gave a little laugh. "Although I'll have to do that as diplomatically as I can or she'll take off like a hare if she thinks I'm telling her what to do."

"Ok, but don't say I told you...maybe, Mormor."

"Don't worry, I'll be discreet."

"And what can I do?"

"Nothing."

"Nothing?"

"Yes. Your parents are not your responsibility." Lauren swiped a fly off her leg in irritation. It might as well be Oka speaking.

"I don't know what that means, Ginnie. If you see someone about to jump off a bridge, you try to stop them, even if it's got nothing to do with you. And Mum and Dad have got everything to do with me!"

"Worrying won't help. I know that's easy to for me to say and won't stop you doing so."

"Too right!" Lauren muttered to herself.

"But have courage. Believe this will sort itself out, one way or another. Spend time with your friends. Be the good older sister to Finn that you always are. And know that all of us, me and Zoltan, Freda and Greg, are here whenever you need us. We all love you and we won't let you fall. You can count on us...you can count on me."

"I know," Lauren said softly, remembering a wave bowling her over when she was little; how it had sucked her under, grabbing and spinning her so that she didn't know which way was up from down, the roaring water in her ears and up her nose as she desperately tried not to open her mouth; and how suddenly, out of nowhere, strong arms had caught hold of her and lifted her out into the air and sun again. And there had been Ginnie, her hair on fire in the sunshine, holding her tight and stroking her cheek, saying, "You're all right, sweetheart. You're all right, I've got you."

She couldn't speak. Ginnie's body had felt so warm against her and her hold of her so secure that her terror had dissolved into sporadic sobs until they, too, faded, as Ginnie gently set her down again and walked back up the beach holding her hand.

"Lauren? Are you still there?"

"Sorry, yes...yes, I'm here," she said at last, a shiver going through her in spite of the heat. Ginnie was saying something, but she didn't take it in. She wanted to be held like that again. She wanted to be held like that right now...and she knew who by! And, even though she laughed at herself for the thought, it brought her back more fully into the present.

"Ginnie," she said, interrupting her, "did you ever fall in love with someone from somewhere else?"

"Where on earth did that come from? And, of course I did! You know I did."

"No, I didn't mean Zoltan; I meant someone different, not European...you know, different culture... different colour."

"Different colour? What's this all about, Lauren?"

Hearing the surprise in Ginnie's voice changing to curiosity, Lauren felt caught out and wished she hadn't said anything.

"No, it's all right, doesn't matter."

"Come on, tell me. Something's on your mind clearly...apart from Jess and Nick, I mean."

"No, it's nothing really." Why had she said anything? Lauren wished she had never started. "It's just about a friend at college."

"A friend? I see."

"Yes, she likes a boy there, but he's Chinese and she's worried getting involved with him won't go anywhere, because...well, because of him being different. Like there's a gang of local creeps out to get him. They broke into his house and..." Lauren stopped; she was saying way too much. "Anyway, thing is, he's staying with relatives over here and after A-Levels he'll be going back to Hong Kong. So, Alice can't see any future in it."

"That does sound difficult." Ginnie's concern sounded genuine. "Has Alice said anything to her parents about it?"

"No, she hasn't told anyone, only Ida..." Lauren screwed her eyes shut and banged her fist down on the arm of the bench. "Only Ida and me, of course."

"And what advice did you give her, as I'm wondering what you might do in her place?"

Ginnie's question threw her.

"My advice?"

"Yes."

"Um, I don't remember exactly. Something like... erm, she should listen to her own heart and...and not let other people's prejudices scare her off...you know, stop her doing what felt right to her." Lauren knew she was talking to herself and it was a strange feeling.

"And what do you think of this Chinese boy? Do you think he's good-hearted?"

Lauren looked away towards the apple tree and imagined Rafi standing in between with his earnest face breaking into a flashing smile, his eyes warm and steady. "Yes. Yes, he is...definitely!" He was trustworthy. She knew it now. Absolutely.

"They'll find a way, then, if that's what she wants. You can trust in that, Lauren, believe me."

Lauren heard the softening in her grandmother's voice and realized Ginnie knew she had been talking about herself. Nevertheless, as she said goodbye and rang off, something settled inside her and she felt easier.

26

The Easter holidays were over and as they waited on the opposite side of the road watching the college entrance, Terry lowered the zip of his body warmer to halfway.

"Aren't you a bit hot in that?" he asked, glancing at John's parka.

"No, I fuckin' ain't!"

"All right, all right!" Terry let it go. John's boss had put him on half-time and cut his pay; it wasn't any wonder he was in such a foul mood.

"Where the fuck are they?" John sent a loose stone skidding across the road with the toe of his boot.

"Patience, Jonno," Terry growled. "They'll be coming any...look, here they are now!"

He soon spotted Lauren and Ida being carried along in the end-of-day flood of students; some dawdling, but most hurrying away and filling the breezy afternoon air with their whoops and chatter and flailing limbs.

"Lover boy ain't with 'em," John said.

"Never mind that." Terry moved out of the shadow of the oak tree, watching Lauren and Ida rounding the bend and disappearing out of sight. "Come on. We'll follow 'em, see where we might introduce ourselves, as it were, on another, more auspicious occasion, shall we say?" He laughed, the phlegm rattling in his throat. "A suitable place for an ambush, if you..."

"All right, Tel? John?" a familiar face, livid with acne, called out as they approached a group of lads, college blazers hooked one-fingered over their shoulders.

"Fuck off!" John said, striding on, forcing two of them in the middle to peel back to make way for him.

"Good afternoon to you and to your comrades," Terry said, pausing among them, smiling and appraising each face in turn, before turning his attention to John, who had stopped to wait for him. "A little civility, if you please, Mr Knight. Surely, you remember these faithful followers of ours when we, too, were part of the Dalby flock."

"Tossers!" John said, pulling up the hood of his parka.

"Gracious, as ever," Terry sighed. "However, we must press on; yes, indeed." He gave a little bow to the group. "Good day, gentlemen."

As they hurried on, two stabbing struts of Terry's to every lengthening stride of John's, they came to a crossroads, where the students in their uniforms were splitting apart and thinning out. Glancing up and down each possible way ahead, they couldn't see Lauren or Ida.

"Where are the fuckers?" John said.

"The question is, have they gone on together? And, if so, where to? To Ms Jackman's or Ms Downes'?" Terry tapped a bent forefinger against his cherubic lips. "Town or country, eh John?"

"Country, 'course. Yer not 'ittin' 'em today, are yer? Yer lookin' for 'idin' places. That's the fuckin' point, isn't it?" Without waiting for an answer, John set off up the lane.

"Wise words," Terry said, starting after him. "Wise words, indeed. We'll make Prime Minister of you yet!"

The idea appealed to him and he chuckled as they walked on together, imagining a Ten O'Clock News report: "During Prime Minister's Question Time in the House of Commons today, the Prime Minister, John Knight, informed Members of Parliament that 'fuckin' Brexit was fuckin' 'appenin', whether they fuckin' liked it or not!'"

"What yer laughin' at?" John snarled.

"Oh, just the vagaries of our democratic system," Terry said.

As the lane twisted and climbed, the sunlit, moorland hills sank from view beneath the rim of the hedgerows. Rounding another bend, they caught a glimpse of the two girls some way ahead of them, framed momentarily in the mouth of a driveway before disappearing again into the shadows and folds of the lane.

"Right," Terry said, slowing his pace. "Now what we need is a good place to conceal ourselves. Somewhere we won't be seen, when they're going home this way."

"It's all bloody hedges!" John muttered.

But, as the lane curved again, it broadened, sloping away on the left to the dark mouth of a drive, shaded by tall rhododendron bushes.

"Ah, ha! What have we here?" Terry veered off towards it and by the time John came up to him, he was standing with his hands linked across his belly and a smile of satisfaction fattening his cheeks. "It's perfect, look."

He walked forward and pushed himself through a break in the bushes into a pocket of undergrowth, soft under foot with fallen leaves. He beckoned John in and they stood side by side, stooping under the canopy, looking out into the lane.

"No-one'll see us 'ere, boy," Terry whispered. He shifted round to look up the drive, which circled a stand of trees screening the entrance from the house. "No-one in the lane; no-one in the house. Yes, indeed; we'll be squirrels up a tree."

He was about to go on when the sound of sharp and tuneful whistling split the afternoon stillness, growing louder as a man on a bicycle whizzed past the entrance and on down the lane, his piping soon fading away.

A thrush popped out of the undergrowth, followed by another, pecking between the leaves and glancing up. Terry stamped his foot and toed a spray of mulch at them.

"Don't!" John shouted, as the birds bolted through the thicket, and his hand flew inside his parka.

"All right, John," Terry said hastily, touching his arm. "It's all right. I'm sorry, didn't mean to upset you."

"I fuckin' like birds," John hissed, "and you'd no fuckin' reason to frighten 'em like that!"

"You're right." Terry kept his voice light, soothing. "Wrong birds entirely! My mistake."

John's hand slowly reappeared from his coat. Terry swallowed and nodded.

"No, the birds we're after have no wings, do they? They won't be able to fly away. They won't even know we're there till our arms go round their necks and our hands across their mouths."

"My back's fuckin' achin'," John said, shouldering his way out and straightening up in the driveway.

"Wait," Terry called, but John marched out into

the lane, forcing Terry to run after him. "Hang on," he said, catching up. He turned in front of him and put his hand on John's chest. "Wait a minute."

John stared down at his hand and Terry quickly took it away.

"What?" John demanded.

"I just want to go through the plan with you, while we're here." He looked back at the entrance and pointed. "Imagine it, Jonno. They go by. We sneak up behind them and grab them. You tie a hood over Ms Downes' head and tie her wrists while I'll introduce Ms Jackman to the bitter lick of my little phial." Terry chuckled. "Oh, yes. And then we'll melt away. No street cameras here. Goodness me, no. Ghosts is what we'll be."

There was no answering smile on John's face, just a hard, unblinking stare.

"Yer plan fuckin' stinks!" he said. "And I ain't doin' it."

"What do you mean?"

John took a step in, thrusting his clenched face close to Terry's.

"There could be other fuckin' people 'ere, couldn't there?" He reeked of tobacco and Terry half-turned his face away as he went on. "But, and this is the main fuckin' thing, I didn't get what you was talkin' about the other day, but I ain't 'elpin' you put no girl's eyes out! All right? And, 'nother thing, she's white, isn't she? Fuckin' one of us!"

Their eyes locked as Terry struggled to think of something to say to get round this refusal. He'd always been able to handle John, ever since junior school.

"Come, come," he said, "let's not be hasty." He

smiled and clapped John on the shoulder. "And I take your point, I do. It's a good one. Other people in the lane at the same time, yes, indeed. That needs thinking about. Yes, yes, our plan needs refining, I can see that. Thank you, John."

"Right, then," John said, stepping back. "Just so it's fuckin' clear, all right?"

"Clear as Ms Jackman's eyes, I assure you," Terry muttered, nodding.

As they walked back into town, Terry wondered whether John's usefulness to him might have come to an end. After all, while it was good to have a savage dog to keep intruders away, once it started baring its teeth at you, surely that was the right time to shoot it, wasn't it? Well, he wouldn't shoot John, of course; but perhaps he should let him go, disentangle himself. No more tip-toeing round his potential violence, no more having to absorb the barrage of his swearing or the stench of his cigarettes. It felt like such a liberation just to think of it...as good as the last day at college...as good as the day his dad left...like dark clouds rolling back and the sun coming out. He started whistling.

"Give it a fuckin' rest!" John said.

Terry laughed. "I may not see you for a while, Jonno. If you're not going to help me, I've got some thinking to do, yes, indeed; how to catch Ms Jackman all alone and how to bring the oh-so handsome Rafael to his knees." He paused, before adding with a venomous gurgle of delight, "To his knees!"

27

Rafi was in the kitchen chopping onions, rocking the Sabatier knife up and down over the board, one hand on the handle, the other over the tip of the blade. He didn't mind cooking supper when his mother had a later-than-usual tutorial, knowing how weary and pleased she would be. Reaching for a bulb of garlic, he heard the soft clunk of the front door closing. Glancing sideways, he saw his mother putting her briefcase on the hall table.

"Hello, Mama," he called out and she gave him a wave, her ring flashing momentarily. "I thought I'd use up the chicken and make musakhan. Is that okay?"

She didn't answer and, peeling the sticky skin from three of the cloves, he wondered where she had gone. Normally, she came straight in and kissed him hello before doing anything else. He looked round to find she was standing just outside the doorway watching him.

"Mama?" he said, brushing his fingers clean and turning to face her.

"I was just thinking how like Baba you are."

"Oh, no," he laughed, "not that again!"

But she did not smile back or move as she went on in a voice that sounded oddly detached, as if addressing someone else.

"Same tight dark curls...smooth olive skin. Same high cheekbones, same jaw...the way it tapers. But no beard yet and you are taller than Baba. And both of you resemble the photos of Jedi as a young man."

Rafi could hear the sadness in his mother's voice as she walked towards him.

"What is it, Mama?"

"I was eleven when my father died, Rafi. I didn't understand it at all...that he had disappeared...that I was never going to see him again...that I would never have the chance to say goodbye to him, to let him know how much I loved him."

She stopped, her eyes molten with tears and Rafi's stomach knotted in sudden dread.

"Baba! Has something happened to Baba?"

"No, no!" she said, raising the palm of her hand towards him. "Baba's fine. But, come, let's sit down, Rafi; I have something to tell you."

As she pulled out a kitchen chair, Rafi took the one across the corner of the table from her.

At first, she sat silently studying him with the same searching expression he had seen earlier as she had stood watching him from the hall. And he sat back, waiting for her to begin, his hands resting against the edge of the table.

"You're already a young man," she said, at last. "In a few months, you'll be 17, and it won't be long before you'll be away at university and then out into the world, which is as it should be, of course. Every chick has to find its wings and fly the nest eventually. But where have the years gone?" She paused and shook her head. "You were such a serious little boy sometimes. I can see you now filling the watering can for your grandfather and carrying it back to him with both your hands, your back arching under the weight of it. And Jedi would take it, bending to say something to you his hand on your shoulder, and a flashing smile would light up your face.

"Yes, I remember," Rafi smiled. "It was heavy and I was so afraid I would spill some."

"I know you were; but he loved having you help him and he was so proud of you."

Without warning, she got up and, stepping round the table, stooped to put her arms around him.

"Oh, Rafi!" she whispered, her cheek hot against his as she hugged him.

"What is it, Mama?" The spicy sweetness of her scent caught in the back of his throat and he coughed. "What has happened? Please tell me. Is everything all right?"

"No, Rafi, it isn't." She released him and sat down again, taking hold of his hand, as she did so. "I have some sad news from Baba."

"What news?" he demanded, pushing his chair back and pulling his hand away, his thoughts jumping to Zak and Jasmin.

"Jedi was late getting up this morning." His mother's voice had calmed and her gaze was steady. "And when Baba went to wake him, he found he had died in the night...a stroke or heart attack, almost certainly. Baba said Dr Amari was on his way." Tears welled in his eyes against his will, and again he pulled his hand away as she tried to take it. "It was peaceful, habibi. He didn't suffer."

"Jedi is dead," he repeated to himself, staring blankly at her. He hadn't even thought of his grandfather. Jedi had always been there, strong and unchanging, as permanent as the farm...as the hills.

"It doesn't seem possible, does it," Maryam said, as if reading his thoughts.

No, it didn't. He couldn't take Lauren to meet him now. The thought was absurd and he pushed it away angrily. The point was they were going home this summer for Jedi's birthday...his 90th. The hookah base came back to him, nestled in its silk-lined box upstairs in the bottom drawer of his mother's desk.

Standing up, he lurched away from the table and out of the house into the light spring evening. Walking round to the back of the house, he crossed the lawn to a path through the rhododendron bushes already swathed in their blousy red flowers and on to the low perimeter fence with its gate to the field beyond. He could hear his mother's voice, "Jedi is dead", but the words wouldn't go in, he couldn't absorb them. They just rang in his head without meaning.

He followed the grassy verge to his left around the ploughed furrows and down to the open woodland at the bottom, pressing on through its filtered sunlight until he came to the stream running through it. Sitting on a fallen trunk, his feet shuffling among the brown-and-rust carpet of long-fallen leaves and twigs and desiccated beech nut shells, he stared into the cross-hatching play of light and dark on the dimpling surface of the water, the last of the sun spooling through the branches with their froth of tender green. Apart from the rustle of water over rocks and occasional sparks of birdsong, he was aware only of the silence and the smell of damp earth.

He wanted to be back at the farm. Surely they

would go home for the funeral? Of course they would. His father would delay the burial till they got there. But, even as he thought of being home again, a new wave of loss and remembrance crashed over him, thinking of his grandfather's strong arm around his shoulders and the graze of his beard against his cheek.

"Tifl aleunz!" Rafi whipped round, hearing the familiar voice behind him, but there wasn't anybody there. "Jedi?" he cried out softly; and then again more loudly: "Jedi!" No-one called him 'little goat' but his grandfather. He wasn't there, but the breeze through the trees seemed to fill the clearing with his presence. Rafi knelt down, resting his arms on the trunk and bowing his head over them.

His family were Christian, but none of them went to church apart from Amti Anoush. He hadn't been since school in Amman and he didn't know if he believed in God or not; he didn't even know what he meant by the word. He moved his hands together and bent his forehead against them. "Please look after my Jedi and keep him safe," he murmured, his eyes closed. "He was a good man...a great man." He paused, seeing his grandfather in silhouette stooping to water his tomato plants, with the sun rising over the hills behind him, drawing back the curtain of shadow across the valley and flooding it with light. "Oh, Jedi!"

The hedgerows and the land were losing definition and dissolving into darkness by the time he reached the gate again and crossed the garden back to the house. Inside, he found his mother upstairs in her study, sitting at her desk, her laptop open in front of her. He went to her, putting his arm round her shoulder and lightly kissing her cheek.

"I'm sorry, Mama," he said.

"It's all right." She raised a hand to his, patting it and holding it to her. Leaning back so that he could see the screen more clearly, she added, "Look, we have flights for Friday afternoon...Royal Jordanian. We'll be home for the weekend."

"Can't we go any sooner?" he said. Friday seemed a long way off. He wanted to leave now. He wanted to be home with his family among his grandfather's things. What was the point of staying here for three more days?

Maryam withdrew her hand and closed the lid of the laptop.

"No, Rafi," she said, standing up. "I need time to make arrangements and we'll have to let Mr Dalby know, as well."

What she said was utterly reasonable. He knew it. But, Jedi was dead! He stood, eyes locked unseeing on his mother, impotent rage boiling inside him. He wanted to go tonight or in the morning. He didn't want to be here. He wanted to be with Baba and Jasmin and Zak. And she should be making that happen, not standing in the way with her ruthless good sense, her calm authority. Rage flared and burned in his chest at her blocking him. He wanted to lash out against her. The walls of his head were rocking and the room was blurring.

He turned on his heel and stormed out, smashing the side of his fist against the landing wall and slamming the door of his bedroom shut behind him. Moving to the window, he glared out into the blackness and pounded at the thick oak sill, glad of the bruising pain of it.

28

He wanted the peace of silence and darkness. He wanted to be still and alone. He turned the lights out, lit a candle by his bed and lay down, his hands behind his head on the pillow, losing himself in the flickering shadows playing across the ceiling.

After a while, he heard a creak on the landing, followed by a soft knocking on his door. Moving his arms down by his side, he didn't answer, hoping she would think he was sleeping and leave him undisturbed. But, through half-closed eyelids, he saw the door slowly opening and his mother's silhouette caught against the landing light slicing in.

Even though he closed his eyes fully, he sensed the room darken again; slowing his breathing, he strained to hear whether she had left or come in. He thought he felt movement, but it was the scent of her that told him she was there. Half-opening his eyes again, he saw her face, gleaming in the candlelight, bent towards him.

"Rafi, do you mind if I sit with you for a while?" she asked softly.

"I'm almost asleep, Mama," he murmured.

"I know, but I feel closer to home in this quiet cave of yours." She turned, pulling nearer the wicker armchair from next to the bedside table and sat down. "You sleep and we'll dream our dreams together."

In the long silence that followed, Rafi closed his eyes, but sleep wouldn't come, a cinefilm of memories of his grandfather at the farm playing across the inner screen of his mind. He wondered whether his mother had fallen asleep instead of him. But she hadn't.

"Death comes like a thief in the night," he heard her whisper into the stillness. "Who said that? I don't remember. But it's true...while you're not looking death slides in and carries your loved ones away...Papa, sister Aisha, my little Casper and now Kamal. Casper and Aisha both alive, but unborn...wombs and rooms all the same to Death."

She was talking to herself, he realized. He felt he should say something to let her know he was awake and could hear her, as if it would be dishonest to let her go on saying her private thoughts aloud, believing he was asleep. And yet, her mention of the older sister she had never known and of the older brother he had never known, one through miscarriage and the other at birth, had touched something inside him and shaken him out of his numbness. He wanted her to go on, to have her quiet voice inside his head, reconnecting his feelings with hers, and he said nothing.

"Time's so short...Jasmin almost 30, you on the cusp of manhood, little Zak only two years behind, and Rashid and me already in our 50s." He heard the rustle of a tissue and the soft blow of her nose as her whispering disappeared into silence again. And he thought perhaps she had finished and found he wanted her to stay, nevertheless.

Opening his eyes, he saw her watching him, smears

on her cheeks glistening in the candlelight.

"I can't sleep," he said, sitting up and pushing the pillows higher behind him.

"You were right," she said, "our family shouldn't be apart. Now, more than ever, we should follow our hearts and be together." She paused. "Ha, some academic, me!" He saw her smile, but there was no humour in it and her words had a mocking ring to them that stirred protective feelings in him.

"Mama," he started, "you..." but she seemed not to hear him.

"All those lectures and papers and conferences, what have they achieved? On the ground? In Gaza or the West Bank? In the minds of Hamas or Likud...Sinwar or Netanyahu?" She shook her head. "No, Rafi, what does all my studying and writing amount to if our own family is split apart? Jedi dead and neither of us there to put our arms around him or say goodbye to him. I should have been there; he was so generous to me, so... so accepting and supportive, right from the start."

She smiled, and, as she raised a tissue to her eyes, the amber stone of her ring caught fire in the candlelight, flaming and disappearing, her hand settling back in her lap.

"What was the start, Mama?" Rafi realized he didn't really know much about the early life of his parents, apart from odd bits passed on to him by Jasmin, who in turn had heard it from Amti Anoush. Something about their mother's grandfather having been Jewish and his wife Armenian and that they had fled to the US to escape persecution a hundred years ago. But he didn't remember their names or why.

"The start?" She closed her eyes, smiling. "Oh, I

remember it so well...as if it were yesterday. We were so young, Baba and I. And I was so frightened of going to As-Salt...to the farm to meet his father for the first time. Huh, but what an oasis of fruit and flowers it turned out to be!"

"What happened? What was Jedi like then?"

"I was studying in Amman then, doing my Master's. I was idealistic, sure of myself. I was going to get justice for the needy and oppressed everywhere. I was going to change the world! And I believed falling in love with a handsome Palestinian builder and marrying him showed, by my own example, how trust in the goodness of others could transcend cultural divides and animosities."

There was something hypnotic in the rise and fall of his mother's voice. Pulling the pillows lower, he slid down in the bed again and turned on his side to face her. No sooner had he done so, however, than the candle flickered, flared and went out, leaving the radiance of her face hanging and then dissolving in the new darkness. Gradually, his eyes adjusted and the room's concrete forms etched in black emerged from the surrounding charcoal.

"Maybe I should leave you to sleep."

"No, Mama, please go on."

For a moment, his mother was silent, then she said, "'I'm going to be sick!'" But before he could move, she went on again: "That's what I told Rashid...Baba, I mean, as we turned in at the gate, crunching over the loose stones and pulling up at the house. Baba just squeezed my hand and said...I can hear his voice now, so warm and certain, 'He will love you. How could he not?' And I told him how not...that his father would not want me as his daughter-in-law when he found out that the baby I was carrying had Jewish blood mixed with his own, because of my mother's father, my dear Zayde Max. I knew what the Haganah had done to Jedi's family and I wasn't just afraid, I was terrified of how he would react...terrified!"

Hearing the tremble in her voice, Rafi stretched out his hand to her.

"I'm all right," she said, giving it a quick squeeze and letting go. "I just remember it so clearly...Baba so calm as he got out. 'You'll see,' was all he said. But the man who opened the door looked fierce to me, with his thick, black beard and penetrating eyes. This was Baba's father...this was Kamal Khoury, younger and more vigorous than I'd expected. I wanted to turn and run...I wanted to disappear. But I needn't have worried, Rafi. He held out his arms to me and embraced me, saying, "Welcome, Maryam. Welcome, my daughter!" His voice was full of warmth and I was struggling not to cry...you know, out of sheer relief. But, after hugging Baba as well, he led us into the house, and as we entered, he turned to me and said, 'My home is your home!' And I burst into tears."

She gave a little cough as if clearing her throat, but Rafi heard the catch in it and pulled the duvet tighter around him. She was always so composed, so solid and dependable, and he recoiled from her crying, worms of discomfort wriggling in his belly.

"So, you didn't need to be afraid of him anymore. He accepted you right away." His tone was more impatient than he had intended and he heard her sigh.

"Ah, Rafi, it wasn't as simple as that. He still didn't know about the baby. But his welcome...his kindness gave me the courage to tell him. I didn't want there to be any secrets. Standing there by the front door, I told him about my being pregnant and about Max Cantor, my Jewish grandfather. I felt like I had pulled the pin on a grenade and I waited for the explosion." She paused, and when she spoke again her voice was calmer and the worms stopped wriggling. "Of course, it was Jedi and there was no explosion. 'When I was young,' he told me, 'my family had many Jewish friends in Jerusalem, and Muslim ones too. We respected each other in those days. We understood we were worshipping the same God in our different ways. It was better then.'"

He saw the dark mass of her hair and face lifting against the shadows towards him. "I hear him so plainly, Rafi, as if it were yesterday. I was naked with fear before him and he covered me with mercy...and those first marks on me of his kindness and acceptance are indelible. They have steered my soul."

In the silence of the night, her words pierced the shield of Rafi's worldliness, opening up a radiance inside him that felt like joy in the middle of sadness. Jedi's avowal, 'My home is your home', became entwined with Amti Anoush's bedtime Bible story from long ago of Ruth's declaration to Naomi, 'Where you go I will go, and where you stay I will stay. Your people will be my people and your God my God.' And he felt the same elation now as he had then, moved to tears by the love embedded in Jedi and Ruth's words.

After a while, as he lay there deeply comforted, his mother began again. "Later on," she said quietly, "we sat out on the terrace. I remember the sun was going down over the olive trees and the air was warm... honeyed with the scent of jasmine. And Jedi leant across and put his palm on my stomach. I could feel the warmth of it. 'We are all of mixed blood', he said. 'This baby belongs here. This baby...' and I can see him now looking away from me and gesturing to the garden, 'this baby will play here and grow strong here.' And she did." She gave a little laugh. "Jasmin did! And so did you and Zak."

But even as Rafi pictured being a boy again playing outside in the sunshine with Jasmin and Zak and taking turns at riding Damiana, their donkey, he saw his mother's head dip. And he knew then...knew with a sinking feeling inside himself where her thoughts had gone; and he waited, listening in the hush to the slow rhythm of her breathing.

"Not you, though, Casper," she whispered at last, but so softly he had to strain to hear it. "You never got to play there, did you? Even so, it is your home, little frog...always was, always will be."

She fell silent for a long time, and Rafi thought about the baby who had lived three days in the gap between him and Jasmin...an older brother forever a baby, which had so confused him. And guilt welled up in him remembering his childhood jealousy of this brother, Casper, who had come before him and whom his mother always spoke of with such affection that he had felt deprived by it, as if this earlier love stole from what she had to give to him. How he had wished him gone! Gone from the garden! Gone from under the fig tree that Jedi had planted over him and under which they had all gathered every spring, even Uncle Sadiq, to celebrate Casper's anniversary. How he had resented that! How he had wished not to be a part of all that sadness, all that solemnity!

Rafi rolled over onto his back and stared into the darkness, understanding his mother's grief better now. Jasmin and Zak hadn't deprived him of his mother's love; the warmth of the sun was always the same no matter how many people it was shining on, and he regretted his hidden hostility towards Casper.

"I'm sorry, Mama," he said. "I wish Casper hadn't died."

She leant forward and he felt the weight of her arm on the bed as she took his hand. "It's all right, Rafi. Often, the dead are as present as the living. You don't lose them; you hold them inside you."

"I don't know," he began, thinking of hearing Jedi calling to him earlier down by the stream. He hadn't been inside him, he'd been outside. And the sound of his voice had been so real, but when he'd turned round he hadn't been there. How could he be? Perhaps...

"It takes time," she said, cutting across his thoughts. "When my father died, I knew he was dead, but I didn't really understand it. All I knew was...was an endless kind of despair." She squeezed his hand and he wanted to pull it away, wanted to stay with Jedi. "Despair and shame," she went on. "I couldn't talk about it, not even to my mother...especially not to my mother."

Her closeness and the insistence in her voice were suffocating Rafi. He couldn't hear himself anymore and he twisted his head away in desperation. He knew she was trying to console him and to give him some kind of advice, but he wished she would go and leave him alone. And, as if sensing his withdrawal from her, she let go of him and hurried on with her story.

"The point is," she said, "Kamal was like a second father to me. He knew what happened and he showed me nothing but warmth and kindness from the very beginning. And I know how much you loved him...love him...as he did you. And you will miss him so much, it will hurt, Rafi...hurt like physical pain. But don't be afraid of your feelings or of talking about them, if you want to. However strange it sounds, those awful feelings make things better...they clean out the wound and let it heal."

"Please, Mama," he broke in, leaning up on his elbow towards her. "Please stop. I'm sorry, but I want to be on my own...I need to..."

"No, I am sorry, Rafi," she said, standing up. "I've said too much. I just...no, enough!" She kissed him lightly on the head and, crossing to the door, she opened it and stood in the light from the landing looking back at him. "Jedi will always be with you," she said.

The light died as the door clicked, and she was gone.

He lay staring into the darkness, letting her voice drain away until there was only silence. He tried to recall hearing his grandfather's voice through the trees, but the memory was only that, somehow sterile and disconnected, no longer vital inside him. "Jedi?" he whispered and lay motionless, barely breathing, listening. But nothing came, not even grief, so all that he knew was an emptiness growing inside him, as if he were disappearing into a black hole. He closed his eyes and tried to lose himself in sleep. But sleep wouldn't come, only a frozen numbness as he stared into the void, not knowing if his eyes were open or shut, until a creak on the landing outside startled him. Glancing towards the door, he saw the crack of light beneath it disappear and a deeper darkness spread through the room.

Knowing his mother had gone to bed increased

his sense of isolation and he grew frightened of the moving shadows of the trees and the muffled moaning of the wind. But worse was the fear curdling inside him of a threatening presence in the room; something malevolent coming after him. Grabbing his phone, he flicked it on and scrabbled to find the number. Hitting the green icon, he held his breath as he listened to the burring.

"Rafi?" Lauren's voice was thick with sleep and, for a moment, he choked up and couldn't speak.

"Hello? Rafi? Are you there?"

"Sorry..." He coughed, trying to clear the gravel from his throat. "Sorry...it's just...well...it's just my grandfather died yesterday and...um..." He broke off, his voice cracking.

"It's okay," she whispered; "just tell me."

29

Terry lay in bed staring at the poster-sized photos of Rafi and Lauren he had Blu-Tacked to the wall, his excitement growing; not only in the erection now pressing against the restriction of his pyjama bottoms, but also in the opening up of the career path he could foresee so clearly before him.

"First things first," he muttered. It was already past 8.30 am and he didn't want his mother bustling in at any moment to wake him up. He got out of bed and wrote 'Bad Night, Let Me Sleep' on his note pad, tore out the page and quietly sellotaped it to the outside of the door.

Back beside the bed, he trod off his pyjama bottoms and slid back under the cover again. He stared first at the picture he had taken of Lauren coming out of the college gates. She hadn't noticed him on the other side of the road and she was smiling naturally as she chatted to Ida. He had cropped the photo so that only her head and shoulders remained, and although her long hair partially curtained her forehead, her eyes were well spaced and clearly visible to him.

As he looked at them, lightly creased in laughter at the corners, he thought how their expression altered the whole set of her face; she looked relaxed and expansive, so different from the day she'd charged after him by the church. No, her face had been tight and angry then glaring down at him, her eyes fierce with the threats she had hurled at him. Well, retribution for that affront would come soon enough.

She was taller than him, although not by much; but would it be a problem, he wondered. He raised his arm and flicked his hand upwards into the air. No, it was only a matter of a few centimetres. Besides, if he stood on the higher side of the track, they would be about level, anyway. He took her in again and smiled. "Your reckoning is coming, Miss Jackman," he told her. "Oh, yes, most certainly! Days of darkness before the flame of insight...trust me."

"But no flame for you," he breathed, swivelling his gaze to the blow-up of Rafi, caught in profile on his bike, "only darkness, my dear Rafael. A darkness as smooth and silky as your skin...but less penetrable, shall we say?" He laughed and slid his arm under the duvet, taking his erection between his fingers and slowly moving the skin up and down. "Yes, indeed!"

Afterwards, he felt disgusted with himself, hurling the scrunched-up, soiled tissue at the bin by the door and missing. This wasn't who he was...this wasn't who he wanted to be. He was responsible for organizing a district network office for NAN. He had an appointment later with Uncle Nathan in Truro, who could very possibly help him achieve this, if he played his cards right, and he'd already applied to the Open University to begin a degree course in Politics, Philosophy and Economics...PPE, yes indeed. John, Lawrence, Matty, they were all behind him now. He had a real future to pursue. He was going to be an MP. He was going to sit on those green benches in the House of Commons; and he was going to make rousing speeches. He could see it...he could hear the clapping and the cheers!

Throwing back the cover, he strode across to Rafi's picture, pulling it off the wall and then folding and tearing it, again and again, until only a knuckle bone against a handlebar looked back at him as he flung the pieces in the bin. "Enough of you," he said, grabbing the tissue and chucking it on top. "Quite enough!"

Showered and shaved, he dressed carefully, removed his note from the back of the door and went down.

"Goodness me," his mother said, the iron she was holding suspended in mid air. "Whatever's got into you this morning?"

Terry flicked a hair from his jacket lapel with the back of his fingers. "I have a two o'clock appointment with Uncle Nathan in Truro to discuss my future."

Cathy's eyes narrowed as she stood the iron on its rest and looked back at him. "What are you up to now, for heaven's sake? You've got that look on your face."

"I don't know what you mean, mother," Terry beamed. "I have a career plan and I'm going to take up Uncle's kind offer of help."

"Career plan! Well, if that means you're goin' to look for a job, I couldn't be 'appier. And where did you get that jacket from?" She looked him up and down. "And those trousers? They suit you, make you look...I don't know...more grown-up, more reliable."

The mixture of pride and anxiety in her voice caused Terry a rare flare of fondness for her. "From the very goodness of men's hearts!" he said, opening one side of his jacket to reveal the Harris Tweed label. "I never knew what a treasure trove charity shops could be. No, indeed. From now on, I shall be swapping BHS for BHF...out with British Home Stores and in with the British Heart Foundation!"

"You're starting to sound like your father and BHS are closing, or so I hear." She glanced at the clock on the mantelpiece. "Anyway, hadn't you better be getting a move on?"

Terry nodded. "Yes, yes; punctuality is a sign of sincerity. Indeed, it is."

"And don't go giving your uncle any of your nonsense, not if you want his 'elp."

"You may rely on me, mother," he said, ducking away as she raised her hand to straighten his tie. "I have put aside childish things...yes, indeed!"

It was two minutes to 2.00 pm when Terry arrived outside the front door to his uncle's offices, and for a moment, before ringing the bell, he stood looking at the brass plaque on the wall beside it: *Curnow Blaine Solicitors*. They were closed on Saturdays, he knew that, and only his uncle would be there. He did up the middle button of his jacket, patted his hair into place and pressed the bell. He didn't hear it ring and, as nothing seemed to be happening inside, he was about to try again, when the door opened and Uncle Nathan's frame filled the entrance.

"Afternoon, Terry. Come on in," he said, turning back into the building. "Shut the door after you and follow me."

As they left the short hallway and crossed a large outer office, all Terry could see in front of him was the checked, cream-and-brown expanse of the back of his uncle's shirt. Dimly aware of armchairs to his right and a reception desk to his left, he followed his uncle into a smaller, but still generously-sized room, their footsteps falling silent as they stepped from tiles onto carpet.

"Right," Nathan said, sitting down on the far side of a large, mahogany desk. The top half of the sash window behind him was open and birdsong floated in on the breeze. "Have a seat." He lifted the papers he was working on to one side and leant forward, resting his forearms on top of the desk and linking his fingers. "Now then, you'd better tell me what's on your mind."

Terry was momentarily distracted by the mass of dark hair lacing his uncle's arms beneath his rolled-up shirt sleeves and struggled to recover the thread of what he had just been asked.

"On my mind? Yes, yes. What's on my mind?" He met Nathan's gaze and smiled. "Thank you, Uncle, I will. The truth of the matter is your advice to me last time we met has had quite an impact on me. Yes, indeed." He gave an exaggerated nod. "I've given it a lot of thought and I can see that the time has come to... well, to plan more seriously for the future."

He paused, waiting for a response.

"Go on."

Terry uncrossed his legs and undid the button on his jacket, letting it fall open more comfortably.

"Have you heard of NAN, Uncle...the National Accord Network?"

"Yes."

His uncle's gaze was steady and unrevealing, and Terry had no option but to carry on with the speech he had rehearsed on the train down.

"I have had meetings recently with NAN's chief

co-ordinator, Tony Gardner, and he has asked me to organize a district office to promote the party and its ideals down here in the South West and to recruit new members."

"Has he indeed?" his uncle interrupted. "That's most surprising. You have no management experience and no political credentials. Why on earth would they wish to appoint *you*?"

Nathan stressed the last word and Terry floundered momentarily, feeling twelve years old again in front of the Headmaster, his confidence undone and his thoughts scrambled.

"Well, Uncle...yes, indeed...that's a very good question...why would they want to appoint me? Who am I, after all? No, no, undoubtedly there are many others far better qualified than me. The thing is, though..." Gradually, as he managed to continue talking without having any idea where he was going, Terry's panic subsided and the threads of his thinking began to untangle. "The thing is that my credentials are that I have none." He saw Nathan's mouth tighten in irritation and he hurried on. "That is to say that I am just the sort of person NAN are hoping will join them: people without credentials; people who have lost faith in the Government and the politicians who are in the pockets of big business; people who have lost faith in a system where the London-based elite drain the wealth from the rest of the country, so that there are thousands of homeless on the street and young people who can't find proper work forced into zero-hour contracts going nowhere, not to mention ordinary working families having to use food banks just to make ends meet...just to survive. And, as Steve Langton, NAN's leader, said, people like me can be the 'vox populi', the voice of the people. We can be the voice for change. The voice that..."

"I get the point!" His uncle broke in sharply. "But don't they have a selection procedure? Was the post advertised? Were you chosen from a list of applicants?"

"Not exactly, no. They have...they have..." Dear God, what do they have? Again the cogs locked, again the cogs turned. "They have a...what shall I call it? They have a more hands-on...yes, a more practical, if you like...approach. I expressed an interest, they sent Tony Gardner down to meet me and he has asked me to prove myself by organizing a district office and raising the funds to pay for it."

An amused smile relaxed the sternness in Nathan's face. "Ah," he said, sitting back, "I see."

As his uncle sat regarding him, Terry felt the stickiness of his shirt under his arms and wondered if he could take his jacket off without seeming disrespectful or, worse still, revealing the roll of fat around his midriff. On the other hand, his uncle hadn't got his jacket on and he could always lay his arms across his lap screening his belly. Yes, he would. Should he do it standing up or staying where he was? Standing up would be...

"So, tell me, how do you propose to find suitable premises for this office and how do you intend to pay for it all?"

His uncle's questions eclipsed the issue of his jacket. This was why he was here...this was the moment of truth. He knew it and his uncle's wry smile indicated that he knew it, too. Very well, then..."Yes, Uncle, those are the very matters I have come to see you about... indeed they are. And I want to ask for your advice and help as to how..."

Rousing, orchestral strains suddenly burst into the air around him, like exploding fireworks, cutting him off mid-sentence.

"One moment," his uncle said, holding up his hand and leaning forward for his phone. "Afternoon, Barry...yes...yes, I am. I have my nephew with me now, but I should be there," he checked his watch, "by 3.15, 3.30 at the latest...good, looking forward to it...see you shortly."

Terry saw the phone's screen go black as his uncle set it down on the blotter in front of him. "Right, you were saying you want to ask for my help and advice. Carry on." He settled back in his chair. "And why don't you take your jacket off? It's warm in here."

"No, I'm all right, Uncle, thank you. But I will just loosen my tie." He undid the top button of his shirt, feeling the sweat from his neck against his fingers as he did so. Clearing his throat and reminding himself to be business-like and to stick to the script he'd prepared, he began again. "When you came to the house after Christmas to tell me off for the way I'd been behaving, you said that if I changed my ways you would help me."

"Yes, I did," his uncle nodded, "and I meant it."

"Thank you...and what I want to say is that, as a result of your visit, I have done a lot of hard thinking... indeed I have." He paused, an exasperated voice inside him hissing, 'No flourishes, Terence!' "And I am making changes. I don't see John Knight or the others anymore. Instead, I have been in touch with NAN, as you know, and I have applied to the Open University to study for a degree in politics."

"Have you?" His uncle's bushy eyebrows arched in

surprise, like two hairy caterpillars, Terry thought.

"Yes. I have decided I want to go into politics as a career. I believe in NAN and I want to help the party establish itself and become a force for good. My ambition is to become a Member of Parliament."

His uncle looked puzzled, his eyes narrowing as he cocked his head.

"And what degree would this be exactly?"

Terry felt the clenched tightness in his stomach relaxing for the first time. The conversation was going entirely as he had hoped and he delivered his answer with complete confidence in its worth.

"It's a Bachelor of Arts Honours degree in Philosophy, Politics and Economics."

"I see," his uncle said with a little inclination of his head, which Terry read as a signal of his approval. "Well, that's a respectable qualification. And have they accepted you?"

"I'm waiting to hear. But I spoke to one of the course tutors and she told me that registration should be straightforward...you know, a formality."

"In which case, I imagine you have come to ask me to help you with the fees. Is that it?"

"Yes, it is," Terry agreed quickly, feeling hurried along by the briskness of his uncle's questions, "although there is one other matter I'd like to ask you about."

"Very well," his uncle frowned, glancing at his watch, "but keep it brief."

"Yes...yes, of course. It's about finding an affordable office space for NAN here in Truro. I wondered if you might know of anywhere suitable or someone I could ask. And I know you haven't much time now, but I'd also like your advice on how best to go about raising the funds to pay for it...that is, for the running of it."

"So, you have come here to ask me for three things." His uncle ticked them off on his fingers as he listed them. "One, to pay for the fees for your degree; two, to find you premises for an office for NAN; and three, to find also the money to pay for this into the unforeseeable future. Is that right?"

"Yes...or rather, no...well, not exactly," Terry shuffled his feet, his face burning.

"What then, exactly?"

"I don't expect you to pay for everything, Uncle, only to help me...er...get the ball rolling, as it were." Disconcertingly, while he was talking, his uncle stood up and walked over to the window, blocking out the light and darkening the room behind him. "I mean I can pay for some of the fees, but not quite all of them. And... um," his voice was shaking and he swallowed, coughing to clear his throat. "Ahem, if you can help me with the office, I have some ideas for how to pay for it through membership subscriptions and fund-raising activities and...and so on."

All he could see was his uncle's back, his shirt stretched taut across his shoulders. In the ensuing silence, with no face to read, Terry didn't know whether to stop there or to go on. He desperately needed his uncle's help; everything depended on it.

"This would be the start of a proper career for me and it would mean the world to mum...she's been so worried about me." It was the last card he had to play and he paused again, not knowing what else to say. "I want to make it up to her...you know, make her proud of me."

On the way home in the train, watching the spreading patchwork of fields as they disappeared and reappeared between embankments and screens of shrubbery, Terry felt a rising sense of jubilation. His uncle's words echoed and re-echoed through his thoughts, "I've seen Steve Langton on Question Time and I thought he talked a lot of sense. I will help you, not least for Cathy's sake. But God help you if you are playing me for a fool!" No more futureless tomfoolery...no more small town dead end...no more empty pockets...no more signing-on...quite soon, no more living with mother...quite soon, no more bloody t-shirts...on the contrary, quite soon he'd be up and running!

"Running!" he said aloud, smiling at his sudden reflection as the train sped through a tunnel. "Yes, indeed," he muttered. "Out of darkness into the light, Ms Jackman," he laughed, as the countryside reappeared, "and your colour blindness cured!" Two women glanced across the aisle at him as they were talking, and he continued his thoughts in silence. 'But how not to get caught, that's the question. I have the means and I know the place...but the getaway, that's the thing...and I also need a disguise.

"We're approaching Liskeard Station. Change trains here for Looe." As the blurred voice completed its announcement, the two women rose, and Terry watched them shuffling into the aisle. What denotes them as women, he asked himself. Hair...earrings... lipstick...bags. One was wearing a dress, but the other was in jeans with a backpack. They bundled past him and out of sight. Women were all sorts of shapes and he couldn't do much about his. But all he had to do was appear to be a woman...a first impression...yes, yes; it would all be over very quickly.

30

"What's up?" Ida asked.

"Nothing," Lauren said, tipping back her head and draining the last mouthful of apple juice from her glass.

"Have you come on? No, forget it; you can't have... too soon, isn't it?"

Lauren didn't answer. She wished Ida would just be there without saying anything. The canteen was packed and noisy; but, for once, she didn't mind the breaktime din with all the clatter and laughter. Sitting at their usual table against the wall, the hubbub provided a kind of shelter and invisibility. She closed her eyes against the glare of the strip lights. She was too tired to think. She wanted to take her head off, wash it out and sink into a no-thought blankness.

"Come on, Laur," Ida's voice was closer and lower... breathier. "You've been off all week. What's going on?"

Coming out of her stupor, Lauren found Ida bending forward, watching her, waiting for an answer, her arms resting on the table in front of her. "Nothing! Everything!"

"Nothing...everything," Ida repeated. "So, what's everything?"

"Really?"

"Really!"

"Okay...where to start? Training's really heavy at the moment. I've got the regional championships coming up soon, followed by the Under 17 Open track and field in Birmingham in July and Oka's really pushing me, which is good. I mean, I know she only wants the best for me. But between college and athletics I don't feel like I have any time for me anymore."

"But things have always been full on for you in the season," Ida said, "and usually you're hyped up and raring to go...you know, 'Olympics, here I come!' So, it's got to be the other stuff crowding in on you, hasn't it? I mean, Rafi and your dad and all of that."

Lauren looked round; she didn't want other people listening in, but no-one was paying them any attention. Even so, thinking about Rafi and her dad caused a kind of panic inside her and she veered away from them. Instead, she said, "Apart from everything else, I've spent hours and hours on applications for a work placement. But, at least, it looks like there's an activity centre in Ottery that'll have me for a week helping kids with kayaking and surfing and stuff like that."

"That's great, Laur! Right up your street." Ida's enthusiastic smile made Lauren think of Finn and she felt warmed by it. "And, talking about placements, I haven't told you, have I? I got a definite 'yes' back from that veterinary centre in Honiton for the last week of term. Small and large animal care, they say; even theatre observation!"

Lauren could see how excited Ida was. "Hey, well done!" she said. "They'll want to keep you forever, I bet." Ida blushed. Despite all her playfulness, even boisterousness at times, Lauren knew how modest Ida was...well, not modest, not quite that, more like unaware how unaffected and kind she was and how good she made people feel just by being in her company.

"No, I'm the lucky one. I can't wait."

"What about Coil?"

"Coil!" Ida laughed. "He's so dozy he won't even know I've been away. Anyway, Dad'll keep an eye on him." She picked up her smoothie and sucked at the striped pink-and-white straw, her green eyes narrowing as she looked at Lauren over the rim of the glass. She put it down and wiped her mouth with the back of her hand. "I know you said Rafi's going back to Jordan for the funeral." She leant forward, lowering her voice. "Is that what's upsetting you?"

Lauren held her gaze for a moment and then looked away. Rafi! She didn't know where she was with Rafi. "I don't know where I am with Rafi," she said, looking back. "That night he rang me, it was weird. There we were in different houses miles apart and yet I felt much closer to him than when we'd been in the same room together."

"Ha, being alone in bed together in the dark sounds pretty intimate to me...not the same bed, but you know what I mean."

Ida was being serious and Lauren sank deeper into herself. "You know what really got to me?"

"No." Ida shook her head.

"It wasn't just that he was crying, it was more the way he sounded...so hurt, so...so raw. He was kind of wailing for his granddad, calling out his name over and over again. And, afterwards, I kept thinking what it would be like if Ginnie or Zoltan died, or Freda or Greg, and it really freaked me."

"Yeah, comes out of the blue, doesn't it?" Ida said. "Death, I mean. Remember when Dizzy died? I know she was only a rescue dog, but I'd grown up with her... she'd always been there. And, that last night, sitting on the kitchen floor with her, I tried so hard to coax her into drinking something. But she just lay there on her blanket looking so...I don't know, looking so feeble, so helpless. But it never occurred to me she was going to die; I just thought she was sick. Anyway, I fell asleep and when I woke up there she was, stretched out..." Ida paused, and Lauren wanted her to stop...wanted to stay with her own feelings; but Ida went on again. "Talk about being freaked! I knew she was dead right away... her eyes were just staring at nothing. And when I went to touch her, she was so cold...so stiff." Ida stopped again, looking down and running her fingers along the edge of the table. She jerked her hand away. "Her paw was caught up and I tried to untuck it, but I couldn't...she was all locked together like a piece of board. I couldn't bear to touch her...she was there, but she wasn't. And Dad had to wrap her up and carry her out...had to dig a grave for her. I couldn't."

Lauren didn't trust herself to speak. Dizzy had nothing to do with it and she felt too angry with Ida to look at her. She knew she was being unreasonable, knew that Ida had been heartbroken when Dizzy died, but she didn't want to think about Dizzy, and anger and guilt boiled inside her keeping her mute.

"Sorry," Ida said at last, breaking the silence and causing Lauren to glance back at her. "Went off on a bit of tangent, didn't I? Sorry. But I still miss her. She was such fun." A slow smile spread across her face and into her eyes. "You know, completely bonkers!"

The affection in Ida's voice cut through Lauren's isolation, reconnecting her. "Yes, she was," Lauren agreed, relenting. "She was a..." Her words were sliced off by the shriek of the end-of-break bell and then drowned out by the pandemonium of students sliding back their chairs, grabbing their bags and jostling for position in a mass exodus from the canteen out into the atrium.

"I've got to go," Ida said, reaching for her backpack. "You coming?"

Lauren shook her head. She didn't want to move. Her whole body felt leaden.

"Ok, see you later."

She watched Ida pushing through the throng to catch up with Nila, a tall Indian girl from Ida's class, already calling and waving to her. Lauren felt a pang of jealousy. Ida was so easy to be with, everybody warmed to her. Something open and straightforward about her that just made people trust her, no matter what she came out with.

'Have you come on?' No she hadn't, although it did feel a bit like it...being irritable, wanting to get away from everyone...well, not wanting to be alone, but wanting a deep connection taking her deeper into herself, not superficial ones trapping her on the surface...no, wanting connection like she'd had with Rafi...naked... not physically, but sort of...skinless...utterly open...no need to pretend or hide anything...no need to say or do anything...just able to be together in the moment... like fusing, all boundaries gone...just a kind of peaceful oneness.

"All right if I clear these away, my lovely?"

A plastic tray slid onto the table and quick hands

reached for the glasses and banana skin.

"Yes, sorry, Annie." Lauren knew the slim, friendly dinner lady well. "I shouldn't be here."

The solitary, cut-off mood shrouded her all day. During Art, Jan had seen her distraction and gently taken the maquette away from her, giving her a sheet of canvas paper. "Paint it out on this," she'd said; and she had, watching the brush in her hand making marks where it wanted to of outcropping shapes in dark moorland colours. And afterwards, in English, she'd read the part of Ophelia in a scene with Hamlet while lost in thought about Rafi's compassionate leave and his going away, at the end of which Mr Tonks had muttered something about her drowning in despair. But she hadn't cared and had taken her lunch to the peace of a shaded bench by the sports field. And throughout the afternoon's double History and Ms Dexter's analysis of Robert Burleigh's relationship with Queen Elizabeth I, as 'a master of Renaissance statecraft', Lauren had wondered how she, too, could learn 'to walk invisible' and bring about a reconciliation between her parents.

At the end of the day, as they stood outside the college gates, she told Ida she wanted to go home on her own. "I'm going to try to get Mum by herself. I don't think she's getting it from Dad's point of view. But I'll go back with you tomorrow, as usual, if that's okay."

"Yeah, fine," Ida said. "I told Dad I'd give him a hand pricking out the tomatoes...oh God, and the weeding!" She screwed up her nose and pulled down the corners of her mouth in a play-face of disgust that Lauren seemed to have known all her life and that she held onto like a talisman as she walked home.

Opening the front door quietly, she paused in the hall listening for sounds of movement, preparing herself. She watched cascading particles of dust swirling in the light from the window halfway up the stairs. All was still and she felt oppressed by the late-afternoon hush of the house. She crossed to the living room door and, gripping its brass knob tightly, turned it and went in.

The room's comfortable, airy spaciousness, with its long sash-windows and high ceiling, brought her instant relief. Her mother wasn't there, only Finn sprawled in front of the television, his yellow t-shirt and ginger curls vivid against the cobalt-blue carpet. But the TV wasn't on, and instead of the usual rubble of homework books surrounding him, bright pots of acrylic paint were clustered on newspaper by the picture he was painting.

Elbow bent from the floor, his left hand cupping his chin, Finn went on painting something she couldn't quite see, totally absorbed in what he was doing. For a moment, she stood taking in all the colours of the room like a balm, soothing her anxiety: rose, mustard and turquoise cushions bright against the soft velvet of the olive sofa and faded brocade armchairs; a tall vase of white lilies on the chest by one window; a translucent, lime-green fern on a stand in front of the other, and both of them as vivid as the rose-and-turquoise curtains framing them.

This was her mother's doing, like the emerald carpet in the music room, the upholstered, scarlet booths at Red Emma's and now the newly-painted, kingfisher-blue walls of The Canoe. Finn liked bright colours, too. Maybe it went with their natures, she thought; both of them vivacious and outgoing, while she was more like her dad: quieter, more reserved...even the clothes they tended to wear were less colourful; mainly jeans with tops in grey or black.

She looked down at Finn again, taking a step closer. "Is Mum home?" she asked.

"Oh, it's you...thought so." Leaning to one side, he looked round at her. "Yes, she is; so's Dad. But they're upstairs having," he paused half a beat, "'a private conversation'." Lauren smiled in spite of herself at his mimicry, recognizing instantly the warning inflection of their mother's voice.

She wasn't sure if it was ominous or a good sign? Maybe Ginnie had got through to her; but Dad wasn't normally back this early.

"What about? Do you know?"

"No idea!" His face split in a lopsided grin. "New mountain bike for me, hopefully."

"You wish!" She took him in again; his cheerfulness, his ease. How did he manage it with all that was going on? Ida always said his cheeks were like apples that made her want to bite them. They were glowing now. "Hmm... might be a good idea, though," she said. "Cycling's good exercise, better than sitting around watching tv and eating triple-decker sandwiches, anyway!"

"I'm not, am I? Look!" Scrambling up, he thrust the pad into her hands. "Tom and I are building a tree-house, right?" He pointed to what looked like a chicken shack in the branches of a tree. "And, if I had a bike that worked, I could be round there all the time helping him with it, not hanging about waiting eons for a lift from Mum."

"And this is Tom, is it?" She pointed to a dark-haired boyish figure in shorts halfway up a ladder, which was propped against the tree and disappeared into the canopy at the top.

"Yes and this is me, up here." He touched the tip of his brush against a smiling face with a ginger halo peering out through the branches.

"And what's this that he seems to be looking at?" She put her finger on a charcoal splodge in midair below Tom.

"It's a bucket...you should've seen it!" He started laughing. "It was full of water and the handle came off. And when it hit the ground..." Keeping the brush clear of the paper, he traced its fall all the way to the bright green grass at the bottom and then punched his arms upwards and outwards. "BOOM! The water leapt out of it in one go like a frightened cat...totally hilarious!"

"Good thing you weren't underneath, then!" Lauren said. But before Finn could say any more the door opened behind them, and as she turned she saw her mother walk in closely followed by the taller figure of her father.

The solemnity of their expressions and their stately progress into the room drained the hope from her and she knew instantly what she had been dreading most was now happening.

"Come and sit down, both of you," Jess said, indicating the sofa, as she took one armchair and Nick the other. "We've something to tell you." She paused as Lauren waited for Finn to put his brush in a jar of water before following him to the sofa. "And, afterwards," her mother went on, "you can ask us anything you want to...anything you're unsure about."

Pulling a cushion in behind her and settling down next to Finn, Lauren studied her mother and thought how strained she looked. Jess was sitting up straight, her back not touching the chair, her face pale and drawn; there was something both anxious and insistent in her "Right, Nick?" as she glanced across at him.

"Okay, yes," he nodded, looking up and clearing his throat. He stretched his legs out and then pulled them in again. For a moment, his eyes caught Lauren's and she saw the desperation in them before they shied away again. "As I think you probably know, I've been going through a bit of a difficult time recently and I...that is, we...well, we feel it might be..."

"Would be," Jess put in.

"...a good idea if I were to take a break on my own for a little while to...you know, clear my head, as it were."

"Take a break where, Dad?" Lauren asked.

"Yeah, but why do you need to go anywhere?" Finn objected, before Nick could answer her. "We can help. Can't we, Mum?"

Lauren saw her father's Adam's apple bob up and down, his eyes blurring, and she wanted to rescue him. This wasn't fair; this wasn't all down to him, was it?

"Look..." she started; but her mother's voice, calm and assured, rode over her.

"Of course, we want to help, darling, and we will. Think of it this way. You know how sometimes, when you're ill, you need to go to bed and rest?" She paused and Finn nodded. "Well, Dad needs a bit of rest...a bit of time out, you see?"

"Yes..." Finn said uncertainly, then added, looking at Nick, "Well, no...not really. Why can't you go to bed and rest here, Dad?"

"It's all right, I'm not going far, Finn; just round the corner over the ironmongers. It's a small flat and you can come and see me any time." He gave a little smile.

"You know, whenever you feel like it."

"Yes," Jess joined in, "and we can all help Dad move his things in there on Saturday. You'll be here, won't you?" Her eyes clashed with Lauren's; it wasn't a question. "And he'll be here for Sunday lunch, as normal."

"But it's not normal, is it, Mum?" Lauren flared. "And, no, I won't be here on Saturday morning...sorry, Dad..." she glanced at him, "because I'll be staying at Ida's and we're going into Plymouth first thing."

"That's ok..." Nick started, but Jess interrupted him, her tone much less conciliatory than his.

"I understand you're upset, but there's no need to be rude."

"I'm not being rude, I'm trying to be truthful. This isn't about a rest, is it?" Lauren looked from one to the other. "What you're talking about is a separation, isn't it? Dad moving out and not living with us anymore!"

Jess shook her head. "No, that's not what we're saying. What..." But Lauren was too incensed against her, against her calmness, her composure, against her allowing her father to bear all the blame, and she cut her off.

"This isn't just about Dad, is it? I mean it takes two. And you're never here. You've been so busy with Red Emma's and now The Canoe you haven't had any time for Dad...or us! Even..."

"Hey...hey," Nick said, raising his voice, "that's enough." But Lauren ignored him and carried on.

"Even Ginnie says so, doesn't she?" She glared at her mother. "She says you need to talk to Dad..." she could hear her own voice breaking up, knew she was crying and didn't care, "and ask him what the matter is, not send him away."

Finn was pulling at her arm, but she lunged away from him, twisting round to face her father. "What is the matter, Dad? What really is the matter?"

"Oh look, sweetheart, don't get upset," Nick said, pushing himself out of the armchair and starting across to her. "Come here."

But, jumping up, Lauren put her hand out to stop him. "No, Dad, don't! Of course, I'm upset! Don't you love Mum anymore? Don't you want to be here anymore?" And, before he could answer, she whirled round on Jess. "And is this what you want, Dad leaving... Dad not living here? And what about us," she flung her arm out towards Finn, "don't we get a say? What about what we want? What about..."

"Stop shouting!" Finn yelled and, as she whipped round, his panicked eyes and ashen face sapped all the rage out of her. "It isn't helping," he added, staring up at her, a plea in his voice.

"Sorry," she said, bending towards him and touching his shoulder, "I didn't mean to..."

"Exactly!" Jess interrupted. "None of us mean to. That's not what any of us want, is it? So, come on... Lauren, Nick, sit down and let's talk this through."

Lauren hesitated, watching her father sit down again. Part of her wanted to follow suit and be supportive of him; but another part was in rebellion at the sight of her mother leaning back in her armchair, seemingly relaxed and confident, her chin lifted against them and a firm smile exerting her authority...her 'school teacher look', as Finn used to call it when she was a teacher before she'd left to open Red Emma's.

"What's important," her mother continued,

meeting her gaze, "is that we listen to each other with respect without jumping to conclusions and flying off the handle."

"Yeah, listening," Lauren muttered and was going to add, "that's what Ginnie's on about", but felt Finn's foot flick against hers and checked herself. "okay, let's do that," she said instead, sitting down. "So, go on, Dad."

"Right," he nodded. And, while he spoke, looking first at her and then at Finn, she saw the tenderness in his eyes and heard it in the warmth of his voice. "Lauren...Finn...the last thing in the world Mum or I want to do is cause you any worry or unhappiness. We love you. Nothing is more important in our lives than you are...nothing." He paused and Lauren dodged his eyes feeling embarrassed. "You're young," he went on, "and it's difficult to explain...to find the right words. It's just things can happen inside you that you don't really understand yourself; and I've been going through something like that...a kind of...I don't know...like losing your bearings and being blown about in a storm, so you don't know where you are anymore. And I know it's made things difficult for all of you, my being here and not being here, as it were, and I'm really sorry about that," he glanced across at Jess, "but..." he drew in a deep breath and blew it out again, "but I am beginning to feel a bit more normal...a bit more myself again. "

"Why go away then?" Finn demanded.

"Just to have some time on my own to try to make sense of what's been going on, that's all. And I'm not going far away, I'll be close by."

The sadness and weariness in his voice rolled through Lauren and she had to lever herself up from the sofa, as if a heavy coat was dragging her down.

"Me, too," she said quietly, turning for the door.

31

Following a delay in takeoff from Heathrow, Flight RJ112 touched down at Queen Alia International Airport, Amman, at 1.13 am on Saturday, 27 April, over two hours late. With a reputation for punctuality, the Royal Jordanian air crew could not have been more apologetic or attentive. For his part, after spending five hours in a pressurised cabin and emerging into the emptiness of the small hours, all Rafi wanted was to close his eyes and go back to sleep. But he could see his mother was alert and impatient, knowing her husband would be there, waiting to drive them home, and that, before long, she'd see Jasmin and Zak again.

"When they wake up," she laughed, as they hurried along, "I'm going to breakfast on their smiles and hug them till lunch!"

The baggage reclaim hall, brilliantly lit and deserted, carried an air of abandonment, something ghostly in its line of blank carousels. Even when one of them eventually jerked into life, causing the other passengers to shuffle closer, the mechanical hum only served to highlight the echoing stillness among the stalking, white columns stretching away around them.

"Wake up, Rafi," his mother said, nudging his arm

as he leaned against her, his eyes closed. "You watch for our cases and I'll find a trolley."

Seeing no spaces immediately next to the moving plates, he waited behind a short man, over whose head he could see the circling bags and cases. Yawning, he screwed his eyes tight and shook his head, trying to free himself from the drowsiness enveloping him like a fog. But it was no use; all he wanted to do was to close his eyes and go back to sleep.

The dreamy unreality of the airport only began to shift with the strong embrace of his father and the rub of his beard against his cheek, followed by their emergence from the terminal into the night air and the splash of the illuminated fountains outside.

The motorway drive into Amman was clear and fast, but much slower as they wound their way through the narrowing road of the suburbs heading northwest towards As-Salt. Sitting in the back listening to his parents' familiar voices, his mother's clear and precise, his father's deeper and less distinct, Rafi had the sense of being truly home again and he drifted into a twilight world of semi-consciousness. Zak and he were riding his grandfather's donkey back through the olive grove, with Jasmin walking beside them. She looked up to say something and the face was Lauren's, lurching him awake again. Opening his heavy eyes, through the swaying windows he saw the shadows of steeply terraced houses rising on either side – the hills of As-Salt, so instantly familiar, as if he'd never been away... as if Devon was already another life and no longer real.

"Ah, the Dwarf of Basra awakes!" Jasmin laughed. "Not dead after all, you see?"

As Rafi lifted himself up on his elbows at the sound of his sister's voice, a pillow hit him full in the face flattening him again.

"Welcome home, brother of mine!" Zak shrieked, walloping him a second time, and jumping astride him on the bed to hold the pillow down, smothering his head.

Rafi bucked him off, twisting onto his stomach and arching his back, then grabbed him from behind as he fell, pinning his arms and hugging him.

"Hello, little brother," he whispered in his ear. "It's good to see you, too."

Releasing him as Jasmin moved towards them, Rafi stood to greet her. Placing her hand on his shoulder, she kissed him on both cheeks and leaned back to appraise him.

"My warrior is growing a beard, I see. Tell me, how have your battles gone with the infidel?"

Rafi ran the back of his fingers along the stubble of his jaw and grinned. "At the news of your summons, my Queen, I travelled here with such haste that I left behind my razor in the throat of the enemy on the battlefield where the wind hovers. The dangers were great, but, as you can see," he bowed to her, "we have survived."

Jasmin smiled. How easy it was to slip back into the playful roles of his childhood. Already a teenager when he was a toddler, she had read him tales at bedtime from 'One Thousand and One Nights', sending him into dreams of flying carpets and magic lanterns, only to be woken early most mornings by his whispered command, 'Open Sesame', and find his soft, dark eyes staring into hers, as they were now.

"It's good to have you home," she said," and Mama,

too. It's not the same without Jedi. And Baba has been so sad. Even Amti..."

"Baba says we're going to bury him in the garden," Zak broke in, eyes wide, waiting for Rafi's reaction. "Near Casper, and plant another tree. Start a...what's it called?" He looked round at Jasmin.

"An orchard of remembrance."

"You mean his ashes?" Rafi asked.

Jasmin shook her head. "No, his actual body."

"But is that legal?" Rafi felt concerned. "I mean I know Jedi would want to stay here, but..."

"First, we will have a service at St George's." Amti Anoush's voice filled the room with the same authority as her ample frame filled the doorway. "And then we will bury him here. No more exile. No more Nakba! This is his home and shall be, forever."

Rafi was taken by surprise, not just by the solemnity of her tone, but also by her appearance. No clay-spattered apron, no cherry-coloured shirt underneath, sleeves rolled; just chin-to-toe blackness, except for the familiar brown leather, working boots poking out. A black kaftan covered her black roll-neck sweater and baggy black trousers, and a loose bun of thick black hair, streaked with grey, squatted like a toad on top of her head. Gone was her habitual energetic smile, if not on her lips, then in her eyes, replaced by a weary heaviness dragging at her features that he'd not seen before.

"Amti," he said, as she wrapped her arms around him and held him close. The unforgettable scent of her, sweet and sour, like nutmeg mixed with sweat, cut him back to childhood.

Amti Anoush, she had always been there; the pivot,

like her potter's wheel, around which they all seemed to spin. Within the family, she had a zone of her own: daughter of his grandparents, Hana and Kamal, yet, at eight years old, after her mother's death, becoming mother to her younger brothers, Rashid, his father, and Uncle Sadiq, as well as housekeeper for Kamal...for Jedi.

Jedi, Amti Anoush, his father; they were the farm. His mother had her professional, university life and Uncle Sadiq had his business and apartment in Amman. Maybe Jasmin would inherit the third leg of the stool from Jedi. Like Amti, his aunt, she was the eldest child, eleven years older than him, a different generation, a second mother.

"It's good to have you home, Rafi," Anoush said at last, unclasping him and holding him away from her, her hands resting on his shoulders. "You look so much like your father." She shook her head. "How can you possibly be seventeen already?"

The intensity of her gaze unsettled him. She seemed to be looking both at him and through him; her eyes meeting his without communication and passing deeper into them, lost in her own thoughts.

"Do I have to go to the service tomorrow? Or should I stay here and help get things ready? For the burial, I mean."

Zak's hopeful voice broke the spell. With a start, Anoush dropped her hands and looked at him. For a moment, she did not speak; and, under the weight of her scrutiny, Zak looked down at his feet, rocking forward on his toes and back, waiting for her to say something. When she did, her voice was calm and serious and her eyes never left his.

"Al Khader, the Church of St George, Zak, represents everything your grandfather believed in. Mutual respect and peaceful co-existence, that's what he wanted...that's what he practised. Of course you will be with us there to honour him and to deliver him into God's care."

Zak chewed on his lip and glanced at Jasmin, who blinked and shook her head, as if in dismay at his question.

"Yes, Amti," he mumbled.

"If Christians and Muslims can pray together in the same church, why not Jews, too? There's no future in hatred and bloodshed, is there, Zak? When Kamal was a boy, there was harmony in Jerusalem. Families there knew they all had Abraham in common, and they accepted each other's customs and beliefs. It was the British who caused the havoc. Ask your mother."

It was the story they had all grown up with; the story of the Nakba or flight of seven hundred thousand Palestinians from their homeland and of their determination – and that of their descendants - to return there one day to reclaim their homes in peace and without hatred.

"But, Amti," Rafi said, wanting to relieve his brother's discomfort. "Isn't that impossible now? Don't the hatreds go too deep?" Even as he spoke, he found himself thinking of Lauren and the steel wall of prejudice and intolerance that separated them. "Jedi never got to go home again, did he? And Israel has occupied Palestine and there's nothing we can do about it. I mean, hand-held rockets on one side and tanks, jets and nuclear weapons on the other! It's not a contest is it? There is no going back, is there? That's the reality."

"With God's help, nothing is impossible," his aunt replied. "That is why we will go to Al Khader, to the Church of St George, together." She looked back at Zak. "All of us! And we will celebrate Jedi's life and we will pray for his soul."

As Rafi passed from the house through the open doorway onto the terrace, he felt immediately relieved of his aunt's heaviness and was glad. He knew it was her grief that had thrown a pall of gloom over them. Nevertheless, having escaped the weight of it, his spirits soared as he took in the scent of orange blossom and felt the warmth of the morning sun.

Moving past the vine-covered trellises, he caught sight of his parents sauntering arm-in-arm along the rows of orange trees, a white umbrella of fragrant blossom above their heads. He paused at the low stone wall by the steps to watch. They were Jedi's fruit trees; he had planted every one of them, as he had the olive trees and vines stretching away below them. And here were his heirs; his mother stopping, turning in profile, her finger raised to make a point, and his father pausing, taking a step back to her.

For a moment, his vision blurred; and, as if outside himself and propelled into the future, the two figures were transformed, refigured as himself and Lauren. The farm was theirs and they would pass it on to their children. This was his home; this was where he belonged. He saw it all, knew it all, felt it all. Jedi would never die. He was alive in the soil he had tilled, in the stream he had channelled, in all he had planted and in his children's blood and his grandchildren's blood.

Rafi saw them all walking along the same donkey

track leading up from the valley, each of them in different decades, but always on the same ancient slope: Kamal and Hana; Amti Anoush and Uncle Sadiq; his parents; Jasmin and Zak; himself and his children. Those coming after were covering the same ground as those who had gone before; all of them caught by the web of time in the one place.

"Come on, little dreamer, we need your help." The track dissolved at the sound of Jasmin's voice, as the soft glow of his revelation faded into the bright reality of the garden.

"Two minutes," he said, turning, "and I'll be there."

He wanted her to go, to be left alone to recapture the fading warmth of his reverie. Instead, she linked her arm round his waist. "I shouldn't tell you this, your head's much too big as it is," she gave him a squeeze, "but it's not altogether unpleasant to have you home again."

He laughed in spite of himself, taking her in with a flood of affection, blind through familiarity to the faint cleft of her hare-lip and seeing only her prettiness and the dark life in her eyes.

32

Meanwhile, in Westabrook Close, Terry was lying in bed, his hands clasped behind his head on the pillows. He was staring at the empty spaces where the posters of Rafi and Lauren had been, while picturing them both as if they were still there.

"I need a plan with an alibi," he said, addressing Lauren. "Yes, yes, a water-tight alibi...so that, when someone throws acid into those innocent eyes of yours, everyone will know, Terry wasn't there!" He laughed. "Only they're not innocent at all, are they? I mean we know what they're dreaming of, don't we?

He rolled out of the bed and walked up close to where her face had been, his mouth twisting between a smile and a snarl. "Only you're never going to have him! He won't want anything to do with you, will he? Goodness me, no. Not with a blind girl...not with a girl whose face is all blistered and scarred!"

He took a step back, tapping his thumbnail against his teeth. Then he stopped tapping, his thumb hovering in front of his mouth, as it widened into a self-satisfied smirk.

"I think Uncle Terry may have the very solution... yes, indeed!"

The idea had only just occurred to him and he wandered over to the window, turning it over. "Light and shade," he thought, watching the end of the garden, where the sun was already slicing across the daffodils and uncut grass. "In disguise where I can be seen and far away where I can't."

Turning back into the room, he moved in front of Rafi's blank space. "Steve Langton and Tony Gardner are going to vouch for me, my dear Rafael," he said, nodding. "Indeed, they are...a private NAN consultation in the morning in our new Truro office...thank you, Uncle Nathan," he bowed to the door and clicked his heels, "before the public meeting in the library in the afternoon. Local...maybe even national, media will be there for Steve's speech." He put out his finger and tapped Rafi's imaginary chest. "And so will I! I will have been in Truro all day, you see."

A whoop of joy carried him back to bed. "All day!" He climbed in and lay back, resting his arms on top of the duvet, the crimson sleeves of his pyjamas discordant against the faded green-and-blue check of its cover.

Tony and Steve would lie for him, wouldn't they? They were as much against interracial relationships as he was. What was that called...miscegenation? He said it aloud, "Miscegenation!" Such an imposing word, you couldn't doubt the worth of it, could you?

"No, indeed, you could not!" he said, raising his voice to the absent Rafi. He paused before going on, his voice lower now. "Such a pretty girl, isn't she, my Rafael? But not for much longer, though...deary me, no! And, really, it is all your fault, isn't it? You shouldn't be here involving your silky brown self, should you?"

He closed his eyes: Matty up the ladder, John

and Lawrence with their shoes off stealing into the bedroom, all of them circling the bed…"Yes, yes…your silky brown self, asleep in your pyjamas…so vulnerable, so unprotected!" A slow smile spread under the closed lids. "I was going to have such…"

A muffled knock on the door stopped him mid-sentence.

"Terry?"

"Yes."

"Time you were up, love. Sun's shining and I need your help to move those heavy pots by the shed."

"You do realize it's the weekend, mother." He opened his eyes and stuck his tongue out at the door. "I was thinking of having a bit of a lie-in."

"Oh, were you?" She tried the handle and he watched the knob turning.

"For heaven's sake!" she said. "What have you locked this door for?"

"Privacy, mother. I'm making plans and I need to think things through…yes, indeed, I need to think things through very carefully."

"What things?"

Terry looked at where Lauren's picture had been and smiled. "Never you mind."

"Suit yourself. I can't stand here all…"

The ring of the doorbell cut her off, followed by two firm raps.

Terry listened to his mother's muffled steps moving away and the creak of the stairs. He heard the front door open and the rumble of voices, soon followed by the door closing again and his mother's clear voice from the hall. "If you wait in here, I'll go and get him."

"Terry," she called, hurrying up the stairs and

knocking on his door again. "It's the police. They want to talk to you."

"I'll be five minutes," he said, kicking back the duvet. "Offer them some tea."

Once he had dressed and strolled downstairs, his mother pointed to the sitting room.

"I don't know what you've been up to, but it's you they want to talk to." She touched his arm, worry in her eyes. "I'll be in the kitchen if you want me."

As he entered, he was surprised to find two figures, not in uniform, but in ordinary clothes. A young man with sandy hair, razored at the sides, was perched on the edge of the sofa, holding a cup; while, standing across the coffee table from him was a slim woman in jeans and a leather jacket, with short dark hair.

"Terence Edward Curnow?" she asked, walking towards him.

"Yes," he said, stopping in front of her, as she showed him her warrant card.

"DS Fran Bannerman, CID, Charles Cross Police Station, Plymouth; and this is DC Jason Kincaid. We're making enquiries about a Mr John Knight, whom we believe is known to you."

"John? Yes, indeed." Terry sat down in the same armchair in which he had faced his uncle in the winter. "Is he all right?" His mind was racing. If this was about breaking into Rafi's house, he needed to stay calm and wait to see what they knew.

"We have reason to believe Mr Knight was involved in an incident in the Barbican in the early hours of yesterday morning, Saturday, during which a man was stabbed." DS Bannerman looked up from the small black notebook she had been consulting. "The victim died in the ambulance on his way to Derriford Hospital."

'That was always going to happen,' Terry was thinking with a mixture of shock and relief, 'but it's nothing to do with me. I'm not implicated.'

Aloud, he said, "That's dreadful; but why do you think John's got anything to do with it?"

"Mr Knight is not at his home address and he's not answering his phone," DC Kincaid continued, ignoring his question. "Has he been in touch with you since half-past two yesterday morning?"

"No, I haven't seen John since...when was it? Not last week, anyway, but the one before...Friday, I think. Yes, it must have been."

"And you haven't been in contact with him since then?"

"No. We..." Terry paused, rapidly sifting ideas.

"You what?" DS Bannerman said sharply.

"Truth is we had a bit of a falling out."

"About?" Her small dark eyes were drilling into his.

"John can be...how shall I put it...impetuous, you know," Terry smiled. It was best to appear relaxed. He folded his hands across his stomach and stretched out his legs. "He suggested we go to Plymouth and... er...enjoy the delights of Union Street, as we used to do when we were younger." He chuckled. "Trouble is those...those outings didn't always go according to plan, if you know what I mean. And, frankly, I didn't feel like doing that anymore and well..." Terry trailed off, shrugging his shoulders.

"And well what, Mr Curnow?" DS Bannerman persisted.

Terry sighed. "Well, let's just say John wasn't very

happy about it. He called me a few choice names and stormed off. I haven't heard from him since."

"Do you have any idea where he might be?" asked DC Kincaid. "Details of any other friends or family he might turn to in times of trouble?"

Terry was glad for the opportunity to turn away from DS Bannerman's unrelenting scrutiny.

"No, I'm sorry I don't. John's quite...quite private, shall we say? Yes, indeed."

"And, for the record, where were you in the early hours of yesterday morning?"

Alibis weren't always easy to come up with at short notice, but on this occasion, Terry felt all the ease of telling the truth.

"I was here. I didn't go out at all last night. My mother can vouch for that."

The young man gave him a thin smile. "She already has," he said.

"Right then," DS Bannerman intervened, taking a card from her wallet and summoning Terry's attention back to her.

He leant forward and put out his hand, but she kept the card back, eyeing him carefully. "If you see or hear from Mr Knight, I want you to contact us immediately. Do you understand?"

"Perfectly."

"Good. And, while we're here, let me give you some advice. Stay out of houses you haven't been invited into."

Terry couldn't stop the blood from springing into his face. "I've no idea what you're talking about, Detective Sergeant. No idea at all!"

"I think you do," she said, and, half-turning, she

nodded to her colleague, who placed his cup back in its saucer and stood up.

"We'll see ourselves out," she added, handing him the card.

"You're not in any trouble, are you?" his mother asked him after the detectives had gone.

They were standing outside the back door, looking at the pots by the shed.

"Not at all," he said. "They want to talk to John and thought I might know where to find him."

"Oh dear, what's that boy gone and done now?"

"There was some kind of incident in Plymouth and they're looking for..."

"Incident?" Her head jerked round. "What kind of incident?"

Worry sharpened her voice and flared in her tired grey eyes. It was a tone and look he knew too well, worry mixed with accusation. How he hated it, ever since he was a boy. Having to stand there and answer her questions, account for himself. He hated being interrogated, hated having to explain himself. The police were bad enough, but nothing like her. There was no umbilical connection to the police; no physical sense of being tied to them, responsible to them. And he felt no murderous reaction to their disapproval either; no desire to throttle and subdue them.

He thrust his hands deeper into his pockets, fury welding his teeth together. Without answering, he swivelled away from her and went back through the house and up to his room, where he lay on the bed staring at the ceiling, his chest pumping, waiting for the rage to unravel.

Gradually, the tension drained out of him and his breathing slowed. Gazing up at the hairline crack in the plaster, his thoughts returned to Lauren. Not long before Rafael would learn his lesson and just as well John wasn't going to be involved. How did that policewoman know about them breaking into Rafael's house? That was worrying. Still, there was no connection to Lauren in that. Good thing he'd changed his plan already. The ambush in Druid's Lane would have been too close to home...to Rafi's home.

He leaned over to the bedside table, opened the drawer and took out a small, blue, plastic wallet. Slipping out the three railway tickets inside, he lay back again, holding them up in the air to study them. "Wednesday 8 May," he muttered, "08.14 from Totnes arriving Truro 10.03, and the innocent return...yes, indeed!" He grinned. Lauren would be attacked on her way to college forty minutes or so after he'd caught the train. He couldn't possibly be involved, could he? He shuffled to the third ticket. "Look, here's the receipt, DC Bannerman. Stick that up your nose and stop poking it!"

Of course, he wasn't going to be on that train; he'd take a later one. But he would have two witnesses to say they were with him in NAN's office all morning from 10.30 on. And, even if the police did want to speak to him, his mother would tell them he'd left a little after 7.00 am that morning to catch the 88 bus to Totnes from the Bull Ring. "Can't be in two places at once, can I?" he chortled, briefly checking the return and then sliding the three tickets back in the wallet.

He put it back in the drawer beside a small wood box. Pushing the reading lamp further back to make space, he picked up the box and stood it on the table. Lifting the lid, he smiled at the glass atomiser resting inside. It was so neat. It would just sit in his pocket out of sight. Nothing bulky or suspicious to carry. Simply step out in front of her and spray it directly into her eyes. The ammonia would do the rest.

33

Lauren hesitated in front of the faded-brown door and then pressed the bell. There was a crackle, followed by her father's voice, "Lauren?"

"Hi, Dad."

"Come on up...hope this works."

Something clicked and she tried the door.

"Yay! I'm in!"

She was halfway up the narrow, dark, uncarpeted, wooden staircase when a door at the top opened and her father appeared in a shaft of light.

"You found me...come on in." He backed into the doorway waiting for her and, as she entered, he put his arms round her and held her tight. "Thank you for coming," he said, his words muffled by her hair, "I'm so glad to see you."

"You don't have to thank me, Dad," she laughed, pulling back. "I've been wanting to see where you are."

"Well, it's not much." He let her go, standing next to her as she looked round the room. "It's just a stop-gap till...you know, till things get sorted out."

Despite the double window overlooking the street, one half open on its catch, the room was dark. What light there was from the window fell on a faded rug and seemed to die there. Her eyes swept over the sagging, brown, leatherette sofa and the upright armchair, with its mustard upholstery and wooden armrests, to the dark wood table and sideboard behind them by the wall, where sombre-framed pictures stole light from the magnolia paint surrounding them.

Despair and shame locked up the words in her. She didn't want to hurt his feelings. But how could he be reduced to this? This wasn't right. This didn't fit. This wasn't him. In desperation, she moved to the window and looked down on the traffic and shoppers in the street below.

"Good for people-watching," she managed, while an inner voice kept screaming, 'You can't live here!'

"Yes. Neighbourhood Watch, that's me." He laughed and she cringed at the falsity of it, aware of his shame before her and feeling heartbroken for him. "Anyway, come and sit down and I'll make you a cuppa."

She looked at the sofa and the armchair; she didn't want to sit on either of them.

"Or have a look around, if you like," he called, disappearing through an open door and out of sight, past a stand-alone cooker with an eyelevel grill.

The bathroom was cleaner than she had feared, with clearly new vinyl across the floor designed to look like black-and-white tiles; yet the room seemed shabby, nevertheless, with rust stains down the bath under the taps and the mirror chipped in one corner over the basin. But it was the bedroom that jolted her with its dingy starkness. The furniture was all dark wood as in the living room: a narrow, mirror-fronted wardrobe; a chest of drawers with one of its knobs replaced in incongruous pine; a small table with a bentwood chair...

and the single bed! Pushed against the wall, with its scratched headboard, one flat pillow and nettle-green candlewick bedspread, it looked mean and lonely. Above it, a framed print of a hunting scene was the room's only adornment, and next to it stood a second bentwood chair in place of a bedside table.

"Lauren, tea's up!"

She heard him call and stood transfixed, staring at the bed, remembering all the comfort and colour of her parents' bedroom at home. How she had loved their luxurious double bed when she was little, with its mountain of squishy pillows and sea-blue duvet; bouncing on it and learning to do tumbling head-over-heels, her mum and dad either side keeping her safe, just as she had done with Finn when he was a toddler.

"Lauren?" He was coming; she could feel the tremble in the floorboards. "Ah, there you are!" His hand was warm on her shoulder and she wanted to reach up and hold it there, but couldn't bring herself to do so and felt cut off again as he withdrew it. "Come on, your tea's getting cold."

She followed him over to the sofa and sat down beside him, taking a ginger nut from the plate between their mugs on the coffee table as she did so. Picking up the chequered mug she recognized from home, she settled back, only to find herself sinking down with no lumbar support, her knees coming almost level with her chin.

"Bloody hell, Dad!" she cried, struggling up again and trying not to slop the tea. "This sofa's crap...lethal for your back!" And seeing his embarrassment, she instantly regretted it.

"Yes, sorry, sweetheart, I know." He glanced round

the room. "It is shit, isn't it?"

Putting her mug and biscuit down, she rounded the table and kneeling down, put her arms round his neck and pressed her head against his.

"You can't live like this, Dad," she whispered. "What are you going to do?"

Freeing his own hands, his arms came round her as he leaned in closer.

"I don't know," he said. "I don't know." And she felt his tears warm and wet on her cheek.

She remembered, back in the winter at home, finding him standing alone in the bedroom upstairs, crying; and how she'd fled into her bedroom, afraid he'd see her. She didn't mind now. She was glad to be there...glad for him to know he wasn't alone. That had been the first time she'd ever seen him cry and it had frightened her, made her feel unsafe. From when she was little riding high on his shoulders, he had always been tall and strong to her, with an easy, light-hearted authority that reassured, rather than oppressed. She'd seen it at college, too; his classes were humorous and relaxed, but people didn't misbehave and the work got done. And now he seemed so broken, so...

"Aaagh!" she cried, letting go of him and trying to push herself up, while desperately massaging her thigh at the same time. "Sorry, Dad," she whimpered, catching her right leg up behind her, "quad cramp!" Grimacing in pain, she closed her eyes until she felt the muscle beginning to unclench. "Ooh, that's better," she laughed, opening them again; and, seeing his worried face, she added, "I'm fine." She flexed her leg a couple of times. "Just need to walk around a bit...ease it off."

"Can I get you anything?" he asked, as she hobbled

towards the window. "Glass of water?"

"Yeah, water'd be good," she said, turning back towards him. "Thanks, Dad." As he headed for the kitchen, she paused, catching her leg up behind her in a thigh stretch before continuing a circuit of the room.

"Do you often get those?" he frowned, coming back and passing her a tumbler midway.

"Only when I overdo it." She emptied the glass and handed it back to him. "Had a race on Saturday." She grinned. "Won it by the way, did I tell you? Means I get to go to the trials in Birmingham. Wish you'd been there. Ida and Henry came, but...you know, not the same as having you and Mum there..."

"Yes, really sorry I couldn't come, but..." he glanced round the room and shrugged his shoulders, "well, you know why."

"And Finn, of course!" she added. "Missed his whoops of encouragement!" She wished he was here now. He always brightened things up, made things feel... she struggled to think of a suitable word...breezier? Easier, anyway! "Was he okay seeing you here?"

"He didn't come. He was at Tom's, getting on with their treehouse. Better that way, really." He shrugged and gave her a wry smile. "But, come on, tea's getting cold."

He went back to the sofa and Lauren followed him, sitting down upright on the edge.

"Very relaxed," he laughed, touching her lightly on the arm. "But I am glad you're here."

"So am I, Dad," she said, knowing it wasn't true, knowing she hated being there and hated him being there, but not knowing what else to say not to hurt him. Instead, she reached for her mug and he took his hand away. The tea was cold and filmy and she put it back on the table.

No words came to her, only the wish to be gone. From the corner of her eye, she saw him sipping from his mug and staring into it, as if he, too, didn't know what to say anymore. He stood up suddenly, the sofa springing up after him and tilting her sideways as he moved to the window.

She checked her watch. "I think I'd better be going."

"Isn't that Terry Curnow down there?" he said, as if he hadn't heard her. "It is...look."

She went across and stood beside him, looking into the street below. A black Range Rover was in a stand-off with a delivery van, the cars parked on either side making it impossible for them to pass each other. The Range Rover flashed its headlights and the van driver's arm shot out gesturing it to back up. Other vehicles were already pulling up behind them and shoppers on the pavement were stopping to watch.

"Where is he?" she asked. "I can't see him."

"Too late! He's gone into that charity shop." He stabbed at the window. "Over there, next to the cafe."

"BHF, you mean?"

"Yes."

She turned away. "He's a creep. I don't want to see him, anyway."

"He hasn't bothered Rafi again, has he?" her father said, still looking out of the window.

"No, and he can't now, anyway. Rafi's in Jordan... for the funeral."

"When will he be back?" Her father glanced round at her. "I mean, he will be coming back, won't he?"

Lauren frowned. It had never occurred to her he

might not, and the thought disturbed her. "Not sure." She hadn't spoken to Rafi since he'd called her in the middle of the night. "He didn't tell me. In fact, he went off without saying goodbye, which is pretty flaky."

"That doesn't sound like him. On the other hand, you said he was very upset. So, I expect...hang on, look, there's Terry!"

"Where?" She couldn't see him.

"Over there!" He stabbed at the glass again. "In the tweed jacket and fedora."

"Oh, my god! What does he look like?"

"Toad of Toad Hall, maybe?"

"A slimy, poisonous toad!" Lauren said, watching Terry as he paused to adjust the stuffed carrier bag wedged under his arm. A woman passing by said something to him and he raised his hat to her, his face wreathed in a smile. Lauren shivered. "He's dangerous," she muttered, turning back into the room. "Maybe better if Rafi doesn't come back."

'But I bloody well hope he does!' she added to herself, collecting the mugs and carrying them out to the kitchen, where she left them on the empty drainer by the sink.

Nick was standing in the middle of the room waiting for her, his arms hanging down and his hair crumpled up on one side. In that moment, she saw him not as her father, but as a man alone and somehow lost, almost boyish in his vulnerability.

"Okay," she said, forcing a smile and going across to him. "Sorry, Dad, but I've got to go."

"Must you?" he said, putting his arms round her, as she went to kiss him.

"Yes, 'fraid so, or I'll be late. But I'll come again

soon...promise."

He relaxed his hold, releasing her. "But one thing before you go," he said, reaching out and taking her hand. "You won't get too involved with Rafi, will you? I don't want you to get hurt."

She stared at him, pulling her hand away. "What do you mean? Why would I get hurt?"

"Nothing. Nothing. It's just..."

"Just what?"

"You know..."

"No, I don't know!" Her neck felt hot and she pushed her hair back behind her shoulders. "And what does *too involved* mean? What are you on about?"

"Don't get upset. Just hear me out for a moment."

"Go on, then," she said, widening her stance and folding her arms.

"Right, well...how to put this? The thing is we're worried about you, about..."

"We? Who's *we*?"

"Your mum and I."

"You and Mum are worried about me?" Lauren laughed. "That's a good one!"

"Listen to me!" he raised his voice and then lowered it repeating, "Listen to me."

Lauren waited.

"We like Rafi; he's a decent, reliable boy...young man, and we're glad he has you and Ida as friends, because the fact is some people...people like Terry and his chums are xenophobic..."

"Racist, you mean!"

Nick threw his arms wide and his mouth curled in frustration. "I don't want to argue with you, Lauren! I'm trying to explain something."

He stared at her, his chest heaving. She saw the anguish in his eyes, knew that he was struggling. "Okay, sorry...go on."

"Thank you," he nodded at her. "So, where was I? Yes...yes, the point is there are people who don't want foreigners here. And yes, all right, many of them are particularly against those who are col...those who are of a different ethnic origin."

You mean Pakis and Blacks and Chinks and Towel Heads! Lauren clenched her teeth and kept the thought to herself. "And so?" she said instead.

"And so," he sighed, "we don't want you to end up getting into trouble because people think you're...think you're more than just friends, if you see what I mean."

She saw his discomfort; and, as the meaning behind his words sank into her, her anger froze into a numbed confusion. She stared down at the frayed stitching of the old boat shoes he wore as slippers, which were both so familiar and so out of place. Not be friends with Rafi because of what other people think...not have him in my life.

"I don't believe this," she said finally, shaking her head and looking up at him. "Not you, too, Dad... surely?"

"Not me what?"

"Because Rafi's got brown skin? You can't mean that."

"That's not it. We're just concerned..."

"Mum, too?"

"It's not us, sweetheart; it's about other people and how..."

She stopped listening, as he took a step towards her, and moved away to the armchair. She sat down, glad of the seat's hardness as if it had a board underneath, and slid her hands along the wooden arms, tightening her grip.

"...your whole future, that's all." He was still talking. She watched him shrug his shoulders. "We just want you to be happy."

She met his gaze without responding, until he shrugged again and went to sit down on the sofa, while she continued to stare into the space where he had just been.

After a while, the racing in her mind eased, her hands relaxed and she sat listening to the coming and going of her own breathing as it slowed, until she couldn't hear it anymore. Rising quietly, she crossed the room, opened the door, closing it softly behind her, and went down the stairs and out into the brightness of the street.

34

"This is a message from Muhammad son of Abdullah, as a covenant to those who adopt Christianity, near and far, we are with them. Verily, the servants, the helpers, and my followers defend them, because Christians are my citizens; and by Allah! I hold out against anything that displeases them."

Rafi sat immersed in the beauty of the church and the solemnity of his mother's sonorous words. He hadn't expected it to feel so cosy, so intimate. Despite the seamless creamy stone walls and vaulted ceiling circling into the matching stone-tiled floor, the church was full of golden light and jewel colours: crimson from the slim, rectangular bench cushions; saffron, olive and azure blue from the holy figures he didn't recognize on the painted panels of the sanctuary partition...even his mother's ring flashing amber as she raised her hand and the rich chestnut of her hair contained under her dark hat.

His father, Uncle Sadiq and Amti Anoush had already spoken, standing where his mother was standing now on the circular mosaic of a double-headed eagle in front of the raised sanctuary step. The quiet emotion in his father's words had reignited his own grief, bringing tears to his eyes. And he had cried and laughed through Anoush and Sadiq's loving anecdotes about their father. About his life-long faithfulness to his wife, Hana, their mother, who had died so young; about his passion for his Nabali olive trees and his reluctance to use pesticides on them to control the fruit fly; and, more than anything, because he remembered them so vividly, about his grandfather's battles with Damiana, which he had named after his mother-in-law, who had been Armenian and looked down her nose at him, much like the donkey did.

"These are the opening words of the Prophet Muhammad, peace be upon Him," his mother continued, taking him away from Jedi, "in his promise to the monks of St Catherine in 628 AD, when they sought his protection. It is known as the Eternal Promise, due to its final injunction, 'No one of the nation is to disobey the covenant till the Last Day.' The 'nation' is the nation of Muslims and the 'Last Day' is the end of the world."

Rafi could sense a growing restlessness among the pews behind him and he wished she would step out of her detached academic role and be more a part of them, adding her sorrow and memories to theirs. She caught his eye and smiled, as if reading his thoughts.

"What has this to do with Kamal, you may be wondering." She caught Rashid's eye and smiled. "When I first arrived in his house, as Rashid's new bride, I told him I was partly Jewish on my mother's side. Although he was a Christian, he was also a Palestinian, with Muslim friends and relatives, who had either been killed by the Jewish militias or who, like him, had been forced into exile by them during the Nakba. And I did not want there to be any potentially poisonous secrets between us. But I needn't have worried. He opened his arms to me and, a few days later, he presented me with a framed copy of the Eternal Promise, saying he wished the Jews had been included in its covenant as he believed the shared God of Abraham would have welcomed that."

Despite the scattered coughing and shuffling of feet that greeted these words, his mother went on again with what she wanted to say.

"What more fitting tribute could there be, therefore, to Kamal's humanity and his forgiving nature than that we are gathered here today celebrating and mourning him in this humble church where, uniquely in the whole of Jordan, Muslims and Christians continue to pray together? It was, of course, his wish that we do so, as you have already heard." Maryam bowed her head and crossed herself. "Bless you, dear Kamal."

Why did it still sound more like a lecture than a tribute? He understood everything she was saying and the importance of it; yet, sentence by sentence, he felt taken away from his earlier emotional connection with Jedi and separated from his sense of oneness with everybody there.

Only later, once they were home and gathered in the garden close to the mound of Casper's grave under the fig tree, did the loving sadness of his grief wash through him again. He stood in a semi-circle of family and friends, arms linked, his through Jasmin's on one side and Amti Anoush's on the other, and theirs in turn through those of his mother and Zak, and so on, like a chain, through those of their cousins and the neighbours, who had walked back with them from St George's. A slow keening grew, like a wind gathering and moaning, as they stood watching his father and uncle, Rashid and Sadiq, lower the wicker casket into the pit they had dug, its lid strewn with the furled white trumpets of Calla lilies. Uncle Sadiq had wanted black irises, the national flower, arguing they were more suitable to the occasion. But Amti Anoush had overruled him, insisting Kamal would want flowers from his own garden, and his father had agreed with her.

Now, as his father and uncle scooped the first spadefuls of earth over the coffin, Rafi felt Jasmin's hand tighten in his, saw her tears from the corner of his eye and felt the heat of his own. Slowly, the fertile reddish earth filled out and levelled the darkness of the pit. The low wailing stopped and, as if on cue, out of the silence came the whistling call of a rose finch. Rashid straightened and, catching Rafi's eye, he smiled, his smile a white breaker in the dark sea of his beard. Confused by the jolt of connection Rafi looked away, surprised and embarrassed by the nakedness of it.

When he glanced back, he saw his father gazing down at the fresh mound of soil, as Sadiq stood back, his round face drenched in sweat. Rafi wondered again, as he had before, if this tendency in his uncle lay behind the air-conditioning business he had started in Amman as a young man. But the thought soon vanished in the expectant hush that followed. He knew some fitting words needed to be said and began to worry where they would come from. As the silence grew, he found himself struggling against a sense of obligation to fill the gap himself. With his heart thumping, he opened his mouth to begin, when his aunt's voice quietly, but firmly, relieved him of the responsibility.

"You too must mingle my friends
since the earth and sky
are mingled just for you and me."

She paused, letting her words drift over them in the afternoon stillness. Then, breaking the chain, she stepped forward.

"Come," she said, "let us eat and drink a toast to my father...," she took in her brothers, "our father...to keep him company on his journey."

"Maybe Damiana'll give him a lift," Rafi heard Zak mutter, and he saw Anoush put her arm around his shoulders, ferrying him with her as she led the way up the garden to the terrace.

"Lines from the poet Rumi," his mother said, arriving between him and Jasmin, and taking their arms. "Simple, but typically elegant and profound...and mercifully brief!" She laughed. "Your Amti Anoush is full of surprises."

Rafi was equally surprised by his mother's levity, and yet, as they made their way to the house, he, too, felt an unexpected lightness and relief from the solemnity of the burial.

35

Lauren was standing by the desk in her bedroom, sorting out her books and homework for college, when her mobile leapt into muffled life in her hip pocket. She slipped it out.

"Hello."

"Lauren? It's Rafi."

"Oh, Rafi, hi. How are you? Thought you'd still be in Jordan."

"Yes, I am...I'm still here."

"You're very clear...sounds like you're in the next room."

"Yes, we have a good connection, I think." Lauren smiled, but he went on speaking before she could say anything. "Is this a good time? I can ring later, if you are busy."

"No, it's fine. I'm upstairs, just getting things ready for college tomorrow."

'*I'm so happy to hear your voice*' is what she wanted to say, but his politeness...his formality made it feel impossible.

"So, how's it been?" she asked instead. "Your family okay?"

"We had the service this morning in St George's

church...quite small really, but with an opening inside to the cave, where a saint appeared to a shepherd telling him the villagers should build a church there. It has a special atmosphere." He paused. "Peaceful, you know...spiritual." His voice dropped for a moment, as if embarrassed by the word. "And, afterwards, we buried Jedi...buried my grandfather...in our garden."

"Right." Lauren looked into the garden below, where twilight was already folding the shrubs and borders into shadow. She couldn't imagine having one of her family buried there and wondered what to say to him.

"So, what's happening now? Everyone still there?"

"No, just my parents and aunt...and Jasmin and Zak, of course. Maybe my uncle, too...I'm not sure, I'm not in the house. But he'll be leaving soon, anyway; he lives in Amman."

"Where are you, then?"

"I'm in the garden by the graves. Casper is buried here, too. I think I told you."

"Yes, I remember." Lauren crossed to her bed, squeezed off her trainers and lay back on the pillows. She waited for him to continue, feeling comfortable in the silence and closer to him. As she waited, she closed her eyes, listening for any sounds where he was and hearing only a constant staccato whirring in the background.

"It's peaceful here," he said at last. "Just Jedi, Casper and me." He paused. "And the cicadas, of course." He sounded wistful. "Always the cicadas."

Ah, that was the thrum! She recognized it now.

"Is it good to be home, Rafi?" she said, without thinking. "Will you stay there?"

He didn't reply at first and she wondered if her questions had been too direct, too personal. He was a private person, she knew that. Yet she'd always felt a sort of unspoken trust between them, ever since the night he'd come running to Ida's, hammering on the door in his pyjamas, barefoot and terrified.

"I'm not sure," he said so softly that she wondered if he was talking to her at all, or only to himself.

Again, she waited to see how he would go on. But the next voice she heard was her mother's emerging from the stillness of the landing outside saying good night to Finn, followed by the click of a light switch and the sound of her footsteps disappearing down the stairs.

After a while, his voice came again, low and dreamy, tickling her ear. "I wish you were here, it's such a beautiful night. The sky is full of stars and the air is...soft...just the scent of jasmine. I'd almost forgotten this...and now it feels like I've never been away. I don't want to leave here...I want to stay here...right here...in this moment."

He wished she was there. She swapped the phone to her other hand and opened her eyes, watching the shadows from the branches of the trees moving on the wall over the chest-of-drawers. Thousands of miles away and yet here he was with her in her bedroom. She got up and opened the window, letting the cool air flow over her face and down her arms.

"Well," she said, when he finished, "if you're not coming back, we'll have to come and see you, won't we? Ida and me, I mean. It'll be an adventure."

She cringed at the false note of her own jokiness. Why had she said that? It wasn't what she wanted to say at all and she wished she could take it back. Certainly, when he spoke again, the tone of his voice was different, less intimate, more matter-of-fact.

"Yes, that would be good. But we will be flying back on Friday and my father...well, and my mother too... they want me to finish my A-Levels. Anyway, Jasmin is calling me. My uncle is leaving, I must go."

While he was speaking, Lauren slid the curtains across with her free hand, one at a time. The closeness was gone and all that remained was a hollow sense of distance and separation.

"Okay," she said, "see you at the weekend, maybe. I'm running on Saturday, but I'll be at Ida's on Sunday. If not, see you back at college."

She heard a woman saying something in the background and Rafi answering her, his voice fading and blurring, then loud and clear in her ear again.

"I have to go, Lauren. Bye."

"Bye," she said, and wanting to end on a warmer note, she added, "I'm glad you rang. It's good to know you're...," the whirring of the cicadas sliced off into dead air, "all right."

She circled back and forth between the window and the door, gazing at the screen of her phone, occasionally brushing the corner of the duvet as she rounded the foot of the bed.

She wanted to call him back. His voice was still repeating in her head, "I wish you were here". It doesn't mean anything, she told herself; it's what people say. They put it on postcards. But he had been in the garden in the dark by himself, hadn't he? By his grandfather's grave and he'd wanted to talk to her. It wasn't politeness, was it? It was what he was feeling. He wished she was there...and she had wished it, too, hadn't she? So, why hadn't she just said that? Why had she changed the subject and brought Ida into it?

She threw her phone on the bed and stood staring at it. This was nonsense. They'd just buried his grandfather in the garden...he was being over-emotional....who wouldn't be? Just as well she hadn't said anything...it would have been embarrassing...he probably wouldn't even remember what he'd said. A moment later, she picked her phone up again and scrolled for Ida. What did she want to say? What did she want to talk about? She shook her head and switched it off.

Sitting down on the edge of the bed, she stared at her bare feet. She wiggled her toes and splayed them. What was it? Why was she feeling so restless... so disturbed? Of course, it was Rafi; but it was more than that...that feeling of closeness and then being cut off. Yes, but...but something else, something more...like a shadow under the water. She was humming a tune. Where did that come from? Something about making up your mind. How did it go? She half-remembered it from the tape her dad used to play in the car ages ago... from a film, wasn't it? What was it called? *Once*, maybe? Yes, *Once*, that was it. She reached for her headphones and searched for the song. The man's voice, when it came, was fractured and difficult to hear at the start.

She tried singing along, but she didn't recall the lyrics, not until a female voice joined in. Then the whole tempo and volume lifted as they hit the chorus which she remembered now and which she had loved to sing out with her father as they drove along:

When your mind's made up
When your mind's made up
There's no point trying to change it

She joined in now and when the track was over, she played it again, singing along all the way through, swept up in the harmony and yearning of their voices, her cheeks wet with tears.

Love, love
There's no pint trying to change it
When you love

After the song had finished, she could hear the refrain looping endlessly in her brain, but when she tried to sing it aloud, she kept losing the melody. Whose love was she crying for, anyway? She shook her head. It didn't make any sense. How could she feel so sad and so...so kind of ecstatic, all at the same time?

So many voices were spinning in her head: the singers' 'Love, love'...Rafi's 'Wish you were here'...her father's 'When your mind's made up...'

"Unmake your mind, Dad!" she whispered. "There's every point...come home!"

A knock on the door startled her and she whirled round, wiping her cheeks as her mother walked in.

"Mum! Why bother knocking?"

"I heard voices," Jess said, looking round the room.

"I was singing."

"Singing?"

"Yes! So nothing to worry about, right?"

Her mother's gaze was fastened on her and Lauren wanted her gone...wanted her intrusiveness gone.

"I'm not a child anymore. This is my room and I don't like it when you just march in. I wouldn't do it to you."

"You've been crying." Her mother rounded the end of the bed towards her. "What's the matter?"

"Mum!" Lauren sprung up and moved away from

her. "Did you hear what I just said?"

Her mother nodded, sat down on the bed and, dipping her head, freed her ponytail from the elasticated band securing it.

"I want to talk to you," she said, shaking out her hair so that it fell around her shoulders, covering her ears and softening her face.

It wasn't something she often did and the intimacy of it took Lauren by surprise.

"What about?" she said.

"I want to ask you a couple of questions and I want you to be honest with me."

"Okay. Go on."

"I had a long talk with Shauna the other day, when I went to pick Finn up, and I didn't like some of the things she said at the time, but I've been thinking about them ever since."

"What sort of things?" Lauren asked, pulling her desk chair round and sitting down. She liked Tom's mum, she didn't want there to be a falling out.

Jess didn't reply immediately and Lauren thought how different she looked with her hair down. Her whole demeanour seemed to have changed. Her mother was always bustling efficiency, always alert and decisive; a quickness...sometimes of fun, sometimes of resolve, often of both...alive in her, in her movements, in her laughter, in her speech. And yet here she was, silent, thoughtful, sitting still; Lauren felt closer to her, more equal, less under her command.

"You know why I gave up teaching, don't you?" Jess said at last.

"Yes, too many exams, wasn't it? Too much red tape?"

"Yes, always the syllabus. Had to fill their heads, not find out what was in them. Only grades mattered, not the subject." Her mother sighed and shook her head. "So stupid...keep the skin and throw away the fruit!"

"So, what do you want to ask me?" Lauren recognized her mother's hobby-horse, 'exams are anti-educational', and tried to steer her away from it.

"Don't worry, I'm coming to that," Jess smiled. "The point is once I'd left and got going with Red Emma, I felt released...energised, like I'd got wings. I could do things my own way, follow my own ideas through, right or wrong. There was so much to organize...builders, banks, suppliers, all of that; it was a big risk, but it was exciting and I felt alive again."

"Yeah, Mum, I get it." Lauren remembered how worn down her mother would seem during term-time and how quickly she sprang back to life in the holidays, like wilting basil given water. "And Red Emma's amazing, but it did kind of take you over, didn't it?"

"Mm," her mother nodded, "that's what Shauna said, more or less. Or, at least, she said maybe I'd seemed...'unavailable' was her word. Is that what it was like?"

Lauren hesitated; she wanted to be truthful, but she didn't want to hurt her feelings.

"Tell me, Lauren. I need to know."

"Ok, yes, it did feel a bit like that. You were out a lot and, when you were here, you were always busy."

"But I was busy before that, wasn't I? I mean marking, making lesson plans, getting materials ready... you know, all the school stuff."

"I don't know, Mum, it was different."

"Different how?"

Lauren could see from her mother's frown of concentration and the way she was leaning forward that she was in earnest, that she really wanted to know.

"How? All right..." her mother's gaze was distracting and she closed her eyes for a moment to think more clearly. "All right, so when you were teaching we were all in the same boat, if you see what I mean. Dad was doing the same as you, and Finn and me were doing homework. It felt like we were all in it together. But, once you got involved with Red Emma, it was more like you'd gone off in a boat on your own."

"I see." Her mother nodded and then, after a pause, nodded again. "And does it still feel like that?"

"Honestly?"

"Yes!"

"Okay, you asked. If anything, it's worse. Since you started with the new place in Totnes, you've been totally absent, like..."

"But that's not true!" Lauren saw her mother's face reddening and the angry flash in her eyes. "I've been here a lot. I'm here every evening, aren't I? And I try my best to be here in the afternoons, when you and Finn get back. Not always, I know but often..."

"Don't get cross, Mum. You did ask."

"Let me finish! And I'm always home on Sundays." Her mother tilted her chin up and glared at her. "And I'm not getting cross, I'm just stating facts."

"Why ask me then, if you don't want to hear my answer." Lauren felt incensed. "You said you wanted me to be honest and, when I am, you get all huffy."

Her mother kept staring at her, her eyes tightening.

"So, what's the point?" Lauren shrugged, looking away to Christine Ohuruogu's poster, taking comfort in her smile and wishing her mother would get up and go.

But she didn't, and when Lauren glanced at her, she saw her mother's head was bent down, her hair obscuring her face as she massaged the palm of one hand with the thumb of the other.

She looked back at Ohuruogu's hand holding up her Olympic gold medal. How was she going to get to Birmingham for the Championships? Would her father still be able to take her or would she need to go with Oka and the others? Was anybody else from the club actually going? Gary Crust, maybe? His qualifying times were...

"You're right," her mother's voice was low, conciliatory; "I did ask...I'm sorry. Anyway, you were saying I've seemed more absent since Totnes."

Looking back at her mum, Lauren saw her smile as she added, "Literally, paddling my own canoe." Her smile faded and she became more serious again. "So, go on, when you say' absent', what do you mean?"

"You sure you want to hear this?" Her mother nodded. "Okay, well obviously there are the times when you're just not here and that's crept up. You used to be here on Saturdays, but you've been over at the Canoe a lot recently. And, when you are home, you're buried in books and paperwork most of the time. It's like you're cut off by some invisible wall of glass or something. You don't really listen to us...you nod and go 'Mm', but you're miles away."

"Does Finn feel like this, too?"

"Yeah, 'Mum's in a trance again', that's what he says."

"And your father?"

"Dad?" She always called him Nick, so 'father' took

her by surprise. "Dad would never say anything against you, but I've seen the look in his face."

"What look?"

"Oh, I don't know, it changes. I mean sometimes, if he's said something to you and you don't respond or even look up, he just shakes his head and looks...what does he look...confused, I suppose."

"What about other times?"

"When you're late...when you're not here and you're meant to be, like the other night, when it was your turn to cook and he had to do it because you were still at the Canoe with the builder, he kind of clenches his teeth together...and I know he's furious and so does Finn. And he just stands there not moving, maybe only for a second or two, but it feels longer...and then it's like he comes to, sees us looking, gives us a smile and carries on as normal."

"Shauna was right, then," her mother said, arching her eyebrows, "and Ginnie and Freda, come to that." She shook her head, and when she went on, she seemed to be talking to herself and Lauren didn't know what to say. "None are so deaf as those who don't want to hear! It's not all one way, is it?"

36

Terry boarded the X38 in West Street. He found a window seat halfway back on the upper deck and put his rucksack down beside him. It was a busy service between Plymouth and Exeter and the bus was full of mid-morning shoppers, most of them 'grey hairs', as he liked to call them. The day was overcast with a chill wind from the north, a last fling of winter in the face of spring, and he was glad of his duffel coat.

Gazing out over the hedgerows at the countryside beyond, he wished the journey was twice as long. He wanted more time to think through what he was going to say. Schools were back. Lauren was back. He'd make his move next Wednesday, the day Steve Langton would be in Truro giving his talk. What he needed to do at the Exeter meeting today was to persuade Steve and Tony Gardner that his plan for the blinding would be good for NAN's follow-up recruitment drive.

"There will be widespread local coverage, maybe even national," he rehearsed under his breath, "and people will want to find out what the note means." The note! He fumbled inside his coat for the breast pocket of his jacket and pulled out a folded piece of paper. Opening it, he studied what he had written there:

OPEN THE INNER EYE
BRITISH PURITY, NOT OBSCURITY

"They'll find it by the girl. It's a kind of riddle they'll want to solve, yes indeed. People like puzzles, the papers are full of them. It'll make them think."

Yes, he'd put it to them like that. He refolded the paper and then opened it again. Maybe the second line should be in red...make it stand out more. And the first in blue, why not? Red and blue on white, national flag colours. "No! Bad idea!" he muttered and saw an elderly woman across the aisle draw her handbag in closer against her. Those were colours NAN used in their leaflets. Not very original, but traditional, which was the whole point. No, the note had to be anonymous and untraceable...no links, just like the clothes and wig.

No links...how was he going to manage that? He closed his eyes and took three deep breaths to calm himself. The cropped puffer jacket and tee he'd got from the charity shop were a common brand; they could have come from anywhere. As for the wig, that was another reason for coming today. Hopefully, one of the costume hire places would have something suitable and he'd simply give them false details, so no come back there. But the note? Handwriting, computers, printers... they could all give him away.

The blast of a horn and sudden breaking, tipping him forward, made him stare out of the window. Weren't these the Marsh Barton lights? Ten minutes or so and they'd be at the bus station. He looked at his watch. He was meeting Steve and Tony in The Ship at twelve for an early lunch and he didn't want to be late. Steve's talk at the Community Centre was scheduled for 3.00 pm and they wanted a couple of hours with him first before they all went on there. That gave him an hour and a bit for wig hunting.

As he left the bus station and made his way to the High Street, Terry pulled a small notebook out of his coat pocket and checked the shop addresses he had jotted down. "Start with the furthest away and work back," he told himself; that way he'd be closer to The Ship when the time came. That meant Fantasy World and The Real McCoy in Fore Street first. The centre of town was busy and several times he had to step off the pavement just to keep up his momentum.

Hurrying wasn't his natural way of being, and by the time he found Fantasy World, his legs were aching and he was feeling hot and bad-tempered. He didn't even bother looking past the SALE stickers in the window, but walked straight in. At first, he was stunned by the assault of multiplicity and colour, with packeted outfits along the wall and costumes on hangers on centre stands and masked heads in rows high up and stands of accessories and life-size models, a Star Trek woman with orange hair, a diminutive Peter Pan.

He stood circling, moving from foot to foot, looking for wigs that weren't orange or lime green or turquoise; all he could see were grotesque masks...pigs' heads, clowns, monkeys, skeletons. A scarlet Devil's tail, next to a tommy gun, caught his eye. And then he saw them in rows on the far wall: packets with pictures of women with different hair. "Thank, God!" he laughed, striding across to them. 'Flirty Flick Wigs', they were labelled and the colours were fine. He wanted dark brown or black; but as his eyes swerved from one to the other, he realized they were all the same style. He wanted something long that would conceal his features and these were all short...no good at all.

When he asked, the assistant said all the wigs they had were out on display. He glared at her in frustration for a moment and then stormed out and crossed the road. Almost opposite was McCoy's Arcade with The Real McCoy just inside. The window seemed full of old-style clothes and, on entering, he soon saw that the shop was an emporium of retro vintage and Americana items: flapper dresses, baseball caps, varsity and baseball bomber jackets, and tees of all sorts...but not a wig in sight. As, once again, he whirled in frustration, he noticed a coral necklace by the flapper dresses and went across to look at it. *Vintage Coral Branch Necklace 17"*, the tag said. He liked the chunky look of it and picked it up. It was lighter than he'd expected, but he liked the deep shade and spikiness of it. He smiled...it was eye-catching, something people would notice and remember. And, above all, it was absolutely a woman's.

"Stunning, isn't it?" said an androgynous figure in black behind the counter. "We may have some earrings to go with it, if you like."

Terry didn't like and he particularly didn't like the oily smirk twisting the black-lipsticked lips or the crinkling emerald-shadowed eyes. "Just this, if you please," he said.

As he marched back towards the High Street, forced into the road one more, this time by double-fronted scaffolding, he checked his watch...11.37. He lengthened his stride and even broke into a trot as he neared Marks & Spencer's and turned down Queen Street. 'Parade Vintage Exeter' was the last entry in his notebook. He hadn't expected it would be so difficult to find a normal-looking, shoulder-length wig. Why did they imagine everyone wanted to look like they'd arrived from outer space?

He spotted the Parade Vintage in a crescent of shops by Central Station and walked straight in. He didn't stop to look round, but went quickly up to a woman rearranging hangers on a stand.

"Excuse me..."

"Yes," she smiled, raising her glasses hanging on a lanyard and placing them firmly on her nose with both hands, "how can I help you?"

"Do you have any long, dark brown or black wigs... for women, I mean?"

"I'm afraid we don't," she said. "Human hair wigs tend to be expensive and are more the province of specialists. And synthetic ones don't suit the ethos behind the items we stock, which are all genuine."

"I see." Terry stood bemused for a moment. He'd used up plan B and C and he had no D. His coat felt heavy and he could hardly summon up the energy to move.

"I'm sorry," the woman said, "I can see you're disappointed. Perhaps you could try a hairdresser or even John Lewis. Yes, it might be worth enquiring there."

He glanced at his watch...11.54.

"Thank you," he said, turning away, "but..." He was going to say, "I haven't got time", only what was the point; he was already halfway to the door?

Once he crossed the High Street and turned into Martin's Lane, the day darkened. Buildings crowded the narrow lane on either side, funnelling pedestrians to and from the brightness of Cathedral Green at the far end. As his eyes adjusted, he caught sight of the pub's dark wood Tudor frontage and its hanging sign of a galleon in full sail with Ship Inn in clear letters above it. Moving closer, painted on one of the cream panels between the woodwork, he read:

Sir Francis Drakes
Favourite
Port of Call

"No apostrophe?" he tutted, smiling at the same time, his spirits lifting. Those were the days, yes indeed; the golden reign of Elizabeth I, Shakespeare at the Globe and Drake singeing the King of Spain's beard. He strode through the *Restaurant* entrance, past the announcement in gold script of *Traditional Cask Ales*, into the welcoming interior with its low ceiling and dark beams, oak panelling halfway up the walls below framed prints of old Exeter: the cathedral, the river, the city walls.

The pub was already busy, a swell of conversation and laughter engulfing him as he made his way past the long polished wood bar, looking ahead for Steve Langton and Tony Gardner, and pausing briefly at a portrait of Sir Francis Drake, an enormous ruff around his neck. "You showed them...by God, you did!" he whispered, before moving on.

"Over here, Terry!" The penetrating voice stopped him a split second before he saw the two men. They were tucked away to his right in a quiet bay with open partitioning, screening them from the passageway. At a table by the wall, Steve was sitting on a padded bench looking straight at him, while Tony was on a chair across the table from Steve and had his back to him.

"Good morning to you Steve...Tony," Terry beamed, walking across to them.

"You're punctual," Tony said, twisting round, the flag tattoo suddenly visible in the creases of his neck. "Good. Here..." he beckoned to the chair next to him, "come and sit down."

Terry unhooked his backpack and struggled out of his duffel coat, looking for somewhere to put them.

"Leave them over there," Steve said, pointing to a small corner table between the wall and a large, open fireplace and chimney breast.

"To save time," Steve went on, as Terry came back, "we've already ordered steak and ale pie for us all. And that's a pint of Abbots; hope it suits you."

"Yes...yes, indeed," Terry said, sitting down. He felt oddly flustered; the food and beer were exactly what he was in the mood for, while at the same time he felt... what did he feel? Aggrieved? Yes, that was the word. He didn't like having decisions taken for him without his say-so, not at all.

"Cheers!" he said, unsticking his glass from the beer mat and holding it up. "Here's to NAN!"

"Yes," said Steve.

"To NAN," Tony said, "and death to the dragon!"

Terry looked at him blankly.

"St George!" Tony grinned.

They clinked glasses.

"Wonderful pub!" Terry added, glancing around. "Great choice! England as it always was...as it always should be."

"Right, to business." Steve put his glass down and pushed his iPad across the table. "Tony, will you take the minutes, please?"

"Sure," Tony nodded, reaching for it.

Steve sat back and looked at Terry. "It's important to

keep a record of what was said and what was agreed."

His expressionless, unblinking grey eyes unnerved Terry.

"Yes, of course," Terry blustered. "Proper records, yes indeed." And suddenly, more than anything, he wished he was back in the Exeter Inn holding court with John and Lawrence...and Matty!

"As you know, I'll be in Truro next Wednesday. We're building up a head of steam down here. Strong turnout in Bristol, more than we'd anticipated," Steve eyes flicked to Tony and back again. "Room wasn't big enough. And registration numbers for this afternoon are encouraging. Now, I understand you..."

"Three steak and ale pies, gentlemen," announced a waitress, sliding a large tray onto the edge of the table, causing Terry to hastily lift his beer out of the way.

Once she had passed round the plates and cutlery wrapped in napkins, she lifted a jug from the tray and set it down between them. "Best bit!" she said, smiling at them. "Beef-dripping and merlot gravy! Can I get you anything else?"

"No, thank you," Steve said, "we're fine."

Terry watched Tony push the jug across to Steve as the waitress turned away, wishing he'd had time to ask her for some mustard. Steve helped himself, then Tony; by the time the jug reached him, there was hardly any gravy left.

"Tony tells me you've booked the larger room at the library."

Terry nodded, swallowing his mouthful quickly. "It has capacity for fifty people and refreshment facilities."

"Fifty?" Steve's eyes flicked up. "You're our man on the ground down there. Is that going to be big enough?

We had over a hundred in Bristol and maybe the same again outside who couldn't get in. We don't want that to happen again."

"Well..." Terry flushed. So far, he only had seventeen registrations. "It's early days, Steve. The office has only just opened, but I have started taking steps to publicise your talk, and I'm confident..."

"What steps?"

"What steps, yes indeed..." Terry's mind went terrifyingly blank. Steve's voice was measured, his demeanour perfectly straightforward, and yet Terry felt under attack. "Wheels are being set in motion...," he needed time to think, "yes, yes. I am following up on the membership list Tony sent me." He glanced at Tony, hoping for some tacit agreement that would feel like support, but he was busy typing on the iPad. Terry's throat was dry and he reached for his glass.

"Keep going," Steve said. "What else?"

Terry took a gulp, wiped his lips with the back of his hand, and sat back smiling. This was the perfect moment. The mist of confusion cleared and, when he spoke again, his voice was stronger, more reliable. I am captain of my own ship once again, he thought.

"Recruitment," he said. "Recruitment, Steve, is the essence, is it not?"

"It's important, obviously," Steve nodded with a frown.

"Quite so," continued Terry. He took a small mouthful of pie. The pastry was beautifully crisp and flavourful...definitely home made. They were waiting. Steve was waiting. Tony was waiting. "One moment," he said comfortably, dabbing his mouth with his paper napkin, before taking another sip of beer. "Yes, indeed.

And recruitment depends on publicity, does it not?" He didn't wait for an answer. "No-one will buy your merchandise if they don't know it exists, will they?"

"Get to the point," Tony snapped, "we haven't got all day."

"Ah, the point, yes...well, the point is that I have a plan which will give rise to a great deal of publicity...oh my, yes indeed, a great deal. And the beauty of it is that, while NAN will not be implicated, it will benefit hugely in terms of new interest and new members."

Terry paused, looking gleefully from one to the other.

"What is your plan?" Steve said, pushing his plate to one side and leaning forward.

"We don't approve of mixed-race relationships and the contamination of our stock, do we? We stand for one nation and that is our accord, is it not? And the nation we stand for is the nation of true Englishmen, blood lines centuries old...the Langtons, the Gardners, the Curnows...the nation of all of this," he swept his arm out in an arc, a familiar swelling of pride and excitement in his chest, "the nation that built the greatest empire the world has ever seen...greater than the Romans...greater than the Greeks..."

"What is your plan?" Steve repeated, cutting across him.

"And cut the theatricals!" Tony added.

"Apologies...apologies," Terry said, lowering his voice. "I get carried away, I know. But it is such a magnificent mission we've embarked upon...you've embarked upon, and I'm just so excited to be a part..."

"The plan, Terry!"

In his motionless calm and the steel in his eyes, Terry

saw Steve's anger. That wasn't what he wanted...not at all. He had meant to impress him, to make the leader of NAN realize that he, Terry Curnow, was someone who was fully committed to the cause and someone he could count on absolutely.

"Yes, of course. To put it simply, we want England for the English, don't we? We want our mother tongue, English...we want English culture, English traditions, English food, the Church of England and..." he paused for effect, "and we want English fathers for the English mothers of our children!"

He looked from one to the other seeking affirmation, but neither of them was looking at him. Steve was quietly surveying the tables filling up around them, while Tony was pushing a last forkful of mashed potato around in his gravy.

"NAN stands for National Accord Network," Steve said, in what Terry was beginning to think of as his public voice, both measured and carrying. "That means we are committed to pursuing a national agenda of agreement and togetherness with power devolved from London to the regions. That is our clear message."

Was he against mixed marriages and parenthood or not? From his conversations with Tony, Terry knew that NAN was opposed to further immigration and in favour of assisted repatriation, even though this was not explicit in its publicity. So, maybe Steve was just being cautious and he should press on. After all, what else could he do? Everything depended on Steve and Tony providing him with an alibi. Very well, risk favours the brave. He took a deep breath and began again.

"My plan is simple..."

"Glad to hear it!" Tony muttered.

"There are a lot of people who think like we do, but who are too unsure of themselves to say so. They need something to spark them into action, together with a place to go where they'll be welcome." The expression in Steve's eyes seemed more interested now than angry, as if they were evaluating him rather than skewering him, and he pressed on. "In Ashbrook, where I live, there are two college students, who are...how shall I put this...in the throes of becoming intimate."

Tony glanced up from his typing, his face a mask of irritation. "Thought you were keeping it simple."

"The girl is English," Terry went on, deciding to ignore him, "and the boy is Palestinian...from Jordan." He put his hand down and squeezed hard above his knee, trying to control the sudden frisson of arousal quivering through him. "I have spoken to the girl and she intends to pursue the relationship." That wasn't strictly true, but he knew it as certainly as he knew a bud was bound to bloom. "My plan, therefore, is to nip it in the bud...yes indeed, to prevent the boy becoming the father of her child and all that follows from that... marriage, citizenship, Palestinian relatives coming to live here and the inevitable contamination and erosion of Englishness and our English ways."

"How?" asked Steve. "How do you propose to nip it in the bud and how will that help recruitment?"

Terry's lips thinned in a sly smile. "I am going to open the girl's eyes by closing them..."

"What the hell does that mean?" Tony exploded, banging his fist against the edge of the table.

"Decorum, Tony," Steve growled and then nodded at Terry. "Go on."

Terry leant forward and lowered his voice. "I am

going to blind her with acid and I'm going to drop an untraceable note at the same time, saying simply, 'NO MISCENGENATION!' The slogan came of itself. It wasn't what he'd written down, but it was snappier.

"You're mad!" Tony's voice was low, yet full of menace and fury, as he shoved his face close to Terry's. "What the fuck do you think that'll do to NAN's reputation? You'll get us all locked up, for Christ's sake!"

"Not at all! Not at all!" Terry repeated, pulling away from him. "That's the beauty of it. There won't be any comeback. I'll be disguised as a woman...I'll be wearing a wig." He crossed his fingers under the table. "They won't know who did it. And here's the thing with the note...the press will pick up on it, not just because of the blinding, but because of the note about mixed marriages. It'll cause a lot of controversy and debate between those who think like us and those who don't... those who don't care if we sacrifice our heritage." His heart was thumping and he paused for a gulp of beer. They were watching him, waiting. He put his glass down. "This is happening the same day as you, Steve, are giving your talk not eighty miles away. And all those people who've been secretly feeling and thinking like us for years are going to hear what you're saying, because I'm going to make sure of that. They are going to know NAN's the party that represents them...that is going to protect their future and their children's future." Terry sat back licking his lips and nodding. "Yes, indeed! We're going to get a lot of new members, you can count on that!"

"A symbolic example..." Steve's eyes narrowed, "the nation in microcosm."

"Yes, absolutely...that's it!" Terry felt elated; Steve

understood...he wasn't rejecting the idea out of hand.

"But, Steve," Tony burst out, "that's crazy...and dangerous! We can't go around putting innocent people's eyes out just to make a point! It'll blow up in our faces, destroy everything we've worked for." He whirled round on Terry. "Your plan's full of bloody great potholes! What if someone sees you do it and grabs you? What if your wig comes off and you're recognized? We're trying to establish ourselves as a serious political party, not a bunch of thugs...the ballot box, not civil war!"

Before Terry could reply, his thoughts scrambled by the venom of the attack, Tony whipped back to Steve.

"We've made a bad mistake...my fault. But Terry's not the right bloke for us. We need to replace him, and quick."

Terry stared at the smear of carrot left on the blade of his knife. His face was burning and he didn't dare look up, waiting for Steve's verdict like a condemned man.

"All finished, are we?" The bustle and cheeriness of the waitress was a relief, as she scraped and stacked their plates. And when she leant forward for the glasses, Terry saw a flash of black lace and cleavage beneath her blouse, before she straightened up again and her breasts disappeared. "Would you like to see the dessert menu? The apple pie's homemade and there's a sticky toffee special."

Her gently cajoling tone and smile reminded him of his mother and he felt a tremor of revulsion run through him.

Steve checked his watch. "We'll have three apple pies with ice-cream, please."

"Right you are," she said, picking up the tray; "three

with ice-cream, it is."

Sticky toffee pudding for me, Terry mouthed after her, a sense of foreboding stealing over him like a shadow as she moved away; and he had to force himself to turn back to the others.

In the uncomfortable silence that followed, accentuated by the drum of conversation all around them, Terry wondered if now might be the right moment to set out his proposed alibi, which would make any connection between him and the blinding of Lauren impossible. Surely, they would see that. He cleared his throat, but before he could say anything, Steve began to speak.

"I'm not so sure, Tony. Hitler burned down the Reichstag to his advantage. The wrong people were blamed and public opinion swung behind the Nazis. So, let's not be too hasty."

"But who would we be blaming?" Tony shot back.

"Far-right extremists." The hint of a smile flickered across Steve's face. "NAN will issue a statement condemning the acid attack and the note as an assault on democracy and reaffirming our commitment to due political process. We will be seen as moderate and reliable."

Terry's heart was doing back-flips. *NAN will issue a statement condemning the acid attack.* That was a yes! Steve was going to back him. As for Tony, he could see the confusion in his face, the muscles in his jaws clenching and relaxing, as he opened his mouth to speak and then closed it again.

"Two points, however," Steve said, addressing Terry, all traces of a smile gone. "Miscegenation is too complicated. Ordinary people won't know what it means and it's not part of the Far-right's vocabulary. No, your note needs to be simpler and more extreme." He paused and looked around. "Something like this," he said, taking a notebook and pen from his inside pocket.

He wrote in capitals, detached the page and pushed it across the table, turning it round for them to see: '*WHITE FATHERS, WHITE MOTHERS, WHITE CHILDREN! IMMIGRANTS GO HOME!*'

"Yes, indeed! Much..." Terry raised his fist in the air and shook it, "much punchier!"

As he watched Tony picking up the note, Terry felt another surge of jubilation. Once he was PM, he'd keep Steve as his personal advisor; but Tony, he would...He coughed to hide the gurgle of laughter bubbling in his throat, Tony, he would let go.

"Devious," Tony was saying, as he passed the note back to Steve, "but, yeah, it might work."

Steve nodded, carefully folding the piece of paper in half and placing it inside the notebook. "The second point," he said, looking up at Terry, "is about Tony's warning that something might go wrong. You must always prepare for the unexpected, as far as you can; what you need, Terry, is a watertight alibi. Have you got one?"

"Yes, yes, I have!" Terry said, his anxiety turning to delight at everything falling so easily into place, and he set out the details of his plan with confidence.

"I see," Steve said, after he had finished. "Your proposed alibi is that Tony and I will lie about being in a mid-morning meeting with you in the Truro office, which will necessarily place you on the train at the time of the attack. Is that right?"

The unblinking grey eyes and non-committal tone gave Terry no clue as to what Steve was thinking, but the word 'lie' filled him with unease. It was bald, it was accurate and it signalled a refusal.

"Yes," he said, "but I think it's fair to say that..." He didn't know what he thought it was fair to say, only that he wanted to turn the idea of lying into something more palatable, only the words wouldn't come.

"Three apple pies with ice cream?" rang out a voice behind him, much to his relief.

"Yes, that's us," Steve nodded, holding out his hand. And, as the young man leant across the table to pass him one of the small dishes, a blanket of pungent aftershave wrapped itself around Terry's head.

"For goodness sake!" he muttered, jerking away from the suffocation of its sweetness.

"Enjoy!" the waiter grinned, setting down the other two dishes, before striding away.

Oh God, *fair to say*...the words came back to him; lifting his spoon, Terry sliced into the pastry and scooped up a generous mouthful, playing for time. "Mm, wonderful!" he crooned, savouring the tangy heat against the creamy cold. But Steve was already busily instructing Tony, a new urgency in his voice.

"Get onto Peter Haig at South West and confirm the live interview for next Wednesday after my talk in Truro and check if Samantha can get us some follow-up coverage in the nationals. I can see this igniting a firestorm in Westminster, if we play it right. It only takes one match," he looked at Terry, "and you may just have handed it to us."

Terry walked to the Community Centre with them encased in a bubble of euphoria. Even once inside and on the platform, as Steve addressed the packed hall, he basked in a golden haze of pure delight. He saw the faces, he heard the voices, but they were all exterior to the glow radiating inside him. Lauren's impertinence avenged, Rafi humbled and his political star not just rising, but soaring! Yes, indeed!

It was only after he had left them and was walking back along the High Street to catch the bus home that he remembered about the wig and his bubble burst. Time was running out; if he couldn't find one here, where was going to get one without risk of being recognized? Totnes, maybe? Bit close to home, though... people knew him there. As he turned into Paris Street, he caught sight of what looked like a cafe on the far side and crossed over. He had almost twenty minutes to spare and a mug of hot, sweet tea was suddenly very appealing. When he reached the Pink Ginger Flower Cafe, however, he saw St Petroc's Charity Shop next door to it and went in.

Several shoppers were moving between the racks of clothes, mostly coats as far as he could see, and he edged past them towards a 'vintage' section at the back with old-fashioned dresses and hats and some wellington boots. What's vintage about gumboots, he was thinking, when his eye snagged on a head with a wig and he spun round to face it. Deep brown and thick and long, it was just what he had been hoping for.

As he put out his hand to feel it, a voice behind him said, "Real hair, that is," and a man in a rainbow shirt with a straggly ginger beard came up beside him.

"How much?" Terry asked, keeping his face averted.

"Twenty-five," the man said. "Pay ten times that at a wig-maker."

"Yes, indeed. I'll take it. Thank you."

On the bus home, he kept his backpack flat on his lap, idly stroking it from time to time as he imagined the wig and necklace on his flickering reflection in the window.

37

Rafi got dressed quickly: black jeans, t-shirt and half-zip sweater. Even though it looked bright outside, with dew sparkling on the grass in the early morning sunshine, the air in his room felt chill after the warmth of As-Salt. Heading downstairs for the kitchen, he caught sight of his mother in the morning room, as she had named it. Of the two reception rooms at Windhover, this one to the rear of the house, facing south over the garden, was where she liked to have breakfast. She was sitting at an oak table in the window eating a boiled egg, with the sun on her shoulders, and he could see the Sunday newspaper folded open in front of her, propped up against the sugar bowl.

For a moment, he stood watching her, as she poured more coffee from the cafetiere into her cup and took another triangle of toast from the rack and buttered it. The familiarity of it made him feel as if they had never been away. Only been back a day and a half and already the immediacy of the farm and Jedi's funeral was fading. He tried rekindling the sensation of their all being together in the garden: Jasmin and Zak, his father, Amti Anoush and Uncle Sadiq. Why she was 'Amti' and he 'Uncle', he didn't know. It had always been that way. But he couldn't hold onto them.

"Sabbah al-khayr, Mama," he said, going across to her.

"You're up early," she smiled, tilting her cheek to him.

He kissed her and sat down. He was going to say he was thinking of going up to Henry's to see Ida and Lauren, but, before he could reply, she tapped the paper with her finger.

"This is worrying," she said. "There's growing opposition among British MPs to a compromise over Brexit. And it's not just the implicit nationalism of the UK's withdrawal from the EU and its hostile rhetoric about immigrants that concerns me, but also the rising voice of the authoritarian right in Europe and the US, too." She looked up at him, shaking her head. "Orbán, Le Pen, Johnson, Trump. Incipient fascism is flaunting itself in populist apparel, once again. It frightens me. Do we never learn the lessons of history?"

Rafi knew it was true; they had discussed it often enough, but he didn't want to talk about it now.

"Is it that bad," he said, "or is it just the media stirring things up?"

"No, I don't think so, Rafi. The Observer is a balanced newspaper and this is not opinion, these are facts."

She sat deep in thought slowly rotating her amber ring and he knew she had more she wanted to say to him. But he had other things on his mind and he wanted to divert her.

"Do you think it's too early to call Ida?" he said, glancing at his watch. "I'm thinking of going round there a bit later to say hello."

"There are more important things," his mother murmured, letting go of the ring, leaving him unsure if she was talking to him or to herself. In any case, his stomach was growling and he was feeling faintly nauseous.

"I think I'll just go and get myself some break...," he started, but she interrupted him, motioning to the chair opposite.

"Come and sit down, Rafi. I want to talk to you."

Sunday today, Bank Holiday tomorrow...it probably was too early to disturb Ida, he decided, giving in. He pulled out the chair and sat down. There was plenty of time and he could always text Lauren later.

"This," she said, flicking the article with the back of her fingers, "is just the tip of the iceberg. We are heading into very dangerous times. Putin's annexation of the Crimean Peninsula is just a first step. It's clear he intends to reclaim the Ukraine. And then what? How will NATO respond to that?" She looked at him, but didn't wait for a reply. "And, in the Middle East, Netanyahu is continuing to extend Israeli settlements in the West Bank. He means to leave Palestinians stateless, a dispossessed people with no democratic rights." She shook her head. "Who will stop him and what will Jedi's key be worth then?"

"But, Mama, I don't understand. This isn't new, is it? I mean, you have talked to me before about both of these, but you always seemed..." Seemed what? The weariness and anguish in her face disturbed him. It wasn't like her, not her usual confident self. "You've always told me we can change things...through diplomacy, through international organizations like the UN. Why are you suddenly so...I don't know, so without hope?"

She gave him a weak smile and stretched her hand across to him. It was warm and her fingers gripped his gently. "I'm tired, Rafi, but it's more than that."

He didn't want more; he wanted some coffee and something to eat. "Forgive me," he said, withdrawing his hand, "but I need some breakfast. Can we go on with this later?" Without waiting for an answer, he reached for the cafetiere, adding, "I'll make some fresh coffee."

"No, no, let me," she said, getting up and taking it from him. "I am a negligent mother, what would you like?"

"It's ok, I'll do it," he said, surprised, "I don't mind. I'm going to have some scrambled eggs, if we have any."

"Yes, we have," she smiled, moving past him. "You read the paper."

Rafi watched her go with some surprise. Normally, she let him look after his own needs and he was as much at home in the kitchen as she was. Even so, it felt good that she was going to cook for him, reminding him of being a child again. He sat back, checking his phone for any messages, hoping to find Lauren there.

There weren't any texts, but there was an email and he opened it.

Hi Rafi,

Glad you got back okay. I'm not going to Ida's today, but I'll be there tomorrow if you want to come round, sort of middayish.

See you then,

Lauren

He was disappointed: disappointed she hadn't rung him and disappointed she wasn't going to Ida's today after all. He went to close down his phone and noticed she'd sent the email at 6.47. At least that explained why she hadn't rung. Even so, his pleasure in the day had disappeared and he felt flat, wondering what he was going to do now.

"Is tomorrow too long to wait, my little Antar?" Remembering Jasmin's teasing whisper brought a smile to his face. "Oh noble poet and warrior, tell her you will be there on bended knee...in all your shining armour. And look, see how you topple over!"

How much he missed Jasmin already. He picked up the phone again and sent a reply.

Hello Lauren,

Yes, thank you...

He paused, searching for the right words. *See you then...*he put and deleted it. That's what she'd said. Only Arabic phrases came to him, as if his thoughts hadn't reverted to English yet. *I will be there*, he tried and looked at her message again. She had said that as well. He highlighted the words and deleted them. This was silly. What did it matter? And yet, some sense of fitness in him, some need for a proper order in things, would not let him repeat her phrases.

Tomorrow will be fine, he added, signing off underneath. He read through the message and pressed send, but it wasn't what he wanted to say to her at all and he pushed his chair back from the table in frustration.

He picked up the paper and put it down again. If he wasn't going to Ida's house, what was he going to do all day? He looked out of the window at the small, scattered clouds drifting high up in the blue. Something moving on the lawn caught his eye, as a squirrel, pouncing through the grass, sat up suddenly like a Toby jug, its tail curled up into a handle behind it. It seemed to look directly at him before scampering away through a ring of daffodils and disappearing helter-skelter up a tree trunk.

"You have a talent," Amti Anoush had said when he gave her the walnut box he had made. "Don't waste it." Rafi picked at a scab on his knuckle and smiled. She had inspected the box carefully and he had seen the skilled potter in her assessing his workmanship. Her approval had meant more to him than any effusive thank-you. Perhaps he should begin another project... something for Uncle Sadiq, his birthday was next... or for Lauren? Yes, why not for Lauren? He stood up, excited by the idea, and walked over to the window, startling two magpies who took off low in a panic before sweeping up over the rhododendrons and out of sight. But what? He'd have to think about it.

He'd rather be outside, anyway. It was such a fine day, he wanted to be out in the open air, not shut away in the garage. There'd be enough dull or rainy days for that. Besides, he didn't feel like concentrating on anything. "The grass needs cutting!" His mother's exclamation their first morning back echoed in his head. She was right; it had sprung up while they'd been away. The freshness of the green was as dazzling as the dew. You weren't meant to mow the lawn when it was wet, but he was going to do it, anyway, and they could go on talking afterwards. He uncurled the latch on the window, slid up the bottom half and was assailed at once by birdsong, the sting of the morning air on his face and the earthy smell of the garden.

Later on, as he came in through a side door at the back of the house where they kept their winter coats and wellington boots, Rafi slipped off his trainers and took them back to the door. Holding them out in front of him to one side, he banged their soles together to try to get rid of the grass still stuck there from his mowing.

"Rafi?" he heard his mother call. "Is that you?"

Carrying his shoes, he found her standing in the hall holding a glass of water, a tasselled scarf around her shoulders like a shawl. He recognized it and it surprised him.

"Ah, I thought I heard you. I was just going upstairs. Perhaps when you are ready, you could come and find me. I have something important I want to discuss with you."

"Yes, okay," he nodded. "Let me just change my jeans. I won't be long."

He followed her up the stairs, taking in the black triangle hanging down her back with its deep red, floral embroidery. He had never really liked it because it made her look old and old-fashioned, and the red clashed with her hair, with the coppery glossiness of it. But he knew Jedi had given it to her and that she treasured it because it had belonged to Jedi's wife, Hana, who had died giving birth to his own father.

He had only ever seen her wear it at home in Jordan, and as he turned off into his room, he was puzzling over why she had brought it back with her. Holding on to Jedi, probably, he told himself, hanging the damp jeans and socks over the radiator, even though it wasn't on. As he slid into his flip-flops, he wondered what the 'important' matter might be.

He found his mother sitting in one of the armchairs waiting for him and he sat down in the other. There was no clutter around her, none of the usual scattered books and papers, and her folded glasses were the only item on the small table beside her, apart from the lamp. The sun had moved round from the back of the house and was now shining through the side window, catching particles of dust weaving their spiralling dance in widening shafts of light.

Rafi watched them, waiting for his mother to begin, aware that she was gathering her thoughts as if uncertain where to start.

"Matters are not as they were," she said, finally. "Your grandfather's death has changed my understanding of what is important for us as a family. I want to go home, Rafi. I want us all to be together again."

As she spoke and the implication of her words became clearer, Rafi felt an immediate excitement at the idea of being back in As-Salt, quickly extinguished by anxiety at the thought of leaving Lauren.

"After A-Levels, you mean," he said.

"Not exactly. Let me explain..."

"But that's not what we agreed!"

"I know; however, if you let me tell you what has happened, I think you will understand." She paused. "It is complicated, Rafi. Feelings are complicated and I was not expecting this any more than you."

Some uncharacteristic desperation tugging at her voice dissolved the opposition in him. She wasn't lecturing him, she was trying to engage with him.

"What is it?" he asked. "What has happened?"

"Let me start at the beginning. I always believed I could affect the situation in the Middle East for the better through publishing academic research, particularly with regard to the Israeli-Palestinian impasse. And, also, my hopes were that the students, or at least some of them who attended my courses would leave better informed and correspondingly more tolerant as they went on to pursue their chosen careers. This has been my ambition and it has preoccupied me for the past twenty-five years. Yet now..."

A burst of ringing from the desk phone stopped her mid-sentence as she rose to answer it.

"Hello, yes it is...I see...Thursday at three...yes, that will be fine...thank you."

Rafi watched her make a note in her diary as she was speaking, her tone brisk and efficient, and her self-control surprised him. But when she sat down again, she stared through him for a moment before continuing, and when she did so, it was as if there had been no interruption and she was deeply involved once again in her own thoughts.

"Twenty-five years. Yes, that is a long time. But Kamal's...Jedi's death has changed my perspective. Or, rather, when we were burying him in the garden, I saw something for the first time, even though," she shook her head, "it's so obvious to me now."

She looked away, her forefinger crooked against her mouth and her eyes glassy. Rafi had seen her cry before, the last time only yesterday when hugging everyone at the farm goodbye. But, on those occasions, she had always been smiling as well as crying, her face flushed as well as tear-stained; not pale and drawn as now. And, in the silence, he felt wrapped round in a heavy curtain of sorrow, not understanding it, but oppressed by it.

"Are you okay, Mama?" he said softly. "Can I get you something...more water?"

At the sound of his voice, she straightened and looked back at him.

"No, I'm all right...thank you." She paused, her eyes closing and her shoulders rising and then falling as she took a deep breath and slowly released it.

"It was seeing Kamal being lowered into the ground beside Casper," she said, her eyes opening again and fastening on his. "It struck me then. All the frenzy of my academic life... all that lecturing, researching, writing, publishing, attending international seminars, all those televised discussion groups, all that travelling, all those postings elsewhere, all those twenty-five years of not being properly at home with all of you was my...," she paused and the flash-flood of her words subsided into a new quietness, "all of that, I realize now, was a defence against the loss of my baby...against my grief."

Rafi didn't know what to say. She was still looking at him, as if waiting for his response. But all he felt was confusion, as if everything he thought he knew about her wasn't true...wasn't true and never had been. Or, at least, that there was a deeper truth, a more significant truth that he couldn't quite get hold of.

"Side by side, like alpha and omega," she murmured, "the beginning and the end." He saw her shiver as a dark shadow chased the sunlight from her, but when she spoke again, her voice was firmer. "This separation is not good for us, Rafi. We are a family, we need to be together. We need to go home."

His skin began prickling in alarm. Surely she didn't mean now...right away. "You mean next year," he said, "after my exams?"

"No, sooner than that. I've been thinking and I..."

"But what about my A-levels and Utrecht?" he interrupted.

"Yes, that is what I have been thinking about

and I have found out that you could transfer to the Baccalaureate School in Amman and take the IB instead." He opened his mouth to protest, but she raised her hand. "Let me finish. Often universities consider IB students to have a wider...a more global understanding; whereas those with A-Levels have...what shall we say...a more specific focus. Given the course you have in mind, I think Utrecht might feel the IB to be an advantage."

Universities were where she worked. She knew more about these things than he did, and he nodded as if agreeing, despite the objections bubbling inside him.

"What is it, Rafi?"

"Nothing," he said. But she went on looking at him in the way she had since he was a boy, when she knew he was concealing something from her. She just waited patiently, her eyes steadily on his until the silence grew too heavy for his conscience and he felt compelled to confide in her.

"It's just I have friends here now and I would be sorry to lose them so suddenly."

She smiled. "Of course. It is never easy to leave behind people you care about. And you have become quite attached to Ida and Lauren, I think."

"When would we go?" He didn't want to talk about Lauren. "And what about your work?"

"Yes, I have been thinking about that as well. My contract here and the rental agreement on this house are both renewable from September. So, we would be free to leave at the end of July, when you break up, which fits well with the start of term at the Baccalaureate in early September. Also, I have an open invitation from my old department in Amman to return, if I want to. But I need to think about that more carefully. There may be other avenues for me to explore now...beyond university life, I mean."

She paused and looked away, her fingers gently tapping the ends of the arms of her chair. As he watched her, he saw her eyebrows lift and a faint smile lighten her face. Turning back to him, she caught his eyes on her.

"I still have annual leave due, which means I can be at home with you all over the summer holidays." She laughed and he heard the delight in it, saw it in her eyes, as she added: "And afterwards, of course! What do you think, Rafi? I'll have to come back briefly at the end of August to tie up the loose ends; but, effectively, it means our English adventure will be over quite soon."

The immediacy of her question confused him. He wanted to stay near Lauren. He didn't want to just to go away and never come back...never see her again. But maybe she could come and stay with them...October half-term wouldn't be too far away. He wanted her to see the farm...see his home, his family. Yet, if he asked her and she accepted, it would be an acknowledgement of something as yet unspoken between them. But what if she refused or was embarrassed, thinking of him as no more than a friend? What then?

Even so, the idea of being home again with Jasmin and Zak and Baba and Anoush and becoming once more a part of the whole daily turmoil of the farm filled him with a sense of ease he hadn't felt since Jedi's death. He felt full and empty all at the same time.

"Rafi?" His mother's voice brought his attention back to her.

"Sorry, Mama, I was just thinking..." He paused as another possibility popped into his head. "Yes, I think it's a good idea to all be together again; but I'm wondering, um...it might be better for me to finish the A-Level courses here that I've already started, rather than starting new ones for the IB. That would put me back a year. Do you see what I mean?"

"I think I may," his mother said, a hint of a smile playing at the corners of her mouth. "Go on."

"Well, supposing we do go home, perhaps it would be a good idea for me to come back here each term."

He stopped, waiting for his mother's reaction. His heart was beating as quickly as the thoughts were coming of what life on his own in Ashbrook might be like.

"A sort of preparation for being at Utrecht University," he added, already sensing the resistance in her.

"You are sensible and I trust you, Rafi...you know that. But, no, I don't think it would be a good idea. Remember what happened when I was away in London? I would be worrying about your safety all the time. Sixteen is too young to be living entirely on your own."

The seriousness and finality of her words drained the hope from him, yet he persisted in trying to convince her, nevertheless.

"I'll be seventeen by then and I needn't be on my own. I could rent a room with a family...with Henry Downes, for example."

Even as he said the name, his spirits rose again. Ida's father was so solid and his mother knew him and had good reason to trust him.

"I'm afraid the answer is still no. Your father would never agree to your being here on your own." As if seeing the rising frustration in him, her voice softened as she added, "Besides, going to university when you are nineteen, rather than eighteen, could be a good thing. Believe me, the stresses on first year students are considerable...living away from home for the first time and having to take full responsibility for looking after themselves. The more mature you are, the easier that will be."

Rafi stood up, angry at her control over him and wanting to be away from her.

"I'm already living away from home and I already look after myself when necessary," he insisted, his voice growing louder and more petulant. "And this...this changing to the baccalaureate would mean wasting a whole year!"

"You've been living with me, Rafi," she said calmly and her answer enraged him further.

"It's my life and I want to start making my own decisions about what's best for me!"

Without waiting for a reply, he spun round and stormed out.

38

The following morning, Rafi was woken early by another fine day brightening through the curtains. Turning away from the light, he lay pondering the day ahead, excited at the thought of seeing Lauren again and wondering whether things would be different between them since his night-time call to her after the funeral. He had felt so close to her then. Was it really only a week ago? It seemed much longer. Well, at least he wouldn't be stuck for things to say...so much had happened...was happening. He could tell her about going back to As-Salt and ask her if she'd like to come to stay at the farm. Would her parents allow that? Would his? Maybe he'd need to invite Ida, too.

He turned onto his back. You could leave home, get married and have sex at sixteen...in the UK, anyway. Mrs Hooper, their Maths teacher, had told them that. And that they could leave school, of course, and get a job...what else? He tried to remember. Get a passport, maybe...but he already had one. Anyway, that was enough. Why shouldn't he do his A-Levels here, if he wanted to? Surely he had a legal right to choose to do that, even if his mother and father disagreed.

He swung his legs out of bed and looked at the

small alarm clock on the table beside it: 6.51 am. For a moment he sat on the edge, legs apart and head bowed staring into the carpet between his feet. If he wasn't going to stand up for his own rights, what use would he be trying to stand up for anyone else's? He could talk to Henry today, ask him about renting a room. And, if that was no good, he'd find somewhere else. Mrs Hooper's voice came back to him, "...and you can also ride a moped at sixteen." He could have transport and a part-time job, live on his own, see Lauren as much as he wanted to and pass his exams, as well.

He shook his head and rolled back on to the pillow. It wasn't going to happen, was it? Baba and Mama would never agree to it. And if he disobeyed them, what then? No, he didn't want that. The impossibility of going against their wishes overwhelmed him. Being estranged from them...not being able to go home, see Jasmin and Zak, Anoush...having no money...no, it was too much.

Frustration burned inside him as he dressed. He wanted to go home, but he wanted to go on seeing Lauren, too. Why couldn't he do his A-Levels here? That would solve everything. His thoughts went round and round in circles and always ended up with his mother's refusal. 'Mm,' he grunted, sitting on the edge of the bed again and tying the laces on his trainers, 'Mama says no now, but maybe Baba will understand... and, if he thinks it's all right, then she might change her mind.'

One thing he was sure of. He didn't want to be around his mother until he had had a chance to speak to his father. So he slipped down to the kitchen for some breakfast before she was up, and once he heard her moving about overhead, he quickly left his plate and cup in the dish washer and ghosted back to his room.

A while later, he heard her study door close, which meant she was working and did not want to be disturbed. Leaving a note on the hall table, *Gone to Ida's – back by 6.00*, he went out just before midday and walked up the lane. The high hedgerows on either side were still full of the pretty flowers his mother had named and he tried to remember them: bluebells, primroses, pink something... but what were those purple ones...like pokers? Anyway, he didn't need to know their names to appreciate them; it was their colour and scent that mattered. Maybe he should pick some for Lauren...well, for Ida too. No, it would be too much, too awkward, he decided, walking on. His nose itched and he rubbed it with the back of his hand.

As he turned in at the gate, he heard Henry and Ida's voices coming from behind the sheds to the side of the house. He made his way along the path, until he reached two long poly-tunnels, their mouths open, but with no-one inside. Skirting these, he saw three figures gathered further down by the chicken coop and he paused. The two girls were standing side by side facing Henry, who was speaking and pointing at the run from the henhouse.

"How?" Rafi heard him say, followed by something from Ida he couldn't make out, then Henry again, "That's three-millimetre welded wire and I put it in deep, deeper than any fox'll dig."

While he was speaking, Rafi watched Lauren. They were all standing sideways to him and she was on the far side of Ida, but half-a-head taller with a dark headband holding her hair from her face. Panicking at the sight of her, he took a step back, intending to slip out of sight again; but, even as he did so, she looked round and saw him.

"Hi, Rafi!" she called with a wave.

He raised his hand in reply and walked over to them.

"Very sorry to hear about your grandfather," Henry said, stepping towards him and holding out his hand. As Rafi felt the warm grip of it and took in the sturdy figure with his rolled shirt-sleeves and tanned forearms, the similarity between Jedi and Henry dawned on him.

"Thank you. I think you and Jedi would have got on well." Rafi saw Henry's uncertainty. "He had a small farm; he grew fruit and vegetables."

"Ah, I see," Henry nodded. "I expect..."

"Didn't keep chickens, did he?" Ida interrupted.

"Hi, Ida," Rafi smiled. "Hi, Lauren," he said, catching her eye and looking quickly back at Ida. "No, he didn't. You see..." He stopped, scanning the chicken coop as the penny dropped.

There were no chickens in the run, no clucking from inside the henhouse, just a couple of feathers caught against the wire on the far side.

"What happened?"

"A fox got in," Ida said. She was standing just like her father, legs solidly apart, weight evenly balanced. Her hair seemed shades lighter than before, almost as pale as champagne now, and the sun had brought out the galaxy of freckles across her nose and cheeks. Yet unchanged, despite the fox, was the air of amused anticipation that glittered in her eyes.

He frowned, trying to subdue his reflexive grin. "Did it kill many of them?"

"All of them!" Henry said. "Took one with him and

bit the heads off all the rest."

"But it's so stupid," Lauren protested. "What's the point? Just killing for killing's sake."

"Defensive maybe, when the birds started panicking," Henry said to her. "But more likely, he was planning to come back...you know, now it's springtime and there are pups to feed." He turned away towards the house. "Anyhow, come on, there's not much more to do here that can't wait. Let's go and have some lunch and enjoy the sunshine."

While Ida and Henry went inside to prepare the food, Rafi and Lauren sat at the bench table on the terrace.

"So, how does it feel being back?" Lauren asked, breaking the silence between them.

"Fine," he said, wondering whether to tell her about his mother's decision, wondering whether it would matter to her. "How was your race yesterday?"

"I lost," she said. "I wasn't concentrating."

A fly landed on the table and hopped onto the back of Rafi's hand. He flicked it away and batted his hand after it.

Lauren was looking away from him into the garden and he watched her secretly, his head bowed. A small, gold crucifix lay flat against her skin in the V of her polo shirt, its chain disappearing into the soft green folds of the collar. It was the only jewellery he had ever seen her wear and he wondered about her choice of it.

Quietly studying her, he couldn't quite put his finger on what it was about her that appealed to him so strongly. She was tall and straight and small breasted; there was hardly any bulge beneath her shirt. But there was something about the openness of her face that drew him to her. She wore no make-up; she didn't need to. Her features were strong and her skin smooth, unblemished, glowing with good health, the whites of her eyes bright. Her whole nature seemed to be revealed there. A kind of unadorned truthfulness that was like beauty, he thought; he wanted to lean over and kiss her and taste it in her, find it in her and make it his own.

"You know when I rang you from Jordan," he started, unsure what he was going to say, but compelled to release the tension building inside him. Her eyes moved back to him and engaged.

"Yes," she said.

"You said you'd like to see our farm in As-Salt."

She smiled and nodded. "Yes, I would."

"The thing is my mother has decided..."

"Here you are, guys!" Ida's voice rang out as she emerged with a tray, which she slid between them on the table. "Same as usual," she said lifting two jugs clear, "cider and lemonade." She set them down, one golden, the other pearly, while they took off the tumblers. "And these should keep you going," she added, plonking down a wooden bowl of crisps. "Food won't be long."

"Go on," Lauren said, as Ida disappeared inside again.

She poured herself a glass of lemonade and offered him the jug.

"Thanks." He took it, but changed his mind and set it down, helping himself to cider instead. "Yes, she has decided she wants us to move back home and for our family all be together again."

Laura's hand hesitated in mid-air, halfway to the crisp bowl. "When? I mean what about college?"

He saw her concern. "When we go home for

the summer holidays. She wants me to change to a baccalaureate in Amman."

Lauren took a crisp and chewed it slowly.

"But I don't want to. I want to finish my A-Levels here. Go home in the holidays and come back again in term-time."

"Can you do that? Will your parents let you, I mean? And where would you stay?" Lauren laughed, in spite of herself. "Sorry...sorry. Too many questions. It's just such a surprise."

"That's all right." Rafi took another drink of cider, enjoying its sparkle and the curiously sweet dryness of it. He would tell her what had happened between him and his mother and see what she thought about it. He put his glass down and sat back. "We had an argument last night. My mother says it's too dangerous for me to live here on my own. She doesn't think I can look after myself, but I can."

"But where would you live? And wouldn't you mind being on your own?"

He lent forward and lowered his voice. "I was wondering whether maybe Henry would let me rent a room here."

Even as he said it, he knew he would never ask him, that it didn't feel right.

"I'm sure he'd want to help you, if he could," Lauren said. "Only, it might be a bit...well, a bit awkward."

"Yes." He nodded several times. He couldn't see what the awkwardness was exactly, but he felt it. "Yes, of course."

"I mean, I know Ida would want to help, too. It's just..." she frowned, glancing towards the house. "It's just people might get the wrong idea, you know; they might think you were Ida's boyfriend or something. It could put Henry in a difficult position."

Her saw her discomfort. Her face was flushed and her eyes were avoiding his, and it excited him...the word boyfriend had excited him.

"Could I stay in your house, then?" The words sprang out before he could stop them and he regretted it instantly as she jerked back as if slapped, her eyes fully on him now, the surprise in them softening into something more penetrating, so that he felt seen through and his own face burned.

"We don't have a spare room, Rafi. I wish we did."

She wasn't offended...she wasn't rejecting him. In fact, she was smiling, and the warmth of it kindled a glow in the pit of him, chasing away the fear from a moment ago. He wanted to find something to say to bring the unspoken between them out into the open, but everything he thought of sounded banal and inadequate. Before he could find the right words, Ida and Henry emerged from the house carrying trays of food and plates, causing him to lean back to make room.

After lunch, sitting round the table with mugs of tea, Rafi told them about his grandfather's funeral and his burial in the garden.

"Buried in your own land?" Henry said, glancing away down the valley. "Why not?" Looking back, he smiled. "We do it for our pets, don't we, Ides?"

"One or two!" Ida laughed and he roared.

"Rats, mice, gerbils, rabbits, frogs..."

"Trumps the tortoise," Lauren joined in, "and that magpie."

"I'd forgotten the magpie!" Henry shook his head at Rafi. "And Curly too, of course, Coil's predecessor."

"And Dizzy," Ida said.

"Yes, Dizzy," Lauren nodded.

"Never be another like her, will there, Ides? Sweet natured, she was."

The laughter and affection had turned wistful and Rafi felt lost, excluded. Who was Dizzy? He had no idea. They had all been a part of each other's lives forever and he didn't really belong here, did he?

"Dizzy was their beautiful dog," Lauren explained, as if sensing his discomfort, "just an out-and-out sweetheart."

"She was my mum's Collie-cross." Ida gave him a rueful smile, which exploded into a broad grin. "God knows what with! Demented Springer or something! Loved to carry huge sticks..."

"Logs, more like!" Henry joined in.

"Whole branches." Lauren held her arms out wide, having to twist not to knock into him. "Used to trip people up coming the other way."

They were all laughing and Rafi felt caught up and included in their warmth again. He didn't want to lose them. There had to be a way to persuade his father.

"Right, I'm going to take another look at the chicken run," Henry said, standing up.

"Can I help you?" Rafi offered.

"No, that's all right. Thank you for the offer, but I'll be doing more pondering than labouring. Got to think how to outfox a fox!" He laughed and held out his hand. "Good to see you, Rafi. Be sure to send your mother my regards, now."

As they watched him disappear from view beyond the polytunnels, the stillness of the afternoon seemed to wrap them in silence; and Rafi wondered if it was due to his being there and whether they would rather be on their own. He could say he'd promised to help his mother with something, or that his father would be calling and he needed to be there. Lies came so easily, it bothered him. Maybe just say that he had homework to do, which was true to some extent, although he could easily finish it after supper as already planned. He licked his lips, drew in his legs and was about to say something, when Lauren pre-empted him.

"Come on," she said, pushing her chair back, "let's clear up and then I'm off. Promised Mum I'd check on Dad."

Lauren washed, he dried and Ida put away. It didn't take long.

"I'll go, too," he told Ida afterwards, as Lauren slipped on her backpack. It looked so small and light, he wondered how she managed a night away with so little.

"Double Bio first thing," Ida grimaced, as she opened the door and stood back. "Meet you in the canteen at break?" Lauren nodded and gave her a hug."And you too, Rafi, if you want to," Ida added, looking at him expectantly.

He froze. Should he hug her, too? Lots of students seemed to be doing that with their friends.

"Come on," Lauren tapped his arm, "see if you can keep up with me."

"Thank you, Ida," he said. "And, yes, I will be there," he added over his shoulder, as he took off after Lauren who was already turning into the lane.

He couldn't catch up with her, but she waited for him outside the entrance to Windhover, walking slowly backwards as he came up to her.

"You're panting," she said, standing still.

He put his hands on his hips, the pink tip of his tongue showing as he tried to catch his breath. She was breathing normally, her face barely flushed.

"I know," he managed, "I'm not fit like you."

"You could be. You should come running with me."

"I'd never keep up."

"It's not racing, just building stamina."

"Okay." He wiped the sweat from his forehead with the back of his hand. "Maybe it would be a good idea."

"Great!" she laughed and checked her watch. "I've got to go, but we can talk more about it tomorrow, yeah?"

She turned away and he watched her break into a long, easy stride, gathering speed down the lane before disappearing round a bend at the bottom.

He stayed staring at the point where she had vanished as if she might magically reappear. The empty lane sparked a loneliness in him and he wanted her back. He would see her tomorrow, he told himself, and they were going to go running together, just the two of them...no Ida, even. But it seemed far too long to wait; and, as he made his way up the drive and into the house, he despaired of the long hours ahead, a mist of boredom already seeping into him.

"Taking up running, I hear," Ida said, when he found them at break the next day, her grin warm and teasing.

"Is this one free?" he asked three lads at the next table, pointing to an empty chair.

"Sure!"..."Help yourself, mate!" chorused the two facing him, and he pulled it across.

"Yes, it is true," he said, sitting down and feigning seriousness. "Lauren told me she needed some extra coaching and asked if I could help her to improve her times."

"Ha, ha!" Lauren whooped, giving his shoulder a push. "You wish!"

"Well, of course, she'll be seventeen soon," Ida's spurt of delighted laughter pierced the canteen cacophony like a peel of bells. "Bones getting heavier... you know, greater density, more to move around."

"Huh, some friend you are! Anyway," Lauren hooked her hair behind her ear, "the stronger my bones, the greater my strength, the faster I run!" She poked out her tongue at Ida, "So, there!"

'Such playful girls! They must like you, little brother.'

Jasmin's affectionate, mocking voice echoed inside Rafi the rest of that day and the next. And once he had arranged with Lauren that he would go to her house after college later in the week with his sports kit, a restless excitement possessed him in a way he had not known since Christmas Eve as a child.

39

Terry rolled over and squinted at the clock. 5.47 stood out from the darkness in vivid green digits. Throwing the duvet back, he stumbled out of bed, putting his hand down to steady himself.

Today was the day. Glancing at the half-filled backpack by the chair, he scrambled into his clothes and lifted the backpack onto the bed. Fetching the carrier bag with the wig from the wardrobe, he placed it carefully on top of the folded remainder of his disguise and gave it a little pat, before zipping the pack shut.

He knew that after a cloudy start the forecast was for a warm, sunny day. Even so, he shrugged on his tweed jacket over his shirt and jeans and patted the inside pocket to check his train tickets were there. They were. Then, turning to his bedside table, he opened the drawer and stood motionless for a moment staring at the small wooden box and the note beside it, which he took out, unfolding it: '*WHITE MOTHERS + WHITE FATHERS = WHITE CHILDREN!*' He nodded, pleased with the cut he'd made. Yes, it was better...more forceful without the 'immigrants go home' bit.

"Moment of truth," he whispered, pocketing it. Stretching out his hand again, he pushed up the lid of the box with his thumb. How innocent it looked, nestled in the cotton wool inside. Apparently, nothing more than scent in a little glass atomiser with a brass cap. He smiled, lifting it clear. There was no need for the box...speed would be everything. So light, so invisible, he thought, slipping it into his jacket pocket for the time being. And, as he did so, he caught sight of the orange cover of an ordnance survey map sticking out between magazines on the bottom shelf of the book case by the window. Going across, he bent down and freed it. "Oh, yes!" he whispered, taking it in. "Yes, yes, yes!"

Closing his bedroom door behind him with a resounding click, he made his way downstairs, whistling as he went, and left his backpack by the front door. Striding into the kitchen, he switched on the glass kettle. "Earl Grey, I think," he chortled, reaching for the tin. "Yes, indeed." This was a pivotal day in his life. He watched the ring of blue light and the first stirrings of the water as it began to bubble. Nothing would be the same again. This was the start of his new life, his new career...day one, effectively, of his political ascent to power. 'Saviour of Britain...', 'Another Churchill in the Making', he could already see the headlines.

Leaving his tea brewing, he started whistling again as he helped himself to a bowl of Cocoa Pops.

"Rule Britannia, for heaven's sake?"

He turned. "Good morning, mother."

"And up and dressed already? Whatever are you up to?"

Normally, her questioning and the sight of her in her dressing-gown and slippers would have made the hairs on the back of his neck bristle in revolt; this morning, however, her appearance in the kitchen for her six o'clock cup of tea was exactly what he had been counting on.

"Up to?" he beamed at her. "Up to? What I'm up to is taking the first step down the pathway to glory."

"Oh, yes? And what might that be?" The knowing suspicion in her tone and the pursing of her lips only delighted him all the more.

"What it most definitely is, mother, rather than what it might be, is my ten-thirty meeting in Truro with Steve Langton, leader of NAN, as you know. And that is why I am up bright and early because I have to catch the early bus into Totnes to catch the eight-fourteen train." He took out the blue ticket wallet, opened it and passed it to her. "Bus and train, yes, indeed!"

"I hope you're not up to one of your tricks," she said, handing it back to him. "You often are when you grin at me like that, same as when you were little."

"Moi?" Terry laughed, pointing at his own chest and pirouetting.

She gave a little gasp of irritation and went round him to the kettle. "Just don't let your Uncle Nathan down, that's all."

After she had taken her tea back up to bed, Terry put his mug and bowl in the sink and went for his pack.

"Going now, mother!" he called out, arm through one strap and struggling to find the other. "Mustn't miss the bus!"

Overcast and chilly outside, he walked briskly, his eyes darting about under the peak of his cap to see if he was being observed. But all was quiet and still, and the only movement he noticed was a grey cat slipping through the bars of a garden gate ahead of him.

Ignoring the turn for the shortcut to the road into

town, he passed the long rear gardens of a row of terraced council houses. He stopped beside the last-but-one of these and pushed back a damaged garden gate with no catch plate for the bolt. Stepping through, he drew it closed again behind him.

The garden was overgrown with brambles and nettles in amongst the long grass, and he followed the flattened trail of his own footsteps from the day before to the shed in the corner. End on to the house, with a flat bitumen roof, it too was derelict, its rotting window frame missing several panes of glass. Edging through the half-open doorway, he slipped off his backpack. Leaving it slumped on the floor, he lifted the door so it didn't drag where it had warped and tugged it closed.

For a moment he stood perfectly still, listening, waiting for his eyes to adjust to the gloom. He could hear nothing apart from the occasional rasp of his own breathing. The shed was musty, the stale smell of rot and decay pervasive. When he had come the day before, he had cleared a space near the window and rigged up a seat, with a plank set across a wooden beer crate at one end and the grass box off a mower at the other. He sat down and peered at his watch; it was almost 6.15.

"Two and a quarter hours!" he groaned, looking at the debris opposite him; a rotary mower twisted backwards on a hook, its blade missing, in between shelves on brackets loaded with pots of paint. He ran his eyes past them, over the rusting tins with paintbrush handles sprouting from them, plastic bottles of white spirit, a stained rag screwed up, a roll of garden wire, some desiccated seed packets and an opaque plastic container with no lid. Nothing at all to amuse himself with. And, in the other corner, all he could make out was a leaning jumble of long-handled gardening tools, including a spade, a fork with a bent tine, a hoe and a broom with half its bristles missing. Beside them stood a metal barbecue stand on a jagged piece of flattened cardboard.

A large spider scuttled close to his feet and he kicked out at it, sending it racing back under a toppled pile of fractured roof tiles to the side of him. He thought of the sandwich in his pack and moved to get up, then thought better of it. It was too soon. He'd have it at seven at the earliest. At eight, he could start to get ready. '*The book!*' He told himself, remembering. '*Read the book.*'

He got up, unzipped the front pocket of his pack and took out the paperback. Sitting down again, he angled the book to catch the light from the window over his shoulder. 'On Speaking Well' by Peggy Noonan. He liked the unadorned simplicity of the cover; the black print on white, the thin blue border and the banner in the same blue two-thirds of the way down carrying the subtitle, 'How to Give a Speech with Style, Substance and Clarity'. When he had asked the woman in the library for a book on rhetoric and public speaking, this was the one she had recommended. He didn't remember her name; but, whenever he went there, she always smiled at him and was helpful. It was one of the few places in town he felt welcome. She was tall, with a posh voice, and she wore colourful scarves. In fact, he had thought of acquiring one for himself and wearing it as a kind of cravat. Her style...her distinctiveness appealed to him and he had trusted her judgment.

As he opened the book, he felt a surge of excitement. This was his future. Oratory would be his passport. He would stand on the hustings, he would stand at the dispatch box in the House of Commons and he would change people's hearts and minds with his eloquence, yes, indeed! They would elect him and they would follow him and he would make Britain 'Great' once again. He began turning the initial pages looking for the start of the text, when a sudden rustling outside made him freeze. The rustling stopped and he closed his eyes, straining to hear more, but couldn't. And then he heard it again. It sounded closer. Standing up, he edged to the window and peered round. The noise came again and he saw a thrush foraging below him.

He had imagined the old man who lived in the house had seen him and was coming. He wasn't afraid of him. Old Jacob was in his nineties, a wartime refugee from Poland. But Terry was afraid of discovery and of having his alibi compromised. He blew out heavily as his panic began to subside. And when he sat down again, he held the book closed, thinking of Lauren and rehearsing the sequence of moves he was going to make before and after.

Less than a mile away, Lauren had woken while it was still dark. Emptiness, like the stasis between lightening and its shadow roll of thunder, had held her in a no-man's land of semi-consciousness, until the memory of her father's absence merged with the nausea of despair. For a while, she lay reliving the day of his going, thinking of her parents' half-empty bedroom next door and remembering seeing his suitcase in the hall and what he'd said to her as he'd hugged her, "I'll just be round the corner, any time you want me...Finn, too."

Everything felt wrong. The house felt wrong, like

an amputee with a limb missing. How could she bring him home again? She had no answers. Something fundamental had been taken from her and she couldn't get a grip on the enormity of it. Yet, who could she take it to? At the time, her mother had seemed cheery and unreachable. "It's just temporary," she had said, her smile like a shield, "while your father sorts himself out. We both need a bit of space, that's all...nothing to worry about." But she was worrying about it and something had changed in her since her talk with Shauna.

And Finn had hidden his feelings when she'd gone to his room to see how he was. She could see he had been crying, his eyes were moist and red around their rims; but he'd spoken in that defiant, self-important tone she knew so well...that he had used since he was little, whenever he was hurt and trying not to show it. "Ginnie says Dad's going through a mid-life crisis," he declared, "and that we're not to worry, because he'll soon come to his senses." Since then, Tom's treehouse had become his obsession. It was all he ever talked about and he spent as much time there as he possibly could.

Eventually, after she had opened the curtains and got back into bed, she lay watching the dark sky slowly lightening into a pearly blanket of cloud. She wished Ida was there to talk to about the muddle of it all. In the end, however, it was Rafi's voice deep inside her that brought her comfort, low and dreamy from the night garden by his grandfather's grave, "I wish you were here."

"And I wish you were here," she murmured.

Well, he soon would be here, she thought, as she dressed in her college clothes. They were going running together and she'd have time alone with him...time to try to sort things out. So much seemed to have happened between them and yet nothing had been said, not clearly, anyway. She needed to get things straight with him and stop this nagging uncertainty in her. She'd lost the race because she couldn't focus. This wasn't her, was it?

After breakfast, Finn left before her, saying he was meeting Tom early. She felt it was an excuse to avoid having to talk to her and she felt hurt and angry that instead of drawing them closer together, their father's leaving had put a wedge between them. Even her mother had delayed coming down, so that she had to call out goodbye to her up the stairs as she was leaving. Rounding the corner into North Street, she paused to look up at the windows where her father was, but the curtains were closed. '*Are you coming home again or are you and Mum really splitting up?*' She wanted to know. Walking on, she decided she'd call in on him on her way home and ask him straight out.

As she passed the familiar shops and cafes, all about her seemed increasingly unreal, as if she was moving through a film set, temporary and disconnected. She looked at the road curving away in front of her and nothing she had known or counted on seemed certain anymore.

Terry checked his watch again...8.07. Time to change. Taking the carrier bag from the backpack, he drew out the wig on top and then the clothes and sandals underneath. Taking off his jacket and shirt, he folded them onto the seat and slipped on the long-sleeved, dusty pink T-shirt. Looking at the striped cheesecloth skirt, he went to undo his belt and then changed his mind. '*Girls wear jeans too, don't they?*' He looked down at the legs of his own. '*No, these'll do...save a lot of time afterwards*' He stuffed the skirt back in the plastic bag and grabbed the sandals. '*You, too!*' he grinned, shoving them in. '*Everyone wears trainers with jeans. Yes, indeed. And this jacket,*' he unfolded it, '*will be fine.*' He pulled it on and wriggled uncomfortably, jabbing his elbows up in front of him against the tightness of it under his arms. Bottle green, in fake leather with a diagonal zip, it barely reached his belt, but it had been the only top he could find in the charity shop that fitted him, more or less.

He turned for the wig and put it on, carefully adjusting it with his fingertips. "Right, moment of truth," he said aloud, moving to the bicycle and angling its mirror up. Dark brown, the hair fell either side of his face, shading his eyes. He stroked it down with his palms to where it curled on his shoulders. "Look at you!" he breathed.

Going to the side pocket of his backpack, he pulled out the coral necklace and a pair of dark glasses with black frames. He bent his head and passed the necklace clear of the wig, straightening it over the tee. Moving back to the bicycle, he slid on the sunglasses. "Perfect!" he muttered. "Thank you, Mother." He'd found them in the junk drawer of her dressing table. She wasn't going to miss them.

He looked at his watch. Almost 8.20...time to go. He had one last look round and went to the door, lifting it and pushing it back. Halfway to the gate, he wheeled round with a grunt of exasperation and went back. '*How could I forget you?*' he muttered, grabbing the tweed jacket and fumbling for the atomiser. His fingers closing on it, he pushed it quickly into his pocket and grabbed the map that was poking out, as well.

"Coming," he whispered, "ready or not."

Three minutes later, walking down North Street towards the town, he turned right on a path crossing the stream that ran alongside the road and stepped off it into the shadows of a private gateway with trees. Virtually invisible, from here he could see the paths from town on either side, as well as the entrance to the cut-through used by dog-walkers and college students which was hidden between the hedgerow and old stone wall, about ten yards down on the other side of the road.

Without prior knowledge, he wouldn't have known it was there at all. The narrow entry to a flight of steps was inset and to the naked eye all he could see was the continuous flow of hedge and stone. But, once up the steps and through the kissing-gate at the top, he knew only too well that you emerged onto a grassy hillside and followed a steeply rising track across it to a wood at the top.

A dark knot of figures to his right came into view round the bend from town and Terry lowered the sunglasses along his nose to see them better. These were a group of lads he recognized from previous surveillance, Mark Ingle and some of his mates. He watched them growing larger, coming closer, one or two blazers already off, their chatter and laughter more distinct. "You too, sheep-shagger!" one with a blond mohican shouted, pushing another. But the rest of what they were saying was lost, as suddenly they darted across the road and disappeared, one behind the other, into the hedge.

Terry glanced down. 8.33. His hands felt sweaty and he rubbed the palms against his jeans. Should he get into position now or stick with his plan? 8.35 – 8.40.

Whenever she'd walked in and not gone with her dad in the car, she'd never been later than 8.40. *'No, wait till you see her and then go. The less time you're there the better. Oh, shit!'*

A woman in a coat with a walking stick and a small, scruffy dog at her heels appeared from the other direction, made her way to the gap and turned in. Glancing up the road again, he saw Lauren coming, already off the bend and walking quickly. He started to run and checked himself. *'You're a woman; walk like a woman...shorter steps.'* Holding the map in his left hand and the atomiser in the jacket's slant pocket in the right next to the all-important note, he crossed the bridge over the stream and then the road. Two girls and a boy passed him from behind, running in the road, before ducking through the opening ahead.

Glancing up, he saw Lauren crossing the road. Two more yards and he was there. He hurried up the steps, pushed through the kissing gate and started up the track. Further along, ahead of him, the last three through were already almost up to the woman and her dog, while away to the left, he could see a herd of cows grazing on the slopes below. After a few paces in, he paused. Opening the ordnance survey map, he folded it back on itself so that he could hold it one-handed. Then he took hold of the atomiser, flicking the lid off it with his thumb.

He stood, head bent as if studying the map, but with a view of the gate through the tumble of hair. And then there she was coming through, striding quickly towards him. He looked up, raising the map slightly as a gesture and smiling. "Excuse me," he said, using the voice he'd been practising...softer, higher up in his throat than his own. She was almost up to him now and slowing. "I seem to be a bit lost."

Reaching him, she stopped. She was taller than him and, as he turned the map towards her, she lowered her head to look at it. In a split second, his hand cleared his pocket and he was spraying the acid directly into her eyes. "He won't want you now, will he?" he hissed. "Dear me, no!"

For a moment, there was silence, but, as he dropped the note and sprang away for the gate, her scream sliced into the back of his head and ricocheted off the hillside. A man in a running vest and shorts coming towards him paused, mouth open. "Emergency!" Terry gasped, running past him. "Got to get help!" Out by the road again, he kept running, his face burning, his chest bursting.

40

'Stop running, People are looking. Just walk...fast. Don't look at anyone. Yes, yes, Skylark Lane, turn up here...less people...much better.'

The lane was narrow and empty, a bend soon carrying him out of sight of the main road. Terry relaxed to a saunter, shrugged the backpack into a more comfortable position and straightened his wig. His head was sweating and he longed to pull it off. '*Not till the train*,' he told himself, '*toilet transformation!*' A triumphant exhilaration swept through him and he laughed out loud. He'd done it! Right into her eyes! He couldn't wait to see Stephen and Tony's faces. They'd know who they were dealing with now.

"Lovely morning." A female voice startled him, and he recognized it, even as he looked up and saw the woman from the library in a large straw hat. She was closing the front door of a small terraced cottage, a brilliant turquoise and scarlet scarf frothing around her throat.

'She's looking at you...don't stop, keep walking.'

"Yes..." hearing his own voice, he coughed and changed register, "yes, yes, it is, isn't it?"

He quickened his pace again and didn't slow down

until he had turned out of the end of the lane and reached the bus stop in the town centre. Several people were waiting there and he joined the queue, keeping his head down, praying the bus would come quickly. As he waited, he heard the wail of a siren growing louder. He didn't dare look up, terrified the police already had his description and were coming. It got louder and louder and then, gradually, he realized its note seemed to have changed, its urgency disappearing elsewhere.

He closed his eyes and blew out his breath. '*Not police...ambulance...must be. Yes, yes, ambulance...for sure.*'

Later, sitting in the train, staring out of the window in his own clothes, Lauren's scream sliced through the numbness encasing him, its pure explosion of pain a horror in his own head, and he was glad for the speed of the ambulance. He wanted her pain taken away. He didn't want her agonised shrieking inside him.

'*You did the right thing. You did it for our Queen and country, and people...the right people...will be proud of you. Yes, indeed!*'

41

"We are going to begin this morning by looking at the narrative structure of The Great Gatsby and the role of Nick Carraway. This is a short novel, elegantly composed in nine chapters. if you turn to the first page, you will see..."

Rafi picked up the Penguin paperback, glancing again at the glass-panelled door as he did so, for although he enjoyed Fiona McLaren's literature classes, with her crisp Scottish accent and the clear way she presented the texts they were studying, he was finding it hard to concentrate. Lauren's desk, slightly to the right in front of him, was empty. She was never late and he wondered if she might be ill; because, if she was, they wouldn't be able to go running.

"Now, Luke," Mrs McLaren said, moving in front of her desk, her movements as neat and precise as her words, "I will ask you to read the opening paragraph as written, in the first person." Rafi was relieved when she looked past him. "And then, Richie, please read it again using the third person, so that we can take note of..."

Even as she was speaking, however, he noticed a shadow outside the door a second before it opened and Jan Rawlings walked in with Ida close behind her. The two teachers turned aside, their heads close together, and he couldn't hear what they were saying. But he was more interested in Ida, who was scanning the class, her face taut and colourless. As her eyes found his, the alarm in them frightened him.

"Rafi," Mrs McLaren said, her voice raised towards him, "you are excused class this morning. Please go with Ms Rawlings and she will explain."

"We'll go to the Art Room," Jan said once they were outside and she set off down the corridor.

"Is it Lauren?" he asked Ida quickly, as they took off after her.

"Yes, she..." She broke off, her voice hoarse, pausing to hold the swing door for him. "I'll tell you in a minute."

They hurried on in silence, a growing dread gnawing at him. Had she had an accident? Had she been knocked down? A car? Was she in hospital? Was she dead? Or, maybe, it was her parents, her dad... maybe, he'd tried to kill himself.

By the time they had crossed the courtyard and Jan was opening to the door to the Art Room, Rafi was both impatient for answers and afraid of what they would be, the fear knotted inside him.

"Here," Jan said, pulling out chairs at the nearest table, "let's sit down."

Rafi closed the door. The brightness of the room, with all the colourful paintings displayed on the primrose walls, and the familiar faintly acrid, but not unpleasant, smell of paints brought a momentary easing of his anxiety. This was a safe place, a warm place and he looked along the shelves for the maquette of the runner Lauren had showed him, but he couldn't see it.

"Right," Jan said, as he sat down, "this is about

Lauren, Rafi. She was attacked on her way into college this morning and she's in Wonford Hospital." Her sombre tone, so at odds with her orange t-shirt and apple green dungarees, stilled him as if he had been slapped.

"Is she all right? I mean..."

"No, she isn't all right!" Ida snapped, and he felt the stupidity of his question.

"Listen," Jan said, pushing back her chair and standing up, "I'm going to let Ida tell you what's happened while I go to see Mr Dalby again. But wait..." She walked across to the sink, filled two plastic beakers with water and brought them back. "Here...we're all in shock, so have a drink, catch your breath and remember," she put her hand on Ida's shoulder, "Lauren *will* be all right." She stressed the 'will'. "Whatever happens, we'll be here for her."

The door closed and Rafi waited as Ida drained the beaker and sat staring at it.

"Tell me," he said quietly. "What has happened?"

"Okay," she said, looking up at him, and paused. Her eyes were as green as ever, but all the freckles across her nose and cheeks had faded and she looked haunted. "I don't know where to begin...it's awful, Rafi." She paused again, shaking her head.

"How did you find out?" he asked evenly, hiding his impatience, and hoping a factual question might help her.

"It was as I was turning into college. Lucy Foley and her brother were in front of me and I heard them saying something about Lauren having been attacked and I asked them what they'd seen. Apparently, they were going across the Terrace when it happened."

"What happened? You said she was attacked."

"They said they were ahead of Lauren walking up the hill and heard her scream..." He heard the quaver in her voice as she stopped and took a swallow of water from the beaker before going on. "So, they... er...they turned round and ran back, because she kept on screaming and there was a man there, a runner, and they thought he'd attacked her, but then they saw a woman running away back to the kissing gate...you know, out to the road."

A woman? It didn't make any sense. "Why was she screaming?" he asked.

"Well, they were saying something about her eyes and that's when Jess rang me. She was at the hospital... Lauren's dad, too, she said. But, at first, I couldn't hear what she was telling me because she was crying...well, no, sobbing and kept breaking off."

"What about Lauren? What about her eyes?" But he already knew the answer, already felt the sickening realization of it in the pit of him. "Was it acid?"

"Yes, I think so. They said the man was pouring water from his flask into her eyes and he told them to do the same from their water bottles; but they said she wouldn't keep still and was going crazy."

"Why didn't they ring for an ambulance? They should have..."

"No, the man did. They said he'd been told to keep running water on the burns particularly the eyes."

"How can they do that in the middle of nowhere?" Rafi crashed his fist down on the table.

"But they did." Ida reached out and touched his hand. "They managed to get her to the stream and they kept cupping water over her face till the paramedics got there."

"And what about the woman who ran away?"

Ida shook her head at him. "I'm sorry I don't know any more."

"But what about Jess...what did she say?"

"Only about the acid and that Lauren had been taken away and they were just waiting to find out more."

While she was speaking, Rafi saw the door open, as Jan came back into the room and came across to them.

"Listen, my next class will be here soon..."

"Yes, of course." Rafi went to stand up, but Jan put out her hand.

"Wait a moment. Mr Dalby had already had a call from Mrs Jackman, and when I suggested you both might need some time out, he agreed. So, you're free to go home, if you want to. But that's up to you. It's your choice."

Ida nodded, taking out her phone. "I'm going to call Dad. I just want to go to the hospital and be there."

"Right. And what about you, Rafi?"

He was looking down at the paint stains seeping like birthmarks through the grain of the wood.

"Acid burns," he said. "She would have been in agony." His eyes and jaw were tight with anger. He looked up at Jan. "Yes, thank you, I'll go, too. I want to find this woman."

"Okay, but don't do anything rash," Jan said and added, as they rose to go, "And you know you're both welcome here anytime, don't you...when I'm not teaching, that is...if you want to talk or just be somewhere quiet?"

Outside in the courtyard, Ida stopped and turned to him. "Do you want to come with us? Dad said he wouldn't be long."

He did and he didn't. He wanted to be near Lauren, but they might not let him see her. Besides, Ida was like part of the family, but Lauren's parents might not want him there.

"Thank you, but I think I will go home first." He wanted some time alone and to speak to his mother, if she was free. Only then he felt guilty, as if he should go out of loyalty. "Actually, I'm not sure what to do," he said.

"I know," Ida nodded, as they made their way through the college and out into the sunshine. "It doesn't seem real, does it? I feel like I'm having a nightmare... but I'm not, am I?"

They walked on in silence as far as the road, where he stood facing her on the pavement, unsure whether to wait with her till her father came or simply to go.

"Please will you call me when you have some news?"

"Yes, sure...of course I will," Ida said, taking half-a-step forward and wrapping her arms round him in a hug so fierce and so prolonged he didn't know how to respond. He put his arms loosely round her expecting her to pull away again, but she didn't and he felt embarrassed by the press of her body against him. Yet, the longer it went on, the more comforting it became.

"We're going to take care of her, Rafi." Ida's voice was low and the warmth of her breath tickled his ear. "She's going to be all right."

Part Three

Autumn 2019

42

Terry enjoyed following the narrow road's twists and turns through the Glynn Valley on his daily drive home from Truro. Leaving the fast, dual-carriageway A30 at the Bodmin turn-off, he was now caught up in early evening traffic on the single-lane A38 towards Liskeard. For the next three or four miles, although the speed limit was 50mph, he knew there would be the usual 40mph procession with a long tailback of exasperated commuters, due to there being a lorry or elderly driver in the lead. But he didn't mind going slowly. It gave him time to take in the countryside, the sloping fields and streams, the rising and falling tides of forest. It also gave him time to reflect.

As the queue approached the bend by the Halfway Inn, an SUV towing a caravan came into view at the front glinting in the early evening sun. The pub looked inviting with people sitting outside by the stream, chatting and relaxing, and he thought of turning off for a pint and letting the traffic thin out. But he decided against it; his mother would have supper waiting and he was hungry. Instead, he slid his window further down to catch the cool of the breeze, turned up the volume and began to hum along with the CD. As the music built to a stirring crescendo, before breaking like a tidal wave into its famous refrain, he joined in with all the gusto he usually reserved for the last night of the Proms on TV: '*Land of hope and glory...Mother of the free...God who made thee mighty...Make thee mightier yet.*'

He delighted in the soaring of his own fruity tenor and broke off laughing. "Yes! Yes, indeed!" he shouted. "Elgar! Solti! I salute you! Magnificent! Absolutely magnificent!" These were men that understood. These were men he'd like to have dinner w... Flaring red lights were coming straight at him. Pushing stiff-armed against the steering-wheel, he stamped down on the brake pedal, screeching to a halt inches from the rear bumper of the car in front. Brushing the sweat from his forehead with the back of his hand, he sat panting and deepening his breath to calm himself, until gradually the cars ahead started moving forward again and he saw the SUV with the caravan disappearing down a side road to the right.

The line of traffic picked up speed up the hill to Doublebois and then accelerated downhill from the roundabout soon afterwards, freed into dual-carriageway again towards Liskeard and Plymouth. He stayed in the slow lane as other cars raced past and started the CD again. He was in no hurry. He liked being a driver; it was a new experience. And he liked the quirky, little Fiat 500 his uncle had given him. "Della's gone for a Toyota Hybrid...a Yaris," Nathan had said. "And we...no, to be accurate it was her suggestion...she thought a car would make life easier for you with all the travelling you're doing now, back and forth. Mileage is low for the year and it runs well. Should last you for a while yet, if you look after it."

Well, he would look after it...he was looking after it. The creamy facia and steering-wheel pleased him; it had so much more charm than all those black interiors in other cars. In fact, the whole car pleased him with its playful character, as if it was having fun compared to most of the dull, look-alike models he saw everywhere... as if, with its impish profile, white paintwork and wine-coloured roll-back hood, it was cocking a snoop at German and Japanese engineering. "Your Noddy car," as his mother called it. But he didn't care. Yes, it was a pity it wasn't British, but he'd just have to wait till he could afford a Morgan.

His uncle's generosity had taken him by surprise and, as he drove on, he thought about it. The truth was Nathan had been impressed by the success of several NAN candidates in the local council elections in May, including Exeter, as well as South Somerset and Harlow in Essex. Five scattered NAN councillors nationally might seem trivial and hardly worth talking about, but it was a breakthrough and the Network's first electoral success, and they could and would build on that. "Oh, yes!" he exclaimed, nodding to himself. That was the point of a network; it was grassroots and growth came from the bottom up.

Again the music swelled, catching his attention, even though he was already singing along with it, without realizing it. '*Not that false joy that dreams content... With what our sires have won... The blood a hero sire hath spent... Still nerves a hero son.*' He grinned. Yes, yes, he was a 'hero son' all right. He had squirted the acid in her face. He had dropped the note. And, after Steve Langton's condemnation of 'this extremist and undemocratic political act' during his televised meeting at the Guildhall in Truro, it was he, Terry Curnow, who had had the responsibility of confirming his leader's declaration to journalists from The Western Morning News, The Cornish Times and BBC's Spotlight South West. And he had particularly enjoyed reading Tony Gardner's follow-up, humble-pie text: *Exceptional coverage I was wrong well done.*

"Yes, indeed!" Terry muttered, slowing past the speed camera into Landrake and checking his watch...6.20, should be home by 7.00. Indeed, it was as a result of his initiatives that membership numbers had grown ever since, rising steadily all through the summer. He'd known how popular pub quizzes were and he'd also known how selective information could be imparted through the questions and their answers. He'd had to be careful, of course, to disguise NAN's agenda and he'd enjoyed the challenge. For example, when he'd asked a question like, *How many more people moved to the UK than left in the year ending June 2018: a) 25,500 b) 137,000 c) 273,000? Answer: c) 273,000*, he'd sandwiched it between two seemingly innocuous ones: *What is the first name of Prince William's youngest son?* and *What is the UK's most popular pub name?* But even these apparently innocent ones were about traditional British institutions, guiding the quizzers' thoughts in that direction.

And the 'Win a Fish & Chip Supper for 4' quizzes he had organized on the beaches in St Ives, Perranporth, Newquay, Polzeath and Bude, as well as one on the Hoe in Plymouth, had been hugely popular. They had set up near the beach cafés, flying NAN's red-and-blue flags on poles to show people where to go, and the holidaymakers had turned up in their sun-creamed hundreds; so much so that he'd had to organize two sessions, one in the morning and one in the afternoon, in order not to disappoint them. And, better still, the people who came had been happy to pay the pound-a-head entry fee, which meant that, after the fish and chips were paid for, NAN had made almost £700 profit and almost twice as much again in follow-up membership fees.

At the time, he had felt elated at this success. But, soon afterwards, dwarfing that achievement into insignificance were not only the cheque he had received for £25,000 from an anonymous donor, but also a further staggering £70,000 in donations deposited with his Uncle Nathan. "Your Steve Langton is attracting the attention of some important people down this way," his uncle had said. "People who want to see a return to traditional values."

"You have a talent for this," Steve Langton had said when he'd rung him to report back. "Your questions are cunning..." He'd paused, and Terry could still hear the dry rasp of approval that followed. "And profitable!"

As he approached the Saltash tunnel, which would feed him onto the Tamar Bridge, Terry turned on his headlights and turned off the CD. He could concentrate better without the music and he liked to take in the view of the river on either side of the bridge. The traffic crawled through the tunnel and it was just as heavy coming the other way. Going home time all round, he thought, as the white van in front of him came to a complete stop. "Isambard Kingdom Brunel," he said aloud, looking across at the double-helix railway bridge running alongside them. He repeated the name. He admired the man, an English engineer of worldwide renown, and he liked the feel of the words in his mouth.

Once he had passed through the toll booths, he put his foot down and stayed in the fast lane virtually all the way to the Ashbrook turn-off, feeling increasingly irritated by the stop-start, bottleneck effect of too much traffic. Yet, by the time he turned off into Westabrook Close, his good humour was bubbling inside him again. What a difference a few months had made! No more dealing in t-shirts, no more trying to stop John and Lawrence from killing each other and no more lectures from his mother or Uncle Nathan. What's more, he had struck a blow for the protection of the nation and shown he was a man of action as well as words. As a result, he had Steve Langton's full confidence and he was on his way.

"Yes, indeed!" he announced to the herbaceous border, going up the path. "And this is just the beginning!"

Singing, '*God who made thee mighty...Make thee mightier yet,*' he was on the point of putting his key in the lock when the door opened, releasing a fragrant waft of fried meat and onions, and his mother was standing there.

"Oh, Terry," she said, staring at him, seemingly lost for words.

"Well, let me in, Mother, and then you can tell me what the matter is."

Clearly something was. He knew that haggard look too well, her face pale but for the burnt hollows around her eyes. Guilt and anger surged through him at the accusation, disappointment, and despair he could see there, just as it had as a boy when he had done something wrong.

"The detectives are here again," she said, stepping to the side and pulling the door further back. "They're in the sitting room...they've been waiting for you."

"No need to get upset," he blustered, brushing past her. "Didn't see their car. Probably here about John, like last time."

Fighting down the panic squalling inside him, he marched through the open door into the sitting-room. The two detectives were standing side by side, their backs to the fireplace, and he recognized them at once; the young man with his razored sandy hair and the sharp-faced woman still in her black leather bomber jacket.

She walked towards him, holding up her warrant card. ""DS Fran Bannerman, CID, Charles Cross Police Station, Plymouth; and this is DC Jason Kincaid."

"I know who you are," Terry said, planting his feet astride and folding his arms, "you've been here before. How can I help you?" He feigned a smile. "John's not in trouble again, I hope."

"No, John Knight is out of harm's way for some years to come. And we are assisting in the investigation into an incident in Ashbrook on Wednesday 8th May, in which a young woman was assaulted." Her small, dark eyes bored into his without blinking. "Where were you on that Wednesday morning between eight and nine o'clock?"

"8th May? 8th May? Let me see." Stay calm, he told himself. Act as if you're trying to remember. "Ah, yes, of course. Wednesday the 8th was the day of the National Accord Network meeting in Truro, where its leader, Steve Langton, gave a speech. I was with him and his deputy, Tony Gardner, all day...all day, that is, from just before ten-thirty onwards."

The more he spoke, the calmer he felt.

"How did you travel there?" DC Kincaid asked, coming alongside DS Bannerman.

"Let me see," he said, looking away briefly and frowning "Yes, that's right, I took the early bus from here to Totnes and then caught the 8.14, I think it was, from there...train, I mean...gets into Truro just after 10.00."

"Is there anyone who can confirm that?" the young detective persisted, his tone neutral, but not his smirk.

"Yes, indeed." Terry turned and beckoned his mother forward. "My mother."

"Mrs Curnow?" DC Bannerman prompted, as she hesitated.

"I remember about that poor girl being attacked." She shook her head. "Terrible thing to do. I couldn't believe it...not here in Ashbrook."

'*No, it wasn't, you stupid, stupid woman!*' Terry wanted to scream at her, blood rushing into his face. He saw Kincaid's smirk widen.

"Yes, it was," Bannerman was saying. "But I'm wondering if you can confirm what time Terry left the house that day."

"Surely, you don't think...you can't do! Not Terry!" She looked across at her son, her face tight with apprehension. Her frown deepened and then cleared. "No," she said, facing the detectives again. "I remember now, 'course I do. My alarm's set for 6.00 and I always go straight down and make myself a cup of tea... helps get me started." She paused, glancing at Terry and shaking her head. "Sorry," she said, turning back to Bannerman, "I'm smiling because as I came down the stairs I could hear Terry in the kitchen whistling Rule Britannia. Not something I was expecting, I can tell you. He's not exactly an early bird," she gave a little laugh, "nor a cheerful one...not first thing, anyway."

"What time did he leave the house that morning, Mrs Curnow?" Kincaid demanded, and Terry saw her bridle at his brusqueness.

"I had just taken my tea back upstairs, Detective Constable, when he called out goodbye and I heard the front door click shut. So, that must have been about ten past six."

"Just as I told you!" Terry burst out. "And now, if you're finished, I'd like to have my supper in peace."

"We're not finished," Kincaid snapped back. "We would like you to explain the CCTV footage we have of you arriving at Truro station at..." he took out a notebook, "at 12.02 pm midday." He looked up, a gleam of triumph in his cold blue eyes, as bile jumped burning into the back of Terry's throat.

"No! No! It isn't me! I have witnesses!" he spluttered, turning to his mother. "Mistaken identity is what it is, yes, indeed, you'll see. Stephen Lang will..."

"Terence Edward Curnow," DS Bannerman interrupted, moving closer, "you are under arrest on suspicion that, on Wednesday 8th May 2019 at 8.40 am, you assaulted Ms Lauren Jackman on Terrace Walk, Ashbrook, by spraying a corrosive substance into her face. You do not have to say anything, but..."

"What's this? What's this?" Terry erupted, as DC Kincaid came towards him and he heard his mother's gasp behind him. The DC's words became a disorienting, rumbling wave bowling him over and submerging him, so that he no longer knew which way was up. He couldn't clear his mind...couldn't think straight.

"No, no, you can't do this!" he protested, as DC Kincaid gripped his elbow.

"You will accompany us to Charles Street Police Station," DS Bannerman was saying, "where free legal advice will be offered to you."

As they escorted him from the room, his mother blocked their way, reaching out and holding his arm. "You didn't, Terry, did you? Tell me you didn't." The stunned pleading in her eyes sprung tears in his own.

"My uncle's a solicitor!" he shouted, blinking furiously as they led him around his mother and out to their car.

43

The evenings were starting to draw in and the curtains in his mother's study were already closed when Rafi tapped on her door and went in. The heavy, brandy-coloured velvet of them reaching to the floor retained some cheer against the empty surfaces of the book shelves and mantelpiece, with their dust-marked air of abandonment.

"Can I help you, Mama?" he asked, gesturing to the packing cases.

Maryam was folding one of Aunt Anoush's pots in bubble-wrap. "Just a moment, while I finish this." She tore off a length of sellotape from the dispenser and smoothed it down along the join; then, revolving the package in her hands and seemingly satisfied, she settled it carefully into place in the nearer of the two wooden shipping crates.

"Right," she said, arching her back and looking around her. "No, I'm nearly there, thank you." She smiled at him. "Two more of Amti's pots," she pointed to the coffee table, "and that's it. Well, in here, anyway."

As she moved to cut more bubble-wrap from the roll across the armchair, he stayed where he was, watching her. He wanted to talk to her, but he didn't know where to begin or even if he should, or whether these were now exactly the sort of worries he was going to have to sort out for himself. He didn't want her to think he wouldn't be able to cope without her.

"What is it, Rafi?" she asked, glancing up.

"No, it's okay, I don't want to interrupt you."

"You're not," she said, with a final snip. "Or, at least, I'd like a break."

Laying the scissors and piece of wrap on the desk, she lifted the roll off the armchair onto the floor and sat down.

"Now," she pointed to the other chair, "come and tell me what's on your mind."

She was leaning back, her hands loosely linked in her lap, watching him attentively.

"It's nothing, really," he started, sitting down. "It's just..." He paused, his stomach suddenly tight at the thought of her going.

"Rafi?"

"Sorry. I was..." He stopped again, looking down at his feet and shaking his head. "It's going to be strange without you here," he said at last, looking up at her. He wanted to say, "I'll miss you"; but something got in the way.

"Yes leaving without you is going to be strange for me, too," she said. "I'm going to miss not having you with me."

It was enough that she had spoken the words for him. Their warmth released the grip of the abyss in him, and he stayed where he was, recovering his thoughts, the silence between them more a communion than a separation.

"There is something else I want to ask you," he said,

after a while. His mother didn't respond and he looked up to find her gazing steadily at him.

"It's about Lauren."

Maryam nodded.

"She rang me earlier. She wants me to go round there tomorrow. And...um..." He took a deep breath and blew it out slowly. "Well, I haven't seen her since the hospital before I went away and her face was covered in bandages then." He paused again and Maryam waited, leaving space for him to go on.

"I don't know what it's going to be like, Mama... what she is going to be like."

For a moment, her eyes searched his face and he felt both the weight and the tenderness of them. "Of course, you are anxious, Rafi," she said. "You know Lauren is blind now, but you do not know how she will look or how she is coping with having her whole life turned upside down."

"Yes, that is it," he nodded. "But also, I don't know what I am going to say to her. I mean, I want to help her, but what I can do?"

His words hung in the air as once again his mother sat quietly regarding him, apparently lost in her own thoughts.

"I was eleven when my father died," she said at last, "and fourteen when my mother married again. That was a very difficult time for me, but I found a strength I did not know I had and so will you." She paused and then went on again, stretching out her arm in a sweeping gesture. "Look at this room. See how bare and bleak it is..."

"Yes, but..." he interrupted, feeling puzzled. This wasn't what he had asked.

"Be patient, Rafi. Listen to me. Even with all its ornaments and rugs and books gone, this room is still solidly what it is; and new decorations and furnishings will soon restore its warmth and welcome."

"Yes," he saw the analogy and it didn't help. "But I am not a lamp shade...I'm not a bookcase," he objected. "What can I do to help her?"

"You do not have to do anything," she said. "You only have to be there for her." And, as if sensing his impatience, she went on, "Lauren will be as anxious as you are, wondering how you will feel about her when you see her and wondering how she will know when she can't see you..."

"Being there," Rafi broke in. "I don't understand what that means."

His mother hesitated and glanced away, as a muffled squall of wind and rain rapped at the window and rattled its frame.

"When Jedi died," she said, looking back at him, "what helped you the most, when you were feeling at your worst?"

He didn't answer at once, letting his eyes drift away to Anoush's pots on the table.

"Being home at the farm again," he said finally.

"And what was it that made things better?"

"Being near Jedi...having all of you there...you know, Jasmin, Zak, you and Papa, Amti." '*Most of all,*' he wanted to add, '*talking to Lauren by Jedi's grave in the dark,*' but the memory of that felt too raw to share.

Maryam was waiting, leaving him space to say more if he wanted to. And when he didn't, she said, "So, can you remember what it was we did that comforted you?"

He got it. Having them all there, without having

to explain himself or say anything, had made him feel safer...less lost. "Just having you there was enough," he nodded. "You didn't have to *do* anything. That's it, isn't it? That's what you mean."

"Yes," she smiled. "Lauren has asked you to go to see her. I don't think she expects anything from you. Imagine if this terrible thing had happened to you, would you want your friends...I mean your close friends, like Yousef and Amal...would you want them to come to see you or to stay away?"

She leaned forward waiting for his answer, but the presence he felt was Lauren's. At home and blind, it was Lauren he would most want to have with him. He could hear her voice, feel the touch of her arm against his and catch her scent of cinnamon.

"Come to see me," he said. If she was there, even if he couldn't see her, he'd feel stronger.

"Maybe that's how Lauren is feeling, don't you think? Why she wants to see you."

"Yes, you're right, Mama. She just wants me to go to see her...and Ida'll be there, I expect. But..." He paused, not knowing how to put it. "How does...no, what I mean is, what will she look like?"

"Ah, yes, of course," Maryam said. "You are frightened what the acid may have done to her face, poor girl," she shook her head, "such beautiful skin. But plastic surgery has come a long way and she will already have had skin grafts where she needs them. I understand they do that very early on...within the first few days, I think."

"But what about her eyes?"

"I don't know; but it will be all right, Rafi. *You* will be all right. Do you remember the little story about fear?"

"I don't think so. Tell me."

"Fear knocked on the door, faith answered and there was no-one there."

The following morning, after his mother had dropped him off by the car park, he rounded the corner into West Street, chanting her words like a mantra. He crossed the road and stood in the shadows near the entrance to the church, looking at Lauren's house on the other side. He remembered how at first, after the attack, there had been no question of his visiting her. And how, later, Ida had told him, when he had asked her, that Lauren didn't want to see anyone yet. Spinning away from her without another word, he had stormed home and immediately booked a flight back to Jordan for the day after term ended. He was going to do as his mother wanted; he'd transfer to the college in Amman and he'd forget about Lauren. He would find another girlfriend, an Arab girl. Someone like him, someone he could trust. But one afternoon, out of the blue, Lauren had rung him.

Recrossing the street, he slowed his pace as he neared the house. He wanted to see her; he'd been thinking of little else since her call. Yet, he was dreading it. He rang the bell and took a step back.

As the door opened, Finn's moon face appeared under a foam of gingery curls. "Hey, Rafi," he grinned, standing aside with a mock bow, "come on in." Rafi crossed the threshold just as Jess appeared, hurrying towards them.

"Hello, Rafi. It's good to see you." The cheeriness in her voice sounded false and, despite her smile, her eyes seemed pinched and tired. "How was your summer?"

she went on. But before he could answer, she gestured towards the music room. "Let's go in here for a moment. And, Finn," she turned to her son, "go and tell Lauren Rafi's here. Thank you." She closed the door behind them. "I just want a quick word with you before Lauren comes down." Her smile faded. "Please," she said, pointing to the armchairs and he followed her across to them.

"Right, where to begin?" She was sitting upright, almost rigid, her back not touching the chair. "The thing is, Rafi, Lauren has had a dreadful time, poor girl...absolute, excruciating agony, I can't tell you!" She paused, shaking her head. "And not just at the time, but afterwards with the skin grafts...she said they were the worst of all, even with the morphine." She looked away from him and then back again. "And she's blind!" she blurted out.

Rafi saw the fury flare in her eyes, heard it in her voice; and he wanted to respond, but couldn't think of anything adequate to say.

"And she's blind," Jess repeated quietly. "No vision at all...well, for now, anyway. Stem cell treatment may be possible later...we don't know yet. But the point is... and this is all I wanted to say to you really is that she's the same Lauren she always was. She's been depressed, of course." She nodded at him and he found himself nodding back at her. "Who wouldn't be? But what she needs now are her friends. Finn's been wonderful, staying by her all the time. And so has Ida...made things more normal again. And now you're..."

She stopped at the sound of a door closing above them. "That'll be her now," she said, getting up. And, as he rose, she smiled at him with genuine warmth for the first time and touched his shoulder. "She's so pleased you're back. She hasn't said so, but I can tell. And she's anxious...you know...about how she looks." Hearing the voices on the stairs coming nearer, she added quickly in a kind of plea, "Be a good friend to her, Rafi. Be kind. I know you will be."

44

Her hair had gone. She seemed to be all neck. And she was wearing dark glasses. She came in past Finn, who was holding the door for her. She wasn't bald, he could see that now; see the stubble coming back along the sides and the boyish crop on top. But the black, square-framed glasses were obscuring half her face.

"Rafi?" she said, turning her head a little, as if scanning for him.

"Yes," he croaked, his mouth dry and his throat like gravel. He coughed. "Yes, I'm here."

He froze, not knowing if he should move towards her or let her come to him.

"Right, well I've got work to do," Jess said, starting forward. "Come on, Finn; you can cut the grass for me."

"Nrrrh," Finn protested. "What about Lauren?"

"Lauren will be perfectly fine." She put an arm round him and escorted him out of the room, closing the door behind her.

"Do you want to sit down?" Rafi asked, taking a step towards her and offering his hand, even though he knew it was a futile gesture.

"I'd rather get some air," she said, tilting her face up. "It's not raining, is it?"

"No." He glanced out of the window at the loose skeins of cloud shuffling past one another behind the steeple. "It's a bit cloudy, but I don't think it's going to rain."

"Okay then, let's go."

"Do you need anything?" he asked, hurrying to open the door. Her jeans and hoodie looked warm enough; but he wondered if she had a white cane she might want.

Again, as she came towards him, he held out his hand, unsure whether or not to take her elbow to help guide her.

"I'll grab my stick on the way out," she said, passing him unaided. Once in the hallway she paused, looking towards the kitchen. "Mum, we're going out for a bit," she called. "Won't be long." There was no response. "Must be in the garden."

Rafi followed her, surprised at her assurance as she made her way to the front door unaided, pulling up her hood and pausing by the coat rack for her cane. Her movements seemed so normal that, as she slid the loop from the handle over her wrist and opened the front door, without planning to, he found himself asking aloud, "Can you see anything at all?"

"No!" she said sharply. "Nothing."

Once outside, he went to take her arm, but she shrugged him off. "I'm fine," she said, walking on and tapping ahead of her with the tip of her stick, feeling her way along the line of terraced houses.

They walked in silence until she stopped and tapped her way to the edge of the pavement. Facing the road, she stood motionless, waiting for a lull in the traffic. As the engine sounds finally died away, she went to step forward, but Rafi shot out his arm to stop her. "Wait!" he shouted, adding more softly, "There's a bike coming."

When it had passed, he touched her lightly on the back. "We can go now."

"I've got to learn to do this by myself, Rafi," she said, as they reached the other side. "I can't count on other people all the time."

Whether it was the earlier touch of her under his palm or the sound of her voice saying his name now, he didn't know, but he sensed the change between them, as if she was letting him in. And as they turned into St Lawrence Lane, he saw Zeno's illuminated sign further up and remembered how frozen they had been that Sunday after lunch the last time they were there. So much had changed since then; but, in spite of everything, he felt she was going to be all right and that he would be there for her, when she wanted that...if she wanted it.

"Dad's moved into one of these houses," she said, pausing and pointing to the right with her cane. "Number 7, can you see it?"

Looking across at the row of narrow terraced cottages, he saw the brass 7 on a maroon front door almost opposite them.

"Yes, it's just here. Do you want to see if he is home?"

"Not right now," she said, walking on. "Let's go to the Rec. We never made it last time, remember?"

"Yes, I do."

"And it's you I want to talk to, anyway."

Her directness panicked him. Was she going to be angry with him for going away? Was she going to say she didn't want to see him anymore?

"But are you sure?" he said. "He must miss you

and..." he didn't know how to put it, "and worry about you."

"Quite sure and I'll tell you why. Dad blames himself for not being at home and driving me to school as usual that day. And he keeps apologising for deserting me, as he puts it, and there's nothing I can say to make it better."

Despite the dark glasses and her hood, he knew from the catch in her voice that she was in tears.

"I tell him it's not his fault...that I'm going to be okay. I tell him the physio's really helping and that I'm getting great support from the eye hospital and the RNIB. I tell him Oka's fixing me up with a running guide, once I go back." Her words were coming faster and louder now, like a chant, and he had to lengthen his stride to keep up with her. "I tell him Mum's finding out about getting a guide dog further down the line. I tell him she's been in touch with some foundation about a rehab course. I tell him I'm learning Braille. I tell him, beyond all that, there's the hope someday of stem cell treatment and, who knows, seeing again. But it doesn't make any difference. He just goes on crying and saying he's sorry and I can't bear it!"

She stopped dead as she shouted it out, head dipping, shoulders hunching. He stood paralysed, looking up and down the street in embarrassment, seeing distant faces turned towards them, and not knowing what to say or do. Overwhelmed by the torrent of her hurt and anger and the reality of her situation, he felt lost and reached for his sister. '*Help me, Jasmin,*' he prayed, but no answer came.

"Do you want to go back?" he said, touching her arm, but she didn't say anything, just handed him her cane, took out a tissue from her hoodie pocket and blew her nose.

"No," she said, stuffing it away again, "let's go on and we take a right at the top."

He handed back her cane, and as they walked on in silence and turned for the park, his mother's refrain kept echoing in his mind, "You don't have to do anything, just be there for her." Well, he was here and he wanted to do something. He wanted to hold her hand, but he didn't know where he was with her so he didn't dare to.

"I may be going back to college," she said. "I didn't want to...you know, people fussing. They're just trying to help, but it makes me feel like a freak." She paused, as if waiting for him to say something; but before he could, she went on. "Anyway, Ida changed my mind really. She told me Jan Rawlings said I've got *good hands*," she gave a little laugh, "and can still model clay. She said if I go back she'll help me and that it would be good for me to get back to normal life and be with friends." She paused again and then added, "What do you think, Rafi?"

But before he could answer, they had reached the park entrance, narrowed by the hedges on either side. "We're here," he said, taking her elbow and guiding her through.

"Let's find somewhere to sit down," Lauren said, reaching for his hand and edging him off the path onto the grass. "Somewhere quiet."

Her grip was warm and firm. But as he steered her between a group of lads playing football and two dog walkers busy chatting, with a third approaching, he scanned the park for people he might know. He had only ever been alone with Lauren once before, as usually Ida had always been there as well. Now, they were walking hand-in-hand; and, even if she was blind, it felt like more than just helping her, as if some declaration was being made.

On the far side, across the path skirting the grass, he saw a bunch of people he recognized from college. They were huddled together in the carcass of a shelter, with green iron posts and corrugated metal roof. One or two of them were looking in their direction, and Rafi had to fight the urge to drop Lauren's hand and walk apart from her.

Yet, at the same time, this closeness to her was what he had been longing for and the live pulsing of her palm against his had sent goosebumps up his arms. Unsettled, he led her past the skateboard bowl with kids on scooters shooting the concrete ramps, and on to the furthest corner of the field by a sycamore tree.

"This looks okay," he said, slowing.

She let go of his hand and sat down. "No cow pats, I hope," she laughed, running her fingers over the grass beside her.

He wasn't sure where to put himself and her dark glasses bothered him. He couldn't see through them, couldn't see what had happened to her. In the end, he sat down near her at an angle, so that he had to turn his head a little to look at her.

There was something he had been rehearsing to say to her all the way from the house; now the moment had come, he couldn't bring himself to begin. He took a breath, opened his mouth and then coughed instead.

"Ida says you're going to be living at the Dilleys," Lauren said. "Are you okay with that?"

"Yes. Yes, it's good. It's a small flat really. It has its own entrance, which means I won't have to go through the house. I think Mrs Dilley's mother used to live in it."

"Hey, that's great! Means you can come and go as you please...and have friends round when you want." She lifted her face towards him and smiled. "That's so cool."

"But what about you?" he started to say. "I mean..."

But Lauren hadn't finished and rode over him. "And I really like Monica Dilley. You know she's a vet, right? Ida always goes to her, whenever there's a problem with Coil."

He didn't want to talk about Coil or the Dilleys.

"What happened to your hair?" he said, steeling himself, then added, "Is it okay to ask you that?" But before she could answer, he hurried on again, everything he'd been holding back now flooding out of him. "I couldn't believe it when I heard what had happened to you. I wanted to see you, but I wasn't allowed to. Nobody was. And then, when they were, you didn't want to see me...and it's stupid, I know...I see that now...but I just felt angry, as if..." His voice faltered and petered out. "As if I didn't mean that much to you," he wanted to say and couldn't. Instead, he went on, "That's why I went home for the summer."

She nodded.

"And I wish I hadn't." Again, he wanted to tell her how he felt about her, but couldn't find the courage. "That's not what a friend should do," he said. "I should have been here for you, so that..." "Rafi, it's okay," she broke in, reaching out and finding his hand. "Really. It's all right."

She was silent for a moment and he waited, his heart racing, glad he had spoken, but frustrated at his own cowardice.

"Just listen to those birds!" she said, letting go of his hand. She drew in her knees and circled them with her arms.

He hadn't noticed the birds before; but now, glancing over his shoulder to the tree and bushes behind them, he could hear the ringing calls and chatter quite clearly.

"When he squirted that stuff in my eyes, I thought I was on fire. I tried to wipe it away, but it got on my hands, my hair...the side of my face." She bent her head, her face disappearing under her hood. "So they shaved my hair to get rid of it."

"But what about your face, your hands?"

"It's a jumble really. What I remember is water... cold water...pouring in to my eyes. My head back in a stream, then a basin, then under a shower for hours and hours."

Rafi watched her hands, looking for scars and signs of damage, but he couldn't see any.

"Your hands look okay," he said, wondering how they had been saved, but not her eyes. Surely her eyes would have been their absolute priority.

She stroked the front and back of her hands with her fingertips, then raised them, making fists, clenching and unclenching them.

"The grafts still feel tight. Finn said they looked like raw meat." She gave a brittle laugh and clasped her knees again. "The grafts were the worst...worse than the acid. They took the skin from my thighs." She paused, shaking her head, then added, as if to herself, "Even the morphine didn't help."

"What about now?" he asked. "What about your face? Does it hurt?"

"Nothing like it did. The creams and the physio

help, but it still feels sore and tight...sort of stiff."

He wished she would pull her hood down and take off her sunglasses. He wanted to see what had happened to her. He could ask, couldn't he? He didn't want to offend her; but, then, she could always say no, couldn't she?

"I don't really want to talk about it," she said, her mood suddenly changing; finding her cane, she stood up. "Let's go back, Ida's coming round."

For a moment, annoyed at her cutting him off, he stayed where he was, taking a sort of vindictive pleasure in watching her uncertainty grow as he did and said nothing. At first, she cocked her head, as if listening for him, and then gently started probing with her cane, searching for him. He swivelled his legs out of reach.

"Rafi?"

"Yes, I'm here." He got up, dusting twigs and grass from the seat of his jeans. But still he stood apart from her. Why had she asked to see him? She hadn't said anything about how she felt about him. And now she wanted Ida.

"What's the matter?" she asked.

"Nothing." He gazed around the recreation ground. Maybe this whole idea of staying in Ashbrook was stupid. He should be going home with his mother and concentrating on the struggle for justice, not chasing after this blind girl.

"Can you help me?" she said, turning away from him. "I'm not sure of my way on the grass. The streets are easier...more to go by."

She held out her hand and he took it; but it felt alien to him now, flesh without connection. And as they headed back towards the lane, an angry silence grew in him and he wanted to wrench away from her.

"I'm taking the shortcut," she said, letting go of his hand, as if sensing his antagonism. "Thanks for coming, Rafi, but you don't have to stay with me. I'll be okay from here." And she walked off, veering left towards the mechanical cawing of the rooks from the trees by the church.

He watched her go, watched her slow progress as she followed the path, with her cane's rhythmic arc tapping from front to the side and back again. With her hood up, she looked like a beetle feeling its way forward with a single white antenna. As she neared the narrow exit to the footpath, he saw her hesitate, and even though he knew he should go to help her, something fierce in him held him rooted where he was.

Changing the cane's leash from one wrist to the other, she set off again, bumping into the corner of the hedge before readjusting for the gap and disappearing out of sight beside the graveyard railings. He stared into the space she'd left, remembering her racing, watching her coming off the final bend and stretching away from the others down the home straight. How could this have happened to her? She'd seemed so invincible then...so powerful...so unbreakable.

He shook his head. All those months ago he had promised himself he wasn't going to get involved with an English girl...well, any girl...not until he had got his degree and chosen the best path forward to fight for Palestinian rights, his family's rights. This was ridiculous! He stamped his foot in frustration. Why shouldn't he have friends along the way? Why not a girlfriend?

'*Yes, good friend you are, aren't you?*' a voice mocked him. '*Abandoning her, not even seeing her safely home, after the promise you gave her mother. What great kindness! Remember the bicycle. What happens if she gets run down crossing the road?'*

"Wait!" he yelled, sprinting after her. "Lauren, wait!"

At first, as he skidded through the gap, he couldn't see her, but as he cleared the bend where the path forked, he caught sight of her up ahead and called out again. He saw her stop and half-turn towards him, a pale flash of skin showing between her hood and dark glasses.

"What is it?" she asked as he reached her.

He stood with his hands on his hips, panting and swallowing, catching his breath.

"Why did you ask me to come round?" The words jumped out ahead of the apology he'd been intending.

"What?" She sounded flustered, as if caught off guard.

"Why did you want to see me?"

She hesitated for a moment.

"I wanted to catch up with you..." she said. "We've not had a chance since..."

"Why?"

"Why what, Rafi?"

He heard the irritation in her voice at his interruption, but something insistent drove him on.

"Why did you want to catch up with me?"

"Well, why do you think? We're friends, aren't we? That's what friends do, isn't it?"

"Is that what we are, then? Friends?"

"Yes, I thought so," she said, her voice losing its edge. But still he persisted.

"No more than that?"

"Don't shout at me!" She wheeled away, rattling the

railings with her stick. "And, no," she added, walking away, "no more than that."

"What about the night we buried Jedi?" he called after her. "When you were there with me..." She didn't stop and he muttered the rest to himself, "even though you weren't."

45

When Lauren woke the next morning, ants of dread were crawling in her stomach and she turned on her back, keeping her eyelids closed and trying to make sense of her fear. She still had recurring nightmares of being on the Terrace looking at the map, her terror and panic growing on waking, lying unable to see and straining to hear if anyone was in the room...if Terry Curnow was in the room. Sometimes, she would cry out and her mother would come, or Finn, or both.

But this was different. She was afraid to open her eyes, because of the wild hope that, when she did so, miraculously she would see her room again, full of light and colour, and find Christine Ohuruogu beaming down at her with her big smile. Still she hesitated, not daring to open them and whispering the prayer that had become her morning mantra, "Please, please let me see again...please help me like before."

She reached out, feeling for the small panda bear Finn had moved to the bedside table for her. She cupped it to her under the bedclothes with both hands. She knew it was ridiculous, but confiding in this soft, little creature had become a comfort to her. She was thinking of the night in hospital, not long after the attack, when pain and despair had overwhelmed her and she had broken down, feeling completely lost and hopeless, and she had begged God to help her. "Help me," she had sobbed, "I don't know what to do." She wasn't religious, she didn't believe in God; but she didn't know who else to turn to.

"I was desperate," she whispered to the bear, "and I kept repeating, 'I don't know what to do'. And then, out of nowhere, came this brilliant white light...I mean, even though I was blind, I could see it...hurtling towards me, growing bigger and bigger. And it was so bright I had to turn my head away into the pillow; but, somehow, it just seemed to flood into me, while a voice was saying...not in my ears, but in my head, 'It's all right. It is all right.' And, immediately, I felt...what did I feel? I felt calm, reassured...that things would be okay...that I would be okay, and I just fell asleep."

She traced the semi-circle of the panda's ear with her forefinger. "I can't tell anyone else, they'll think I'm mad. Only crazy people hear voices, right? Only crazy people," she snorted, "talk to stuffed bears." But she held onto him, like she held onto the secret comfort of her vision. "Please be with me," she prayed, as she held her breath and opened her eyes; but there was no light, no beaming smile, only the unchanging darkness.

She let her arms and the panda slump down beside her and lay listening to creaks in the landing outside, soon followed by the muffled flush of the loo whooshing and fading. Still the ants crawled, even beyond her disappointment, and she closed her eyes, trying to locate the dread. But the useless, reflex habit only exasperated her and she kicked back the duvet and swung her legs out of the bed, the panda falling onto the floor. And, as she leant down groping for it, she heard him, "Is that what we are then? Friends? No more than that?"

"Rafi!" She was in with the ants now. Why had he pushed her when she was so angry with him? His pretending to disappear in the park had made her panic. It wasn't funny; she'd been terrified. She felt for the edge of the bedside table and slid the bear onto it, shaking her head. "No, no more than that!" He had opened the door and she had slammed it shut. But he'd deserved it. How could she trust him again when he'd been so mean? Even so, after all this time, after all this wanting and hoping, she'd ruined everything. Because that's what he'd meant, wasn't it? He wanted to be more than friends. He couldn't have made it plainer, could he? And she'd said no!

"Stupid! Stupid! Stupid!" she shouted, thumping the mattress with her fist. Almost at once, she heard running and the door banging open.

"Laur...Laur, what's the matter?" Finn's breathless voice was flying towards her. "Are you all right?" His hand was on her shoulder, his knees were knocking into hers and she felt his breath warm on her cheek, smelling of toothpaste.

"Yes, yes, I'm okay, just...just freaking."

"Are you sure?" He drew his hand away. "I heard you shouting and..."

"Yes, really, I'm fine."

"You don't look fine, you look...and now you're crying!" He seemed to be moving away and she heard the muffled click of the door being closed quietly before he came back again and the bed dipped as he sat down beside her. "What's up?"

She shook her head. She didn't want to explain.

Besides, her eyes were dry and uncomfortable.

"Can you see my eye drops?"

"Yes...here." His warm fingers slid the small, slope-shouldered dropper into her hand. She unscrewed the cap and hesitated.

"Could you do it for me?"

"'Course," he said, taking it back again.

She swivelled round and lay back. "Two drops in each."

"I know," he laughed, "up the nose end, right?"

She pulled the bottom of each eye wider open with a finger and tried not to blink as the drops landed, flooding her eyes, first one and then the other.

"Mm, that's a relief," she crooned, blinking furiously trying to spread the drops and keep them from sliding out down her face. "What would I do without you?"

"Not a lot," he laughed.

"No, I mean it," she said seriously, turning her head towards him. "You've been great...really great."

And he had. She wanted him to know that. When she'd come home, he'd hardly left her bedside. And once she was up and moving around, it was his hand she'd felt in hers and his voice she'd heard so often, accompanying her, guiding her, "First step coming up... bannister on your left". Even after school had started, as soon as he came home again, he'd come to check on her.

She wanted to say more. She wanted him to know how easy he had been to have around. Her mother had been too worried, too anxious to have bright things to say about the future...about support from the Katie Piper Foundation, about getting a running coach, about the possibility of stem-cell treatment. Her dad, when he came round, was too upset, too full of apologies for not having been there. They both drained her with their emotional demands on her, even though she knew they were suffering, too, and trying to show their love. When they left her on her own again, she could relax.

It was only with Finn and Ida that she felt comfortable. They weren't sentimental, didn't pussyfoot around her. They were their normal selves, all their affection for her plain in their usual friendliness and jokiness. They didn't make her feel fragile and broken like her parents did, just wounded and on the mend. But she couldn't tell Finn all that; it would just make him feel embarrassed and awkward.

"Anyway, I'm okay," she said instead, swinging her feet round and sitting up, "and Henry and Ida are coming to pick me up in a bit and I'll probably stay the night, so you're free to go round to Tom's or whatever."

"Yeah, I will. The treehouse is almost finished. In fact, we're going to have a grand opening; coke and vegan burgers at 20 feet and you're invited!"

The gurgle of delight in his voice made her smile. "Not sure I'm up to ladders yet."

"No, you'll be fine. Tom'll lead the way and I'll be right behind you. It'll be exciting. And we've got chairs and a table up there, so you can sit down if you want to. We're going to take our sleeping-bags and spend a night up there. Mum doesn't know yet, but Shauna says we can. It'll be magic...just need a moon-clear night!"

"And owls hooting!" Lauren laughed.

"And foxes barking!" Finn joined in.

"Treesss whissspering..." she hissed.

"And ghossstsss..." he mimicked her.

"Ghossstsss what?"

"Sssnacking!" he gurgled, barely able to get the words out for giggling. "Ghossstsss ssssnacking!"

"What on earth's going on in here?"

Jess sounded almost angry; but Finn's laughter was infectious and Lauren couldn't catch her breath to reply.

"You're invited too, Mum," Finn gasped.

"Invited to what?"

"The grand opening of the Tofin treehouse," he said, which set them off again. "The Tofin haunted treehouse!"

"For goodness sake, you two!" Lauren caught the tremble in her mother's voice and knew she was on the verge of being swept into laughter, too. "Tofin! What's Tofin?"

"Tom and Finn, that's what we've called it...the Tofin."

"Tiffin at Tofin, brilliant!"

Lauren heard her mother's pleasure in the remark, but didn't get it. "What's tiffin?"

"Oh, a sort of chocolaty treat from the Raj...Indian. Anyway, doesn't matter. The point is your father's coming round for coffee this morning. So, time to get dressed."

"Coming round for coffee," Finn repeated, as soon as they were alone again. "Do you think Dad wants to come back?"

Lauren heard his hopefulness and swallowed her own doubts. "Maybe," she said. She knew the attack on her had brought her parents closer together again, but she didn't want pity for her to be the reason for any reconciliation between them...not unless they'd sorted out whatever was the problem in the first place...not unless her father no longer wanted to put Jan Rawlings on like a sweater...not unless her mother could tear herself away from her paperwork and meetings.

After Finn had gone, she got dressed slowly. She could move around her room quite confidently now, although she still stubbed her toes against the leg at the foot of the bed from time to time. However, choosing what she was going to wear had become much more complicated. Her mother had helped her every day at the start, making suggestions she thought were helpful, "Oh, look, here's that pretty smock Ginnie gave you...you know, the rust-coloured one. Let's put that on, shall we?" And although Lauren had been grateful at one level, it had made her feel like a child again at another. As soon as she could, she had clawed back her independence, getting her mother to leave fresh underwear on her chair and to colour code the individual garments in each drawer of the chest into three piles from left to right: black, dark colours and light.

With no way of checking herself in the mirror, she had to rely on her sense of touch to select the clothes she was looking for, her hands and fingers her eyes now; as a result, to make things easier for herself, most of the time she dressed in black jeans and her black hoodie. She knew both her parents liked her to dress more colourfully, particularly her dad. She could hear his voice, 'Those conker, chestnut colours really suit you... bring out the highlights in your hair', and she hesitated, wondering whether she should forsake the hoodie for the russet, roll-neck sweater he had bought for her as a peace offering after their row. But she liked having the hood, liked being able to put on her sunglasses and pull it up over her head against the sides of her face. It made her feel more protected, safer.

She heard Finn's excited voice below and knew her father had arrived. By the time she'd brushed her hair and gone down, she heard them all in the sitting-room and paused. "Hang on, let's wait for Lauren," her mother was saying so clearly that Lauren knew the door had been left open for her.

"Here she is," Finn said, as she walked in and the conversation died. Five paces at ten o'clock would take her past the coffee table into the centre, but she'd only gone three when she felt her father's arms go round her. "Lauren," he said softly, holding her tight, his stubble warm and scratchy against her cheek; the familiar smell of him, something earthy and sweet like autumn, brought a visceral pang of yearning, a longing for the certainty of the past.

"How are you, sweetheart?" he murmured, holding onto her.

"Not great, Dad, but I'm all right." Gently untangling herself, she turned for the armchair.

"Left a bit," Finn called out, as she found the arm and sat down.

"Your father's got some news." The exaggerated cheerfulness in her mother's voice grated on Lauren's nerves. "Haven't you, Nick?"

"Yes, well, I thought you would like to know, Lauren...no, I mean all of you, really, would like to know that Terry Curnow has been arrested and is on remand in Exeter jail."

"Yey!" Finn hooted, stamping his feet.

"Lauren?" Her mother's hand was on her arm. "Darling, what is it?"

Lauren rocked forward, linking her fingers and

pressing her hands together as hard as she could between her knees, trying to stop the trembling quaking through her.

"Breathe!" Her mother's arms went round her. "You're okay. You're safe. We're all here."

Lauren ducked her head away from her mother's coffee breath, but the warmth of her embrace calmed her and gradually the shaking eased into sporadic shudders as she took deeper and deeper breaths.

"I'm okay," she said at last, looking up and leaning back. "It was just..." She broke off, feeling foolish. 'Terror!' was what she wanted to say, but couldn't. How could just his name cause her such blind panic...'blind' panic? She laughed, a short, bitter snort of shame and self-mockery.

"He'll be going away for a long time," her father said, his voice coming closer. "Apparently, Annabel Howard, you know from the library, was coming out of her cottage in Skylark Lane as he was going past and she recognized him. Told the police he had a woman's wig on, but she knew it was him from his build and the way he walked. It seems she'd often seen him in the libr..."

"It's not enough!" Lauren interrupted, heat rising in her again. "They'll say she didn't have her glasses on or...or that she's short-sighted, if she did. He's slimy; he'll slide out of it."

"No, sweetheart, there's more." Her father's hand was on her knee and she knew he was squatting level with her. "They have CCTV footage of Terry...or, rather, the woman he was pretending to be...at Totnes station catching a train after the attack on you and much later than the one he said he was on that morning. But, not only that, they've also got footage of him getting off that train in Truro as himself...no longer in disguise, I mean."

"He can't get out of that, can he?" Finn cried. "They've got him, Laur! They've absolutely nailed him!"

Finn was right she told herself. He couldn't talk himself out of this one, not now. And yet, what was filling her vision were the woman's dark hair and sunglasses looming up large in front of her and that voice, "He won't want you now, will he?", and the screaming pain, "Dear me, no!"

"No!" she yelled, lashing out as strong arms, her father's arms, encircled her, pulling her into his chest; followed a moment later by her mother's warm hand on her hair.

"I'll kill the bastard!" Finn shouted, and the outrage in his voice jumped heat into her eyes, but no tears came.

She expected her mother or father to tell him off for swearing, but neither did and his words were left hanging in the silence that followed.

After a while she grew calmer and her father's grip softened, letting go finally as she sat back. "Thanks, Dad, I'm okay...I'm okay."

"I'll go and make some coffee," her mother said, withdrawing her hand and leaving a chill at the nape of Lauren's neck. "Come on, Finn, you can help me get out the biscuits."

"How about the brownies?" Finn was asking as their voices faded from the room. "They're totally awesome..."

Once they were alone, her father said: "By the way,

I meant to tell you, Jan Rawlings says you're welcome to go back to her classes, whenever you feel like it...says you might enjoy modelling clay again, make things feel more normal. What do you think?"

"When did you see her? Are you back at college?"

"No...no, er, she came to the cottage...wanted to know how you were."

"Does Mum know?"

"Mum?" He gave a little cough, clearing his throat. "Well, no...I mean Jan just called by, that's all."

"What's happening, Dad? I thought maybe you and Mum were sorting things out."

"We are, sweetheart. We are."

"But having Jan to your house isn't going to help, is it?"

"It's not like that. I didn't ask her, she just dropped by. She's a friend and she cares about you. This is silly."

"No, it's not! For heaven's sake, Dad, do you want to come back home or not?" She could tell how uncomfortable he was feeling, she could hear the anxiety in his voice. But she was angry with him. Why the hell was he involving Jan again? Mum would never believe it was innocent, and then what?

But before he could answer, two sustained rings of the doorbell shattered the spell between them. Lauren heard Finn racing past shouting, "Coming!" A moment later, a cool current of air blanketed her legs as a familiar voice ducted with her brother's in the hall, followed by more footsteps and her mother's voice. "Oh, it's you, Ida, hello. I'm just making coffee. Would you like some?"

"Hi, Jess. And thanks, but Dad couldn't find a space, so he's waiting in the car."

Lauren stood up. "I've got to go, Dad," she said, pausing for him to come to her.

"Things are going to be all right, chick," he whispered, hugging her. "Try not to worry."

He hadn't called her that since she was little and she hung onto him for a moment before letting go.

Out in the hall, she felt suddenly surrounded and jostled, with Finn brushing past her, followed by Ida's hand on her shoulder, as she leant in and kissed her cheek.

"Hi, Laur, sorry to rush you, but..."

"Henry's waiting outside, I know," Lauren said. "That's okay, let's go. Can you get..."

"Here it is," her mother interrupted, touching her to let her know where she was.

"Thanks, Mum." Lauren reached out for the backpack and looped a strap over her shoulder. "I'll ring you in the morning."

"Okay. I've got to be in Totnes by ten, but I'll have my phone. And, here, take this, it may rain." Her hiking jacket was pushed into her hands and she turned to go, eager to escape the fussing. "Have you remembered your cream?" her mother called after her.

"Yes," Lauren groaned, "and a spare pair of knickers!"

"Gross!" Finn gurgled, as he came up beside her, taking her hand and placing her stick in it. "Don't forget this."

46

At Windhover, as Rafi stuffed the last of his things from the wardrobe into the black holdall on his bed, a familiar nausea and emptiness curdled inside him. He knew the feeling. Whenever he was packing to leave the farm in As-Salt, there was this same sense of loneliness. Pressing down hard on the college blazer folded on top, he tugged the zip across, trying not to snag the fabric in its teeth.

Tomorrow, his mother's taxi would drop him off at the Dilleys on her way to catch the train for Reading. From there, she would take the coach to Heathrow and fly on to Amman. He checked his watch; it was almost midday. He heaved the holdall onto the floor. By tomorrow night, she would be at the farm with Jasmin and Zak and his father and aunty Anoush, while he would be on his own in the flat at the Dilleys.

There was a soft knock at the door. "Rafi?"

"Yes, Mama, come in," he said.

"This just came for you." She held out a plain white envelope as she entered, and he went across to take it. "There's no stamp, no proper address."

He turned it the right way up and his heart lurched. *Rafael*, it said, and underneath, *Windhover*. Terry! Who else could it be? He ripped it open and unfolded a sheet of lined A4 with its ruled margin and filing holes.

Greetings Rafael,

I trust this finds you well and in the pink. Oh, dear me, no! That won't do at all, will it? You won't ever be in the pink, will you? Never mind. No doubt you will be surprised to hear from me, confined as I am at Her Majesty's pleasure. But your heart would be lifted at the...what shall I call it?...at the camaraderie you find in a place like this. Yes, indeed. One way or another, you can get most things in and most things out.

Of course, until the trial, I'm not allowed to write to you or to anyone else involved in the...how shall I put it?...in the incident. Yes, yes, 'the incident', that's certainly what it was. However, a friend of mine who likes to travel...best not use any names, as I'm sure you'll understand...has said he'll drop this through your letter-box next time he's passing.

The thing is, Rafael, we've had our differences, you and I. Indeed, we have. But the point is (and this is why I'm writing to you) it's not personal. Not individual. What I mean is, if I happened to be in the desert and met you on your camel, we might well become the best of friends. I certainly felt we might the night we called in on you at your house and found you in your pyjamas. Yes, I certainly felt a kind of rapport developing between us then...a kind of mutual understanding and regard, don't you think?

"No, I don't!" Rafi blurted out, jerking the letter away from him, as if wanting to be rid of Terry's rhythmical, repetitive voice and his insinuating grin. He wanted to rip the paper to shreds.

"What is it?" Maryam asked, touching his arm. "Who is it from?"

"A rat, that's who!"

"Who is a rat?"

"Terry Curnow!" He spat out the name and held the letter up to look at it again.

"Don't read any more." She held out her hand. "Give it to me, I'll deal with it."

"No, I want to see if he says anything about Lauren." He moved away to the window and held the page to the light.

So, no, it's not personal, not at all. It's about purity, Rafael. It's about pedigree. After all, dogs need to stick to their own breeds or we'll end up with a world full of mongrels. And, of course, it's the bitches, the female dogs, who are the problem. Once they come on heat, goodness me, every dog in the street is after them. So, they've got to take responsibility. Yes, indeed. They've got to be selective.

I mean, you don't want an English Setter or a British Bulldog...what shall I say...mixing with a Saluki or a Chow, do you? 'Course not. It won't do at all, will it? Who wants a setter with a ruff or a bulldog that thinks it's a greyhound? No, no, no. I mean, you wouldn't cross a camel with a horse, would you? You can't go hunting with a hump, can you? No, 'course not. You're a sensible person, I'm sure you'll agree. "Each to their own", as my gran used to say.

Same with people, it's no different. But the trouble is our young women aren't seeing it, are they? They're mixing with anybody, whoever they are, wherever they come from. So, I'm not blaming you, not at all...quite the opposite. This is all Ms Jackman's doing...yes, indeed...leading you on, as if blind to the need for the purity of our breed...of our stock. So, I have opened up her inner eyes to help her see more clearly. Yes, yes, the wisdom of insight, I've read about that. And she'll thank me later, you can be sure of that.

So, there we are, Rafael. Yes, indeed. Go back to your own country with a clear conscience and find a young woman with the same smooth brown skin as you. And Ms Jackman will have plenty of time to think about her duty to her own kind. My word, yes. Plenty of time without other...other distractions, shall we say?

And, don't you worry about me. I'm pleading guilty. I don't mind this, not at all. Brexit has set us free. Soon, we'll help all the immigrants go home and then the old bulldog spirit will rise again, you'll see. And I have a plan. I'll be going into politics... help move things along a bit. Yes, indeed. Make this my university, if you like, and continue with my degree.

So, you see, Rafael, you've had a big effect on me. No doubt about it. You've made me think much more deeply about things. Indeed you have.

But, goodness me, look at the time. I must stop or I'll miss the post! So, this is the end of the line, Rafael. This is thank you and goodbye. Although, who knows, I may visit your country one day and look you up. I think of you quite a lot. Indeed, I do. Quite a lot.

Au revoir,
Terry

"He's vile," Rafi said, thrusting the letter at his mother. "He attacked Lauren because she was friends with me...deliberately, in cold blood. He's a racist dog and they ought to shoot him. I would!"

"Wait," Maryam interrupted him, holding up her hand. "Let me read this."

When she had finished, she refolded it in three and slid it back in the envelope.

"This is disgusting, fascist nonsense," she said. "It is also incriminating evidence. He says he'll plead guilty, but you can never be sure. Unfortunately, I haven't enough time to do it myself; so you must be sure to give this to the police as soon as you can."

She held out the envelope to him, but, as he went to take it, she kept hold of it, making him look at her. "Remember, Rafi, none of this is your fault," she said, her eyes softening, "not in any way." She let go. "The blame and the madness are all Terry Curnow's."

After his mother had gone, Rafi sat on the edge of the bed, staring at the blank screen of the phone in his hand. He wanted to speak to Lauren. In the small hours, he'd gone over and over her final words: "No, no more than that." Had she said it in anger or did she mean it? Had he misunderstood her that night in the garden? His thumb moved and the screen lit up. There were no texts and he clicked it off. No, she had just been being kind because Jedi was dead...it was "no more than that". Even so, she was the one he wanted to tell about the letter. He wanted to talk to her...he wanted to make things right between them.

Again his thumb moved as if of its own volition, the screen lighting up. There was her number...there was the little green telephone. Yet, he couldn't bring himself to press it and he let his hand slump onto the duvet. Why on earth would she want to hear Terry's letter? How stupid could he be? He must be the last person she'd want to hear about. But he didn't have to mention him, did he? Why else was he ringing then? To apologise. He brought the screen back up in front of him. He could say he was sorry about yesterday, that... that what? His hand fell back on the bed again.

What was he afraid of? Why couldn't he just do it? Yet every time he raised the phone, determined to ring her, panic overwhelmed him and he let it sink down again. Finally, disgusted with himself, with his cowardice, he threw it down and shoved it away from him. If she had meant what she said, there was no point calling her. And if she hadn't, then he just needed to wait and she would contact him.

He picked up the letter instead and stood up. He'd go to the police now and get it over and done with. But as he moved for the door, Jasmin's voice stopped him, "Come on, little brother; be brave. She is a kind girl and, mystery of mysteries, she seems to like you." He smiled, in spite of himself, and reassured by the familiarity of his sister's gentle teasing, he went back to the bed and rang Lauren's number.

47

Chariots of Fire shattered the silence, startling her, and her thumb jumped against the clay, smearing Ohuruogu's finger. She grabbed along the bench for her phone, but couldn't find it.

"It's on the bed, I'll get it. Here..." Ida's hand brushed hers, tapping the back of her hand with the phone, "it's Rafi."

"Not now," Lauren snapped, as she felt for the contours of the flattened finger.

"I'll leave it here." The phone, still ringing, clicked dully against the bench. "What's up?"

"Nothing."

"Why don't you want to speak to him?"

"I'm doing this."

The repetitive jingle sliced off and Lauren wished Ida would stop hovering and go back to what she'd been doing. She felt safe being with Ida, but she didn't want to talk; she just wanted to concentrate on the maquette and not think about anything else.

"I'm okay," she said. "You go back to sorting Coil out...must be his time for a chat."

"Have you and Rafi fallen out?"

"Look, sorry Id, but I don't want to talk right now,

okay?"

Ida's arms came round her from behind and she could feel the warmth of Ida's face against her own even through her hoodie.

"I know," she said, "and you don't have to. It's just I can't bear what's happened to you and I want to make it better and I don't know how to. You've been gone so long and I want you back!" Her hug tightened and her voice was cracking. "I don't want that fucking creep to have broken you!"

"I'm not broken," Lauren said, stiffening.

"But you're so cut off, Laur. You sit there so straight and still with your back to me and I don't know why you even want to be here." She broke off, letting go, and Lauren could hear her rapid breathing, almost like panting.

"Because you make me feel safe and want nothing from me." She turned her head towards her and reached out for her hand. "Because doing nothing, you do everything."

For a moment, there was silence and just the warm pulsing of Ida's hand in hers.

"Ok, nothing it is," Ida said eventually, giving a last squeeze and letting go. "Time for lunch, anyway. You coming?"

"No, I'm not hungry."

"You've got to eat, Laur. All you've had so far is a glass of juice."

"I'm fine."

"Right, well, I'll leave the door open in case you change your mind."

Lauren listened to her going and felt a flicker of fear at the growing stillness and emptiness surrounding her.

Holding the maquette loosely with both hands, she sat lightly circling her thumbs over the figure's torso and wondering why she hadn't answered Rafi's call. What was she afraid of, after all?

The distant thuds and clinking, followed after a while by muffled voices, came as a relief. Henry's calm presence in the house reassured her. "Treat her normally...best way," she'd overheard him telling Ida, when they had brought her back to stay for the first time. And, after the dark, timeless days, first in hospital and then at home, it had felt like the first flicker of light from her old life.

"You didn't call me then, did you?" she whispered, remembering the interminable days of pain and despair, when she had longed to hear from Rafi, as much as she had dreaded it.

She let go of the maquette, took off her sunglasses and, leaning back, eased a slim tin from her jeans' pocket. Taking off its lid, she took some cream on her fingertips and began massaging it into the skin around her temple and under her eyes, where the graft still felt tight and sore. What did Rafi want? She regretted the way they'd parted the day before, but she wasn't ready to deal with all that. She didn't have the energy.

On the other hand, he might keep ringing till he got her. Better to get it over and done with and off her mind. She pressed the lid back on the tin and felt along the bench for her phone.

"Siri, call Rafi," she said and waited.

"Hello. Lauren? Is that you?"

"Hi. You called me."

"Yes, I did...um...there's something I wanted to tell you, but I'm not sure if this is the right time?"

His hesitancy irritated her and she felt an antagonism she didn't understand.

"What is it, Rafi? What do you want to tell me?" Her voice was harder than she'd intended.

"Maybe this isn't a good moment. You sound in a hurry."

"No, now's fine. Just tell me."

"Okay, the thing is...well, there are two things..." she could hear how difficult he was finding it to come to the point, wriggling like a worm on a hook; part of her didn't care, didn't mind hearing him squirm. She wasn't going to help him and she waited silently, until he went on again. "The first thing is about yesterday... are you still there?"

"Yes."

"Okay, it's just it didn't feel right after you'd gone and...um..." He stumbled again, clearing his throat, but she didn't say anything. "So, I'm wondering if I could come over or meet you somewhere to...to talk about it."

Why was she being mean to him, she wondered. Other boys wouldn't have tried to ring her like he had. He might be a bit old fashioned and serious, but he was sincere. That's what she'd liked about him, she trusted him. Except yesterday in the park, when he seemed to vanish; she'd been so frightened, groping around trying to find him, so exposed and alone. And then, when he revealed himself, under the relief, she realized she'd felt stupid and humiliated.

"Law-ren?" How foreign her name sounded in his mouth, 'Law-ren'. She hadn't really noticed it before.

"I'm here. I'm just thinking about yesterday. You said there were two things. What's the other one?"

"I don't know whether I should tell you this. I mean,

I thought I wouldn't...didn't want to upset you, but then I thought you might want to know. And secrets get in the way, don't they?"

"So, what is this secret?"

"I got a letter this morning...from Terry."

Lauren froze. Slowly lowering the phone, she held her breath, on edge for the faintest sound.

"Law-ren?" Rafi's muffled voice came from her lap.

Leaping up, she whipped round, dropping the phone, and stood with her back to the bench.

"Ida!" she yelled.

Rafi's voice came again, but all her attention was on the sound of Ida and Henry's distant voices growing louder as the floor began to tremble with their running.

"Lauren, what is it?" Ida seemed to reach her as quickly as her words, stretching her hand out and grasping her arm.

In the same moment, Henry was beside her, too, the solidity of him palpable through her blindness, his voice warm and reassuring. "Are you all right, love?"

She reached for Ida and held onto her, her whole body shaking.

"Law-ren?...Law-ren!" Rafi's voice came from the phone by her feet.

Henry grunted as he bent down for it. "Hello, Rafi. ...Yes, she's here with us. She'll ring you back in a bit, I expect, all right? Yes, I'll tell her."

He exchanged glances with his daughter and nodded. "I'll go and make some tea."

"What happened?" Ida asked, after he'd gone.

Disengaging herself, Lauren drew in a deep breath and shuddered.

"I was so scared," she said at last, her chest heaving.

"I thought he was here...in the room. I could feel him."

"Who?" Ida said.

"Terry...Terry Curnow. Rafi says he's had a letter from him."

48

As Rafi stood in the middle of the living room looking around him, he felt nauseous; empty as if he needed to eat something, but sick at the thought of it. He didn't understand it. The room was friendly and comfortable, with its fitted blue carpet, generous sofa and colourful paintings on the wall. And even though the day was dull and overcast, the table and chairs by the window had plenty of natural light from the wide panes of glass overlooking the drive and front garden.

He picked up his case and went through to the small bedroom at the back, hoiked it onto the single bed and started to unpack his things into a small chest-of-drawers with a mirror and a wardrobe with two deep drawers under the hanging space. A faded scent of something flowery hung in the air and he squeezed round the end of the bed to open the window, pushing the chintz curtains further back on their rail. A damp, leafy spool of air flowed past him with the tang of autumn in it.

"It's probably a bit feminine for your taste," Monica Dilley had said, as she showed him round. "It was Mum's, of course, so a bit old ladyish, I'm afraid."

Well, the bedroom certainly was very pink, from the deep-rose carpet to the pale-pink walls and the faded-pink flowers on the cream curtains. But it didn't matter, did it? Because Lauren couldn't see, could she? He took out his phone, but there were no messages. Why had he mentioned the letter? How could he have been so stupid!

He stared out at the telephone wires crisscrossing against the sky, desperately wanting to ring her to apologise and make sure she was all right; but his mother's words rang clearly in his head, he could hear her voice. "There's no hurry, Rafi. Give her space. Let her come to you in her own time."

Come to him, it's what he had imagined so many times; but would that ever happen now? He turned and took in the single bed with renewed disappointment. He had so hoped for a double, like the one he'd had at Windhover.

"Enough!" he said aloud. That was never going to happen; he was just a friend, "no more than that!" She could not have been clearer. Even so, ever since his parents had agreed to his staying on alone, he had felt a growing excitement. And, when this apartment... well, flat the Dilleys called it...had been offered to him, he had pictured Lauren coming round and their having time together on their own. They would talk, watch TV, listen to music, eat together. He would buy wine and cook for her in the galley kitchen. They would be private, the space was theirs and they could do whatever they liked.

How often he had been aroused just thinking of touching her, kissing her, burying his face in her hair and smelling the lemony-cinnamon of her. He had never had a girlfriend of his own, never had any sexual contact, not like Yousef and Amal...or, at least, that's what they claimed. Amal said his elder brother had picked up a prostitute in Al-Jubeiha and paid for him as well. Knowing Amal's brother, it was probably true; but he wasn't so sure about Yousef's story of having an erotic massage in a hotel by the sea in Aqaba when he was on holiday with his family.

He turned the candlewick bedspread back, revealing the pillows. So what if it was true or not, anyway? He was still a virgin! And that hadn't mattered before at home in As-Salt. In fact, when Amal and Yousef teased him about it, he had told them he would not sleep with a girl until they were married, and he had meant it. It hadn't been about religious obedience, but about an impulse to be true and do right; because, when he thought about his grandfather's key and the murderous expulsion of Palestinians from their homes during the Nakba, he had realized that all he had to offer against division and injustice in the world was his own behaviour.

He lifted the edge of the duvet and bedspread and looked at the taut white sheet underneath. It had all seemed so clear back then. He would work to join the UN and he would find a wife to have children with and he would commit himself fully to both of them. But now, ever since he had felt Lauren's arm brushing his that first evening at her house, he had become possessed by a longing to be with her, to make love with her, to feel her skin against his. And, yes, he did want to marry her and be at the farm with her, but that would be after university and that was then and now was now.

His phone rang, throbbing in his pocket; dropping the covers, he carried it quickly through to the living-room, as if caught out.

"Hello, Mama."

"Rafi, my flight's just been called. I want to check that you have settled in all right and have everything you need."

"Yes, I'm fine."

"Good. And don't forget to give that letter from Terry Curnow to the police. It's incriminating evidence."

"No, I won't."

In the background, the airport tannoy blared out some distorted announcement, and a sudden panic at her going swept through him.

"It feels..." He hesitated. There was no point worrying her with the emptiness he was feeling.

"I can't hear you. What did you say? You're feeling..."

"Don't worry. It doesn't matter. Have a safe journey... and please ring me when you're home and everyone's there."

"I will. I've got to go. Take good care of yourself. I'm very proud of you."

After she had gone, he felt listless. He made a cup of coffee, opening a pack of chocolate digestives and carrying them back to the table by the window, sitting there watching a grey squirrel darting about the lawn. A familiar red Royal Mail van turned into the drive and the squirrel raced up the nearest tree, circling the trunk, before disappearing.

Taking the mug with him, he went back into the bedroom to finish unpacking. At one end of the case, in an elasticated inside pocket, he was surprised to find his mother's leather-bound, folding photo wallet. Normally she kept it in her handbag and took it everywhere with her. Lifting it out, he held it to his nose and the musky scent of it sent a shudder of grief through him. He opened its two wings and saw the three photos she always kept there: in the centre was one of him, Jasmin and Zak, caught with unposed smiles as they made their way up the track either side of Damiana, their father a little behind. A grin broke across his face at the sight of the donkey. How he missed her and the awful roaring protest she used to make at times.

"Poor Jedi!" he laughed, his eyes sliding across to his grandfather in the left frame. He was sitting at the head of the table with Amti Anoush and Uncle Sadiq on one side and his parents on the other. A wave of longing crashed over him to be at that familiar table, eating those spiced dishes so alive in his mouth at the thought of them. He brought his attention back to his grandfather, who seemed to be looking directly at him. And, as he sank into the warm strength of Jedi's gaze, he felt a stirring of guilt at his sexual thoughts about Lauren.

"To be respected, Rafi, you must be respectful." Jedi's voice came back to him, with all its loving seriousness. "Value your life and the lives of others, even of your enemies."

He wanted to be like his grandfather. He wanted to be as warm-hearted and steadfast, but he felt trivial and lightweight by comparison. When had he last thought about Gaza or the West Bank or the dispossession of his own family, of all Palestinians?

"I promise you I will," he told his grandfather. "And we will return. We will be an independent nation again with our own homeland."

He set the open photo wallet down on the bedside table, propped up and tilted back like a travelling alarm clock in its own case. And, as his eyes left his grandfather's, he noticed the striking face in the third frame to the right. A young woman, with a mass of wavy auburn hair around a strong face, was smiling out at him, her lips wide and generous under a prominent nose and deep-set eyes.

At first, he didn't recognize her, although there was something in her expression that struck a chord in him, and then he realized. "Grandma!" he laughed. It was his mother's mother, Naomi. He had only ever known her as an old woman with grey hair and a loud American voice. How strange to see her so young. He must have seen this picture before, but he didn't remember it. Perhaps in the past he hadn't known who it was at first glance and ignored it, too caught up in the other photos to bother with it.

He hadn't thought about her properly in ages and he stood staring at her, sipping at his coffee until his phone blared suddenly. Putting the mug down, he ran through to the other room to answer it.

"Hello," he said, not even looking to see who was calling.

"Hi, Rafi, it's me."

"Oh...Lauren, it's you...yes, hi." His blood was racing. "How are you? I mean, look, I'm sorry about yesterday. I shouldn't have..."

She cut him off. "It's alright, I'm fine. Are you okay to talk?"

"Yes, I'm at the Dilleys...in the apartm...or flat, I mean. I'm just unpacking my things."

"Has your mum gone, then?"

"Yes...yes, she has. In fact, she rang a little while ago; her flight had just been called." He checked his watch. "She's probably in the air by now."

"Must feel strange being in a new place on your own."

"Yes, it does a bit."

He paused, thinking of asking her over, but wondering how she could get there, even if she wanted to. Perhaps he could go to her house and bring her back on the bus. But how often did they run on a Saturday? He'd have to make the journey there and back twice. If only...

"Anyway," she said, "the reason I'm calling is I want to talk to you and Henry's going to drop me home after lunch. So, are you busy this afternoon?"

"No, not at all. That would be great. What time do you want me to come over?"

"No," she laughed, "I'm going to come to you; I want to see the flat."

Her words hung in the air between them before she corrected herself, saving him from his own embarrassment.

"Well, I can't see it, can I? But you know what I mean."

"Yes...yes, I do. But how will you get here? Shall I come over and catch a bus back with you?

"No, that's okay. Mum wants to have a chat first and then she's going to give me a lift. Pity we're not old enough to drive yet..." She stopped abruptly.

She was never going to be able to drive, was she? He stared out of the window, desperately looking for inspiration. "Yes, so come when you're ready, I will be here. And..." He paused. What could he possibly say that would make things any better? But he had to say something...anything.

"And what?"

"I was just thinking you'll have to learn to ride pillion."

It was unplanned, a throwaway remark to lighten the mood; but it didn't work.

"Will I? Why's that?"

"Sorry, that didn't come out right." He sat down. "What I mean is my uncle in Amman, Uncle Sadiq, is sending me some money to buy a moped to help me be more independent. So I'll be able to give you a lift...you know, if you want one."

"Thanks, but I don't think so...not yet, anyway."

"No, no. I'd be very careful, I'd go slowly. You'd be safe with me...really. I've been riding motorbikes since I was thirteen...you know, back home, on the farm."

"We'll see," she said. "Not sure it's legal. Anyway, got to go now, see you later."

He put the phone down, but didn't let go of it. That word, there wasn't any way round it. It popped up all the time, and yet no-one said it. "Blind!" he said aloud. Why was it unsayable? No point being embarrassed by it, was there? It was the truth and they'd just have to get used to it. But what did she want to talk about?

49

"Let's go and sit in the garden," her mother said and Lauren heard the suck of the dishwasher door closing. "It's a beautiful day out there."

"Great," she said, easing her chair back. She liked being out in the fresh air; she felt less cut off there, more connected to the world, freer in a way.

"Door's open, but mind the step," her mother warned, holding her elbow as she passed.

"I know!" Lauren said, jerking her arm away and immediately regretting it. "Sorry."

Her mother laughed. "Don't like me fussing, do you?"

And Lauren was glad she hadn't taken offence, glad, too, at her good mood. She seemed lighter.

"Is Dad coming over?" Lauren asked, letting her mother take her arm and guide her to the bench.

"No, he's had to go up to see Mormor. It's one of the things I want to talk to you about. Here we are." Her mother let go, and, finding the warm, wooden edge of the garden bench, Lauren turned to sit down, kicking something that spun away as she did so.

"Whoa, not apple time already!"

"Yes, and plenty of them," her mother said, touching

shoulders as she sat down. "It's an amazing tree...how it goes on producing year after year, I mean. There'll be enough for some specials at the restaurants again...keep Ben happy."

Lauren leant back against the hardwood frame and waited for her mother to come to the point.

"Oh, look! That damn squirrel's been at the bird feeder again! I only bought it last week and it's meant to be..."

"Mum!" Lauren put her hand on her mother's arm. "Come on, tell me about Dad and Mormor and whatever else it is you want to talk about or we'll run out of time."

"You're right...you're right." Jess paused. "The thing is..."

'Divorce!' Lauren thought, panicking at the new gravity and hesitancy in her mother's voice.

"...Mormor rang earlier, while Nick was here. She said Pop has pneumonia and he's in hospital...in fact, that's where she was phoning from. Anyway, she told Nick that Pop's lungs are congested and he's having difficulty breathing..."

"Oh, Mum, he's 90 years old!"

"I know...I know, but he's tough and they've given him antibiotics...apparently, the earlier the better."

"And Dad's gone to see him?"

"Yes."

They weren't divorcing! Lauren dipped her head. But, Pop! Pop had been there for ever... 'Mr Volvo', who'd set up the manufacturer's first dealership in the UK...who'd escaped the Nazis at night crossing from Norway to Sweden in a fishing boat...who'd given her a Volvo pedal car the year Finn was born...who smelled like wood shavings and was as dependable as the oak tree in his garden, where he'd hung a swing for her.

"Just when you think things can't get any shittier, they do!" she blurted out.

For a while, nothing was said. As the sun's warmth slid from her face and she felt the first sting of autumn in the air, she pulled up her hood and slid her hands into her sweatshirt pockets.

"It's good Nick will be there, whatever happens," her mother said quietly. "And Ginnie and Zoltan are driving over as well; so, Mormor won't be on her own."

At the mention of her other grandmother, a great wave of love and longing swept through her. She wanted Ginnie beside her, right now! She wanted to hold her hand and hear her voice, right now! 'Please, please don't let anything happen to her,' she pleaded, remembering the angel or whatever it was that had come to her.

But before she could give Ginnie any more thought, her mother went on, "Yes, life must seem pretty shitty to you after all you've been through, but..."

"*Is*, not *seems*!" Lauren interrupted.

"All right, 'is'. But things aren't just black and white, are they? There's a moon at night and clouds in the day, and it's not all bad news. The..."

"Certainly feels like it!" Lauren broke in again, exasperated. "You're just...you're just...oh, I don't know...they're just words, that's all! They don't mean anything."

"Actually, they do. Because, as I was saying, the other thing I wanted to talk to you about is good news, I think."

Even through her anger and frustration, Lauren heard the sincerity in her mother's voice and relented.

"Go on then."

But as she waited, a sharp clap ringing through the air made her jump.

"Mum!" she cried.

"Sorry," her mother's shoulder nudged her. "Just that tabby after the birds again. I didn't mean to startle you. Did I tell you I found a dead pigeon round by the bins the other day, although I don't suppose..."

"Mum, what were you going to say? What's the good news?"

"All right...all right. But this is in confidence, you understand? I want to tell Finn in my own time."

"Mm," Lauren nodded, half-listening. She didn't like having secrets from Finn, but she didn't have time to argue about it. She wanted to know what the good news was and then to get a lift over to Rafi. She wanted to get away from home. She wanted time and space to clear her head and untangle the rage that kept erupting inside her. Most of all, she wanted to be alone with Rafi in his own flat...he was calm, he was trustworthy and he wasn't family.

"Are you listening to me?"

"Yes, I am. You were saying Dad came round for lunch and you had leek and potato soup."

"The soup's not the point..."

"You're telling me!" Lauren snorted.

"The point is that we were able to talk without arguing and to hear each other. I felt he was being more open with me...you know, less defensive."

"Maybe because you were listening to him, not attacking him?"

"I don't attack him!" Jess flared, and Lauren waited, wishing she'd put it differently. "Well, all right, yes, I was upset about his obsession with that Jan Rawlings. I was hurt and I couldn't see he was hurting, too. Not until Shauna pointed it out to me.

"Shauna?" Lauren was surprised. She liked Tom's mum, but, as a working nurse, she saw her more as hands-on practical than marriage guidance. "What did she say?"

Her mother let go of her breath, as if blowing out candles, and laughed. "What didn't she say! She told me I was obsessing about Jan Rawlings, that I'd been so wrapped up in the restaurants that I had taken Nick for granted, that I hadn't looked at my own part in what was wrong and that the problem was communication... or rather, lack of it."

'Sounds pretty well spot on to me,' Lauren was thinking, but said instead, "And what did you say?"

For a moment, not only was her mother silent, but so, too, were the garden birds. And all she could hear was a distant thrum, as if the universe itself was breathing, until, somewhere high to the left of her, a seagull's triple-repeated screeching ripped through the silence, jolting her with its insistent, demanding cries.

Her mother laughed again, only this time Lauren felt the warmth in it rather than the bitterness. "I told her I had to go."

"Oh, you didn't?"

"Yes, I'm afraid I did. Cowardly, really, but I was angry...offended." She paused. "The truth hurts sometimes, but Shauna was...Shauna was...what was she? She was kind. She saw through me...said I wasn't letting her in and maybe that's what Nick was feeling, But she said it...oh, I don't know...gently, as if was she putting her arm round me, not attacking me, anyway.

And it helped me see what had gone wrong and what I needed...still need to do to try to put it right again."

While her mother was speaking, Lauren felt a shudder through the frame behind her, as if her mother had sat fully back for the first time, and she noticed the change in her tone from her usual briskness to something softer, more reflective.

"And what has gone wrong, Mum? I mean, is it just about not talking to each other, like Shauna said? Is that it?"

"I don't know...maybe. But, no, it's more than that... it goes way back."

"What do you mean?" Lauren asked. And, as her mother went on, she felt oddly embarrassed, but excited too, just as she had when she was little and had secretly watched her parents cuddling and kissing. Only this wasn't quite the same; her mother knew she was there and was treating her like an adult, not a child...like an equal almost.

"Well, we met when we were trainee teachers together...I think you know that. And one of the first things that attracted me to Nick was his openness...no trying to be cool, just behaving as if we were already friends, which we soon were. We were on a placement together in a comprehensive in Manchester...Moss Side, really tough area, difficult kids, not their fault. Anyway, I was struggling, thinking of chucking the whole thing in. But Nick...I mean, the kids took to him right away and he was just breezing through it...and yet every evening he came and helped me prepare for my classes the next day. He was just so kind and supportive. He kept telling me I could do it and he got me through it...I passed. But without him..." Her voice trailed off.

Lauren waited for her to continue, and, when she didn't, she said, "Go on, Mum."

"What? Yes...yes, sorry..." she tapped Lauren's leg, "memory lane and all that. No, what I was trying to get at...or, rather, what I'm trying to get at now is where did that ease between us go...that openness? Where did the fences go up and why?"

She seemed to drift off into silence again, and, without planning to, Lauren reached out, feeling for her hand and finding it. "Do you want to know what I think?" she said, squeezing lightly.

For a moment, her mother didn't reply, but, as Lauren went to let go, she held on to her. "Yes, I do. Tell me."

"It's nothing new, Mum. It's just that after you gave up teaching and got involved in opening Red Emma's, you became less and less available...more and more sort of cut off."

"But I was always there, wasn't I? I mean, giving you breakfast, dropping Finn off first thing on my way to the restaurant...and being home again by the time you both got back in the afternoon. Didn't I?"

Lauren heard the plea in her voice. "Look, I know you were doing your best, but you asked me...what was it...where the fences went up, right? And what happened was that...yes, you were home those times you just said, although not later on when you got The Canoe and started getting back later and later...but, even when you were home, you were so absorbed in all that stuff to do with banks and builders and the rest of it that you might as well not have been. In fact, all that paperwork was like a fence."

"Was I? I see...I do see...and I wish I could put the

clock back and do it again, do it better..." She paused. "Thing is you don't notice it at the time. Two young children, both of us working, we were too busy trying to..." She broke off again. "We stopped having time for each other. We got bogged down, didn't see the crack... didn't see it getting wider and wider."

The resignation in her mother's voice, devoid of all its usual bright certainty, made Lauren worry that she'd been too blunt.

"I know you were doing it for all of us, Mum. I know how hard you were working."

"I was...I was. And I thought Nick knew that, too, and would hold the fort for me, until everything was up and running and I could step back a bit."

"But he would ask you things and you didn't answer... it was like he hadn't spoken. And then you started coming back late and he had to do all the cooking, as well as all his marking and everything."

"I know." Her mother sighed, moving Lauren's hand back into her lap and letting go. "But we have started talking about it and I'm biting my tongue and trying to understand what he's telling me." She gave a little laugh. "I am listening and I think it's working, because he's being more responsive...not just going silent on me."

"Does that mean you're not going to separate?" Lauren said so softly, it was almost a whisper. "Not get divorced?"

"No, no...neither of us wants that. We just have to..."

"Does Finn know? Have you told him?"

"Well, not in so many words, but he knows Nick's been coming round."

"Mum, have you any idea how worried we've both been? For months!"

Lauren felt clearer and lighter. The dark cloud squatting at the back of her head for so long was gone, but she couldn't understand why she felt so angry, when she was feeling so happy.

"Yes, look, I know...this must have been...well, has been...very hard for both of you. I do realize that, and..."

"Not hard, Mum, bloody awful! Imagine how you'd have felt if Ginnie had kicked Zoltan out when you were a kid!"

"I didn't kick your father out! We just agreed..."

"Yes, well, we didn't, did we? Did you even think about us?"

"Yes, of course, we did. Nothing was...nothing is more important..."

"Ha! I don't think so. It certainly didn't feel like it!"

She hadn't planned to say any of it; the words just flew out. In the silence that followed, Lauren already began to regret her outburst. Worst of all was not being able to see her mother's face to gauge how she had taken it. Everything was true, but she didn't want to be mean.

"Sorry," she said, finally. "Just venting! It's great you and Dad are going to be okay. Really."

"Come on," her mother said, leaving a tangible vacuum, as she stood up. "We need to be going." And, as her mother reached down to take her hand, Lauren caught the familiar scent of her, vanilla and almond like hawthorn, and was filled with an aching sadness that made no sense.

Once they were in the car and on their way, she

grew apprehensive and was relieved every time her mother had to stop to give way to on-coming traffic in the narrow streets. She wanted to sit there, warm and comfortable and safe, and for the journey to go on forever; not because she didn't want to spend time with Rafi, but because she dreaded what his reaction would be when she pulled down her hood and took off her sunglasses.

'Everything's okay,' she argued with herself. 'Why are you stressing? Looks like Mum and Dad are staying together, so Finn's going to be fine. And Rafi wants to see you.'

'What about Pop, then? What about being blind? What about running? What about the rest of your life?'

'Pop? I don't know about Pop. I just pray he'll pull through. But I do know I'll run again. I may be blind, but, one way or another, I am going to compete at the Olympics, or Paralympics more like, and Terry bloody Curnow isn't going to stop me!'

'What about Rafi, though? Who's going to want a girlfriend who's blind and grotesque?'

She felt in her pocket for the tin of cream and, taking off her glasses, scooped a small amount onto her fingertips and gently stroked it over the rough and crinkled skin around her eyes.

'I am who I always was, so it's up to him.'

50

A little after three o'clock, Rafi heard the buzzer and went to open the door. Like some nightmare crow, Lauren was standing on the platform at the top of the external, metal staircase, a black apparition in hoodie and dark glasses,

"Hello, Rafi!" a voice called out from below.

Peering down, he saw Lauren's mother smiling up at him.

"Oh, hello, Mrs Jackman. Won't you come up?"

"No!" Lauren growled.

"Thanks, but I'm in a bit of a rush right now. Maybe later, when I pick Lauren up again, if that's okay."

"Yes, of course."

As he watched Jess turn away with a quick wave, Lauren stepped forward, bumping into him.

"Sorry," he said, shuffling back. "Look, give me your hand and I'll show you the way."

Her fingers were cool, gripping him firmly as he guided her through.

"This is the living room," he said. "There's the sofa or one of the chairs by the table at the window, whichever you like."

"By the window," she said.

He led her across and she sat down, leaning her cane against the edge.

Taking a seat across the corner from her, he watched her, trying to gauge her mood, but the glasses and hood obscured her face and he couldn't read it.

"Would you like something? Tea...coffee? Or there's some orange juice?"

"What's it like having your own place?"

Her question threw him. "I've not had much time to think about it," he said, looking around at the room. "Mrs Dilley's mother lived here, so I've been thinking of it as her place, rather than mine."

"Juice would be good. Thanks."

He went to fetch it, feeling off-balance and unsure of what to say.

"Anyway, I'm glad you're here to see it," he said, coming back. He touched her hand with the glass and she took it. "I'll show you the rest, if you like." He frowned, cross with himself. She couldn't see anything, could she?

"Okay." She felt for the table-top and put the drink down.

When he took her hand again, her fingers were damp from the condensation on the glass. He led her into the kitchen and the bathroom and, from there, into the bedroom.

She sat down on the edge of the bed, bouncing slightly to test it.

"It's a single, isn't it?" she said, stretching her arm back and finding the other side.

"Yes." He looked away from her, as if she could see him and read his thoughts. "So, that's it," he said, turning back, expecting her to get up. But she stayed where she was, turning her face up to him, as if she could see him.

"Rafi, what happened at the Rec the other day?"

"What do you mean?"

"You know what I mean."

He couldn't think what to say; the truth was too uncomfortable and he didn't want to lie.

"I don't know," he said. "There was a lot going on. My mother was leaving, I was moving and it was the first time I'd seen you since...you know..."

She waited for him to finish, and, when he didn't, she did it for him.

"Since I had acid thrown in my face, you mean?"

"Yes," he mumbled, wishing to get away from her, just as he had in the park.

"What are you afraid of?" she asked, raising both hands to push her hood back.

He felt again the shock of it, of her short hair revealing the shape of her skull.

"It'll grow back," she said, as if reading his thoughts, and took off her sunglasses, resting them on the bed beside her. "How do I look?"

The lower part of her face, her mouth, looked almost normal, but her eyes...her beautiful eyes! He clenched his teeth to choke off the protest clawing at his throat.

"The skin round your eyes," he managed, "it looks sore. Does it hurt?"

"It's not so bad now," she said, raising her hand and running her fingertips across the tops of her cheeks and the bridge of her nose. "I've got some cream that helps and I'll be having more grafts, later on. But my eyelids," she touched one, "feel almost normal. Amazing, really...

from my own tissue."

As he took in the sallow skin like a mask across her eyes, he tried to quell the images of her burnt and blistered face before the grafts. He wanted to cry for her. He wanted to magic back her healthy, easy face. But what he wanted most of all was eye contact and there was none...nothing to read, nothing to interact with.

"And my eyes?" she asked, as if she could feel the weight of his staring. "What are they like? Be honest, I want to know."

They looked smaller; or, at least, not properly open and tighter somehow. And he couldn't really see a pupil, just a milky lens.

"Well?"

"They're still brown, only..." He hesitated.

"Only what?"

"Um...they're not quite clear; they're a bit filmy."

"Filmy," she dipped her head. "Okay, I know what you mean."

"Do you want to go back in the other room?"

She didn't answer. As he waited, seeing her vulnerability, a wave of anger engulfed him.

"This is shit!"

Her head jerked up and she laughed.

"You never swear, Rafi."

"I know," he said, "but this stinks! It's so unjust!" But her laughter, as free and ringing as it had always been, shattered both his pity and his outrage, touching him like fire and fusing him back to her.

She patted the bed beside her. "Come and sit down."

As he did so, she felt for his arm, ran her hand up to his shoulder and then down again, finding his hand

and linking her fingers with his. The coldness and the damp in them were gone now and what he felt was the warmth of her.

"We're friends, right?" she said.

"Yes."

"And friends look out for each other, don't they?"

"Yes."

"So, why did you stop looking out for me at the Rec?"

He went to move his hand away, but she tightened her grip.

"You have to tell me, Rafi. If you're not open with me, we've not really got anything, have we?"

"I am being open."

"No, you're not." She relaxed her grip, but he didn't let go of her, and when she spoke again, her tone was softer. "Look, you've got to take your hood and glasses off, too, know what I mean? You've got to trust me or we'll never get any closer, will we?"

He closed his eyes, his chest heaving, as if he'd been running. God, closeness! He could feel the warmth of her wrist against his, smell the spicy scent of her. Every hair on his body felt electrified; yet he sat immobile, fear freezing the longing in him.

"Be brave, little brother!" Jasmin whispered in his ear and he flicked his eyes open.

"I am your friend," he started, needing to say something, "but...at the Rec, I don't know why, I just got embarrassed...the other kids from college being there...seeing us together."

"Embarrassed? Why?"

"Because..." Rafi's chest burnt like a furnace, pumping heat up through his neck and shoulders into his face. "Because...I don't know why 'because'! When we were on the phone together that night after Jedi died, I felt so close to you, like you were right there beside me...like your mind was in my mind...like we were alone together in the universe, bound together, just the two of us. That sounds mad, I know, but it was different...I'd never felt anything like that before and..." As he hesitated, trying to make sense of what he was saying, the stream of remembered feelings in him dried up, leaving him back in the moment. "But, anyway," he went on, "when I ran after you...you know, by the church... you said we were just friends, nothing more."

It was strange, but now that he'd said the unsayable things he'd wanted to tell her for months, he felt calmer, bolder. "So, what did you mean just now about us getting closer?"

Lauren let go of his hand and shifted her weight round towards him, her knee against his. She reached out for his face and, finding it, traced his cheekbone with her fingers.

"You feel hot," she said, taking her hand away again. "Do you mind me touching you? They told me not to do that."

"Who did? And, no...no, it's okay."

"One of the nurses at the hospital, she said it was too personal." Lauren shook her head. "No, not personal...too intimate, that's what she said. But then that's what being close means, isn't it? And touch is good." She stretched out to him again, cupping the side of his face in her palm. "It's what we have now, isn't it? Closeness, I mean. And there's nothing to be afraid of or embarrassed about, is there? Not if we trust each other."

She slid her fingers round behind his neck and drew him towards her. "Kiss me, Rafi," she said.

Clumsily, he put his hand on her shoulder and leaned into her, bumping his nose against hers. He pulled back. "Sorry."

"It's all right," she said. "Just close your eyes and imagine we're back in the night garden with the cicadas." She brushed his closed eyelid with her thumb. "We wanted to be together and now we are."

Gently, she pulled him towards her again, and when her lips touched his, their warmth and softness snuffed out his fear and ignited a joy in him.

Acknowledgements

Charlotte Richardson is a friend from the Plymouth Writers Group, who moved abroad some time ago. The first draft of this book owes its existence to all the support and encouragement she gave me from her new home in the south of France. For her thoughtful feedback and suggestions, chapter by chapter, I am more grateful than I can say.

Similarly, I want to offer huge thanks to my niece, Trisha Becker, for all her hard work in editing and proofreading the second draft from the other side of the world in Fremantle. Her interest in the story and in seeing it come to fruition has been irreplaceable.

After the first draft, I sent my manuscript for appraisal to The Literary Consultancy, who passed it to their Reader, author and creative writing lecturer, Vicky Grut. Her incisive and comprehensive critique, affirming my prose while criticising the narrative structure, led me to a complete rewrite. Thank you, Vicky, for your very detailed analysis; I have tried to make good use of it – fingers crossed.

One difficulty I had, once the story was told, was finding an appealing design for the cover. To my absolute delight, my granddaughter, Hannah Broadley-

Becker, took a pivotal scene from the book and created a beautiful illustration of that moment – thank you so much, Hannah.

My thanks are also due to Ric Salmon of ATC Management for his permission to quote the chorus from Markéta Irglová and Glen Hansard's wonderful song, 'When Your Mind's Made up', from the inspiring film 'Once'.

In addition, I want to acknowledge and thank Jim Bruce of Ebooklover.Co.Uk for his contribution to the development of this book.

Finally, I would like to pay tribute to the warm help I have received from Julia, Alice and Cat M at Rowanvale Books in turning my manuscript into a publishable paperback and eBook.

Author Profile

Charles Becker grew up in Maidenhead and St Ives, Cornwall. He now lives in Devon with his wife. Formerly a wine merchant, English teacher and University Counsellor, he has been writing full-time since his retirement. His first novel, *Murder at Royal William Yard*, is a detective thriller set in the Ocean City of Plymouth. *The Little Fishery: Love and Loss by the Riverside* is the story of his childhood home by the Thames. This love story, *Lauren and Rafi*, is his second novel.

Printed in Dunstable, United Kingdom

65490503R00272